LAWYER FOR THE DAMNED:
FEAR KNOT

by
Darwin E. Farrar

To Buster, Monte, and the public-school teachers who shared the joy of reading with me. To Tannis, Denise, Carron, and the Tribe - who've shown me the strength of love. To Digene, Drake, and Jack who've lifted me up through all the phases of my life. To David and the rest of my martial arts family who keep me moving forward. And to the crazies: Jo, Ki, Lisa, and The Race Doctor - who help me live outside my box.

CHAPTER 1

SIC INFIT

(So It Begins)

THE TWO GUNSHOTS sounded like dueling cannons in the narrow confines of the hallway - so loud that they alone should have been at the forefront of my thoughts. But no, even as the sound of the last gunshot reverberated through the strangeness of my new surroundings, it was the speed with which he'd drawn and fired his weapon that my mind struggled to understand.

It was like being in a car crash when the air bags deploy. There's no sense of movement, progression of time, or series of events that allows the mind to perceive change. There's just an instantaneous shift from one state where there is no air bag, to another where the airbag is fully inflated. Here, one moment his hand was relaxed and empty at his side, the next it was holding a smoking gun. Somewhere in between the two states he had drawn and fired, twice.

And, just like that, two people had been shot. One, a chubby guy dressed in a long frock coat and frilly shirt, was slouched forward, precariously held upright by his substantial gut, a sword still held in hand. The other, a much younger guy with bad teeth and *Grapes of Wrath* hand-me-down clothes, was laid out on the floor. He'd fallen on top of some sort of hatchet. Both had bullet holes right about where their third eye would be.

This was killing more up close and personal than I'd ever seen. But for the nickel sized holes in the front of their heads, and the much larger holes in the back, I'd have thought they were drunk-sleep. Like when you come home too drunk to take off your clothes, fall onto the bed, or the floor if you're less lucky, and sleep in whatever crumpled up position you land in.

These guys wouldn't have the luxury of waking up with crooks in their necks and a bad hang-over.

Two more would-be assailants stood to the right of the dead guys. One, a squat man with thick undefined forearms held a crude club, the other, a well-dressed, falcon-eyed man had drawn a slender Tuck Sword. Like me they stared at the bodies.

Where I was transfixed by the bodies on the floor, they were merely waiting. I understood why when the bodies folded in on themselves and well, just kinda dissolved. There was no smoke, sound, or warning of any kind. When it was over all that remained were the clothes, roughly posed as people, shoes and weapons.

"What the fuck?" I heard myself say.

Apparently, everyone else heard me say it too. I realized I'd neglected to use my inside voice when all eyes shifted to me - except his. This man, my guide turned killer, kept his eyes on the falcon-eyed man. When he regained the man's attention, he broke the silence with a question.

"Me, him, or it?"

The falcon-eyed man answered with a flit of his eyes toward the gun.

"Ah, yes. Well, …"

My killer-guide un-cocked the gun and spun it three-quarters around in his hand, so the barrel pointed down and the butt faced him.

"Now that we're all clear on the what's what, …"

Right hand still holding the downward pointed gun, he moved with a slowness that marked it as deliberate, and with his left hand drew what looked like a cross between a knife and a sword from under the back of his poncho.

The blade, at least twenty inches long and two-inches wide, ended in a narrowed double-edged point. The handle, which looked to be made of some kind of bone, was separated from the blade by a worn and dented metal guard that ran from the base, over the handle, and ended at a sharp stud at the butt of the sword/knife.

"… the who's who, …"

Without taking his eyes off the two assailants, my killer-guide bent fully to place the gun on the floor then kicked it to a point halfway between them.

"… and the stakes at hand, …"

My killer-guide twisted the knife around in his hand and closed his grip into a fist around the handle so that the blade ran almost parallel to his forearm and the curved guard covered his knuckles. Then he raised his fists like a boxer and crouched into a left leg leading fighting stance.

"... shall we proceed?"

With a guttural yell, club wielding guy lunged into action. Club raised high, he charged forward for a killing blow.

As the club started down my killer-guide bent his front knee, pushed with his rear leg, and punched.

The straight line of the punch was faster than the arc of the club. Where a punch alone might have grazed the arm before connecting with the head, held as it was, the blade of the knife went through the arm just before the metal guard struck the assailant's jaw. Dazed by the blow to the jaw, the assailant spun to the ground unaware that he'd lost several teeth, and that his arm was now only barely attached to his body.

The falcon-eyed man wasn't just better dressed, he was also more skilled. He held his Tuck Sword with familiarity and joined the fray just as the first attacker spun past my killer-guide. The falcon-eyed man stepped wide toward my killer-guide's weaponless side and swung his sword parallel to the ground. It was a decapitating stroke or at least it would have been had my killer-guide not bent at the knees, lower into his fighting stance. Instead, the blade whistled by overhead.

Pivoting on both feet with blade in hand, my killer-guide threw a hook toward the falcon-eyed guy's body. The blade followed the arc of fist, but where the fist didn't make contact, being longer, the blade cleaved a deep ridge across the attacker's torso. At the end of his swing, my killer-guide raised slightly and reversed his arm direction. What would have been a vicious back hand resulted in the sword stabbing into and through the assailant's skull.

Though he'd pivoted into his strokes, my killer-guide's feet hadn't left the spot where he started. As the falcon-eyed man's limp form fell, my killer-guide begrudgingly took a step back, so that the man didn't land on his boots.

He then turned back to the squat, now nearly one-armed guy.

Sweaty and in a panic, the guy had crawled over to the wheel gun which he now held in his one remaining hand. Though his eyes fixed on my killer-guide with relief and glee, the unsteady gun in his hand showed fear and desperation.

The odds weren't in his favor but given the speed with which he'd drawn and fired the gun, a quick lunge might have brought my killer-guide to within striking distance before the gun went off. Instead, he stood tall and square, making himself an easy target for the unsteady shooter. A brief glimmer of hope passed over nearly one-armed guy's eyes as he drew the gun's hammer back, and a smile brushed the corners of his mouth when the gun's hammer started down. Both vanished when the gun misfired with a "piftt."

A second misfire was followed by a jam and any hope the guy had had was replaced first by desperation then resolution. My killer-guide walked almost casually, sword/knife in hand, swinging smoothly with the rhythm of his stride. He stepped to the outside of the gun and with an easy up-stroke lobbed off the guy's remaining arm at the elbow. In the same motion he circled the blade around and with a backhand, cut through the guy's head from medulla to mouth.

The top half of the head landed near me, just as the

arm, gun still in hand, landed at the foot of the crowd that had gathered to watch. Along with the body to which they were moments ago attached, the head and arm shriveled and dissolved into nothingness.

The gun, no longer possessed by the hand, lay on the floor between my killer-guide and the crowd, pointing at him. He made no move for it. Instead, he let his eyes, sparkling with clarity but lacking any compassion or joy, bore into the crowd. This was an invitation to any would-be challengers and a message to all.

"Gunfighter." A nervous greeting by a few became a realization by some, then a murmur that both passed through and hushed the growing crowd. He sheathed the knife as he slowly walked over to retrieve the ancient gun, neither acknowledging nor ignoring the crowd.

Absent challenge, they didn't exist for him.

He bent, picked up the gun, reloaded and holstered it, and started walking all in a single smooth movement. He didn't glance back and, though he could have been talking to anyone, all knew he was talking to me when he said,

"Gather up the clothes and weapons."

I gathered up the dead guys' belongings and fell in behind him without hesitation. I had a million questions, but I figured they could wait until I was sure he was done shooting and decapitating.

This was my introduction to Purgatory and my first meeting with The Gunfighter. It happened just over a year ago, depending on how you count; right after my 'accident.'

᠀

Given my reputation, I'll understand if you take all this with a grain of salt ... or more.

DE TENEBRA

CHAPTER 2

OMNES UNA MANET NOX

(One Night Awaits Everyone)

To THIS DAY, whenever I hear a rusty bearing, a loose fan belt on a car, a bad wheel on a shopping cart, or anything making that irritating, irregular squeak that says, 'I need fixing,' I cringe at the memory of my when I first met The Gunfighter.

That irregular sound - squeak, squeak, ... squeak, ... squeak - pulled me from a blackness darker than nothing, into a blur of sensory inputs.

Like combat veterans, kids who grow up in rough places, and others that live where sleep is both a precious and precarious proposition, I typically wake and fall asleep quickly. This wake-up call was different. Rather than "instant on" clarity, I had to fight to focus my mind and vision. If you've had your bell rung in a fight enough times, you know the drill. You can't tell if you're moving or things are moving around you, so you find the first thing you can that probably isn't moving and focus on that. Now, if that thing just happens to be the floor of the ring - or worse, some parking lot black-top or barroom linoleum – well, you're screwed.

It took me more than 90 degrees of head rotation before I found something to focus on.

Dark blue scrubs walking alongside a wobbly old wheel told my slow-on-the-uptake brain that I was headed down a hospital hallway in a badly maintained wheelchair.

I knew this was bad. But I didn't realize how bad it was.

"Welcome back."

It was a cheerless voice, not at all muffled by the surgical mask that I couldn't seem to focus past.

"Where am I? What's happening?"

These seemed like reasonable questions, even in my impaired state.

"Ah yes. Well, it seems there was an accident."

"An accident?" The last thing I remembered was having drinks with Christina at The Line Hotel in Los Angeles.

Christina was the first woman of color hired by the San Francisco law firm where I worked - Fulsome, Rucker, and Taft, which pretty much everyone whose name wasn't either Fulsome, Rucker, or Taft referred to as the FRAT. The FRAT was a smaller-than-it-liked, wanna be contender for the "A" list of law firms.

Christina was a Mocha-colored woman from one of the island countries. She wasn't pretty in an obvious or traditional way, though she could easily be described as handsome. At 5'10" weighing 190 pounds she was more 'thick' than fat. Strong jaw bones and the sharp nose she'd inherited from her mother drew attention if not admiration. Smooth, skin gave way to the unblemished whites of her eyes in a stark contrast that hazel or green irises could have moderated. Instead, darker than black irises exacerbated the contrast and added an unintended intensity to her every glance, thought, and expression.

In another life Christina might have been an athlete or model; in this life she was a high-strung, caustic woman who grated on her peers, supervisors, and subordinates alike. While such personalities are not foreign to law firm life, and coddling is often part of the compensation package for rainmakers, prima donna litigators, and managing partners, it's not a good career advancement strategy for new associates. For Christina, a second-year associate who lacked the business connections or pedigree that promised great things to come, it all but guaranteed that she'd be let go as soon as optics and liability allowed.

As a Senior Associate, I was "asked" to have her work with me on a big case that was headed to trial in Los Angeles. But you don't get to be a senior associate without learning to read between the lines and speak to the partnership's real concerns. What the partnership actually wanted was for me, the firm's only other black person, to be the one that fired her.

It made sense. After his 'Angel' client's departure, the Senior Partner that had insisted on hiring her made his disappointment in her clear and suggested that Christina wasn't FRAT material. Following his lead, the firm's newest and only female Partner, had taken to publicly criticizing Christina and her work. Having me, the firm's only veteran attorney of color, agree that she couldn't cut it was the next logical step toward limiting the firm's exposure when she was let go.

It made sense. But it wasn't right.

Over the long days of trial preparation, two things became apparent. First, Christina was damaged goods. While this was fairly obvious, I didn't fully appreciate the extent of the trauma she'd suffered until much later. Second, Christina had plenty of potential. What she lacked was training and an understanding of how the practice of law differs from the study of law. While she'd done well enough on the three things that are necessary to become a lawyer - the Law School Aptitude Test, law school, and the bar exam – she, like a lot of rookie lawyers, had yet to realize that these things have little to do with actually practicing law.

Unlike the study of law, practicing law is about understanding your client's and employer's interests, building their confidence in your understanding of legal processes and strategy, and making them comfortable enough with you to trust your advice on how to protect and further their interest. This is especially true and all the more challenging if you don't come from money, don't have an ivy league pedigree, or are black, female, or a member of any protected class.

By transactional litigation standards, our case was fairly straight-forward. A large corporation had made a hefty buy offer for an innovative new biotechnology company whose heavy investments in R&D had produced several potentially lucrative patents but left them short on operating funds. After repeatedly extending the closing date for the deal and conducting numerous "due diligence" reviews of the patents, the corporation publicly stated that the patents were near worthless and backed out of the deal.

Having expended its operating reserves during the protracted negotiations and now unable to sell any of its patents because of the bad press, the biotechnology firm soon went under. The corporation then bought the bulk of the firm and the firm's patents for pennies on the dollar.

With the facts and law on our side, we sought actual and punitive damages and asked the court to enjoin the corporation's future licensing and sales. As with most cases that should be settled instead of tried, rather than being about right or wrong, the facts or the law, resolution was about the relief sought – the dollars.

The Line Hotel was one of my Los Angeles favorites. Located in Japan-town, less than a ten-minute drive from the downtown courts, it was close enough to be convenient. Yet, with its ultramodern, concrete-everywhere décor, full-wall windows, and Asia-themed amenities, it was different enough to provide a reprieve from work. That it had a gorgeous bar that was usually well stocked with top shelf booze and even better eye-candy, further added to the Line's appeal.

In the morning on the fourth day of trial, just after we'd presented the bulk of our case, defendant's counsel decided he'd milked his client for all he could without risking being sued. He made a settlement offer that left the corporation in about the same position it would have been in if it had just paid our initial demand – minus his legal fees. The judge granted an adjournment for the afternoon to allow negotiations, and by close of business we'd agreed to settle for more than the purchase price originally offered, plus a sizable stake in defendant's new biotech subsidiary.

Even after FRAT's hefty cut, our client would have more than enough cash to start a new business and a steady new revenue stream. It was time to celebrate.

By the time we got back to the Line, it was near dinner time. By way of thanks, the client had arranged for Christina and me to dine at a trendy and exclusive Japanese restaurant nearby and given us an open tab at the hotel bar. Not to be outdone, the firm had moved us from our two "deluxe" rooms to the hotel's best two-bedroom, three bath, master suite. It came complete with in-suite Jacuzzi and spa. They also gave me strict orders to take the next day off.

With a little guidance here and a suggestion there, Christina had done very well with the work I assigned her. Rather than fire her, I'd gotten her an interview with Kommins and Canudsen, a small firm in Oakland known for doing big things. She'd leave for a good job with a solid reference, I'd get credit for moving her out without any drama or severance pay, and the firm would have zero exposure. It was a win, win, win, that I thought she'd jump at.

Unfortunately, when I first broached the idea of leaving before the trial, Christina's response was awkward to say the least.

"But I like working under you. If you'd like, I'd be happy to do more for you."

I couldn't tell if she was joking, trying to be flirty, or just expressing some latent insecurity. It was a moment we were both happy to let pass.

I decided to press the topic of Christina's going to work for Kommins and Canudsen again after we'd settled, toward the end of our meal, over a lackluster bottle of Verdelho.

"I'm impressed by and appreciate the hard work you did on this case. I think, with more one-on-one training and case exposure, you will make a very fine lawyer.

Unfortunately, I know for a fact that the FRAT isn't willing to give you the time and training you need to advance. But I think I can help."

She looked down and went silent.

It made sense; I was delivering bad news. Even sugar coated and offered with a lifeline, being told that you're not going to make it on the job is a hard thing to hear. I'd expected and braced myself for sadness, possibly a few tears, and maybe even a bit of anger, but not what came next.

Still looking down, she unclasped her hands, lifted one off her lap, then slid it across the table till it touched mine. Only then did she glance up and even then, not directly into my eyes.

"I understand. And I would like for you to train me when and as you see fit. I will do any and everything you ask of me, without question or condition. I will be yours to 'train.' And of course, I will be very discreet."

I was floored, offended, and flattered at the same time. What's the portmanteau for that … flafendered? I tried to rally my thoughts but all I managed to produce was a disorganized stream of consciousness that started with me mumbling out …

"Umn, ah, that's not what I had in mind. I mean, well, you're really not my type."

Apparently, there was nothing wrong with her hearing. She went from demur and subservient to vindictive like someone had flicked a switch.

"Wait, what! You, a wanna be like them midnight-man, are trying to say that I'm not your type? What, is my butt too big? Am I not 'light-skinneded' enough for you? Or could it be," and she added air quotes here to make her sarcasm clear, that I'm just too "exotic" for you?

I'd never seen air quotes look so much like I was being flipped the bird.

This was yet another in a series of times that I wished I'd grown up on the east coast. East coast folks, especially New Yorkers, are masters of the quick comeback. We west coast natives are lucky if we even experience *esprit de l'escalier*. Having been born in Californian, the best I could muster in response to her race-based, arrogant rant, was the truth.

"You're not my type because you're a woman!"

Though I tended to keep my personal life separate from my work, I wasn't closeted. Indeed, I was "out" enough for the partnership to tout the diversity this brought to the firm when wooing their more progressive clients. But between my being both preoccupied with work and not interested in anybody I met through work, my sexual preference was generally overlooked.

I startled Christina into unintentional eye contact. Before she could rein it in, momentary confusion then calculating anger flashed in her eyes. When it passed, we were left sitting in mutually shocked silence. When that silence moved beyond awkward to become painful, I picked up the over-priced and underwhelming Verdelho, poured myself more than enough, then waived the bottle over her glass in the universal "care to join me?" gesture. She nodded a bit too enthusiastically and, after the pour, downed the wine in a single lift. With the glass drained, she took a deep breath, then exhaled slowly.

"Ok, I don't know which is worse, my being mortified by the way I put myself out there sexually, or how embarrassed I am at my reaction when I thought you were rejecting me."

I tried to jump in, if only to suggest the latter as a more appropriate reaction, but she waived me off.

"There's no way I'm going to recover from that kind of *faux pas* over wine. How about we head back to the Line and take advantage of our open tab – I've been told that Mescal raises my groveling, apologizing, and mea culpas to near artistic levels."

It was a good recovery and a great lead-in to an apology; I doubt I could have done better. But there are some things that an apology just won't cover - things that may be forgiven but will never be forgotten.

Going through the world not seeing or denying differences is an act of privilege. Lip service liberals' claims that "we're all the same" are typically rooted in expectations of conformity that don't actually embrace diversity or grant equality. Bad as that is, this was worse.

It wasn't that Christina hadn't heard that I was gay, it was that she believed her island ancestry gave her higher social status. That plus the deviant, 'over sexed nature' that she, like many in our society, attributed to homosexuals in general, and Black men in particular, led her to think I would jump at her offer. That I didn't was an affront to her and the marginally higher, and therefore all-the-more precious, social status she clung to.

I was going to the Line's bar with her, I was going to have a drink with her, I was going to assure her that it was nothing personal, and I was going to tell her that she needed to start looking for another job.

I got the bill and signed for the dinner while Christina arranged for a ride back to the hotel. Since a hired car is never more than a minute or two away in downtown Los Angeles, we made it to the Line Hotel fifteen long minutes after we finished our meal.

When we got to the hotel Christina said she had to run up to the room. By Los Angeles standards it was still relatively early, so by the time she returned I'd been shown to a seat at a table far enough from the bar to give us some semblance of privacy. When she returned, she stopped at the bar to pick up our drinks.

It took two trips for Christina to bring all our drinks. First to arrive was a lovely chocolate porter for me and a very light and hoppy IPA for her. Her next trip produced two hefty shots of a reposado mescal that she insisted we down immediately.

"Here's to those we meet, cheat, and beat along the way." She said it as we raised and clinked classes. After we tossed back the smoky concoction, she paused to give both of us a chance to brace ourselves, then started in on her apology.

Three or four sips into my beer I wasn't following what she was saying. Less than half-way through the beer, feeling over-drunk and slightly nauseated, I announced that all was forgiven and suggested we call it a night. That's the last thing I remembered.

"I don't remember any accident."

"Well of course not, that's the whole point of roofying someone. Ok, technically speaking, you were given gamma hydroxybutyric acid, something that apparently your body does NOT play well with. That you went into a coma rather than waking up with a bad hangover and some compromising pictures that would have kept Christina at the firm, well, I suspect that was an accident.

Maybe God didn't just give us something called a soul.
Maybe he gave us a small part of his infinite self.
And for lack of a better name, we call that the soul.

DE TENEBRA

CHAPTER 3

UBI JUS IBI RENDIUM

(A Remedy For Every Wrong)

So, Christina had drugged me. I had a hard time believing it at the time but knowing what I know about her now, that she would resort to such a thing to advance her career makes sense.

"And, … here we are at the elevator. Do you think you can stand? It would look much better if you did." Before I could, he hauled me to my feet and tossed me into an old elevator.

I wanna say I landed cat like on my feet but honestly there was more than a little stagger and sway involved. What I lacked in grace, however, I more than made up for in lawyerliness.

"Ok, Mr. doctor, nurse, or whatever type of healthcare provider you are, if I've been in a coma why did you just yank me out of the wheelchair? What hospital is this anyway? And where the Hell is this elevator taking us?"

He responded in less time than it took me to debate whether it was too late for me to fall on the ground to pad the malpractice claim that seemed to be presenting itself.

"Nicely organized. However, we're not in an elevator or a hospital and I'm not a doctor, nurse, orderly, or other healthcare provider. I said you were in a coma, and your body still is. You however are a detached soul, and I am here to guide to judgement."

My mind hadn't fully cleared, but I'd regrouped enough to understand that this guy was completely serious, and therefore completely nuts.

Rather than the awkward silence you'd expect after someone drops a bomb like that, the pause that followed was more about to two men sizing each other up.

He was a little bigger than me, but truth be told, I prefer to fight above my weight class. A small man that is game to fight usually knows what he's doing, knows how to take pain, or both; he won't stop till one of you is out cold or dead. Big men are easier - most think they'll be stronger and prevail because they're bigger. They tend to fold when they learn the hard way that there's little correlation between size and strength. Even when they are stronger, they're quickly frustrated and easily intimidated by a fighter that knows how to work the angles to neutralize their strength and make their size work against them.

Two things about this guy made me hesitate. First, he seemed to have freakish strength. Yanking me out of the wheelchair should have been a chore but he made it seem almost effortless - there was no pause to gather himself involved. We've all heard of drugged and deranged individuals doing things normal folks can't do. He didn't look drugged, but clean, sober, and crazy strong is still a big problem.

Second, the location was to his advantage. You need space to make a big man's size work against him. As anybody who saw George Foreman fight in his second iteration can tell you, a patient big man that's intent on cornering you is a big problem.

I glanced past him to the elevator door. It hadn't started to close but I figured it would at any moment. With two strikes against me it was time for dialogue.

"So, if I'm a detached soul, where is this elevator going?"

He paused before answering. Whether this was to take in what I'd said, to listen to some non-existent voice, or maybe just to let the door close, was anybody's guess. I thought to myself, "give me a 'C.'"

"We're not actually in an elevator" he said.

Give me an 'R.'

"What you see is the result of your own efforts to find or manufacture familiarity in this wholly unfamiliar situation."

Give me an 'A.'

"When you get past your current state of denial, you'll see things more accurately. No doubt I'll look different to you then too."

Give me a 'Z.'

"As for where we're going? This elevator is one of your attempts to understand your passage. As your guide I can say that if you haven't already, soon you will likely sense that this elevator is going down."

Give me a ... wait, what? Down! WHY?!"

Souls fear moving on for the same reasons people fear death.
Both represent the unknown.

DE TENEBRA

CHAPTER 4

RES IPSA LOCQUITUR

(The Thing Speaks For Itself)

Oĸ, I'll admit, the down thing, or at least the implications of my going down, threw me. As the door closed, sweat lit my brow and I started looking around the elevator for the emergency stop. Since I now had the distinct sensation of downward movement, this was definitely an emergency.

I feared the answer and had a hard time asking, but since I needed to know, I just threw it out there.

"So, are you ... the Grim Reaper?

"No."

"The Boatman?"

"No."

"The Ferryman?"

"No."

"Him of Many Faces, The Stranger?"

"No, and no."

I was dizzy, sweat soaked and tired, even though all

I'd done was ask a few questions. With one hand on the elevator wall to steady myself, I closed my eyes and took a couple of deep breaths.

When I opened my eyes I saw that he'd cocked his head slightly to the side and raised his hands in a manner that seemed artificial yet intended to calm and placate. I guess he was trying to be helpful.

"It may help to focus on the where and why of our journey."

There was neither malice nor judgement in his statement.

Hands still up to placate, he reiterated, "Focus on the where and why."

For lack of other ideas or options, I went with my movie-based knowledge of religious dogma. My mind raced through *The Ten Commandments*

Thou shalt not steal? Geez, I was ten years old in a candy store – that's gotta be entrapment.

Thou shalt not covet thy neighbor's wife? What 'just gone through puberty' teen hasn't lusted for the Hottie next door? And what exactly does covet mean anyway? Do no-way it'll ever happen, wouldn't even begin to know how to act on it, and would be mortified if anyone ever found out about it fantasies count?

Thou shalt not take the lord's name in vain. OMG, if "Jesus!" counts I'm done for. Wait, did I just do it again?

Thou shalt keep the Sabbath day holy. Is that Saturday, the Jewish Sabbath, or Sunday, the Judeo-Christian Sabbath? Not that it mattered, like most lawyers, I routinely worked both.

I was 0 for 4 and couldn't even remember the other six Commandments - I needed to switch tactics.

"So what, am I supposed to contemplate which of the Seven Deadly Sins I've committed?"

"Actually, they are called the Seven Cardinal Vices: Greed, Gluttony, Lust, Wrath, Envy, Sloth, and Hubris. And, if you were to do so, would you start with greed, envy, or hubris Counsellor?"

Out of everything he said, all I really heard was the last word. He'd reminded me that I'm a lawyer and - call it hubris if you will - a damn good one. In my panic I'd almost forgotten the holy trinity of lawyering: 'Admit nothing, deny everything, and make counter accusations.'

I threw him a changeup that most major-league pitchers would envy.

"I don't know why I'm here. I'm sure I haven't done anything worse than most people, and you don't seem to be either willing or able to point to anything in particular that I've done to warrant going down!"

To my surprise, rather than strike me down, start in on that whole torment thing, or do whatever it is they do in Hell, he agreed with me, sort of.

"I am not one to judge or be judged by. I don't know how you define right versus wrong, so I have no idea what you've done that you think would warrant a soul penance, what that penance should be, exactly where your soul will go, or how long it will stay there."

His response made at least two things obvious. First, my movie-based knowledge of judgment day wasn't gonna cut it - I had no idea what this guy was talking about. Second, while this wasn't the guy that was gonna make the call, he seemed to know how things worked, and certainly knew a lot more about what was going on than I. So, I needed to keep him talking.

"Ok. You said I should focus on the where and why. According to you we're in an elevator that is a construct I've created. So why are you here with me? You said you're not The Grim Reaper or The Ferryman, and you're not like any construct I could imagine. So, who are you?"

"Those are mere names - transient associations of the past. Even on the mortal plane, one's name is a thin guestimate of who and what we really are. Just as mortals are often given nick names by those who know them, here souls are referenced on a relational basis. With that in mind, the better question is, what am I'm doing here with you."

"So, you're not Death by any name?"

"No. Typically, I come along shortly after that point."

"Ok, so you're the guy that pushed me down the hall in the wheelchair, picked me up and shoved me in this elevator, then casually let on that you're my guide."

I conveniently left out the part about my being headed to judgement.

"If all this is a construct of my own creation, why do I need a guide and how do I know you're not one of my constructs?"

"My job is three-fold. First, I'm here to help you figure out where you're going. Second, I'm here to help you get where you're going. And lastly, I'm here to make sure you know what's going on when you get there."

"Ok. So where are am I going?"

"Earlier you said you don't know why you're here and that you're sure you haven't done anything worse than most people. Though they're often slow to admit it, souls that go to Heaven, Hell, or the almost infinite number of other places in-between genuinely believe they belong there. Those that need time to reach that, or some other truth require a place to do so. That place is Purgatory."

Ok, you can't bullshit a good bullshitter, which would be almost any decent lawyer, and like I said, I was several steps above decent. I called bullshit.

"You're pretty much cribbing from *Dante's Inferno*. Or are you trying to tell me Dante went to Hell, somehow got out, and then wrote *The Inferno* before he died?"

"Given the detail and depth of Dante's writings, a past life memory is but one explanation; we can't rule out possession, an out of body experience, psychic nightmares, or even a near death experience that provided him a glimpse beyond the veil. Imagination or in this case what appears to be fiction, is often driven or influenced by a memory that lies at the edge of conscious recall."

"So, Dante was right? Hell is a place of infinite pain and suffering?"

"Like the hereafter, Hell is vast and varied. Few can or would speak to the true nature of either. Those souls that are sent to the hereafter, or who "move-on," aren't known to return so who's to say if or where Dante's river of blood, shades, or horrid forest might be found. However, whether he knew it or not, Dante got a lot right about Purgatory including the idea that our sense of whether and where we belong in Hell is a product of our beliefs about right and wrong.

"In Dante's time the Catholic Church frowned upon charging for loans, casual sex, and suicide, among other things. People of his time and place were taught, and most believed, that such acts were sins. While those from Dante's time and place will see themselves as having sinned by such deeds, souls from another time or place may not. The Samurai that commits ritual suicide will more likely see sin in the failure that led to his suicide than the act of suicide itself.

"Dante's Purgatory also reflects the practices of his life and times. Branding, flogging, burning, and self-flagellation were not uncommon. Confessions often involved an early variant of waterboarding - the dunking stool, or breaking on the wheel, and hairshirts weren't a fashion statement. That such practices exist in both Purgatory and his book should come as no surprise. Souls in Purgatory inflict and seek punishment at least in part because, in their experience, it is how the truth is extracted."

I think I have a high tolerance for pain but I gotta admit, I was more than a little unnerved by the prospect of being tortured into admitting that I belong in Hell.

"Am I to be tortured till I either admit that I belong in Hell or survive it long enough to get into Heaven?"

"If you wish.

"First and foremost, Purgatory is where souls go to come to grips with their fate. The lesson to be gleaned from *The Inferno* is that most souls use the same truth-seeking methods in Purgatory that they used on earth: academics do research and write papers, intellects debate, fighters fight. The result is usually the same, papers, resolutions, physical contests that, over time, lead the soul to, and to accept its fate."

"And since I'm a lawyer ...?"

Yeah, it seemed obvious to me too, but when you're headed to Purgatory, the saying that 'the devil is in the details' takes on a far more significant meaning. His look confirmed my suspicions even before he started to speak.

"While there are many ways fate can be decided, those that had no calling or passion, those that never pursued their dream, those whose sense of self was tethered to base interests, and those who are lost must still find their way. Those who've no other means will often have their fate decided in a courtroom, alongside those who've found their calling in the law."

"This court, does it follow state, federal, or international law? Am I the defendant? If so, what am I accused of and what's the applicable standard of proof, reasonable doubt or a preponderance of evidence?"

"I'm not the lawyer. All I can tell you is that you will appear in court at what is called an arraignment. At the arraignment, it will be presumed, res ipsa loquitor, that your soul should remain within the jurisdiction of Purgatory for a period not to exceed eternity."

"How can res ipsa loquitor possibly be used to justify my being in Purgatory."

"In Purgatory it references a fundamental presumption - that a soul goes where it believes it belongs. You are, of course, free to argue that you don't belong in Purgatory, as many do."

"So all I have to do is say that I don't belong in there?"

He paused and let the silence ask, if I really thought it would be that easy?

"No. Many new souls say that they don't belong in Purgatory, though few can articulate why. The difficult part, the part where most souls eventually falter, is proving the point. A lapse in judgement, a drunken night, or just being dealt a bad hand can tarnish the soul."

I took a moment to tally this up. I was going to trial, where I didn't know the local court rules, what law applied, or what exactly I was accused of; but I had to win.

Scared and exasperated, I closed my eyes, took another calming breath, and when I opened them, he'd changed.

Before me was a weathered looking man that looked to be somewhere in his forties. From afar he might seem to be one of the homeless. A poncho that could easily be mistaken for a blanket was draped over broad shoulders, and brown jeans that seemed to have faded to a dusky color fell without wrinkles to brush the top of dirt brown boots. Thick dark hair and a five o'clock shadow furthered the misdirection. But, in the close confines of the elevator I could see the shirt under his poncho was freshly laundered. Rather than faded jeans he wore soft brushed leather pants, and his well-worn boots showed the comfort and quality of hand-made craftsmanship. He stood at an angle that allowed me to see that a wide-rimmed sombrero rested on his back, held fast by a leather strap around his neck. An old wheel gun rested low and comfortable in a holster on his hip. Like him, it was weathered and scarred on the surface, but ultimately a thing of brutal beauty.

He stood tall. Thickly corded muscle rippled across his forearms. Dark brown almost to the point of black eyes, bordered by crow's feet, watched me take him in. There was no mercy, kindness, or joy in his eyes or anywhere about his person; his gaze was that of a predator - dispassionate, and unflinching.

"You see the more real me now."

He said it like shifting form was an everyday thing.

"That means you're beginning to accept this reality. I suspect we'll be arriving shortly."

Right on cue, the elevator chime signaled our arrival.

It's one thing to be told you're going to Purgatory and quite another to find you have arrived. Terror ran through me like a racehorse leaving the starting gate

I didn't realize I'd backed away from the door until I felt myself pushing against the rear wall of the elevator and felt my feet take turns sliding across the floor, unable to gain sufficient purchase to move me through the wall and further away from the slowly opening elevator doors. Terror had gotten ahead of and was about to consume me. Eyes wide and frantic I searched for another way out. Like a drowning man grasping for a sword, I locked eyes with him in a plea for help. He stared back, unyielding and dispassionate as ever.

Rage at his indifference and the wrongness of it all welled up within me with just enough force to give pause to my terror. I peeled myself off the wall and met his hard gaze with one of my own.

"Ah."

He said it with a hint of what I told myself was respect.

"This is the hard part for most people. Even those that understand that they've brought themselves to this point and that with or without my 'assistance' they're going forward. Some need the threat of force to alleviate whatever guilt they're feeling, others feel they shouldn't go down without a fight, some need pain to take the edge off the terror they're feeling. That we may proceed without such theatrics bodes well for you... at least as well as one can hope for here."

With that my guide, the Gunfighter turned and headed out the elevator door into Purgatory.

Head down, resigned to a fate of which I was still unclear, I willed my feet forward and fell in after him. I was a half-step behind him, with one foot in and the other out of the elevator, when the shooting had started.

*This needn't be a place of eternal torment and suffering.
This could be heaven just as there could be heaven on earth,
were that the collective will and need.*

DE TENEBRA

CHAPTER 5

ET TIMIDUS EST, UT MANE DOMI

(The Timid May Stay At Home)

I PICKED UP the eight shoes, four shirts, three belts, seven socks, two sets of bloomers (don't ask), four weapons, and four pairs of pants that was all that was left of the assailants that attacked when he exited the elevator, and fell in behind The Gunfighter. As we walked down the hall of what appeared to be a standard issue government administration building, I chanced a glance around.

I'd seen a lot in my first few minutes in Purgatory. Other than being brutal and uncomfortably hot and humid, Purgatory was not at all what I had expected. There were no sheer cliffs to be thrown from or pits of lava and fire to burn in. Instead, there were worn wood floors, and empty counters guarded vacant desks that were stacked high with files and documents.

The other souls that I saw, well they looked like extras on a studio lot from a hodge-podge of movies. In addition to the Grapes of Wrath look, there were some Starsky and Hutch, several porn set rejects wearing nothing, a few in Game of Thrones medieval, even a woman clad in a fur bikini à la 10 Million Years BC.

I was like a tourist in New York, looking everywhere but where I was going.

I turned just in time to avoid running into ... Patti LuPone.

Patti LuPone here? in Purgatory?

I was stunned, really stunned, and not just because I was pretty sure Patti was still alive. I lost focus and have may even let out a yelp. Before I could stop them, the swords and knives slid off the stack of clothes I carried and fell to the floor in a loud ruckus.

She looked at the tangle of swords and clubs on the floor, smiled gleefully, and in an all-wrong voice asked, "play you pick-up sticks?"

When The Gunfighter stopped and faced her, I braced for more shooting. Instead, he spoke with seeming familiarity.

"No games witch."

Patti's face fell with disappointment.

Witch? "Patti LuPone is a witch?"

"That's not Patti LuPone. She's called May. She's my Beldam Witch."

My face fell with disappointment.

Then I realized what he'd said and blurted out. "Witches are real?"

He spoke as he turned to resume walking.

"They're real, diverse, and sharp of wit. The lesson you should have learned in the elevator is that in this place what you see and hear is more, and with time hopefully less, a function of what you expect. If you only speak English, you'll hear English unless you need or expect to hear something else. May here guessed you'd like to see Patti LuPone so she influenced you to see that form."

Again, he didn't bother to look over his shoulder.

"May, you will show him your real self."

Where Patti was, now stood a tall, bone-thin, woman with bright red claw like fingernails. Matching bright red lipstick, applied with abandon, accentuated a smile that bordered on maniacal. Her outfit, a low plunged peplum blouse and hip hugging black pencil skirt with white tear-drop shapes instead of polka dots, hung from her emaciated body, highlighting her odd points and angular form. She had jet-black hair, cut in an inverted bob with points so sharp they could have been weapons. Thick black kohl liner, apparently put on with fat fingers, surrounded black button like eyes that had no white sclera. Instead of a pupil four thinly connected dots formed an "X" in the center where the iris and pupil would be. Cracked and dry, white powdered skin stood in contrast to her eyes and lips.

She looked almost comical, kind of like a Morticia Adams meets Raggedy Ann, but in a far scarier way.

I'd forgotten all about the clothes and equipment that I'd dropped to the floor, until he started giving her directions.

"May, leave one outfit, sell the rest, then meet us at arrivals."

With a dexterity that took her freakiness factor up yet another notch, she bundled the shoes and weapons in the shirts, used the pants to make a strap, and tossed the whole lot over her shoulder. She then bared pointy white teeth at me in what I think was a smile, turned and seemed to glide-float down the hall.

I picked up the few things she'd left behind and followed The Gunfighter as he walked off in the other direction. We'd only gotten a few feet before my curiosity got the better of me.

"That is your employee?"

"No. I won HER."

I bristled at both his correction and the thought of one person owning another, but given his recent display of violence, I made it a point to keep it out of my voice.

"How does one come to win another person."

He ignored what I thought was the obvious question – were people really being brought, sold, or in this case won.

"Shortly after I arrived, she bet I couldn't shoot a rock off a nearby wall. It was a sucker's bet."

"She bet her freedom on your shooting ability?"

"No. I bet my freedom on my shooting ability, she bet all her possessions.

Mostly she was betting that my gun, like most complex tools, wouldn't work here. She lost that bet when it did, and I hit the target. She lost her freedom when she went double or nothing against me shooting someone in the head. Again, it was a sucker's bet."

Having just witnessed him in action, I passed on the question of whether she was betting that he wouldn't do it.

"But the gun didn't work when that other guy tried to shoot you with it?"

I belatedly realized that I was pointing out an incon-

sistency in a story being told by a guy who'd just shot and/
or decapitated several people, so I made a hasty addition.

"Is there something different about the gun?"

"The gun is a Remington New Model Army .44
caliber revolver. In my hands, it's one of the few weapons
that works here. Some say it is cursed, some say it's bonded
to me, most say the two are the same. I got it off a dead
Calvary officer somewhere around 1863, and had it converted to cartridges a few years later."

"Wait, you were guiding souls to Purgatory in the
1860's?"

"No. I was in the Calvary in the 1860's."

"So, you were once human like me?"

"Human, yes. Like you, no.

"I was born in the mid 1800's. Back then life was
shorter and people grew up faster; at fourteen most folks
were working for a living, and few folks lived beyond sixty.
By the time I turned 16 I'd found my calling as a hunter.
By the age of 23 I'd hunted and killed just about every
creature on the North American continent, except man.

"I joined the Calvary because it offered a legal and
lucrative way to hunt and kill humans. As a soldier in the
Indian wars, I hunted and killed Comanche, Cheyenne,
and other Native American men, women and children for
a living."

"Children? "

I was incredulous.

"Is that why you're here?"

He ignored both my question and incredulity.

"By the time I turned 40 killing had become as habitual
and exciting as shaving. Once the wars ended my brand of

fighting was no longer needed and, having seen the things I'd done, the white soldiers refused to have anything to do with me. I was promoted and reassigned to 9th Calvary Company K, a group known as the Buffalo Soldiers.

"My unit got sent to Wyoming as part of a 'peace keeping effort' that became known as the Johnson County War. The locals didn't take well to having the army policing them, especially when the army consisted mostly of blacks. When a few of the boys under my command were beaten by some locals we'd been sent to protect, I decided to send the townsfolk a message.

"I went to the homes of the four men that were involved. I gutted the two single men, and left them to die, beat the wife of one of the married men to death in front of him before I shot him, and made the couple that had kids watch me feed their offspring to their hogs, before I shot first her, then him.

Word of what I'd done spread through town before I finished that night's dinner."

"You fed the kids to the hogs then went and ate dinner?!"

A wave of nausea rolled over me that threatened to buckle my knees. I closed my eyes, took a few deep breaths, and prayed he'd stop talking. He didn't.

"By dawn the next morning a lynch mob had gathered outside the fort and was threatening to burn it down if I wasn't turned over. The Captain of the fort and I had been through a lot together. When he asked, I didn't mince words about my deeds. He went out and talked to the crowd, then came back and gave me a choice. I could either be hanged on the spot, something he didn't think would satisfy the crowd and would likely lead to several soldiers and locals being killed, or I could take off my uniform and walk off the base as a deserter, into the hands of the mob.

"He agreed to let me keep my gun provided I pocket all but a single cartridge. He said it was out of respect for the things I'd done in battle, but I suspect he, like many others, believed the gun was cursed.

"I'd hanged and lynched people before, so I understood and respected his offer. I took off the jacket I'd been issued on the spot. Then let the captain see me take out all but one cartridge from the gun and put the rest in my pocket. After a nod from him and a salute from me that went unreturned, I turned and walked out the fort's front gate.

"I shot myself in the head with this gun in front of the crowd just outside the gate of the fort. I was buried in an unmarked grave a stone's throw from the fort with the gun in its holster and the remaining cartridges in my pocket."

Eyes closed tight, I rapid-fire swallowed to keep from throwing up. When I opened my eyes, I took a deep steadying breath, stood up straight, and decided I'd rather talk about May.

"If May knew the gun worked for you, why would she think you wouldn't kill someone with it?"

"A soul can't be killed. But, if there's enough damage done to the self-projection, by say a bullet to the head or decapitation, the soul will abandon the projection and move on. Thing is, most souls that move another on, move-on themselves. I suppose it has something to do with the gravity of the act and balance on this plane.

"May was counting on me shooting someone with it. She'd already been paid a handsome fee to get a particular guy moved-on. If I moved-on, I couldn't collect on either of her bets with me and she'd keep what she'd been paid. If I didn't move-on, she would quite happily become my property."

His claim conjured images of plantation owners claiming that their slaves had happily forfeited their freedom for the master's care. Again, I bristled unobtrusively. "Happily? Why would anyone be happy to be a slave?"

"She's not a slave, she's under contract to me as an indentured servant.

"My being able to move others on with impunity is a valuable commodity here. The few of us that can do so generally work for the state. The few of us that can do this kind of work are generically referred to as Reapers. Between the job, the always available side jobs, and our ability to bring some basic goods back from the earthly plane, we're well paid. And as long as she's my servant I'm obliged to provide for her. The war paint and fancy outfits she wears, like the clothes she took and the ones you're holding, were imported … at no small cost.

"Purgatory is full of imperfect souls, all of whom arrive here without any worldly possessions. Call it vanity, shame, or ignorance, warm though it is here, few are willing to walk around as a naked self-projection, like you're doing."

Initially I was more shocked than embarrassed. I even had to look down to accept the truth of what I'd heard. I know, I know, you'd think I'd realize I wasn't wearing clothes pretty early in the game. But what can I say, somewhere between finding out I was going to Purgatory, witnessing multiple killings, or move-ons as they call them, and meeting freaky-indentured May, I guess I got distracted. I'd just kinda assumed that I was still wearing the hospital smock that was part of my elevator construct.

When the truth of it hit me, I cringed, blushed, and quickly repositioned the clothes I was carrying. Replaying key events since my arrival, like the crowd looking at me after the shooting and May's freaky bared teeth smile, brought another wave of embarrassment.

"You might want to put those clothes you're holding to their intended use?"

Though, as usual his tone was unengaged and his eyes showed complete indifference, something told me he was enjoying my predicament.

I dropped everything except the pants. In my rush to cover myself it wasn't until after I got one leg all the way in and the other down to about mid-calf that I realized I'd made a mistake. These were the fancy old pants of one of the first attackers. There were buttons instead of a zipper and they'd been vacated without being unfastened. There was no way I could get both legs in with them fastened while standing. I teetered briefly on the verge of falling over before adopting the universally ridiculed solution of hopping around on one foot while I simultaneously tried to unfasten them and/or extract my partially inserted leg.

After three or four graceless hops I realized both that the pants were buttoned all the way up and that the foot of my half-in leg had passed through the pant leg bottom and wasn't coming out without a fight. Absent something to lean on, I was going down.

I'd have settled for a wall or desk but there was nothing

even close. Instead, I took another hop to get within arms-length of the Reaper called The Gunfighter, then reached for his shoulder to balance myself.

He moved, with the same speed, balance, and indifference he'd shown earlier in his killing spree, and stayed just outside of my reach. My hand made just enough contact to appreciate the softness of his poncho; it was like pushing against water, there was nowhere near enough substance to offer balance or support.

Faced with the inevitability of my fall, I opted for the least bad outcome; a respectable, but by no means pretty, forward roll that ended with me sitting on the floor still holding on to my half on pants. It wasn't the perfect position, but it allowed me to undo the pant buttons and slide my other leg in.

While there, I made the best of being on my ass and scooched over, grabbed the shoes, and put them on. They were worn, ugly, and stiff with dirt. My foot fought against them because they were too small, and my stomach threatened to join the rebellion when my sockless foot felt the toe patterns that had been worn into the sole of the shoe by prior owners.

Just when I resigned myself to going barefoot my foot acquiesced and slid all the way in. I briefly considered trying to extract my one foot but found that even more unappealing when I realized I'd have to carry the shoes in my hands. After coercing my other foot into the other shoe, I stood and, in an effort to retrieve a modicum of dignity, fixed The Gunfighter with my 'you're the worst wingman ever' look before putting on the shirt.

The clothes May left were borderline functional but

far from flattering. The coarse material of the pants fought against movement and, absent belt loops, which like the zipper was a subsequent invention, they sagged and promised a plumber's crack at every reach, stoop, or bend. The shirt was stained, worn paper thin, and like everything except for the shoes, a size too large.

I didn't need a mirror to know that I looked like shit.

Admittedly, I was over-extending the rule that 'if you feel bad you should try to look good,' but since I both looked and felt bad, I decided I should act bad.

I pushed past The Gunfighter, headed for who knows where.

"Well, let's get this ass-show on the road."

I didn't bother to look over my shoulder when I said it.

There are many places where the soul
goes seeking growth or grace.
Some are called Purgatory some are called something else.
Some aren't called anything at all.

DE TENEBRA

CHAPTER 6

IN REM

("Against Or About A Thing")

It was an old building. Hard wood floors polished by eons of foot traffic reflected dulled images while cracked and broken Latham-like plaster hid rough stone walls. We walked down the hall passing room after room with non-descript desks and individuals doing non-descript jobs; people seemingly moving papers from right to left then left to right, talking to people that didn't appear to be listening, or being talked to while clearly not listening. Every now and then voices would rise or tempers would flare and a head or two would pop up to peer over the stacks.

Those that chanced a glance up at the spectacle that we would have been anywhere else would, on seeing The Gunfighter, inevitably look away and speak in hushed tones.

Rounding a corner brought a long line of mostly naked people into view. The line stretched the length of the hallway, perhaps beyond, and took up most of its width. Hanging from the ceiling at regular intervals were faded gray-black signs with red writing that read, "New Arrivals." After walking along-side the line for about half the length of the hallway, we turned and entered a sturdy, unmarked door.

The door opened into a sea of mismatched desks that were bordered on the far end by shoulder high cubicle walls next to a series of cell like offices. Most of the desks were vacant but every so often a head would pop up or I'd see the slouch of someone's shoulders.

Walking past the cubicles and in front of the offices, The Gunfighter turned, opened a door, and entered. He hadn't knocked so I assumed it was his office.

I almost bumped into him when he stopped short.

In front of him, behind a battered old desk, was a guy that was both fat and thin at the same time. His skinny arms rested atop a contrasting gut while beady eyes looked out furtively over pink patchwork cheeks that evidenced an alcohol-medicated life. Sparse gray hair on his head and discolored splotches on his arms suggested a long, slow end to a short and uneventful life. In the ever-present humidity, his ill-fitting clothes clung to him. He was constantly fidgeting and pulling at his clothes, in a poor and humorless Rodney Dangerfield impersonation.

He sat ensconced in a makeshift fortress of boxes that was fortified with stacks of paper. Behind him, a dust laden bookshelf was populated with several law books. Though divided by the occasional manila folder, piece of paper, or random object, they weren't arranged in any discernable order. An old-fashioned ink container and wood stick pen sat to the side of the desk - evidence of its use was smeared randomly across the papers on the desk, and liberally across his hands and shirt sleeves. Almost lost among the clutter on his desk was a wooden block with his title carved into it.

I don't believe I read his title, and I'm sure I don't remember it if I did.

Two chairs completed his office ensemble. Strategically placed too near the front of the desk was a broken and ratty hardwood chair. Being slightly shorter than his desk chair and obviously uncomfortable, it appeared intended for subordinates. More to the side, where conversations could be had without the desk interceding, was a relatively plush, high-back chair. Dusty for lack of use, it sat in wait for the hoped-for visit from a superior, colleague, or conspirator.

He sat up too straight in his chair - body ready for flight having never consider the fight option - and his eyes searched to and fro, unconsciously looking for an escape that he knew wasn't there. After he accepted that there was no getting out of whatever was going to happen, he greeted the Reaper with a false familiarity that did nothing to mask the fear he was trying to hold in check.

"Hey, … Gunfighter."

The Gunfighter rebuffed him silently, briefly fixing him with predatory eyes that passed through him before moving back to their eternal search for threat.

"So um, what can I do you for?"

Yeah, he actually said that.

Sullen and silent, the Gunfighter stepped to the side, leaving me standing before the bureaucrat in answer. When he saw my ill-fitting clothes, he was visibly, if only marginally, relieved.

Suddenly on the spot, I stammered out the only thing I could think of that might be pertinent.

"Um, I'm a new arrival."

After looking me up and down he smiled disingenuously. "Well with all those clothes you can't be too new. You've even got nice matching shoes."

Ignoring our vastly different interpretations of both clothes and nice, I jerked my head in The Gunfighter's direction.

"He gave them to me."

"Did he now?"

With a smile that bordered on salacious, the bureaucrat turned toward The Gunfighter.

"That true? You gave him clothes?"

The Gunfighter was deadly still. His eyes vaguely on the door where we'd entered. If I hadn't seen his lips move, I might not have known The Gunfighter was speaking when he answered.

"They're his half of the take from a four man move-on we just did."

"You split a move-on 50-50 with a newbie? I don't know, sounds a lot like a gift to me."

Greed had gotten the better of him. This guy was fishing for a bribe, and not being at all subtle about it.

The Gunfighter stepped forward quickly and slapped him with a backhand that neither of us realized was coming till we heard, and in his case felt, the crack of the blow. The Gunfighter paused, perhaps to consider it, perhaps to allow the man to appreciate that it was coming and that he couldn't do anything about it, then slapped him again … harder. Then The Gunfighter grabbed him by the shirt and pulled him close, so close that there was no doubt The Gunfighter would be heard through the man's slap induced fog.

"There's a lot you don't seem to know.

"You don't seem to know that you got this job after I moved your predecessor on, and you don't seem to know that your underlings have pooled their resources and are offering a bounty to anyone that's willing to move you on.

"The bounty isn't much, an amount that's generally beneath my kind, so I'll offer you a deal: I won't collect the bounty right here, right now, if you stop blathering on and give him all the information he needs.

"What do you say?"

The Gunfighter dropped his slapping hand to his gun as he released the man.

"I'll take anything other than 'ok' to mean you decline my offer."

Eyes watering from the slap, fear, or both, the fat-thin bureaucrat stared in shock, opened his mouth to say something, then caught himself. Realizing how close he'd come to getting moved on he stammered out, "Ok."

When The Gunfighter released him, he slumped-fell back into his chair.

Humiliated, mad, and bathed in a fresh new coat of sweat, he turned more on me than to me. After running his hand through the few hairs that had yet to flee his scalp, he gestured toward the ratty chair in front of his desk and all but yelled,

"Well. Sit your ass down!"

At 180 pounds and just about six feet tall I'm not particularly intimidating. But my family has fight in our genes and, with golden glove and professional boxers throughout the family tree, I have a legacy of ring work. Every man, woman, and child in my family was expected to be ready and able to throw down if, and when necessary. That I was gay brought me no quarter; some tried to beat it out of me, while others tried to prepare me for the risks of the life before me. The result was the same – long, hard, and often brutal training sessions. Growing up poor and black almost to the point of blue skinned only upped the ante - by the time I finished high school I'd survived gangs, knife-fights, being shot, at and way too much to take crap from this cowardly bureaucrat.

Besides, I was tired of people yanking my chain.

I locked eyes with him, then leaned forward to rest my knuckles on his desk - sending a message of aggression and dominance deep into his lizard brain.

"I'm sure you're going to ask, so yeah, I've already spent most of my share of the move-on, yeah I could use another pay day and, yeah I work cheaper than he does."

It was a bigger bluff than I then realized, but one that I knew he didn't have the nerve to call.

"Oh, ok, yeah, well um, the first thing I'll need to know is whether you'll be contesting your time here. I mean, it's ok if you are, or if you aren't, you know, either way is fine. I just need to know so I can, you know, figure out what all to tell you."

As I'd hoped, he assumed The Gunfighter was working with me because I was a newly arrived Reaper. I eased myself into the nicer chair at the side of his desk.

"Tell me everything."

At that, The Gunfighter touched hand to hat and walked out the room.

"Yeah, well, um, since you seem to know how moving-on and being moved-on works, we'll go over the rules first. They're fairly simple but any soul that gets caught breaking them will be beaten, dismembered, dipped, or moved-on."

I knew I shouldn't, but I asked anyway. "Dipped?"

"Yeah, dipped - in lye that's made from wood ash."

He glanced up and to the left - recalling some memory that he'd worked hard to repress.

"It feels cool at first, almost a welcome reprieve from the heat here. Then your skin starts to itch. That itch becomes a burning sensation that gets worse and worse. In the earthly realm, after your skin is eaten away it would start in on the muscle and eventually eat through to the bone. Here, you get all the pain, but instead of eating through flesh and bone whatever is dipped slowly and painfully dissolves away, layer after layer.

"An arm, both legs, your entire body, they just get smaller and smaller, and lose form. If you're lowered slowly or dipped repeatedly, the process can take weeks. The good news, if you wanna call it that, is that other than the Reapers and the state, nobody's likely to dip you until you fully dissolve. The bad news is people have been dipped at the same rate that they heal, until their sanity or will to be here is long gone."

I shouldn't have asked. I'd already heard and seen more than I wanted, so I prompted him to move on.

"Ok, tell me about the rules."

The rules were straight-forward, but odd to say the least. Rule Number 1 was that everybody must work. So, while sloth will get you into Hell, it isn't tolerated in Purgatory. It seemed ironic, but oddly appropriate. Obviously, somebody here had a since of humor.

Rule Number 2 was that things like altruism, mercy and kindness were forbidden. This rule gave new and literal meaning to the adage that, "no good deed goes unpunished." It also explained both why the Reaper reacted the way he did to the insinuation that he'd given me a gift, and why he'd let me fall when I was trying to put on my hideous pants.

Rule Number 3, that "pleasure for the sake of pleasure is not permitted," is exactly what you'd expect to find in Purgatory.

Rule Number 4 was the exception to Rule Number 3. The "schadenfreude exception" allowed and even encouraged taking pleasure in other's harm or pain. This exception was fundamental to Purgatory's economy. Wealth could be accumulated, as long as doing so harmed others; flaunting, excess, and elitism gave rise to jealousy and oppression.

Rule Number 5 was that valid contracts must be honored, and work must be paid for promptly. As a rule of thumb, it had to be paid for in about the same amount of time it took to incur the debt – so a job that takes a day must be paid for within a day of completion. While this initially struck me as a basic economic provision of law, Purgatory's definition of "valid" and "debt" made this a far more nuanced proposition.

Finally, Rule Number 6 prohibited new arrivals, souls that had been here less than six days, from contracting with servitude or bond, for anything more than the number of days they had till their arraignment. Apparently, this was intended to stop new entrants from either being conned into long servitude contracts with offers for things that they didn't need, or entering into long-term agreements for extravagances when they knew they were going to departure soon.

I scanned his bookshelf with growing interest as he went on but gave him my full attention when he started talking about the hearing schedule.

"You'll have a retention arraignment in front of a magistrate five days hence. This will be the first step toward determining residency. If you wish to remain, some sort of trial will be scheduled for about six weeks later. If after that you still want to stay, it will be about six months till your next trial. Any more process will be scheduled at the end of your month six trial, but as a rule your next appearances would come six years, six decades, then six hundred years after that."

"Six hundred years!

"What am I supposed to do during that time and where will I stay while I'm waiting?"

"Oh, well I assumed you'd already secured lodgings and, um, would continue in the line of business you seem to have started in. If you can't afford something, we can put you up in our new arrivals facilities. But I'm sure ... ."

He was cut-off by a knock on the door. I turned and there stood The Gunfighter's freaky looking indentured servant May. Her button-like eyes were so intensely focused on the bureaucrat that I looked back at the fat-thin bureaucrat to see what was going on. To my somewhat horrified amazement, his eyes had lit up, his mouth reformed into a leer of a smile, and he'd sat up a bit straighter; he even tried to adjust his sparse hair.

Remembering what The Gunfighter had said about May, and figuring he couldn't possibly be seeing what I saw, I guessed May was showing him something he really liked.

Apparently, May was the sweet to the Reaper's sour. She seemed to bat her button eyes and even managed to make her broken dialect sound almost coy when she said, "Two done? Take to lodging."

I figured I'd gotten all I was going to get from the fat-thin bureaucrat, but knew I needed more. I decided I'd take advantage of his "agreement" with The Gunfighter.

"I'm going to borrow a few of the books you have on your shelf."

That seemed to break the spell. He shook his head and for a moment looked almost like he'd been slapped again.

I cut him off when he started to stammer out a refusal.

"That is, unless you want The Gunfighter to know that you broke the deal you made with him by refusing to give me some of the information I need?"

May's cracked, blood-red lips parted into another pointy-toothed smile. And I left the fat-thin bureaucrat's office with Corpus Juris Infernum, Corpus Justinian Infernum, and Corporis et Ainima, three books that would help determine my fate.

With May leading the way, we exited through thick wooden doors that swung on well-oiled hinges and headed out of the building for my first real glimpse of Purgatory.

We walked out into what at first looked like a bad air day in Delhi. The unmoving air was so thick and smoky with particulates that I couldn't see much beyond a hundred yards or so.

As we moved down the stairs into the streets, I saw several rough-hewn stone buildings. Some, two or three stories tall, that gave way to smaller one-story affairs, were braced against each other, others were separated randomly by stone streets, alleys, or vacant patches of gravel and dirt. Unlit heavy wooden torches were lodged in stone cut-outs on buildings here and there, where streetlights should have been.

The air borne particulates gave the humid air a subtle scent of smoke and earthy decay. Fallen particulate formed a fine layer of soot on the ground so pervasive that its presence was evidenced most by its absence. Soot darkened both sides of the pale masonry streets; foot traffic had roughed out an irregular center section. Looking outward toward the horizon cast the streets in stark relief; like railroad tracks, they seemed inexorably headed towards some dark fate.

But the thing that struck me most was what I didn't see. There were no pits of fire or demonic imps inflicting torment on writhing souls. No booming voice or third eye looked down on us from some perch up high. Instead, it was like walking through one of those old black and white movies shot in some small European town.

We walked among rough but diversely dressed people, headed here and there along the cobblestone streets. My ill-fitting shoes found and frequently abandoned purchase on the irregular surface. They constantly teetered and threatened to slip from under me in a most treacherous fashion - forcing me to walk with a wonky, misaligned stride. Neither my odd gait, ill-fitting outfit, or May's oddly stylish ensemble drew the slightest attention.

Rounding a corner, I slip-skidded to an abrupt stop, barely managing to avoid a bent and dirty man struggling to keep a wheelbarrow upright as he pushed it up the inclined and uneven stone street.

Looking back in the direction we'd come I was again struck by the absence of things. There were no cars, plants, overhead wires, or any of the things I'd come to associate with civilization. I was beginning to grasp the full import of The Gunfighter's gun being a working machine.

"No machines?" I said.

"No machines." May replied.

"No plants?"

"Dead tree forest outside town."

I turned a full 360 degrees to look at the streets anew. There were no complex tools, powerlines, plants, or animals anywhere in sight. Sensing that she was a good if not my only source of reliable information, I turned to her.

"I have lots of questions. But let's start with just two. First, how much do I have left from my share of the move-on, and second, is it enough for a guy like me to take a girl like you somewhere for a drink?"

Sensing either that a new game was afoot or that I was playing into her hand, she picked up the pace and flashed me that pointy-toothed smile of hers.

"Bar. Room near."

❧

*And temptation? Is the perfect soul that has
never faced temptation truly perfect?*

DE TENEBRA

CHAPTER 7

QUANTUM MERUIT

(As Much As Deserved)

WE WALKED DOWN a maze of unmarked, rut-ridden, look-alike streets until we came to a building that was set far back from the street. It was bordered on two sides by the solid walls of the buildings next to it. In front, a low stone wall created an outdoor seating area between the street and the front of the building. Half a dozen or so wood hewn tables were surrounded by large stone blocks that served as seats.

Groups of two, sometimes three, were seated at the tables. Stepping through a gateless gap in the low stone wall, May moved toward a seat that put her back to one of the side buildings and provided good views of the street and the bar. She pulled a small but dainty hanky from her sleeve and, after slapping the dust off the stone, seated herself with the grace and practice of a high society woman.

Almost immediately, and without any discernable prompting from May, a short, squat man scurried out with an empty bowl and two heavy, sand-made glasses. Each glass held about two fingers worth of a light brown liquid. After placing the items on the table between us, he half bowed and left without a word.

Following May's lead, I picked up one of the glasses, albeit without extending my pinky finger as she had, and took a sip. It had no smell but a bad, scat-like, gag-inducing taste. That, and the acid like burn it carried when I swallowed it down, induced a coughing fit that left me gasping and teary-eyed. Sitting up, through bleary eyes I watched May watch me, her odd stillness interrupted only by an occasional dab at the side of her mouth with her hanky.

This was my first taste of Forus, the drink of choice and indeed, the only drink to be had in Purgatory. Though it's a simple distillate, made by burning wood to produce pure methyl alcohol, it differs widely in quality; a better grade, improves the bad after-taste but does nothing to improve the post-consumption burn. Bad as my drink was, turns out I was drinking one of the better grades.

Just a few sips left me bleary eyed and pathetic looking. This was the perfect time to ask my questions. With a Forus-induced hitch in my throat I warmed May up with a simple inquiry.

"Pleasure for pleasure forbidden, but we sit having a pleasant drink?"

Disappointed by my diction, my ruse, my inability to handle my liquor, or all three, she shrugged toward her glass and queried, "Pleasant?"

I conceded her point with a nod and another sip.

After another round of coughs, gags, and tears, I paused to catch my breath and took in the crowd. It wasn't particularly obvious, so it took me a moment to notice. Most of the patrons would casually lean forward and spit into the bowls shortly after taking a swig. A few wouldn't bother spitting into a bowl, they'd just lean to the side and spit on the ground. Turns out, the Forus being spit into the bowls would be resold as Et Forus, or Ad Infernum - depending on whether it was spit out once or twice.

Rather than lean forward or to the side to spit, May sat up straight, her posture perfect. Pinky out defiantly, sipping the vile concoction as though it were a fine reposado tequila. Almost rhythmically, after each sip she'd put the glass down, and repeatedly dab the side of her mouth with her hanky.

I was surprised. So much so that I fell into her dialect effortlessly.

"Spit drink no?"

Button-like eyes downcast and with modesty and a hint of indignation she said, "Dab. Spit no ladylike!"

"May" I said, "you are truly a gem among stones." Then I raised my glass in toast, took a swig, swished it around my mouth, then picked up the bowl that came with the Forus and spat. Gone was the acid burn, and the scat after taste was reduced to more of a scat essence.

May flashed me her pointy toothed smile, took another sip, then daintily dabbed at the sides of her mouth again.

When I asked how I was supposed to pay for our drinks, she placed two dark coins on the table. She identified one as a Horis the other was a DieBus.

The Horis represents a common hour of work while the DieBus represents a full day of work at the common wage and is equivalent to 9 Horis.

This went a long way toward explaining why some of the morning's assailants seemed hesitant and unprepared for the undertaking – they were conscripts paying the penalty for amassing more debt than can be paid off in a day to avoid being dipped. Dipping as punishment also explained why there was no forgery or other crimes against the state in Purgatory; the punishment for such crimes was repeated full body dipping.

I picked up the Horis to get a closer look. Rather than metal, it was made of hardwood. Burned and carved into it were intricate and detailed designs. The front showed a pan balance scale with a fire in the pan on one side outweighing stone blocks in the pan of the other side. On the back of the coin was what appeared to be blood-stained wings with feathers strewn about, as though they'd been ripped from an angel's back. Along the bottom, Herculaneum style lettering spelled out "Non Est Spe." My very rusty Latin roughed this out as saying something about there being no hope.

The DieBus was a slightly larger coin. It had the same blazing fire and stones on the scale pan on one side, but on the other side, above the same Latin inscription, was the Leviathan cross - a cross with two horizontal lines instead of one and what looks like an infinity symbol at the bottom of the vertical line.

After examining the coins, I asked, "Do I have enough to buy us another round of drinks?"

May shrugged her shoulders.

"Today."

Turns out, May was a very good bookkeeper. After the cost of my "clothes" and our drinks, I had 1 DieBus and 2 Horis left from my share of The Gunfighter's move-on.

I wondered out loud, "how am I supposed to eat for a week on that?"

As she dabbed away her last sip of her Forus May casually asked, "Hungry?"

And it hit me. Though I'd been in Purgatory for almost a full day and hadn't eaten since just before I was drugged, I wasn't the least bit hungry. I looked around at the other patrons and saw that no one had ordered any type of food.

"No eat?"

May leaned forward, nodded toward no one in particular, and whispered conspiratorially. "Eat pleasure."

I paused for a second to take that in, then ordered a second round of drinks.

May proved to be a wealth of information. She schooled me on the economics, politics, and general workings of Purgatory and its legal system. By her best guesstimate, about half the souls agree to move on at their first appearance before the magistrate, this percentage drops with each court appearance after that.

May didn't know of any instance where someone either exhausted their appeals or won their case. She was of the mind that people got to keep trying until they gave up. Though she'd heard that prosecutors often offered enticements for souls to move on, May thought that most folks sought to stay in Purgatory because they understood or at least accepted it.

Our conversation took a bit of a surprising turn when

I asked, "how many Reapers are there?" To my surprise, May didn't know how many Reapers there were, she just knew there were several. In addition to The Gunfighter, May mentioned Hatchet, Jester, Scythe, Farmer, Blade, and Samurai.

Those that took the job as a Reaper - and pretty much everyone that was qualified was offered the job and ended up taking it - were given the ability to move between Purgatory, Hell, and the earthly plane. Most brought with them the weapon that they'd mastered in life but, until The Gunfighter's arrival, the weapons had been basic tools, all of which could, with sufficient materials and varying degrees of effort, be produced here in Purgatory.

The Reapers were a tightknit but generally antisocial group. Though they sometimes worked and regularly trained together, they weren't what anyone would call friends. As far as May knew no Reaper had ever moved another Reaper on. Most thought this was by mutual agreement but May knew for a fact that they were all under contract, most for an eternity, and apparently the boss forbade such things.

The punishment for breaking a servitude contract was dipping for as long as the contract principal determined or up to the length of the contract. The Reapers' boss had been known to dip people that disobeyed him until they were about to dissolve, then they'd be pulled out and allowed to recover just enough to continue the punishment. Depending on the offense and the boss's temperament, the process had been known to go on for decades.

I was as impressed by May's knowledge as I was by her candor. And, while I think of myself as a good schmoozer, this type of reveal was way beyond my skill level. I was out of my depth and I had the distinct feeling that it was I who was the mark. So, rather than beat around the bush, I just asked.

"May, why are you giving me all this information?"

"Accept drink, obligation implied. Share information, obligation satisfied."

Narrowing her button like eyes she declared and all but waved her finger in my face as she admonished, "No frees. No favors!"

May explained that since performing or accepting favors was a punishable offense, whenever someone offers something, it's assumed that they want something in return. So, accepting the offer implies that you agree to give something in return. Unlike the explicit deal, which generally has well defined, if not clearly stated mutual obligations, implied obligations are neither clearly stated nor mutually agreed upon. Implied obligations have many layers and nuances; even unsolicited acts carried an expectation that the beneficiary would give something in return.

So it was, that for a couple of Horis and the agony of a few sips of Forus, I'd learned the subtleties of the implied deal and, more importantly, not to underestimate May.

If spiritual growth is the objective, free
will is the catalyst it requires.

De Tenebra

CHAPTER 8

QUI FACET PER ALIUM FACIT PER SE
**(Who Acts Through Another,
Acts Through Himself)**

I WAS ABOUT to launch into another round of questions when May sat up straight...er. She dropped, more than put her handkerchief into her purse, then leaned to the side as if to hear better. When she recognized what she heard, she straightened up and smoothed her skirt before crossing her hands over her knees and assuming a most lady-like position. I leaned in the direction May had oriented, and strained to hear a faint but rhythmic clop, clop, clop - like hooves making their way along the stone streets.

Moments later, a coal-black creature came into view. It was big, easily almost ten feet tall at the highest point, a large hump in the middle. Thickly matted hair around the neck and head gave-way to an elongated snout and long shaggy hair covered its body and legs. Even in the heat and humidity of Purgatory, its every exhale produced a plume of steam from its nostrils.

As my mind labored to understand the sight, what I'd thought was a large hump on the beast's back, shifted to the side and glide-slid to the ground. It was only after they stood apart that I realized I was looking at a shaggy horse and its rider rather than some strange Hell beast.

The rider had a long shaggy cowl draped far over his head and wore a dark wooly cloak that was matched to, if not made from, the horse's hair. He stood motionless in the street for a moment, then he moved forward and faced the horse. There was no saddle or stirrups. Burried in the shaggy mane was a chain that connected to a black metal guard that ran between the horse's eyes and down the top of its muzzle. In purpose and appearance, it was more a helmet than a bridle. Similar guards ran along the horse's forelegs, and another black plate was just barely visible on the furry chest. Standing face-to-face with the hairy, plate-covered horse head, the rider pulled the chain that served as reins forward over the horse's head as though he were going to tie it to a post, but instead let it fall. Horse and rider stood still for a moment, then both leaned forward to touch heads. When they straightened, both turned and looked toward the pub.

All eyes in the now-silent pub that had been on the duo sought interest elsewhere when the rider approached. Though the long cowl hid his features completely, I'd have bet my last Horis that he was staring at me. I suspect other patrons felt the same way.

Many hands drifted to inner pockets; most sought

coin to pay their bill and quickly leave, while some sought the false assurance of a secreted weapon.

As he approached the low stone wall that defined the seating area, the rider pulled back the cowl, exposing smooth bone-white skin stretched taught over an emaciated head. He wasn't just bald, he was hairless; there were no eyebrows, no stubble, no hint of his having any hair anywhere. The smoothness of his head and face was broken only by the two small openings of his nose, a slit of a line that was his mouth, and dark, sunken eyes. Those eyes were offset by high cheekbones, that left hollows in his cheeks.

He scanned the pub crowd with the same dead-eyed, predatory look I'd seen in The Gunfighter's eyes. By the time he reached the pub's seating area he'd sized up and dismissed everyone in the bar. Except me.

Having seen the hardened stare of The Gunfighter, I'd like to say that I was not inclined to wilt under his gaze. In reality, he was too much of a spectacle, and I was too naïve, to avert my eyes like everyone else did. As it was, I didn't realize I was staring till he came to a stop right in front of me. Standing close as he now was, my eyes were on the same plane as the axe that hung at his side. It was a beautiful, intricately etched, single-edged affair with a black wooden handle that ended in a metal spear tip.

I'd just taken a sip of my Forus and was appreciating the bone-like polish of the black wood handle when I felt his predatory gaze and realized both that he saw desire in my appreciation and that in Purgatory to openly covet is to challenge.

He withdrew the hatchet slowly, with an all too

familiar sense of deliberateness, and placed it on the table between us. This triggered a post-traumatic stress like flash-back to The Gunfighter's post killing spree offer of his pistol to anyone brave, foolish, or desperate enough to try and take it.

Rather than awkward, the silence that followed was one of pure terror. What should have been a quandary, about how to defuse the situation, was resolved by an involuntary swallow of the Forus I'd forgotten was in my mouth.

A brief squint of his eyes suggested my bold drinking move had caught him off guard. This was followed by obvious disappointment when I teared up just before I erupted into another round of Forus-induced coughs and gasps.

May broke the now embarrassing and increasingly awkward moment with a greeting that suggested familiarity.

"Rider."

As though I no longer existed, he nodded toward May in acknowledgement, picked up and sheathed his hatchet, turned, and entered the pub.

After wiping the Forus-induced tears from my eyes, I took a deep breath to recompose myself before turning to May.

This was the first time I questioned her. I mean, yeah, I'd asked her questions and, sure, a part of me still had questions about her very existence, but this was the first time I doubted something she'd told me.

"May, I thought you said there were no animals here?"

She answered without missing a beat.

"No animals."

I nodded over my shoulder toward the beast on the street.

"Animal."

She didn't even bother to look in the direction I'd nodded.

"No animal."

Incredulous, I looked to the shaggy black beast in the street, then back at her, then at the horse again, and finally threw up my hands.

Her tone was one generally reserved for kids and simpletons.

"No animal, Grim."

That name almost made me forget about the animal question.

"Are you saying that guy is The Grim Reaper?"

"Grim and Rider. Reapers."

It seemed May was either confusing the horse with the rider or had seriously bought into the image of the two-as-one. I was beginning to suspect that she'd had more than enough Forus for a while.

I was getting tired, so I suggested we continue our discussion on our way to where I was staying. That I'd avoid seeing that Reaper again as he left was itself reason enough for me to get going.

May dropped a couple of Horis on the table and we left. As we passed through the opening in the low wall and into the street, I saw four men headed our way. At least two were armed, all of them looked desperate.

May let out a low hiss when she saw them and began muttering something I couldn't quite make out. As they drew nearer it became clear that they weren't the least

bit interested in us; their focus was on the animal, ...
Grim, ... or whatever it was.

Ignoring us as they passed, the four quickly moved to
surround the beast. The two holding weapons stood on
opposite sides of the horse that wasn't an animal. Another
guy stood in the street farthest away from me, in front of
the horse, and the last man completed the surround by
standing behind the beast. I wasn't exactly sure what the
point of all this was, so I looked to May. Seeing my confusion, she explained their intentions with three words.

"Steal. Eat. Sell."

Even ignoring the fact that the souls in Purgatory
didn't need to eat, this seemed all kinds of wrong. Having
made my way in Purgatory thus far by being a silent
partner on the right side of a fight, I came up with a quick
and completely half-baked plan.

With the implied obligation theory in mind, I figured
I'd call The Rider, he'd save his horse, and I'd get a few
Horis out of the deal.

I headed back toward the gate, to call for The Rider.
Of course, this being Purgatory, I shouldn't have been
surprised when or that things quickly went sideways.

As I approached, the guy nearest me, the one in the
back, either mistook my approach as an attack or just
decided to send me a message. He turned and lunged at
me with a long, rusty knife.

Luck and muscle memory saved me. Before I could
think about it my hands came up like a boxer and I stepped
to the outside of his attack, blocked his lunging right arm
with my left, transferred his wrist to my right hand and
pulled him by the arm while he was still thrusting forward.

This accelerated his momentum in the direction of his attack, throwing him off-balance. Before he could stop his forward momentum, I reached across his back and over his shoulder with my left arm and added my weight to that of his own now out-of-control body. To his credit, he got his feet underneath him in time to avoid crashing face first into the uneven stones. Unfortunately for him, as he pushed back to regain his balance, I pulled back with my left arm and suddenly off-balanced him in the direction he was fighting to go. The foot sweep I added took his feet out from under him and converted his stumbling backward to a high and painful fall.

Though he landed hard on his left side, his right-hand still gripped the knife. I still had a grip on that wrist, so I dropped down onto his jaw with my left knee and his ribs with my right knee, with enough force to break both. From this kneeling position I slipped the knife-holding arm into an arm bar.

In spite of his ungainly landing, likely broken jaw and ribs, and arm-barred arm, he kept struggling and managed to move his wrist enough to slash my shoulder. In response, I thrust my hips and arms forward into the arm-bar with enough force to dislocate his elbow, and the weapon went flying.

I looked up to see where the weapon landed and realized a few things. First, I'd broken a fundamental rule of street fighting – 'don't go to the ground if the assailant might have friends around.' I dive-rolled forward and used the should-have-been dislocated and now spaghetti-like arm, to pull my attacker over, onto his stomach. This brought me close enough to the knife to grab it. When

I got to my feet, knife in hand, I realized that I'd gotten away with breaking the rule about going to the ground because the other three attackers had their hands full with the horse that somehow wasn't an animal.

The attacker in front had wrapped the reins-chain around his hand and was trying so hard to pull the horse forward that when, after some resistance, the horse took a sudden step forward he lost his balance. When he threw himself forward to keep from falling backward, the horse took advantage of the slack and, with a roll of his head created a circular wave along the chain that looped the chain around the guy's neck. With a turn of his head and a hard yank on the chain the horse took the guy's head off.

With a turn away from the pub and another quick whip of his head the horse lashed out with the now-free chain at the next attacker in the street. The guy moved, but not quickly enough. The chain cleaved a deep gash in his thigh that left him crawling.

The attacker on the sidewalk between the street and the pub made his move when the horse turned, exposing its flank. Rather than turn to face the new threat, the horse unleashed a series of rear leg, mule-like kicks. Though none of the kicks landed, they drove the attacker back, across the sidewalk, toward the low stone wall of the pub. The guy never saw the intricately etched, black wooden handled, single edge axe that swung from the other side of the wall and took his head off.

Far too late and much too slowly, the guy with the gashed leg was trying to crawl away. I watched as the horse casually walked over and with a heavy hoof, cleaved his head in with less interest than if he were pawing at the ground.

That's when I understood what May meant. This was not some dumb animal. The horse - Grimm, and the Rider had a symbiotic relationship; they were a Reaper.

It was also when I realized that the guy who'd just chopped off a guy's head with an axe, the guy that actually looked like death - the Rider, Rider Reaper, or whatever May called him - was headed toward me, axe in hand, walking casually, and looking disinterestedly deadly.

My spaghetti-armed assailant was on the ground between me and The Rider. Though his right arm was useless, and he couldn't talk very well with his messed-up jaw, he mumbled and pointed at me with his free hand clearly trying to tell the Rider that I, the guy holding the knife, was part of the attack crew, not him.

The Rider seemed to get the message.

Desperate and near panic, I looked to May. She stood wide-eyed, clutching her hanky, and actually looking, I don't know, concerned ... ish? It was almost sweet. But it was also obvious that she couldn't or wouldn't do anything to help.

I quickly considered my options. Saying it wasn't me probably wouldn't fly, what with me holding the knife and all. I could fight him, but if he was anywhere near as fast and skilled as The Gunfighter, I knew I didn't stand a chance. I seriously thought of running away, but between my janky shoes and his having a horse, I'd no doubt the guy would catch me.

It was the thought of the horse that saved me. I hurriedly stuck the knife in the waist of my pants - without any unintended slicing thank-you. Then, using a generally under-valued skill that I picked up in grade school, I put my thumb and forefinger in my mouth and whistled loudly toward the horse.

Hearing what I'd hoped was either a familiar or foreign enough sound, the horse turned in my direction and, with an indifference that suggested more obligation than gratitude, nickered twice. The Rider, seeming not to have noticed any of this, continued his deadly casual approach. He didn't break stride when he got to where Spaghetti-arm lay between us still pointing at me; he stepped on and then through the base of Spaghetti-arm's skull with less interest than an animal pawing at the ground

Two steps later, just as Spaghetti-arm was starting to turn to goo and dissolve, he came to a stop in front of me. I didn't assume a fighting stance, raise my hands, or even flinch when he shifted his grip on the hatchet.

I wasn't being brave, I just didn't have it in me to control my shaky legs, Forus-queasy stomach, and flinch at the same time. He took a long moment to stare me through, then put the hatchet away and dropped some Horis on the pile of clothes that moments ago had been worn by Spaghetti-arm. Having acknowledged my contribution and satisfied our implied obligation, he simply turned and walked away.

May stepped off the sidewalk and rushed forward, looking for all the world like a damsel from an old western - albeit with weird eyes, pointy teeth, and way too much makeup - who's overcome with joy that the hero survived the gunfight. She rushed toward me, arms out-stretched only to stop, stoop, and gather up the clothes and coins.

Looking at me gleefully she said, "one third, I sell for."

Exhausted and shaking slightly with what felt like the

mother of all adrenaline come downs, I said 10%. In short order, we agreed she'd get 25% of the sale, the knife and coins were mine, and she'd tend to my shoulder injury.

Purgatory has gotten a bad reputation.

DE TENEBRA

CHAPTER 9

CUI BONO

(Who Benefits)

WE WALKED DOWN several unmarked, look-alike, rut-ridden streets before May stopped, seemingly at random, at a non-descript two-story stone building with a small hand painted sign that read, *Dark Light Inn*. I couldn't tell if it was the Forus, if Spaghetti-arm had done more damage than I'd thought, or if it was a combination of the two, but I was completely spent; I felt like we'd hiked for miles.

Out of habit I grabbed the heavy wooden door to open it as May stepped forward. Somewhere in the back of my increasingly fuzzy mind it dawned on me that this type of chivalrous act was probably forbidden in Purgatory. Since May was leading me into who knows what, I could always say I did it because I didn't trust her and wanted her to enter the room first.

As she passed by me, my hand slipped off the handle

and I stumbled back a couple of steps into the street. I looked up from my mid-street vantage point and noticed that in the time since we left the pub the sky had changed from an opaque redish-white, to a smoky dark grey. There'd been no burnt orange-sienna sunset, no first star of the night, the sky had just faded to grey; I doubted there'd be a twilight blue dawn.

May graciously acted as though she hadn't seen me stumble. Holding the door easily with one hand, she followed my gaze upward then captured the moment with a word, "Darkening," as I walked through the door in front of her.

I was tired. So tired I could barely stand up straight, let alone take in all the details of the room I'd entered. What I did notice, what I couldn't miss, and what provided a reinvigorating adrenaline jolt was the monster of a man standing behind the counter in front of me. He had to be near seven feet tall and at least half as wide. The top of his bald head marked the start of a tapering outward that ended in broad shoulders without pause for any discernable neck. He had an anchor goatee that seemed to grow out of his ears only to meet at his chin, and his nose had been crushed in and knocked around so many times that it was little more than a squiggle connected to two holes in his face. With arms the size of ham-hocks, the monster sized man reached for an equally monster sized club. I almost wished I'd let May enter the room first.

My people have a long and unpretty history when it comes to finding travel accommodations. Though the Green Book is no longer a travel necessity, "welcome" remains a tempered term. I've lost count of how many times hotel security has more, and most often less politely stopped me in the hall and asked for proof that I was a hotel guest.

As my lethargic mind went back and forth, debating between backing out of the building and reaching for my newly acquired knife, May stepped around and in front of me.

Without any of the staring, muttering, or obvious signs of concentration that I'd come to associate with what seemed to be May casting a spell, the giant of a man immediately softened. He involuntarily started to raise his hand to say hi, stopped it halfway up when he realized what he was doing then, caught with his hand half-way up, hunched his massive shoulders as though he were trying to hide from the hand next to his head. Since he couldn't hide the half-raised hand, he raised one finger and pumped it up and down a few times. As any primary schooler will tell you, the "one finger wave" is the aspirational equivalent of getting to first base. Being no stranger to school ground politics, it struck me that "One Finger" hoped to but hadn't yet made a move on May.

Fighting valiantly against a smile, May hissed at One Finger and began muttering and making finger signs of her own. Even to my untrained eye her signs seemed more for show than effect.

Club now in hand, One Finger tightened his grip on the club till even the solid old hardwood made cracking sounds. Try as she might, May couldn't hide the fact that she was impressed. Her now trademark hiss gave way to a brief titter, and she succumbed to a blush that, thanks to her pasty white make-up, was only slightly obvious.

Even in my exhausted state, I recognized this exchange for what it was – Purgatory's twisted version of flirting.

Strange as it seemed even to me, I'd taken a liking to May; she was the closest thing I had to a friend in Purgatory. Besides, truth be told, I've drunk less and made more questionable choices than the one she seemed ready to make. I say this so that two things are clear. First, I would have happily served as May's "wingman." Second, it certainly wasn't my intention to "block" the action she had going. Unfortunately, I did just that, literally, when I staggered forward and collapsed to the ground between them.

My subsequent snippets of memory include a huff of air being forced out of me when I was tossed over One Finger's shoulder, wooden stairs creaking under our combined weight, and being dropped like a sack of potatoes onto a none-too-soft surface that I would later learn was my bed. At some point I tried to sit up but was stopped by May's slight but surprisingly strong hand on my chest. As her face slowly came into focus, in a voice far clearer than I'd heard from her before, May changed my protests and pain to blackness with a single word. "Rest."

I woke fully in my usual fashion, but with a start. I was alone in a stone-walled room that for an instant let me think I was back in one of the Line Hotel's finished-concrete rooms. I'd slept on a cot made of thin strips of wood that were interwoven and attached to a wooden frame. At the other end of the room was a roughhewn desk and chair. On the desk was an alcohol lamp, some sort of writing tool, a pad of paper, and the books I'd borrowed. A small, shuttered window above the desk was open. It provided air and enough ambient light to let me know that the skies had reverted to the smoky red color that seemed to mark Purgatory's daytime.

Remembering the fighting and drinking I'd done the day before, I sat up slowly in anticipation of the dull ache of a hang-over and sharp pain that follows a fight - either as a pleasant reminder of victory or sad recollection of defeat.

To my surprise I felt nothing. I shook my head in search of telltale signs of having drunk too much, then rotated the shoulder near where I'd been cut. Again, nothing.

I realized I'd slept in my clothes and was glad of it. Having either May or One Finger undress me would have raised a whole other set of questions and concerns. I pulled off the shirt I was wearing and, after seeing the hole in the shirt made by Spaghetti-arm's knife, ran my fingers across my back and shoulder. There was nothing - no bandages, no stiches, not even a discernable scar.

My respect for May climbed another notch.

After briefly considering my usual morning routine I realized I had no need to use the toilet, no morning stubble to shave, no morning mouth to brush away, and no water with which to make any of that happen. So I put the ratty, knife holed shirt back on and left the room.

Standing in the hall outside my room I heard a faint humming. It struck me that this was the closest thing I'd heard to music since my arrival in Purgatory, so I headed down the stairs to investigate. Halfway down, a creek from the wooden stairs announced my impending presence and brought the humming to an abrupt halt.

Continuing down the stairs brought One Finger fully into view. It wasn't the strangest thing I'd seen in Purgatory, but the sight before me was certainly one to remember. With ballet-like grace and an economy of movement that belied his size, One Finger was on the verge of corralling a cloud of the black, dust-like soot that seemed to be everywhere in Purgatory.

This was Zen in its purest form - a moving meditation, that both focused and transcended the task. After a final stroke of the broom, the soot swirled like a mini dust-devil and coalesced into a neat pile.

When he turned to face me, I half expected him to say something like, "there is no spoon" or in his case, there is no broom. Instead, he greeted me in a melodic, velvet soft baritone. "Ah. Mornin' sir. Ah trust ya rested well. Er da commodations up ta yer needs? Do lemme know if ders' anytin' ya require."

His accent was thick and unlike anything I'd heard; just following his meaning required dedicated attention and active listening. Though I wondered why I was hearing him as I was, I had to admit, the whole Barry White bass - Idris Elba tough thing was … stirring. His appeal to May was obvious – when you looked beyond the obvious. They were near exact opposites on the surface - where he was large and loquacious - May was slight and terse of diction. But beyond the surface each had a depth and refinement that contradicted both their diction and outward appearances.

Caught off guard, my response was a tick slow. I could only hope that I recovered quickly enough to hide my surprise.

"Yes. Thank you for asking." I said, "Have you any idea where I might find May?"

"Ah yes. Mite is da operative word der, no idle ans on dat one. But she did say she'd stop by inna day er two."

After a pause, he quickly added "… to check-in on ya."

His belated clarification caught my attention, but it was the general lack of cleaning water that gave him away. A none-too-close inspection suggested I'd slept through the adult portion of the night.

With feigned ignorance I said, "Oh, it looks like dust from sweeping has gotten on your shirt." Then, with a brief lingering glance at the white powder around his zipper I added, "and … pants." Pointing out the traces of May's white facial powder in this way earned me a nod and an almost friendly grunt.

Turns out the flirtation between him and May had been going on for quite some time - even by Purgatory's near infinite sense of time. Apparently, One Finger suspected my fainting last night was an act.

In Purgatory, you generally lay where you fall; helping someone up would either be a favor, or something intended to force an obligation. May's job was to get me to my room, not just to the inn's lobby. Since she couldn't do this without his help, a deal had been struck. The deal obliged May to do something she could claim she didn't want to do – him, in exchange for his helping her complete her assignment. And, with May 'acting under duress' he could claim the *schadenfreude* exception. So, thanks to me they were finally able to hook up, without breaking any rules.

Having inadvertently provided him ingress to May - yeah, pun intended - I declared myself the best wingman in Purgatory. More importantly, I figured One Finger and I had an implied deal and, since I was without a job and unprepared for trial, his end was now due.

I went for broke and laid it all out.

"This is my second day here. Other than your roof over my head for the next few nights and too few Horis, I've got nothing - no job, no job prospects, and more importantly, no idea what I'm going to do at my arraignment. So, I guess the thing I 'require' is some help; possibly in the form of a job, certainly in the form of information, and ideally both."

"Ah yes, bein a new arrival, tis a tryin time no doubt. Well, ah cain't elp you wit a job, der's not much needin doin ere and ah'm already workin a side job to supplement da coin da inn provides. But ifin yer interested ah'd be appy ta bend yer ear fer a bit."

With nothing to lose I nodded for him to continue.

"First and foremost, stick ta wot ya know." Then, after a wry smile. "Now, ah ain't enny more a lawyer dan yer a fighter. But, in ma dealings wit boff da denizens of Purgatory and da local judiciary, ah've found it prudent ta keep da four A's in mind."

I bristled slightly at his assessment of my fighting skills, but held my tongue, and looked on questioningly when he raised a single fat finger.

"One, *ambiguitas contra stipulatorem est* - ambiguity, especially yer own, will be construed against ya. Ah'm fraid dat round ere da ole 'innocent until proven guilty' ting is a kit a rubbish."

With that he turned his hand-paw palm inward and raised a second sausage finger. "Two, *allegans contraria non est audiendus* - contradictory statements will na be eard. Dis place is full o ninnies dat claim dey don't belong ere cause dey did some good deed er spent a small bit of an ill-gotten fortune on a good cause. Do try not ta be one of dem sorts."

His disdain for this approach was evidenced by the international gesture he was making. Bringing his other hand up palm-in, he raised another fat finger.

"Tree, *allegans suam turpitudienem non est audiedus* - allegations of yer own infamy will na be eard. Odds are ya won't, but uders ave tried ta treaten or intimidate dare way out of ere. Don't boder. Given enough time folks around ere will recover from just bout anyting dat won't get boaf parties moved-on. Dere's only two tings folk ere really fear, bein dipped and moved-on.

Four, *allegatio contra factumnon est admittenda* - allegations contrary to deeds will na be eard. Don't boder tryin ta convince da judge dat you're a saintly bloke dat's nere done a questionable deed. You're da one dat as to be convinced of yer innocence, lies will nah serve ya."

And with that he raised the second finger of his left hand. That he was making the international gesture with both hands wasn't lost on me.

"So, you're saying I'm hosed if I don't pay attention to the four A's?"

"Dis ere is Purgatory - yer 'osed' regardless of wot ya do. But doubly so if ya don't pay tention ta da four A's."

"Fair enough" I said. "Did you use this approach at your arraignment?"

His eyes drifted toward the floor and his massive body heaved with an uneven sigh.

"Na. Tings were simpler back din. Ma 'arraignment' consisted of me beating some poor slob ta a pulp."

I was still bristling from his earlier, 'you're no more a fighter than I am a lawyer' quip so I asked, "And this makes you a fighter?"

He laughed at my barb, seeing humor in it that went beyond my perception, then shook his head.

"Naw, tis da uder way round. Ah chose ta be tested in da arena because ah've always been a scrapper.

❧

Purgatory, like the rest of Hell,
is where the soul goes to find and foster growth,
in its own time and fashion.

DE TENEBRA

CHAPTER 10:

CONFUSA EST POTESTAS

(In Chaos There Is Opportunity)

"Truth is, ah've always enjoyed a good dust up. Probly cuz da fights ah ad in da streets were nuttin compared to da beating ah got from ma da. As a kid, even doe ah ad no money nor equipment, ah became a regular at ery dirty, sweat soaked boxing gym dat got tired a trowing me out.

"Sure, ah was a gamer, but ah was mean and ah took tings too personally. Da bigger and stronger ah got, da more real boxers avoided fights wit me. Ma brief and uneventful pro career was most notable fer da number o times ah lost by disqualification. It dint even matter wen ah lost ma boxin license; by den no respectable boxer would ave anyting ta do wit me. After dat ah took ta bare knuckle street fightin. It paid well and ah flourished under da minimal rules and blind eye dey turned toward dirty tricks. Unfortunately, da better ah got, da worse da bettin odds went, and da smaller da purses got. At da 'urgin' of ma mob andlers ah trew a few fights. T'was profitable but painful."

He took a deep breath before continuing. In his eyes was a sad, almost wistful look that let on that the pain he spoke of wasn't just physical.

"Comin off da losses and seemingly vulnerable, ma andlers told me ta win again. Pride driven, ah killed da next guy ah fought, … and da next guy. Dat proved to be da end o ma bareknuckle career.

"Since no one would take a match wit or bet ginst me, ah transitioned ta full-time mob work. Ah worked ma way up from leg breaker, ta crew chief, and eventually ah got my own territory. Da latter proved ta be ma undoing.

"Wen you work fer criminals, performance reviews er pretty-straight forward; just do wot yer told and ya will stay wer yer at, a bit o initiative and maybe a bit o business acumen are like ta move ya up, fall-down on da job and dey'll beat er bury ya.

"Ah got ma own territory after a couple decades o beating and breaking people, but by din ah'd grown tired o violence. It's not dat ah were na still capable o it, but radder dan ma go-ta response, violence came ta be just one a several managerial tools at ma disposal. Instead o beating and killing ah undersold and bankrupted ma competitors. Debtors' assets were sized and sold, and ma distributors were given financial incentives ta improve sales, quality, and ultimately profits. Dat led some o ma employees ta tink ah'd gone soft. It woulda been unfortunate fer dem stead ah me if ma 'betters' adn't come ta view me and ma increasing revenues as a tret ta dare territory and position."

"And even though you'd moved away from violence?"

"Like ah said, you can na buy yer way outta dis place on da basis o a few belated good deeds.

"So, on ma sixth day ere ah was told ah ad ta fight some guy if ah wanted ta stay – ifin ah lost er refused to fight, ah would be dipped fer a long time. T'wasn't a ard decision or match; ah beat da poor slob ta a pulp n barely broke a sweat.

"Ah was called back six weeks later fer a two ganst tree bout. Da guy ah were paired wit ad some skill, but he liked da work too much and got carried away. When he stomped one guy's ed-in dey both went down, and ah was left goin two ganst one. Ah certainly learned a lesson dat day."

Somewhat surprised, I interrupted and asked, "Was that your first two-on-one fight?"

He brushed the question off with a wave of a meaty hand.

"Ah been fightin gainst odds since secondary school. Unless dey've practiced togeder, two again one is almost easier dan one-on-one; ah spect ya know dat. Dat day's lesson were bout bein in control a ma-self.

"Between my first and second bouts ah'd made use of ma old skill set to survive ere. Ah stole and/or acted as muscle whenever da need er opportunity presented itself.

"Ting is, wile it ain't sactly frowned upon, stealin ain't counted as work. After ma second fight ah tried real work. Wit my size t'was easy fer me ta get ard labor work – auling, breakin stones, and construction. And ard, spirit breaking work dat tis; ya ask me, dat and da tret of a good dip as prompted more n a few ta move-on.

"After six months of breakin and carryin stone, ah was

strong, bitter, and an odds-on favorite when I was called back in. It were supposed ta be two against six, but my 'partner' was inept and kept getting in da way, so ah tossed him aside and took care a da six me-self.

"Ah did six more years of eavy labor din were called back ta face 20-30 oter souls dat ad opted ta fight ta stay, in a survivors' melee. By din ah were more'n uninged, ah were a lost soul, an emotional void. Most ad formed alliances and some ad smuggled in weapons, ah'd done nothing ta prepare fer wot ah knew was comin."

His voice lowered, his head followed, and his eyes lost focus for a while, as he starred into his past. Not wanting to interrupt, I didn't speak or move. He took a moment to rub something off his hands that hadn't been there for a long time, then cleared his throat and continued.

"Ah'd ave ta say ah weren't concerned wit much at dat point; winning, loosing, wot ah was, or who ah ad been. Ah didn't know wot da hereafter would be like and ah couldn't seem ta bring myself ta care. It sounds strange ta say it, and ah didn't recognize it at da time, but fer da first time ever, ah felt free. Ah knew ah'd fight, but ah weren't worried bout dat, revenge, making a statement, being disrespected, er any of da oter petty tings dat ah usually carried in me noggin.

"When ah showed up dey sent me to da arena. It was just wot you'd spect - a big open space with a dirt floor and only one-way in and out. Dair were a viewn area above da raised dwall dat defined da circular arena. Fin dair were spectaters dair ah din't pay dem no mind

"Everyone knew why we were dere. When da door closed, no one said go, dere were no bell, announcement, er 'moment' o any sort. One minute we were a group o men milling about, da next we were a group of animals goin at each uder.

"Dem dat ad formed alliances worked in teams o two or tree again da few udders dat were big er skilled nuff to go it alone. Ma reputation and size ad got me marked as a target well before ah stepped inta da arena. Dat din't make me no never mind. Fer me it were only bout angles o attack and opportunity. Ah fought intuitively, blending skills, tricks, and strategies learned over ma decades in a stream o violence dat was boaf pure and terrifying. Witout da fear o goin down, da damage ah inflicted were tempered only by opportunity and da needs o da fight.

"Ah didn't even realize da fightin was over till ah spat out a finger dat was beginin ta dissolve in ma mouth. I looked round and wot ad been a ardy group o combatants was now a scattered collection o unconscious and cowering men. Many ad twisted or missing limbs, all wanted nothing more dan da chance ta be dipped just ta get away from me.

"Ah left da melee numbed by da violence and disappointed dat ah'd survived. Ah ad six decades till ah'd ave ta fight again, but no idea wot ta do wit myself. T'was almost like da melee ad drained dat last bit o violence from me. Ah got cleaned up and went ta a bar ta drink - not spit - and figure out wot ta do wit myself.

"Six monts later ah was drinking Et Forus full-time, trying ta avoid doin wot ah taut ah mite do wit myself. Ah'd spent wot little ah'd saved while working as a laborer and was running tabs at bars and inns dat ah knew ah could na pay. Wile ma size and reputation kept most creditors at bay, ah figured t'was only a matter o time fore a Reaper came ta take me in fer a dip. Ah was more-n a little surprised wen two mostly average lookin guys came up insisting dat ah go wit em.

"Now wen ah says mostly average ah'm being generous. Da smaller one was on da pudgy side, and da taller one mite could'na weighed more dan 10 stone. Da small one was leant on an old walkin stick and lookin at me in disapproval wile da taller one was smilin at me like ah was da bell o da ball and e wanted ta dance."

With a half laugh he added, "N lookin back on it, ah guess ah kinda was and he kinda did.

"Ah knew rite-off da two weren't Reapers; Reaper's usually got no range when it comes to emotion and, oter dan da Rider Reaper, dey almost never work togeter. So, ah asks dem ta leave me be wit a variety of colorful spressions. Wen dey don't, ah tells dem if dey want da stuffin kicked outta em all dey gotta do is wait till ah finishes me Et Forus.

"Quick as a wink da tall one grabs up me glass, trows da Et Forus in ma face, and tells me ah'm done drinkin.

"Well, much as ah respect quick ands, ah won't abide a waste a good booze, er even bad booze wen its alls ah got. So, after wiping ma eyes and upending da glass ta make sure it were truly empty, ah licked ma lips, trow'd da glass toward 'Stickman,' and lunged at 'Speedy'. Ah weren't surprised dat Speedy side-stepped ma lunge, ands dat fast usually come wit quick feet ta match. Ah lunged just ta get close enough ta Speedy ta neutralize is speed and maybe get a grip on em. Wot ah didna anticipate was stick man ducking under da glass and wedging dat walking stick a his tween ma legs as ah lunged.

"Ah tripped over da stick but mite ave regained ma balance, if speedy ad't caught me wit a spin kick ta da back of ma noggin. Knocked me tru da door and out onta da patio outside he did. Ah ended up on all fours on da soot-dusty stone floor.

"T'was dark inside but brite nuff outside ta blind me fer a second. Ah figured dat would give me vantage since my eyes would be more adjusted dan me two new friends wen dey came out after me. As ma eyes began to adjust wot ah saw almost cost me dat vantage.

"Da usually empty patio were full, and da patron nearest me were a Reaper. So were da one next to im and da near dozen oters dat formed a loose circle around da edge o da patio. Most sat casually, a few even sipped Forus, uders stood, like late arrivals at ah concert. All der death-disinterested eyes were on me.

"Ah figured dey were dair ta finish me off and drag me in after Speedy and Stickman wore me down a bit. Now, wile ah might'a lost da desire fer violence, ah still ad me pride. Ah figured da opportunity ta take on a group of Reapers don't come round ery day so's ah might as well get da preliminaries over wit.

"Bright blinded as ah ad been, wen dey came out neither Speedy nor Stickman saw me grab a andful of dirt while ah crawled on all fours over ta a stool. Wen dey got near me ah swung da stool toward Speedy in a wild lookin backanded arc. Speedy ducked under da stool easily and came in wit a Muay Tai style round ouse kick aimed at da back of me knee. Ah took da kick to da amstring but bent and leaned in so's it looked like e'd it is target. Is follow up brung him in closer, still out of grabbing range but close enough fer me to trow da dirt in is eyes. Wen e raised is ands up ta wipe at da dirt, ah closed and got a old o is wrist. Ah'd a ended Speedy's part o da fight rite der if Stickman adn't ad at me.

"Stickman swung at an angle dat woulda near knocked me ead off, broke me arm, er maybe both. Ah saw it comin' and lifted Speedy's so e took da blow on is arm. Ah could feel da power o dat blow trew my grip on Speedy and was almost surprised dat is arm stayed attached ta is body; judging by da way e was owling, so was Speedy. Ah twisted is limp arm around and slid ta Speedy's back, din grabbed is collar so's ah could pull im in close ta use as a shield. Stool in one and, Speedy eld fast wit da udder, ah turned on Stickman.

"Stickman nodded a bit and almost seemed ta smile. When Speedy struggled in protest, ah settled him down wit a tap er two o da stool on is ead. Dats wen Stickman went on da attack.

"We was a study in contrast. Stickman's attacks, tempered by a lack o desire but not unwillingness ta urt Speedy, were calculated and accurate. In contrast ah swung boaf da stool and Speedy around wit abandon. Ware e was grace and efficiency, ah was power and fury. Fer a time it looked dead even; e couldn't get past ma defense and ah couldn't mount an effective offense. But is was da long game; it took a wile but e gradually reduced da stool ta a single leg and, in da process, turned Speedy inta dead-weight on ma arm. Ah was starting ta feel da time ah'd spent drinking wile e was untouched and looking fresh as da day.

"In da end, t'was ma experience trowin matches dat saved me. Da trick of losin is ta convince everyone, including yer opponent dat der actually winnin. Ya let dem beat you gradually, by makin em tink dat der doin more damage dan dey are. Dis was no different and no less painful. Ah sucked air loudly, turned a little slower, left ma flank exposed a bit too long, and ventually took a blow to da same leg dat Speedy kicked me in: Switchin ma defense ta protect da leg made da injury believable. Dat ah fell after takin anoter shot ta da leg weren't just believable, t'were spected. So, wen ah dragged Speedy down wit me and trew da remains of da stool at Stickman, wile strugglin ta get up, eryone taut it were da last act o a beaten man.

"My trowin da now barely conscious Speedy at Stickman was incongruous with da injured and beaten man ah'd show'd dem. I was opin dat Stickman would be caught completely off guard."

One Finger leaned in conspiratorially and with a smile in his voice said, "as ah sprung at Stickman from my crouch, ah swear ah even saw a bit o'surprise on da face o a Reaper er two.

"Unfortunately, Stickman weren't much surprised.

"But, wile e were na fooled inta droppin is guard, he did miscalculate da physics of Speedy as a projectile. He stepped to da side of ware Speedy was eaded but apparently didn't take inna account dat in addition to coming at em, Speedy was spinning in a circle parallel to da ground. Stickman had to take a second step ta da side ta avoid being it by Speedy's limbs as dey came flail-spinin around. Dat's owe he lost is advantage.

"Instead o being positioned ta strike wen ah dove

at em, e adda do a *passata sotto* – a defensive move dat involves duckin under and turnin away from yer attacker. It works great in fencin, but not so well when yer totin a walkin stick. Ah went over im sure nuff, but ah got a solid old o is stick on da way. Stead ah getin pulled off balance and avin ta close wit me, he let go o da stick. Ah rolled out of my dive and came up wit da stick firmly in and. Dis time wen he smiled, e weren't shakin is ead. Ah mite dare say e looked a bit impressed.

"Aving gained da vantage, ah took a moment ta preciate da weapon dat ad caused me such trouble. She was a beaut – da ardest wood ah'd ever seen, worn to a polish by regular use, but still wit nary a nick. Ah figured she might come in andy if ah ad ta deal with all da Reapers dat were still sittin around watchin us, and a little practice on Stickman seemed in order.

"Wen ah feigned left and he didn't move, ah swung her one anded wit my right. Radder dan duck e blocked wit is left forearm and broke er clean in two.

"T'was ma turn ta be impressed.

"Quick as ah could, ah swung da now stump of a stick at em wit a backand. E ducked under ma swing and stepped so close dat we both knew ah'd grab em. Fore ah could get old o em, e combinated on me; it me wit more blows dan I could count. Da parts ah member most er a knife-and strike ta ma troat an a left palm-eal ta ma nose. Dem two left me choking, blinded by tears, and specting an attack dat ah likely wouldn't see or survive. Ah staggered back a few steps and, wit no udder options, took a defensive stand while ah listened fer him ta come.

"At first ah taut ah was earin bells. Ah figured not

being able ta breath were takin its toll on ma earing. But wen me eyes cleared, ah realized ah was earin da sound of DieBus hittin da stone floor as da Reapers left.

"Stickman, who was now smiling, bent ta pick up a coin, din turned ta me and said, 'Anudder Forus?'

"Well, who am ah ta say no ta dat! T'was a much better deal dan aving ta go on fightin. Besides, ah liked da symmetry of startin and endin a fight wit drinks.

"When ah nodded ma greement Stickman turned to da barely conscious Speedy, shook is ed in disapproval, din told em, 'pick up da coins, pay fer da damage, and go. We fighters are going ta drink.' Speedy was crawl-stumblin around, gaddering coins wit is one good arm when me and Stickman eded back in ta da bar.

"Over drinks Stickman explained ow dis ad been a job interview. He were a fight instructor fer da Reapers. Dey ad eard ow ah ad used ma size and wot e politely called an 'opportunistic' - rather dan dirty - style of fightin, ta walk out a da melee wit barely a scratch. Oping ta boaf learn from da experience and impress is instructor, is student Speedy ad asked ta elp with da interview; a request Speedy was now regrettin. Da little dance we tree ad done was da interview dat led ta wots now ma side job as a fight strategy instructor fer da Reapers.

"It were a paid interview too. Da coins dey dropped were ma signing bonus, minus Stickman's recruitin fee. Dat bonus more dan covered ma outstanding debts. Da remainder and wot I'm paid ta train da Reapers, as allowed me ta buy dis tidy lil slice a Purgatory."

Sure, he was big, imposing, and a maestro with a broom, but I'd seen two of the Reapers in action. They were fast and highly skilled. The doubts that crossed my mind must have shown on my face.

"Ting is, da Reapers is unique mostly cause dey can move folks on and remain ere. Sure, some of dem, like yer friend wit da gun or da Rider Reaper, er extra special, but most of wot ya sees is da result ah practice and discipline. Dey, like us, can be moved-on, and dey, mayaps even more dan most, er fraid o wot comes next.

"So, dey spends most of dare time practicing and more dan a lil coin learnin strategy, technique and da mental focus needed ta go beyond da limits of mortal world tinkin so dat dare ready fer wot er dare next encounter olds. Dey'er like cruel, violent, and in dare own way, artistic versions of yer Boyscout, always prepared.

"Dey don't like surprises. Dey don't wanna come cross someone like me, wit size and power dat deys likely ta underestimate, balance and technique dey won't expect, and a dirty, er opportunistic, way of fightin dat dey aint familiar wit. So, when they learn bout someone wit valuable fightin skills dat ain't got themselves moved-on, dey sees an opportunity ta learn and reduce risk, and look ta ire dem.

"Dey ired me to elp em understand da mind set one learns ta adopt after years o less dan onorable, and ighly disorganized street fightin. I don't so much teach fightin moves – they've some of da best boxers, swordsmen, and martial artist ever walked da planet fer dat - I elps em wit tinkin outside da box, takin wot yer opponent and da environment give ya, and da most difficult thing fer most of em, understanding wot yer opponent is feeling and how it influences wot dey are like ta do."

He'd given me an opportunity, so I took it.

"So, what would you say I'm missing or not understanding in my new environment?"

He leaned in conspiratorially again.

"Well now, dat dair's da ting of it all now it-in-it!

"Work, trial, and da possibility a getting dipped – dem tings, like da system itself, er designed ta wear ya down, so's ya accept yer fate. Ah says gents likes us, we're da lucky ones. We're comfortable in da venue we select; we knows wot we are and cain do wot we do.

"Doctors, priests, n most professional sorts can't get passed da second A."

And by way of reminder, he again held up two fat fingers in what wasn't a peace sign.

"Some a dem professional type blokes talk bout good deeds dey done till dey realize just ow little good were actually done. Tis even worse fer everyday folk. Most of em don't know wen, let alone ow ta stand fer demselves. Now days, more often dan not dey just shows up at da court on da six day wit no idea wots gonna appen or wot dey wants out of it. Even if dey constest goin down, less dey ask fer sumptin different, da best dey'll get is ta ave ta come back ta court six weeks later.

"But makin sure yer fightin or contesting ware yer comforable, wether it's in da ring, da street, or da court-room, is only alf da battle. Da key ta winning any fight anyware is ta fight on yer terms, but not just ta ware yer strong. Ya also gots to go ta ware yer oppoent's weak n vulnerable; ya gots ta take yer oppenent well outta dare comfort zone.

"Da courts ere ave been around purt-near forever.

Dey'll let ya wear yerself out wit talk bout yerself till ya accept yer fate. Da less obvious and mite ah say more important ting is dat da courts, from da judges, prosecutors, bailiffs and intake workers, to da buildin itself er also worn down. Dey er lookin fer da easy way out. Be da one dey've never seen before, da one dat demands dat dey tink, and dat makes dare normal way o doin tings risky. Make em fight on uneven ground; befriend chaos, master da unusual, and advance da unexpected. Din dey'll be lookin fer a way out well fore you."

Still clinging to the idea that I was something of a fighter, I waxed philosophical.

"I think I get it. It's like what Sun Tsu meant when he said, *fight where your enemy isn't.*"

A cloud briefly passed over his face and for a moment he almost looked cross. But it went as fast as it had came. He sat back with a sigh, then said,

"Dat's not sactly wot he said, and it certainly ain't wot he meant.

I've read enough Sun Tsu to know that there are multiple and disputed interpretations of this and several other sections of his writings. So I offered a gentle correction.

"I think that depends on who's interpretation you're reading."

He rose slowly, like an old challenge weary bear that must once again stand to its full height, then reached for his broom and started to walk away, apparently done with our conversation. At the doorway he stopped, turned, forced a smile before speaking.

"I don't know wot dem oter fellers wrote bout is words,

I only know wot da bloke told me just before e decided t'was is time ta move on."

*It is true that the soul doesn't measure
time, only growth. And why is this?
Because, to the soul the shell of the body is
nothing, as is the time that it lasts.*

DE TENEBRA

CHAPTER 11

LONGA EST VIA, ET QUE DIFFICILIS

(Long Is The Way, And Hard)

I STAYED SEATED, listening to the rhythmic swish of his broom fade as he cleaned other parts of the inn. It dawned on me that the burden of his thick accent patois demanded that I pay close attention and brought with useful information. I sat there quietly, reflecting on my situation and the conversations we'd had for what may have been hours. Eventually I reached two conclusions. First, my new friend One Finger was wrong about one thing - he was definitely more of a lawyer than I was a fighter. Second, I was gonna lawyer the hell out of, well, Hell!

I decided to follow his advice ... to go with what I know. While I didn't know the ins and outs of Purgatory's judiciary, I had a general understanding of how the law works and a few good books courtesy of my intake worker. So, I went to my room, took a seat at the small wooden table, and began learning the law of Purgatory.

Once, while in law school, with a passing grade on the line, I read the course's 500-page constitutional law textbook in a single night. Now, with my soul on the line, I pulled out all the stops. By the time I needed to light the desk lamp I'd gotten most of the little Latin I knew back and almost finished the first book I'd borrowed - *Quod Lex Corpus: Inferos* (The Body of Law: Hell). When the sky lightened and I blew out the lamp, I'd finished *Praxi Ante Iudicium* (Practice Before Trial) and was well into *De Tenebra* (Of Darkness). More importantly, I had a working theory for my defense in mind.

If I was going to take Purgatory's judiciary outside its comfort zone I'd have to go on the offensive with non-traditional arguments.

I agreed with One Finger that fighting to stay was an oft fought and always losing battle. But agreeing to go to some other level was just another form of defeat. And those that argued that they shouldn't be in Purgatory struggled to overcome the res loquitor presumption and ran afoul of One Finger's second rule if they argued that they should be in Heaven because of various good deeds they did. That's where I found my opening.

I was different. As far as I knew I still had a body on the early plane that was very much alive. In a coma sure, but alive nonetheless - I figured I'd cross the coma bridge if and when I got to it. Getting back to my body and the earthly plane was the first order of business. While arguing that I shouldn't go to Hell was typical, and effectively conceding that I wasn't worthy of entry to Heaven would be somewhat unexpected, demanding that be sent back to my body on the earthly plane was novel enough to create chaos – just what I needed.

Unfortunately, my around-the-clock studying had come at a price. I was crook'd back, saddle sore, and intellectually spent. I couldn't digest any more information, had lost all sense of creativity, and was probably missing obvious points. I needed a break from sitting, from reading, and from my tiny room. Since I also needed more books, I decided to head out and explore this bit of Purgatory while I made my way back to the fat-skinny bureaucrat's office.

I grabbed the two books I'd finished and pocketed the few Horis I had. I figured the street rules here were likely the same as in every poor neighborhood: If you look like a local or like you don't have anything folks want, they'll most likely leave you alone. Being dressed much more shabby than chic as I was, I doubted anyone would think I had anything of value. Though I hoped not to need it, I stashed the knife I got when I helped the Rider-Reaper in my pants and pulled my shirt over it.

I made my way downstairs from my room and found One Finger reviewing his books at the inn's counter.

He sized me up quickly and with a wry smile asked, "ya been workin ta see where yer enemy ain't fightin?"

I smiled and nodded, both in deference and gratitude.

"No, just tryin to get uphill of where the fight is gonna be."

He chuckled his understanding and was about to return to his task when I asked if I could trouble him for directions back to the intake building. His stern look told me I'd mis-stepped.

"Ya cain't trouble me by asking fer what ya already

paid fer. Are ya suggestin' I'd break a deal, or dat ya don't know what all ya paid fer when ya rented da room?"

I'd dropped my guard and asked for a favor - his stern chastising was, by Purgatory's standards, a gentle reminder. I recovered as quickly and cautiously as I could.

"Given the state I was in upon arrival, we should probably go over the details of my stay here again."

He accepted my feeble explanation with a knowing nod. "Ye paid fer six days shelter. Dat means a room and protection wile yer inside, and me best efforts if'n yer in earin distance. For a lot more I can arrange it such dat Reapers won't come for ya wile you're inside – but I spect ya won't need n really caint afford dat service."

He paused to let the import of what he'd said sink in, then went on.

"Ya also gets our complimentary concierge service dat includes directions, introductions ta ma connections, and a drag back guarantee – If ya get da stuffin kicked outta ya and can't drag yer self back, anyone dat drags ya in will be compensated fer dare time. Dat is, unless dey were instrumental in causing da arm. In dat case dey'll be beaten so's dey'll need da services a someone like May ta get back up and about."

I nodded both to show that I understood the deal that had been made on my behalf, and to acknowledge the warning inherent in his information.

"Good. Now, gettin to da intake buildin is easy. Dis wole place is built like a toilet bowl. We're top front n center. Da intake, administrative building, court-ouse, n executive offices are inna alf-circle at bottom center. Just keep edin downill n you'll end up at da far end o da plaza opening. You'll likely come in at da end o da plaza by da new entrant lodging. I spect you'll smell dat befer ya see it, n by da time ya sees it dare'll probably be a bunch a good fer nutins lookin at ya wit ungry eyes. Stay to da center of da plaza n walk toward da raised area at da far end. Da intake building will be on yer rite.

"Gettin back is a bit more o a trick. Just keep goin up da ill from in front of da intake building after ya cross da plaza. Yer gonna pass stores, wareouses, bars, and flops fore ya get ta dis level. Most decent inns ere on dis ere street and dis is just about da end on da street."

He pointed left and said, "da oter inns er dat way and da street market is ta da right. If ya get ta apartments ya gone too far, if ya gets ta single omes ya gone way too far."

That said, he turned to one of two small kegs on the shelf and poured out a shot's worth of what appeared to be a darker than usual Forus into a glass. Before my hand could come up to decline his offer, he pulled a towel from his waistband and dipped it into the liquid.

"Ad Infernum. Taint much fer drinkin, but she's good kit fer a clean n polish."

I nodded in acknowledgement and thanks then headed out the now open wooden door to the same spot in the street where I'd stumbled two days before.

It was my third day in Purgatory. Maybe I should have gotten used to it, but I hadn't. With no breeze to speak of, the smell of ash hung heavy in the air, and a light dusting of soot covered everything. I took a few steps away from the inn then stopped and turned to get a good look at my new and hopefully temporary residence, and the nearby surroundings.

The inn was a relatively small structure, made of stone like every other building I'd seen. Its smooth stone wall had no gaps, ledges, or other features that would either make it unique or give purchase for climbing, and the heavy wooden door was both sturdy and unremarkable. Higher up on the building front, well beyond jumping distance, were openings in the stone that served as windows. But for the occasional sign and torches that were placed at seemingly random intervals, it was almost impossible to tell one building from the next.

Luckily for me, the inn had a wooden torch between two upstairs windows, right over the door. I scanned right, left, then right again, taking in the small differences; a banner here, construction there, the occasional open space, a broken-down cart, all the things that made a neighborhood, unique. With this visual firmly in mind, I walked along the street then took the first street I came to that went downhill.

After a few blocks I noticed a gradual decline in both the slope of the street and the neighborhood, and an increase in foot traffic. Well-kept inns gave way to stores and flop houses. Banners gave way to signs, and disrepair was evident in the crumbling stones and soot that collected at the edges of the walkway.

As is the case in most major cities, the closer I got to central administration the more the neighborhood seemed to decline. A few blocks down any street near the L.A. court houses the neighborhood quickly goes to shit; San Francisco's City Hall is only a few blocks from Polk Street and the Tenderloin where hookers work and the mentally ill live; and New York has the subterranean world of the subway. Here, the flop houses that had replaced the inns were replaced by places where beds were rented by the hour. Shops were replaced by liquor stores then bars, and the bars became smaller and less appealing. Eventually the area devolved into groups of small shacks and stands where one could buy rags, crash for the night, or purchase Et Forus and Ad Infernum by the shot.

When the ground leveled I knew I was close but I was sure I hadn't seen the temporary housing. Then, true to my host's warning, I smelled it. Its oppressive odor, a mix of fear and sweat, seemed to weave itself into, and all but overpowered the ever-present burnt smell in the air.

A few blocks later I rounded a corner and the city center stood before me. I'd come in at the far end of a stone plaza that was about the size of a football field. At the end of the plaza were the three administration buildings. Four other buildings, two on each side, ran along and parallel to the plaza. The center building had an additional floor and the window openings looked larger, but even from afar it was obvious that the buildings were of that uniformly bland architecture common to governmental offices.

A line of dead and leafless black limbed trees ran down the center of the plaza. Where the black of the tree limbs provided much needed contrast to the pervasive grey of the plaza stones, an occasional stone bench provided a muted transition between the two.

I followed the line of trees down the center of the plaza walking past derelicts of the kind found in every major city, albeit a little dirtier and perhaps more scantily clad. They lay, sat or huddled on the stone benches, not bothering to beg or threaten, all but oblivious to the clippity-klank sound with which my ill-fitting shoes marked my passage.

I walked down the plaza to where the trees ended, just behind the centermost of five benches. These larger benches curved away from the rest of the plaza and referenced an identical set of benches that abutted the end of the plaza. The equal spacing of the benches created a large circle that, at about 30 yards across, nearly spanned the end of the plaza.

In the center of the circle was an elevated circular platform. Two smooth stone ramps spiraled up to the top, one along each side. At the top of the platform three half-arches met over what appeared to be a square raised stone platform with a step up toward the front, facing the plaza. Curiosity, whimsy, and the fact that I wasn't sure which of the buildings I'd been in before prompted me to climb up the ramp to get a better look.

After only a few steps up the ramp the plaza derelicts began to take note. Like small prairie creatures, sometimes one by one, often in unison, they sat or stood up, surveying first the landscape of each other, then settling their gaze on me. By the time I reached the top of the platform, the purpose of the elevated stones and arches was as clear as the reason the derelicts were watching me.

Rather than the raised platform I'd imagined from the ground, the stones marked the outer edges of what looked like a Roman style stone bath. It was easily more than 6 feet in length, depth, and width. There was a smooth, rounded stone at the bottom center covering what was likely a drain, but there were no stairs leading into or seating benches along the sides of this bath. The bath itself was filled with a pungent, light brown liquid. Even though it was open to the elements, there was no soot or debris afloat.

Any questions I might have had about what this was were answered by the ropes, cranks, and pulleys attached to the ends of the arches that hung over the bath. Though currently tied-off slack, next to a large block of wood that no doubt served as a platform, the ropes and pulleys were ideally positioned to be used to lift, position, and lower individuals into the liquid that filled the pool. This clever design allowed the victim to be lowered slowly or all at once, in whole or part.

In the brief time it took me to figure out the dark purpose of this public "bath," my small audience of derelicts lost interest. I was just another tourist taking in one of Purgatory's grisly sights - the public dipping bath. I mounted the raised stone at the front of the bath-pit, a perch from which I'm sure there'd been many ghastly pronouncements, took a moment to orient myself, then headed down the ramp and toward the far side of the right-most of the three buildings where I had walked out into Purgatory for the first time, three days and an eternity ago.

How long is forever?
Sometimes just a matter of seconds.

DE TENEBRA

CHAPTER 12

NON EST FACTUM

(It Is Not My Deed)

THOUGH I WAS sure I entered the building through the same door I'd exited, I didn't have a clue where the fat-skinny bureaucrat's office was. I wandered the labyrinth of same looking doors and floors randomly until I saw the tail end of a line of nude and semi-clothed people. This was the new arrivals line, the line I would have waited in but for The Gunfighter's intervention.

I attribute my first mistake to a lapse back to earth-side etiquette. I got in line to wait my turn to get in to see the bureaucrat. After what felt like much too long, the line had grown longer but hadn't moved forward. My next mistake was trying to follow the line to the beginning to get to the fat-skinny bureaucrat's office. I followed the line down the hall, around the corner, up one flight of stairs, and down another before asking one sorry looking soul how long he'd been in line. When he told me this was the beginning of his second day, it struck me that this was yet another of Purgatory's petty torments – allowing souls to waste most of their precious first six days standing in line.

Three flights of stairs and eight hallways later, though I still hadn't reached the front of the line, I'd learned that some of these folks had been waiting for almost four days, and I had the beginnings of a plan. I gave up looking for the front of the line and went in search of the door The Gunfighter had used, which I at least knew was somewhere on the first floor.

The door was unmarked, so after a tedious process of trial and error that led me into several storage spaces, a few bustling offices, and one "comfy" room that offered both pillows and whips, I lucked upon the right suite of offices. I went through the door, past the sea of mismatched desks and cubicles, to the fat-skinny bureaucrat's door.

Though genuinely and pleasantly surprised to learn that I was returning two of his books, he balked at the idea of "lending" me others. A none too subtle hint in the form of a finger-gun point was all it took to remind him that his "deal" with The Gunfighter required him to give me all the information I needed. I left his office with two more books, *Ortus est ex Spiritu* - The Onus of the Spirit, and *Usu Apud Inferos Iudicii* - Trial Practice in Hell. When I asked for the courts' calendar and directions to the front of the line, I got the court schedule for preliminary hearings like mine, and a dismissive point in the direction of a door almost directly across the sea of cubicles from his.

A quick walk by the maze of empty desks and through yet another unmarked door brought me to one of the outer intake offices. Six desks were crowded into a room that should have held three, four at the most. The walls were blank and the only light came from an open door on the other side of the room. Each desk had stacks of paper piled high enough to form a barricade between the over-worked civil servant type that sat on one side, and the new arrival seated on the other; in most cases the two were distinguishable only by the fact that the civil servant wore clothes. After a brief, disinterested look in my direction, those that had bothered to look up went back to their tasks.

I exited through the open door on the opposite side of the room into what had to be the main intake office.

I came out next to a vacant, battle worn counter. Five other counters lined the walls and served as reception points and barricades to other intake rooms. An amusement park style line of people snaked from the hallway into all the corners and open spaces of this office, then came to a stop at a line in front of the counters.

The scent of humanity hung heavy in the still, soot-soaked air. Two of the counters had "back in 15 minutes" signs on them, the other three counters were "staffed". At the counter next to me a disinterested civil servant who, having just directed a new arrival to one of the waiting rooms, held up a hand to stop the next new arrival from approaching. Another new arrival sat at one of the two other manned desks. He stared off into space while the civil servant that was "helping" him, a full-figured woman, made unattractive by the condescending way she spoke, sat on the edge of the desk complaining to the coworker next to her as though the new arrival weren't there.

This was Purgatory's DMV equivalent. Of course,

the DMV, with its hard-plastic chairs, random and near-infinite alpha numeric call system, and occasionally helpful staff was a five-star experience in comparison.

It was obvious that I wasn't going to get any information from the civil servants so I did the only logical thing I could think of. I sat down behind one of the vacant desks and called out. "Next!"

I spent the next few hours talking to the new arrivals at the front of the line. I told them I was doing a "pre-interview," asked a few questions, then sent them to a new line - which started in front of the line they were just in. I figured this was a 'no harm - no foul' approach to getting information.

Those at the front of the line that had kept count were usually on their fourth or fifth day in Purgatory. Most of them knew or had heard just enough of the basics of Purgatory to be in a panic. A few knew that they would be given the opportunity to contest their presence, but far fewer had any inkling of how they would do so.

On a hunch, I chose instincts over training and asked a question that I didn't know the answer to, why they thought they were in Purgatory. I don't know if it was because they were out of their element, seeking forgiveness, panicked and afraid, or all of the above, but most went with partial honesty rather than an outright lie. Even though I wasn't getting the whole story, they said enough about their lives to give me a pretty good idea of how they'd come to be here. Pride, wrath, greed, envy, these classics, and a few sins I'd never even considered were well represented.

One woman carried on about how she'd left the money

and prestige of the private sector, for a life spent working as a legislative aide *helping stupid people with stupid problems.* Though it wasn't clear if she was talking about her bosses or constituents, it was obvious that she felt the people she was "helping" were beneath her. Another cried and went on and on about all the charitable donations she'd made, ... all the while complaining that it barely made a dent in the ridiculous amount of taxes she paid.

Over what felt like just a couple of hours, I was lied to, begged, propositioned, and told so many sob stories, that I found myself starting to sympathize with the disinterested civil service workers. My eyes had started to get that glazed-over bureaucrat look, and I was once again considering heading back to the inn when I happened on what I didn't really know I was looking for. It'd been a while since I'd seen it, so long that I almost missed it.

Rather than rush into the seat or conversation, he approached casually, sat easily, then took a moment to situate himself; all the while subtly sizing me up. Even dressed in tired and worn clothes, as he was, one look and you knew this guy was going to figure out and work the system. He was a fixer.

He was that indispensable part of the machine that exists across cultures and occupations. They're procurement specialists in business; on the streets they're hustlers; in restaurants they're expediters. When someone says, 'I know a guy,' before you can finish telling them exactly what you need done, he's the kind of guy they're referring to. Take two parts negotiator, add a lot of brains, some diplomatic and grifter tendencies, and maybe a pinch of muscle, then screen out conscience, and just like that, you have a fixer. Information and angles were his stock and trade, and I needed both.

He sat comfortably before me, dark eyes sharp and calm. After a moment of silence - just long enough to show that he was comfortable - but not long enough to let it become a test of wills, he invited me to begin with an almost gracious wave of his hand.

I opened without greeting or introduction, using a line I'd developed over the course of my earlier conversations.

"This is an informational interview. It may expedite your subsequent processing. Please answer each of the following questions to the best of your ability. Firstly, do you know where you are?"

He answered without hesitation. "Yes. I'm sitting in a large smelly room in Purgatory, talking to a guy that's working an angle."

Unnerved, impressed, and hoping I wasn't showing either. I moved on to the next question. "And what did you do before you came here?"

"Just before I came here? Correct me if I'm wrong, but I think death is pretty much the price of admission here. What about you? I'd love to think you were some sort of white collar grifter – that would be taking the "die with the lie" thing to a whole new level. But if I had to guess, I'd say you were either a lawyer, a cop – probably a detective, or a detective cop turned lawyer. Am I warm?"

He was baiting me. But this was one of those times when nibbling at the bait was a good way to chum the waters. I feigned irritation.

"If you're warm it's only because you're in Purgatory,

where you seem to belong. Now tell me, what, if anything, do you think you did to warrant being here?"

"Not a cop, definitely a suit. The whole 'admit nothing' - make counter accusations things is a dead give-away; a cop would have just ignored what I said and asked another question.

"But, in answer to your question, if you're asking what I did before I came to this place, I think it would be fair to say that I worked for a powerful organization making sure that things that maybe shouldn't be done, got done, without any blame getting back to the boss."

He looked me over again then added, "I suspect you know a little bit about that sort of thing."

With his dark, wavy hair and deep brown skin, I figured him as a mid-level member of one of the Latin cartels or mafia groups. His educated but not-too-educated diction and manner said he was probably second generation; most likely the son, nephew or whatever of someone who knew enough people to get him trust and access, but not a free pass. He fit right in with Purgatory's grifters, miscreants, and rough and tumble.

My brief stint in the Public Defender's office proved useful here. I was hoping it wouldn't work, but I need to see where he'd go with it, so I asked. "Leyva? Los Antrax? Sinaloa? Stop me when I sound a familiar note."

He casually leaned forward, marking his intrusion into my space as more conspiratorial than threatening.

"I don't think this is the time or place for confession, and I'm not in the mood for a stroll down memory lane. The fact that I'm here should tell you that my last job didn't end well for me."

He'd called. So, I raised.

"Perhaps we should end this interview and move you on to the next line."

He didn't miss a beat.

"Naw, you don't want to do that … it's too soon. You've had a nice little rhythm going. After your first few "interviews" you moved people out of one line, then back to their same place in another line, more or less fast enough to keep pace with the career do-nothings at the other desks. Put me back early and your fake new line will grow, and the sheep won't feel like they're making progress. "Some might even figure out that you've got nothing to do with this finely run bureaucracy and then where will you be."

"Ok, if you think I don't work here, why are you wasting your time sitting here talking with me?"

He took an obvious glance toward the stagnant line.

"Our time chatting isn't costing me anything. It seems you want to know about the folks waiting in line. That's information I have. I wanna know what you know about what goes on behind the door back there and what happens next. That's information you have. I'm thinking maybe we can strike a deal. So, if tryouts are over, perhaps we can get down to business?"

Rather than smile (and I was sorely tempted to do so) I answered with a single word.

"Terms?"

He smiled, "Tit for tat." Then, with slight nod of mock graciousness, "I'll start.

"The people behind me are new arrivals waiting to

be processed. But there's a lot of confusion about what "processed" means. So, what is the story with this place?"

I nodded to accept his terms and told him something equally trivial. "Each room has about six more bureaucrats, they go over the basic rules. The first Rule … "

He interrupted me to quote the first rule, "… everybody must work." I recited the second rule, "Altruism, mercy and kindness are forbidden." We took turns doing this until we'd recited all six of Purgatory's rules. Since he already knew the rules, I added that the punishment for breaking the rules is being beaten, dipped in a wood lye that slowly dissolves you, and of course, one can be moved-on by The Gunfighter or one of the other Reapers.

My mention of The Gunfighter by name, and the Reapers in general, seemed to confirm his belief that I was worth talking to.

He leaned in and cocked an ear, waiting to hear more. I'd piqued his interest, so I upped the ante.

"What do people think is going to happen to them?"

His answer was slow and insightful enough to let me know that I'd picked the right guy to talk to.

"Most people are looking to convince someone or everyone that they don't deserve to be in Hell. They seem to know they can't stay here but are too scared of what comes next to move-on. Maybe it's because of what they were taught in life, maybe it's what they've seen since they got here, maybe it's just that the ever-present burnt smell has gotten to them. Whatever it is, there's a growing level panic in that line."

Then, with just enough hesitation to suggest that he

feared the answer he'd get, he asked, "Do you think they're right? Are the folks back there callin the shots?"

It was my turn to take the time to respond with a thoughtful answer.

"Not so much. If you want to stay here, you'll have to make your case for it. If you're smart, you'll start thinking about how you're gonna make your case now. All they'll tell you at the desk is when and where to show up.

"And from what I've seen, nobody knows what's next for anyone."

My answer neither comforted nor caused concern. What it did was put the ball back in my court. So, with an eye toward finding clients and work I asked about the public housing.

"If by housing you mean the 'bare-acts' on either side of the plaza … I've already spent a little time there.

"If the mob ever took over public housing that's what it would look like. Even though somebody gets paid to provide housing for newbies, all the newbies get there is a roof overhead; no clothes, no information, and definitely no privacy. The rooms they have go to people that are either able to pay, or that work for one of the unit bosses. The more you pay or the higher up you are, the better the space you get. Newbies that aren't willing or able to pay, are left to fight for whatever floor space there is. Come darkening, bodies fill every corner and crevice; people sleep head to foot, and shoulders to ankles on the hallway floors."

He then circled back to the Reapers, asking if I'd developed a connection with them in the time I'd been here. I told him how The Gunfighter had brought me here, some of what I'd learned from May and One Finger, and about my run-in with The Rider.

He played his cards close, but when I confirmed that a Reaper had brought me here, I could tell something about my story piqued his interest.

It was my turn again, so I asked, "How are people planning to make their case for staying?" His answer was simple and direct.

"They're all old dogs – they got no new tricks. Most folks fall into one of three camps. Camp one, are the guilty sheep. They're just waiting to be told where and when to go."

As he spoke he made the same kind of finger-gun that I'd pointed at the fat-skinny bureaucrat and drew a bead on a few people in line.

"I guess they believe they deserved whatever comes next.

"Camp two seems to be the largest group. For them whether or not they belong in Purgatory isn't the question. They fear what comes next and will say or do whatever they think will keep them from being moved-on. Most of them don't have a plan; they'll fight, lie, cheat, steal, or do whatever else it takes to stay right where they are.

"Camp three consist of those that don't think they belong here. Some don't think they've done anything to warrant going to Hell, some claim they should be in Heaven, none are willing to take a leap of faith and agree to move-on. About half these folks have convinced them-selves that someone somewhere made a big mistake. They plan to stay here until the mistake is corrected, i.e. until they're sent to Heaven or its equivalent. The other half see their being here as a test of faith. They say they're willing to stay here in Purgatory for an eternity because agreeing to go would amount to a loss of faith. None of them have any idea how long a thing eternity can be.

"In my book, these folks are the worst. Since good deeds are forbidden, you'd think they'd do us all a favor and skip right over penitents and ascetics and go straight to mortification. But no, that would be too easy. I can't figure out if they're still trying to get 'in the bosom of Abraham' or have come to realize that they aren't there and are bitter. Either way they spend most of their time arguing scripture and going on and on about their savior, be it Christ, the Rock-God, Buddha, The Light, Muhammad, or whatever. Maybe they're trying to preach their way out. Now that would be one hell of a con.

"And, speaking of cons, what's your angle here."

My answer affirmed his earlier assessment. "Rule one, 'everybody's gotta work.' I'm tryin to figure out how to build a client base."

"Lookin to build a client base huh. Not bad, but what about the other side of the coin? This is Purgatory, if ever there was a place that's lousy with lawyers, it'd be here. How you gonna compete? What's your angle? You got some sorta benefactor or what?"

Like I said, he was sharp. He'd circled back and was trying to connect me to the Reapers. One thing was becoming clear, a formal association with The Gunfighter or even May, could pay substantial dividends. Rather than risk overstepping my bounds, I put him off.

"That's three questions. The answer to the first is that

based on the line behind you, I don't have to compete. The rest of the answers are trade secrets."

We went on like that for a while, giving a piece of information, then calling for a bit of information in exchange. After a while I figured I'd gotten what I needed, and our business was done. When the person before him got to the front of my line, I suggested he get back in line so as not to miss his turn to see the people that really worked at the intake center.

He smiled in response and told me that wasn't his place in line, that he'd sold some information to the guy that was now second in line in order to have this talk with me. But he took the hint. He paused as he stood up to leave.

"And by the way, as one professional to another, I suggest you take notes next time. It's one of those small details that rounds out the con."

Then, after a brief pause, "you got any advice for someone like me?"

Rather than think about strategy or what I wanted in return, I gave him the best advice I had. "Yeah, get a good lawyer."

You say tomato, I say tomato.
You say pain and suffering,
I say penance and growth.

DE TENEBRA

CHAPTER 13

ACTA NON VERBA

(Actions, Not Words)

RATHER THAN HEAD straight back to my room for more reading, I decided to sit in on some hearings to get a first-hand look at the local judiciary.

I made my way down the same halls I had walked through with The Gunfighter when I first arrived, on my way toward the center-most building which housed the courts. Though there were still plenty of naked and poorly dressed people, the transition from the administrative buildings to the judicial division was obvious. The worn wooden floors were now polished to a sheen and, where there'd been irregularly spaced, non-descript doors on both sides of the hall, the judicial division had large double wooden doors at regular intervals on just one side of the building.

I walked past the first-floor doors to a stairway at the far end from where I'd entered, went up a level, and found a slightly better looking version of the same lay-out on that floor, and the floor after that. Where there were people on the first floor, and a few on the four floors after that, the sixth-floor hall was vacant. Instead of the five courtrooms that lined the opposite side of the street on the other floors, this floor had two sets of inward swinging doors opposite the street side and a single large door on the street side of the hall. The frame of that door was ornately carved with symbols, writing that went well beyond my resurgent Latin, and pictures of creatures that seemed to combine artistic elements of Keith Herring, Salvadore Dali, and Ziggy the Pin Head. I starred at it until I felt a bit of nausea coming on, then headed back downstairs.

On my way up the stairs I'd assumed that all the courts handled the same types of cases and were ancillary to the ones on the first floor. It wasn't until I was on my way down that I noticed the docket cards posted outside some courtrooms. Unlike the first-floor courts which were dedicated to preliminary matters and arraignments, the docket cards showed that the morning session of these courts had hearings scheduled. Even more surprising was that several of the afternoon sessions had civil proceedings scheduled. Figuring that I should start where I was going to start, I headed back down to the first floor.

I started by checking the schedules posted outside the first few courtrooms I came to. The three-line docket card outside these courts simply said: "Early Session," "Break," and "Late Session." Judging from the crowd that had gathered in the hall while I was exploring the upstairs, I'd arrived just before the late session.

I entered the first courtroom I came to by passing

through two soot-stained side-by-side swinging doors into a small, non-descript antechamber. When I attempted to push forward on the inner antechamber doors to enter the courtroom proper, I realized that the two sets of doors opened inwards toward each other. The doors barely cleared each other and made it almost impossible for people coming from opposite directions to pass through at the same time. I stepped back to the first door to open the second door, then followed a foot-worn furrow in the stone floor through the antechamber into the courtroom.

The courtroom was empty, so I walked down the center isle that separated several rows of stone seats, to the front of the courtroom. There was no rail or banister separating the seating area from the hearing area, instead three medium sized blocks of stone both signaled the end of the isle and provided seating at a badly battered and often repaired desk. While the decision to replace easily broken and possibly thrown chairs seemed to have been made long ago, a similar policy had not been adopted for the battered desk. A sign that said "Counsel" hung askew, partially detached and spinning slowly, from one side of the table.

The bench, which was a 'bench' only in the loosest sense possible, was immediately opposite the desk, at the far end of the room. An identical plain wood table, albeit slightly less battered and perhaps marginally better repaired than the counsel's table, sat atop a slightly raised platform. On both sides of the platform were smaller desks. If my prior experience held true, and this was a big if, the clerk, court reporter, and/or bailiff would sit there.

On the left side of the room there was a large rectangular area defined by three ropes and the wall. I wasn't sure what this was for, but I was pretty sure that it didn't serve as a jury box.

I left the empty courtroom and went to the one next door, in the middle of the building. Again, two soot-stained swinging doors led to another small, non-descript antechamber. I entered the antechamber through another set of poorly designed inward swinging doors, on the tail of a harried, hungry-eyed guy, and followed him into the courtroom after he shoved past someone on the other side of the door.

Though almost identically appointed, unlike the first courtroom I entered, this room was full of people and activity.

The first thing I noticed was that the roped-off area on the left was now full. A dozen or so people were corralled into the less than two square meter area defined by the rope. All were so emaciated that they wore what looked like leg irons around their necks.

Seeing them chained and beaten like that reminded me of what my least favorite auntie and occasional care-taker once told me.

"Those who know true despair will accept anything. Like a dog that's regularly beaten, not for any reason, but for no reason, they accept the next blow, and the next, and the next. They no longer fight, flee, or even flinch, they simply fold. For them, hope is long gone and questions of fairness, like appeals to reason are foreign concepts."

These souls were broken. Whatever spark they'd had was dulled if not extinguished by despair. This type of despair, 'true despair' is rare. It is a quality generally reserved for the chronically beaten and well broken; an ugly, sucking thing that exist in its own vacuum-like void that drains the light of the soul more thoroughly than space steals heat and oxygen.

Their despair and defeat were both tangible and infectious, and I immediately regretted my decision to come to this courtroom. After a brief struggle with the flight part of my fight or flight response, I walked down the aisle and joined a smattering of others in the audience. After a few calming breaths I was better able to take it all in.

The rut-worn floors, gavel-dented bench, and just about everything else about the courtroom said it was a high-volume court; one that disposed of lots of cases each day. Like traffic courts, workman's compensation hearings, and other high-volume courts, this court would provide minimal due process and primarily serve to hear but not heed individuals' pleas.

To my right, near the defendant's speaking area, a clump of people in varying states of both dress and anxiety milled about in what probably once was a line.

In front, at the raised desk/bench was a figure in black that I assumed was the judge because that's all I could see. It wasn't that they were supernatural or shrouded in secrecy, that I'd been drinking Forus again, or even that they were too far away for me to make out details. I couldn't see or tell much more about the person at the bench because, in spite of all the goings-on in the room, they appeared to be sound asleep.

Staff Counsel was readily identified by his natty, by Purgatory's standards, legal attire. He wore a vaguely matching coat and pant combo and a shirt that was tucked in and, even though he'd missed one, buttoned up. He stumbled into the courtroom, as though he'd come up short in the ongoing contest to get in or out of the courtroom first, then scanned the inhabitants with a look of confusion similar to the one I had had a few minutes before.

His entry sparked a brief new round of jostling and jockeying for position among the people lined up near his desk. When he saw them, his eyes darted about, as though looking for an escape. Seeing none, with a sigh and slouch of the shoulders, he forced himself toward the counsel's table.

In my years of practice, I've seen all sorts of attorneys. From the new to the savvy veteran, the egotistical to the insecure, and even a few I'd describe as good. This guy wasn't any of those; I've seen criminals more at home in a courtroom than he was. At best he was incompetent, more likely he was faking it. Either way, he was out of his element.

Not surprisingly, or perhaps only somewhat surprisingly, there is no Bar Association in Purgatory. This, coupled with the fact that most souls are loath to do the kinda thing that got them here, opened the field to fakes, cheats, and wanna-bes.

As a legal professional, I was appalled by this guy; as soon-to-be opposing counsel, I looked forward to some "full contact" litigation with him.

The judge, likely roused by the commotion created by staff counsel's arrival, sat up quickly and in a single motion tossed back a thick mane of black hair and pulled it back and out of her face. She was a dark-red complected woman, possibly of Hispanic but more likely Aboriginal lineage. Stern eyes stared out from a too plump face that spoke of a life spent blaming others for unrealistic expectations and unmet desires.

I lost whatever train of thought I had when the judge, for lack of a gavel, slammed a block of wood on the desk several times then said, "You may sit, stand, or leave, but if you remain, you will shut-up and come to order." She made her authority clear with a nod that prompted two stout, club wielding guys to rise from the back of the room and approach the bench. They occasionally paused to beat people into silence or just to beat people as they made their way to small desks on each side of the bench.

When all were quieted, the judge continued. "This is the time and place for arraignment on retention or immediate disposition. You have two and only two options to choose from. You may demand immediate departure, or you may state how you wish to prove your desire to remain in Purgatory. This is neither the time nor place to present your argument, seek absolution, or rail against the injustice of the system.

"If the past continues to serve as a predictor of the immediate future, there are those among you that will attempt to circumvent this process by refusing to select one of the two available options, or that have already done so by failing to show up within the time allotted. In the hope of dissuading others from this course of action, we will start today's proceeding with an example of how not to proceed and follow that with examples of what we may all aspire to."

With a wave of her hand the judge directed the group

waiting in the roped off area on the left side of the court-room to step forward. "These are those who showed up or were brought in after their initial six days had passed." Much to no one's surprise, most of the folks in this group were still waiting in the intake line when their six days expired. Some had come as soon as they'd reached the front of the line and learned that they were late, those that just blew-off the arraignment had been brought in by force.

One of Purgatory's more simple and effective rules was that individuals that fail to make a timely appearance forfeit any and all of their assets to whoever brings them to court. Reapers occasionally, and groups of thugs routinely supplement their income by tracking down and bringing these no shows to trial.

You could tell the ones that were brought in by force; in addition to being naked - like I said all possessions were forfeited – they were typically bruised and battered.

The judge addressed them as a group.

"You are hereby sentenced to be dipped for one half day for each day or fraction thereof that you are late. After dipping those of you that have appeared before this court before will be directed to the proper venue for disposition of your continued presence here in Purgatory. If this is your first appearance, when you return you will be given the opportunity to state how you wish to contest your dispatch from Purgatory. If you wish to request immediate departure you may do so now and avoid being dipped. Otherwise, this order is effective immediately."

She paused to let that sink in then, after another bang of her wood block, "Bailiff, show them out."

Almost on cue, without regard to the warnings they'd just received one of the new arrivals in the group tried to argue that the ruling was unfair because it had taken him more than six days to get through the new arrivals' intake line. I say 'tried to argue' because all he had the opportunity to say was something about fairness before one of the bailiffs clubbed him into submission and drove him from the courtroom to be dipped. The other bailiff smiled in anticipation of a similar opportunity to inflict damage and seemed genuinely disappointed when the group moved out the door without further protest.

Once the late shows were gone one of the ruffian-bailiffs walked over to the group nearest the corral and beat-shoved the broken souls to the center of the courtroom.

As they stood before her the judge, with a look that perfectly balanced disdain and disinterest, asked a simple question. "Do each of you, of your own volition, agree that you will immediately depart Purgatory?"

After a moment of silence, during which both ruffian-bailiffs stepped forward with raised clubs, one, then several members of the group nodded their agreement. Almost without missing a beat, the judge monotoned what was obviously a well-practiced script.

"Ye who now appear before us, having determined of thine own free will to depart Purgatory for what lies beyond, are free to go."

That said, she again banged the block of wood on the table and, after a nod, the ruffian-bailiffs herded this sad and broken group from the courtroom.

After another bang of the block of wood on the desk,

the judge announced, "we will now hear from those who have come forward to request immediate departure without state prompting. As is our custom, in deference to the wisdom of your decision, we offer you a moment to speak your peace."

The people that stepped forward were as varied as the remarks they made. Some were well dressed while others were naked. There were lost looking newbies with little to say, and savvy looking veterans who'd seen and knew more of Purgatory than I ever hoped to. One woman spoke eloquently for what seemed like half an hour. Another soul simply looked back at the audience and said, "Goodbye and good luck." When it was all said and done the Judge gave the same speech she made to the prior group; this time without a hint of disdain.

"Ye who now appear before us, having determined of thine own free will to depart Purgatory for what lies beyond, are free to go." Then she added, "We honor your choice and, thank you for your words of wisdom."

After a nod from the judge the bailiffs escorted the group out of the courtroom with nary a raised club.

Another rap of the block of wood on the desk brought the court back to order and signaled the end of the prelims.

After reminding those that remained that they could only either agree to depart immediately, or state how they wished to contest their dispatch from Purgatory, the judge decreed that those making their first appearance would be divided into three groups. Again, the focus was on the fast and efficient resolution of cases.

The judge banged the wood block on the desk then called the first of this group, those who had entered into agreements to move on. Mostly these were souls that had initially contested leaving Purgatory and subsequently been convinced - by time, beatings, or the general ambiance of the place - to accept moving-on. Some agreed to go to a particular version of the hereafter, most had sought general conditions, like not having to stay in Hell for all eternity, while others negotiated more specific conditions, like no flaying or eternal burning.

These were sucker deals if you believe the soul seeks its own level, a better deal if you don't, and insurance for those who were of a mind somewhere in between. Either way, they were time-consuming affairs as they required the recitation, approval, and sometimes renegotiation of the terms with the staff attorney.

The next group was those that hadn't opted for immediate dispatch and were appearing for the first time after being dipped for being late. On cue, one of the ruffian-bailiffs led the procession of freshly dipped souls out of the corral.

Without looking, up the judge asked, "how do you wish to contest your dispatch from Purgatory?" Spurred by a jab in the back, the first soul from the corral stepped forward. He or she - at this point it was difficult to tell - picked up on the not at all subtle hint, briefly took in their surroundings and, as more a question than a statement said, "trial?"

Once again, with more than a hint of disdain, after banging the wood block on the table the judge said, "Trial it is. You are ordered to appear exactly six weeks from today in division number two to argue your case. Next."

She went quickly down the line like this until one

soul deviated from the script. Rather than the one word allotted he said, "I understand your rules and that I have to choose, so I choose trial. But the fact that I have to choose means this is not a choice made of free will…" The judge interrupted him before he could finish.

"No, apparently you don't understand. You will now be taken back and dipped again. Perhaps by the next session you will understand that when I ask for an answer I want an answer, not a speech."

'Too Many Words Guy' was dragged from the court-room screaming. After that, things generally went without a hitch. While the vast majority of this group chose trial as what appeared to be the default option, there were the expected exceptions, combat, scripture, philosophy, and debate, as well as unorthodox challenges such as chess, and poker; one guy even chose roe-sham-boe.

Almost lost amid all of this, were the few souls that stood strong and steadfastly refused to make a choice. Even after several "prompting" blows from the ruffian-bailiffs, they steadfastly refused to choose - one said only that he did not belong here, two others refused to say anything at all. All three were taken away to join Too Many Words Guy for a dip.

The last and clearly most frustrating group were those that had managed to get to court on time and were con-testing departure. Perhaps as a courtesy, more likely as an inducement for them to waste what little time they had left, this last group was given more leeway to enter their plea. Most struggled with the idea of how they would contest departure." Maybe they'd watched too much or too little television, or maybe the same skills that got them to court on time got in the way. Either way, rather than answer the question, most folks took this as an opportunity to launch into a more or less practiced presentation of all the reasons they should not move-on. It was like in My Cousin Vinny when Joe Peschi is asked for his clients' plea and he tries to explain how the whole thing is a mistake. They tried "to skip the arraignment process, go directly to trial, skip that, and get a dismissal."

The process irritated the judge and made those further back in line antsy – as they worried that they might not have their matter heard during this court session. Since this was the last session of the day, this meant certain dipping for those that were on their last day. Every now and then one of the folks further back in line would break rank and either approach the attorney in a belated attempt to accept a deal or try to cut to the front to increase their chances of having their case heard.

Such tactics were met with deaf ears or ready clubs.

As I watched the souls come and go, I came to better appreciate the depth and value of what One Finger had told me. This system was designed to lock souls into a cycle of punishment and abuse that would foster despair and wear down even the stoutest resolve.

Waiting till the last day to make my appearance would put me at a real disadvantage. Besides, if I was going to claim that I was wronged by the state, I didn't want to look like I was delaying things. Rather than wait two more days till my sixth day, I needed to enter a plea tomorrow, the day before I was required to appear.

§

Most fear the unknown.
And even from the small perch that is Purgatory,
the true nature of the hereafter remains an unknown.

DE TENEBRA

CHAPTER 14

ESSE QUAM VIDERI

(To Be, Rather Than To Seem)

I'D SEEN ALL that I could take and far more than I wanted. Luckily, with things well underway inside no one was trying to enter the courtroom as I was leaving. I pushed pulled through the double doors and headed out the courtroom with a purpose. Rather than retrace the circuitous route I had taken to get there, I went out the nearest doors and came out behind the raised center round at the head of the plaza. Compared to the oppressive air inside the courtroom, the soot-thick, burnt air outside was almost refreshing.

Though little had changed since I went inside some long but indiscernible time ago, things seemed somehow different. Sure, a few of the bench derelicts had moved, and the sky might have gone a shade or so darker, but that wasn't it. As I walked across the plaza back in the direction I'd originally come, I realized it was me that was different.

In a moment of clarity, I saw Purgatory for what it was - a drab, indifferent place made weighty and oppressive by the flawed and fearful souls taking refuge there. Where I'd strategically avoided eye contact when I first passed this way, I now took the time to take in the souls I passed through this new lens.

My earlier expectation to see rampant greed, wrath, lust, and the other cardinal sins now seemed laughably simple. Still, some part of me expected Purgatory to be populated by villains, baby killers, sociopaths, politicians, and other caricatures of some universal evil.

What I saw was far more subtle and therefore all the more disconcerting. Sure, pride and wrath were apparent, and the envious and greedy were well represented, but these were the scents, not the source. Underlying these and a wealth of other behaviors was fear; the fear of not having what you need, of not being good enough, or that one belonged in Hell was present and made all the worse by its proximity. Like an earthquake or lightning strike, the longer this unknown is delayed, the more time it has to gather, and the more the fear of it manifests.

The lateness of the day presaged the coming of the darkness. Fewer heads lifted as I traversed the plaza, and the mass of people trying to force their way into the public housing seemed to push closer together - as though my passage posed a threat to their places in line. I walk- wandered uphill toward the inn, stopping occasionally to shift the load of books I carried from one arm to the other. On every street, shoppers exited and merchants closed for the night, while laborers meandered to their flops or Forus. Though I walked among hundreds of souls, I'd never before felt so alone. In time I found myself back at the inn. Even the inn's big wooden front door seemed weighty. I reached forward and, with a grunt, pulled it open and myself inside.

There was no meditative sweeping or happy humming there to greet me. The front desk, the foyer, and seemingly the whole inn was empty. The small table where I previously sat and acquired valuable information from my host bore the only discernable evidence that things had changed since my early morning departure. In the center of the table, sat a glass with a fat finger's worth of Forus and a bowl for me to spit it out in.

I collapsed into the chair and, after taking a brief moment to steel myself, took half the Forus in my mouth. I knew better than to swallow it but having committed to getting back to reading and trial prep when I finished, I kept it in my mouth as long as possible.

It was everything I'd come to expect from Forus – my throat burned, my eyes watered, and my mouth took on a vague scat like taste. At some point my taste buds threw in the towel. Though the scat taste was all but gone, my eyes continued to water, my tongue began to itch like crazy, and my nose was running like a faucet. This proved to be my undoing. The runny nose triggered a gag reflex and I was forced to quickly decide whether to spit or swallow.

I spit the Forus into the bowl, then leaned over and took a long shaky breath while I waited for the burn to subside. I genuinely considered sticking my finger in my mouth to scratch my tongue; tasting was nowhere on the horizon.

"Careful now mate, dat aint da good stuff. You old it too long and yer tongue'll likely dissolve."

That said, One Finger pulled out the chair opposite me, then paused awaiting permission to join me. After a nod from me he gracefully lowered himself into his seat.

"You take yer Forus like a man dat's seen more dan da day should old. Got a good look at da court place did ya?"

I swirled the remaining Forus around in the glass trying to formulate a question or statement that captured the day's experiences. I had nothing.

So, I said the only thing that seemed to matter. "Tomorrow is the day."

The gravity of my statement seemed to weigh on and compress the conversation that followed. Long pauses followed short sentences and meaningful nods.

"Yer early." He eventually said.

I nodded. "Element of surprise and all that."

He grunted his approval. "Staying?"

I gave a curt shake of the head. "No."

He nodded slowly, "On then."

I shook my head in disagreement. "No."

He looked at me askew and with equal hints of doubt and disdain. "Up?"

After a guffaw and head shake, that answered "no," I looked him in the eyes. "Back!"

He slapped the table hard enough to make the glass jump up from the table as he barked out a laugh.

"Yeah, dat'll take em a while ta figger out."

"Not if I can help it." My disagreement brought him up short. "I'm demanding expedited hearings."

He slapped the table again, this time causing the glass

to tumble over, then let out the most genuine laugh I've heard in Purgatory.

"Well, dat oughta get dare knickers in a bunch." He picked up the glass and rose in one smooth motion.

"Dis calls fer a shot of da better stuff."

He returned with two glasses and a small wooden keg, and poured a finger's worth of a slightly less brown liquid in each glass. I followed his lead, both when he raised his glass and tossed the shot into his mouth, and when he swished the burning drink around in his mouth before spitting it out.

When he raised the keg to pour out a couple more shots, I raised my hand to decline. I pointed to the new books I'd obtained, which remained neatly stacked on the table in spite of One Finger's table slapping quakes.

"I've got some more prep work to do."

With a nod and a smile, he cleared the table and left.

I picked up one of my recently acquired books and started reading. I didn't notice that I was squinting, trying to read as the darkening set in, until the room gradually brightened. He entered soundlessly; his gait so smooth that the small flame from the alcohol lamp he carried didn't waver. He put some paper and a pencil on the table and left just as quietly. But for the light and the writing instruments, I might not have known he was there.

The lamp burned slowly and well into the night. When I finally rose from the courtyard table, I'd read all three books and taken some useful notes. I made my way up to my room by the light of the now almost exhausted lamp. After integrating my new notes into my prior work, I laid out my clothes in the small hope that I'd look more presentable if I didn't sleep in them, took a moment wipe off the soot and rub a bit of a shine into my shoes, then blew out the lamp and laid down to rest.

I woke early and unrefreshed before the sky lightened. I put the best shine I could on my shoes, donned my still wrinkled clothes and left the inn before first light. Though it was the earliest I'd been out since my arrival, the heat, humidity, and soot were already pervasive. As was the case with the evenings' darkening, there wasn't much to the dawn – the dark sky gradually gave way to a light-red sky. It was the first time I'd seen it, and I held little hope that it would also be my last.

Though a few were in the beginning throws of opening, most of the shops I'd passed the day before had yet to open. The plaza was quiet and nearly deserted. Of the few people that were there, none bothered to lift their heads in the groundhog-like fashion of the previous day.

I arrived at the courts early and though the building was open, they'd yet to unlock the badly designed courtroom doors. For better or worse, I'd underestimated the popularity of the early morning session. Between the just-missed-it yesterday and today's my sixth day souls, and the 'seen my last light of dawn' departures, there was already a good size crowd waiting to push their way into the courtroom.

Several souls were gathered around the slip-shod lawyer I'd seen in court yesterday. He was offering various terms and making multiple deals at the same time. The brief snippets of conversation I overheard told me these were bad deals; deals that desperate people make.

My cheap clunky shoes reverberated off the stone

floors drawing unwanted attention. Though my garb was ill-fitting and worn, the fact that I was fully clothed and carried law books, led many in the crowd to assume that I too was staff counsel.

A few people stepped up with questions. I gave them the best answers I could and the few became some. The some quickly became a small group and in short order I was on the verge of being besieged by a small panicked crowd.

Was I the public defender? Could I arrange for an extension? Was dipping really mandatory if you're late? The questions came faster than I could answer. And, as more and more questions went unanswered, things started to get ugly. Jostling turned into pushing, pushing turned into shoving, and questions gave way to shouting.

On the far side of the crowd, one of the court's ruffian-bailiffs had unlocked the doors from the inside. Apparently early morning crowds were the norm and, in the ruffian-bailiff's experience this usually resulted in the doors being pushed in on him when he opened each morning. This didn't happen because of the distraction my presence had created, so he took the unusual step of pulling the doors open to see what was going on.

His opening the door drew the crowd's attention and brought me a small reprieve. I took advantage of the distraction and yelled "Listen up!" to silence the crowd.

"For those of you that haven't figured it out yet, you're in that part of Hell often referred to as Purgatory. There is no public defender here and I'm not some court appointed lawyer that's here to help you. Nothing here is free, favors are not given, and mere courtesy is in short supply. If this is your sixth day and you want to stay, you better start figuring how and where you want to make that claim because that's all they want to hear from you here."

With that I walked through the crowd and into the courtroom… with both more and less sympathy for the attorney I'd seen the day before.

I do not make the rules here, I simply make them clear.
Nor do I create the penalties, I simply enforce them.

DE TENEBRA

CHAPTER 15

CHARITAS ABSQUE ETHICAM

(Ethos Without Ethics)

ONCE INSIDE THE courtroom, I made a beeline for counsels' table. I spread my papers out on the table with no regard to opposing counsel's needs, then used the books I had to form a makeshift barrier that marked my territory and at least partially blocked counsel's view of my notes. Once situated, I alternated between reviewing my notes and watching the scene unfold before me.

Little was changed from the day before. The burnt smell was perhaps a little stronger – likely owing to the wretched individuals waiting in the corral being fresh from a dip. The judge was again face down at her desk seemingly asleep. And what had started out as a line on the right side of the court had already devolved into a mass of people jockeying for position.

Opposing counsel entered late and came rushing down the aisle, only to pull up short when he saw me sitting at what he no doubt considered his table. After a brief pause, his confusion gave way to exacerbation, and he stalked forward.

I stood to meet, not greet him.

Rather than extend a hand to shake, I made sure the knife in my waistband was within view and reach. In Purgatory, a warning like this was about all the courtesy one could expect.

He faltered when he saw the knife then, after cautiously putting his things on the table in the little bit of space I'd left him, addressed me.

"I'm Staff Counsel, who are you?"

I paused long enough for him to get uncomfortable, drummed my fingers on the handle of my knife a few times as if I was trying to decide whether to use it or answer, then sighed in feigned exasperation.

"I'm an attorney appearing on my own behalf to request immediate departure and a few minutes to speak my piece."

I put my hand on my knife and added, "Do you object to that?"

"I have no objection." He said it respectfully, either in deference to my apparent decision to move on, or well aware that those intent on moving on have nothing to lose.

After a brief pause to take full account of things, he offered me a deal.

"Rather than depart and leave your belongings to those two" he said with a nod toward the ruffian-bailiffs, "if you give me the knife, clothes, and a copy of that Spanish book, I'll make sure your shoes get to whoever you want."

It was a shit deal. The kind of offer you only expect

someone that's ready to give everything away anyway to accept. Truth be told, I might have taken it if I'd planned on leaving and had any reason to believe he'd honor the deal. But, bad as the deal was intended to be, knowing that opposing counsel didn't know Latin from Spanish was worth much more than my cheap clothes, borrowed books, and knife combined.

The judge's loud clearing of her throat brought our attention to the bench. Apparently, she woke-up somewhere in the middle of our one-sided bartering session and was less than thrilled at the prospect of losing out on her share of my potentially unclaimed goods.

The lawyer genuflected and spoke before the judge could say anything.

"Good morning your Honor. This gentleman is here to request immediate dispatch. I was negotiating in your interest, trying to ensure that he didn't give his possessions away or destroy them, in the hope that you'd let me keep one or two of his rags. Of course, the knife and books were for you."

"I don't read whatever language that is so, unless he's got some Shakespeare hidden in there I don't want the books. And, be advised counselor, in my courtroom my bailiffs will handle all negotiations on my behalf."

With that she brought the wood block down, banging it on the table.

"Well now that we've got that settled, let's come to order."

She then launched into the same opening statement I'd heard the day before.

"You can sit, stand, or leave, but if you remain, you will shut-up and come to order.

"This is the time and place for arraignment and immediate disposition. You have two and only two options to choose from. You may demand immediate departure, or you may state how you wish to establish your qualifications to remain in Purgatory. This is neither the time nor place to make your argument, seek absolution, or rail against the injustice of the system.

"Now, if the immediate past continues to serve as a predictor of the immediate future, there are those among you that will attempt to circumvent this process by refusing to select one of the two available options. In the hope of dissuading some of you from this course of action, we will start today's proceeding with those who by compulsion or convenience are appearing late or who've previously declined to enter one of the two available pleas. Bailiffs, call the first group."

As was the case the day before, the no-contests and late arrivals were dispatched for dipping with little compassion and lots of clubbing. After another monotone recital those that had been coerced into departing by being dipped, were dispatched.

Finally, the Judge turned to those making a voluntary appearance.

"We will now hear from those who have come forward to request immediate departure without state intervention. As is our custom, in deference to your wisdom, we offer you the opportunity to speak your piece."

After these scripted remarks, the judge nodded in my

direction. I stood to address the court and found myself reliving my first court appearance like a PTSD flashback.

As a rising second-year associate doing pro bono housing litigation, I was called into an eviction proceeding at the eleventh hour. I struck a hallway deal with opposing counsel that would delay the eviction hearing long enough for me to research and develop the case but because of the last-minute nature of the deal we had to go before the judge and I had to ask that the trial be held over to allow for settlement discussions.

Things went well. And by well, I mean I squeaked out a win - the judge agreed to hold the matter over - in spite of myself. The truth of the matter is, I was so nervous that I almost forgot to stand when addressing the court, then I stood up so fast that I knocked my papers, including the page with my scripted lines, off the table.

In my hurry to pick up my papers I tripped and wound up on all fours. When I regained my footing, I was so aware that I was making a fool of myself that I couldn't remember the scripted lines I'd written down just moments before. In short order I was stuck in an anxiety loop - circling back and forth between feeling like a fool for not remembering what I wanted to say, and not being able to focus on what I wanted to say because I was thinking about what a fool I was making of myself.

I don't know if it was out of pity, for the sake of amusement, or just so she could get back to work, but I know it wasn't a good sign that opposing counsel came to my rescue.

"Your honor, at the risk of interrupting counsel when he's almost literally on a roll, the parties have jointly agreed to ask that your honor remove the hearing from calendar or reschedule it, to allow for continued settlement discussions."

It was a spontaneous and well delivered line that got a chuckle out of everyone in the courtroom and broke my anxiety loop. No longer distracted by my own anxious thoughts, when the judge asked if I agreed with the request, I was able to 'finish strong' and answered, "Yes your honor!"

I've thought back on that day hundreds of times over the years; whenever I'm dealing with newly admitted attorneys, being interviewed by potential clients or, as here, starting an important trial. It never fails to bring a smile to my face.

As you'd expect, smiles are few and far between in Purgatory, especially in the courts. My smile caught everyone off guard. Opposing counsel stopped scribbling notes about the deals he'd made and turned to focus on me; the judge put down her block of wood, clasped her hands together, and leaned in to listen; the audience stopped talking; the bailiffs even lowered their clubs and took a seat. In a moment, all eyes in the courtroom were focused on me.

Without a word, I'd brought the court's proceedings to a halt and set the stage for the chaos I was about to create. I made a mental note of this victory.

Having learned the hard way not to rely on written remarks, given the audience and judiciary I was dealing with, I decided to open with one of the classics.

"May it please the court. I am an attorney admitted to the bar on the earthly plane. I was brought here less than six days ago and am making an appearance here *pro hac vice* – for the sole purpose of requesting immediate departure or, in the alternative, to contest the court's jurisdiction."

The last part of my statement caught everyone off guard and got the audience talking. The judge picked up the wood block and started banging it on her desk and yelling at the audience. "Shut up and come to order."

I couldn't tell if she was talking to me, admonishing opposing counsel, or just talking to herself when she said, "long winded, big-word-wielding lawyers must be part of my punishment here in Purgatory."

There was no doubt that she was talking to me when she said, "Just so everyone here is clear on the matter, you are asking for immediate departure, are you not?"

"Yes, your honor. In fact, with all due respect, I am demanding immediate departure." I said it without missing a beat then, after a slightly pregnant pause, just as she started to nod in either satisfaction or agreement, I added, "and concurrent relocation to my former life on the earthly plane."

I want to say the audience in the courtroom went wild and make a bad pun about all Hell breaking loose but really, nothing much happened … at first. Sure, the bailiffs seemed to tense in anticipation, and out of the corner of my eye I could see opposing counsel doing a guppy imitation – opening and closing his mouth but not saying anything. The judge just stared at me as though I hadn't spoken or she hadn't heard me. It was like nobody knew how to react or what to do, I certainly didn't, so everybody except me just sat there dumbfounded - I was standing.

Eventually, some clearly confused soul somewhere in the audience timidly asked of no one in particular, "can I get that?" In short order and despite the judge's calls to come to order, souls starting shouting that they too wanted to go back to the earthly plane. Some yelled out to opposing counsel, demanding to renegotiate their deals.

With the less than subtle help of the bailiffs, and at no small cost to the desktop, the judge gradually brought the court back to order. She glared at me so long and hard that I figured I should say something. But as soon as I started to speak, she cut me off. Turning to opposing counsel she demanded, "Is this something you negotiated?"

In his rush to answer, opposing counsel started talking before standing, caught himself, then jerked himself upright and out of his chair, knocking over his chair and a stack of papers in the process. Difficult though it was, I fought off the urge to smile again.

Wisely, rather than stop to pick up and organize his papers, opposing counsel left them where they fell and responded.

"No ... no your honor. This is the first I've heard of this or any request like it. I don't even have the authority to agree to something like that."

After a moment of what seemed like genuine thought, he added, "And, with all due respect, I'm not sure that you do either. That is, I don't think the court has jurisdiction over matters involving the earthly plane."

Then, as more of a contemporaneous utterance than a legal conclusion he added, "I should probably object. Yes. Your honor, I object to his request."

Satisfied both that opposing counsel was not part

of, and would be of no help in resolving this delay, the judge adopted a more helpful posture and told him more than asked, "and the basis for your objection is what, res ipsa loquitur?"

"Um, yes. Yes your honor." He picked up, then fumbled through some of his papers. After, a grunt that seemed to be his equivalent of 'ah hah' he tried to explain.

"Yes, your honor. Counsel is here therefore, res ipsa loquitur, he cannot claim that he doesn't belong here."

Opposing counsel's cliff note version of the rule lacked any analysis, but that seemed of little concern to the judge. To the audience in the courtroom as much as to me, she all too quickly stated why and how she was going to rule.

"Counsel is correct. The soul knows best. The presumption that coming here speaks to the soul's need to be here is non-rebuttable. As you are here, you are deemed to belong here."

When she reached for the wood block to signal that she had ruled, I interceded.

"Your Honor, may I be heard on the objection?" A nod and a sigh signaled her begrudging consent. I picked up one of the books I had, flipped through a couple of pages, then nodded and put my finger on the page as though I'd found what I was looking for. This was all theatrics but since neither the judge nor opposing counsel knew Latin, they couldn't call my bluff. I addressed the judge, opposing counsel, and the audience as one.

"Taken literally *res ipsa loquitur* means 'the thing speaks for itself.' Here, the fact that a soul comes to Purgatory establishes the presumption that the soul belongs in Purgatory – the thing, or in this case act, speaks for itself. Thus, your Honor is correct where she notes that 'the soul knows best' doctrine is construed to support a non-rebuttable presumption that having come here of its own volition, a soul cannot be heard on claims that it does not belong here.

"However, while the presumption itself may be irrebuttable, whether the presumption is applicable is a question of fact." I stole a fake glance at my finger marked page. "The learned texts of Purgatory make clear that the presumption that the soul that comes to Purgatory belongs in Purgatory is premised on said soul's voluntarily coming to Purgatory. For example, Section 12.2 of the *Charitas Absque Ethicam* expressly provides that, ... 'the choice of where and when to go must be made by the individual soul.'

"Similarly, *Ortus est ex Spiritu* or The Onus of the Spirit, which provides the philosophical underpinnings of Purgatory's legal system similarly makes clear that Purgatory is intended only for souls that freely choose it where it states: 'Unfettered by the trials of the physical world, upon death the soul will seek to perfect itself. Each soul knows its path to perfection. A soul that brings itself to Purgatory will leave Purgatory when it is ready.'

"As I noted earlier, I did not come here of my own volition. I now make an offer of proof - if allowed to do so I can and will provide evidence showing that I took no steps to come here but was instead brought here by force and under state authority. Since it cannot be said that I in any way chose to be here, the non-rebuttable *res ipsa loquitur* presumption is inapplicable here.

Opposing counsel was quick to object - apparently, he'd warmed to the occasion.

"Your honor I object. Counsel is basically arguing that he doesn't belong here in violation of the very rules you established moments ago. I request that he be immediately taken to be dipped and brought back to choose between the two options at this afternoon's session."

I quickly responded. "Opposing counsel opened the door to this discussion. I was merely responding to his claims of *res ipsa loquitur.*"

The judge attempted to resolve the matter neatly. "While I agree that he did open the door, I have neither the desire nor time to engage in legal debate. I take his objection as offering that your statement be accepted as a request to argue your qualifications to remain in Purgatory in a court of law at a later date."

"Thank you, your honor. However, I do not wish to remain in Purgatory. I am making this appearance to demand immediate departure and relocation. I make this appearance *pro hac vice* because, by its own rules, this court lacks jurisdiction over my soul. Accepting your generous offer to stay in Purgatory would require that I waive both my departure demand and submit to the jurisdiction of the court. I will do neither."

"Well so much for professional courtesy. Let's see if you're more willing to acknowledge the court's jurisdiction after half a day's dipping."

That said, the judge banged the block against the desk, the bailiffs stepped forward, and the crowd laughed off my efforts; the first two gleefully anticipating resistance on my part, the latter group reveling in my apparent failure.

Much to the bailiffs' chagrin, I said, "Thank you your honor, and counsel" and began gathering my possessions as though to be taken away. With possessions in hand, I took a step away from the table as though willingly heading out to be dipped. Just before the bailiffs put hands on me, I said to no one in particular, "And so, 'misery acquaints a man with strange bedfellows.'"

Before I could turn to resume my walking bluff, the judge banged the block against the desk so hard that she didn't need to tell the once-again-unruly crowd to 'shut up and come to order.' With menace rarely seen coming from that side of the bench she asked, "counsellor, what did you just say to me?"

With just a hint of false naivety I said, "I'm sorry your Honor. It was a line, from a play, Shakespeare I believe.'"

"The Tempest, scene 2, act 2. It is what Trinculo said as he was asking a monster for shelter!" She spat it out like Forus that had been held too long.

"Are you calling me a monster ... in my own courtroom!?"

Somewhere in the back, someone barked out a laugh that set the audience chuckling. Taking that as a cue, the bailiffs stepped toward me. Malice lit their eyes.

"A monster? No. No your honor, that is not what I meant." And it wasn't. I was talking fast, not needing to fake lack of intent or fear.

"The quote was meant more collegially. I meant that we – that is you, your court officers here, and opposing counsel will all likely end up getting dipped along with me, as a result of your ruling."

"Dat'd be rite fittin!" Someone behind me yelled, causing the audience to erupt in laughter again.

To no one in particular, opposing counsel whimpered more than said, "Me? What did I do?"

The bailiffs now more confused and afraid than intent on doing harm, stopped in their tracks, took a step back, then looked to the judge for guidance. The judge sat back then guardedly directed, "say more."

"Yes, your Honor." I returned to counsels' table and opened the book I'd examined at the start of the hearing then read the passage I'd had in mind.

"Section 12.2 of *Usu Apud Inferos Ludicii*, or Trial Practice in Hell, provides that the court's discretion in this matter is quite limited. As your honor is no doubt aware, subsection (a) requires the timely execution of the court's duties." I could have skipped this section and gone right to the part about jurisdiction, but I wanted the court to feel the need to act quickly.

"My Shakespeare reference relates to subsection (b) which admonishes against attempts by the court to act outside its jurisdiction or authority. It specifically provides that, 'No court or officer of the court shall act, attempt to act, or suborn an act that is in excess of the court's jurisdiction and/or authority.'"

I paused for a minute to let that sink in, and the crowds' more or less creative taunts filled the void.

"And of course, subsection (c) provides that '… any act in violation of subsection (a) and/or (b) above shall be punishable by dipping for a period of not less than one day, and each violation shall be deemed a separate offense for each day it continues.'

By my calculations if you order me dipped till this afternoon without addressing the jurisdictional issue, the four of you will be subject to a full day of dipping. And if you then make me wait six weeks to argue the jurisdictional matter, you could each be dipped for more than forty days."

Again, a bark of laughter provided the opening for a series of hoots, hollers, and jeers that gave way to a "dip the judge" chant from the audience.

"Of course, as your honor has already suggested, the court could approve an agreement between the parties that defers the issue of my departure until after the jurisdictional issue is resolved."

I looked over to find opposing counsel slouched in his chair, head in hands. Apparently, the thought of being dipped for more than a month was too much for him. He'd mentally checked out and was in no condition to take the lifeline I'd thrown out, so I went on without him.

"If opposing counsel is agreeable, I might be willing to stipulate to the court's holding my departure/relocation request in abeyance pending resolution of the jurisdictional question."

"Might?" asked the judge as she waved the bailiffs back to their seats. Unlike opposing counsel, she saw past the threats, had assessed her position, and was ready to negotiate. Now we were just talking terms.

"Yes, your honor. While I'm willing to defer the departure/relocation issue, my fundamental interest lies in departure. I don't want to wait six weeks for a trial. I'd like an expedited hearing on the jurisdictional matter; tomorrow or the next day would be preferable.

With a nod and grunt the judged responded. "Yeah, and I'd like to be almost anywhere but here. The best I can do is get you the next available date."

"Fair enough" I said, "provided I get at least a day's notice in advance."

"Agreed. Advance notice will be provided."

When I didn't move, she sighed. "What else?"

"Well, should I lose on the jurisdictional issue I will need time to prepare for my return to this court. I'd like assurances that I will be afforded the customary six days to prepare should I need to return."

"You've already used some of your six days. I can't restart the clock, but I can toll it. The tolling will start today so, after receipt of the adverse judgement on the jurisdictional issue that I'm sure you'll get, you will have the same amount of time you did this morning to appear for arraignment. Do we have a deal?"

"I believe we're close your honor. Again, with all due respect, might I request assurances that there'll be no interference, retribution, or acts in frustration of the agreement."

I couldn't tell if she was disappointed because I felt the need to make the request, or because I'd had the foresight to make it, but her disappointment was unmistakable.

After a pause she acquiesced, "I don't control what goes on outside this courtroom, after all, you are in Purgatory, but," after a hard look that left the two bailiffs who were now studiously inspecting the floor around their feet, "nothing like that will be sanctioned by this court."

"Thank-you your honor. Now, if opposing counsel agrees… ." With barely a look in opposing counsel's direction the judge said, "Counsel agrees," then banged the block on her desk. "Now get out."

Again, I heard a familiar bark of laughter from the

audience, this time coupled with some clapping. I turned to see where the laughter and heckling had come from and was pleasantly surprised to see One Finger and May sitting side-by-side in the audience. Not wanting to risk snatching defeat from the jaws of victory, I quickly gathered my things then only half looked back to the bench to utter a perfunctory, "Thank you your honor," before heading out.

Distracted and hurried as I was to leave, I only half registered her, the bailiffs' and even opposing counsel's laughter.

Somewhere in the back of my mind an old saw registered: If everybody is laughing and you don't know why, the joke is probably on you.

⤫

The desire of the most advanced soul
is to join and help others,
while the lowest souls of Hell are destined
to dissolution in a pool of souls.
Are these similar fates mere coincidence?

DE TENEBRA

CHAPTER 16

DE BENE ESSE

(Of Well-Being - Under The Circumstances)

I GATHERED MY two hecklers and, with One Finger cutting a wide path before us, we quickly made our way out of the courtroom through the tricky swinging doors, and into the relative calm of the hallway.

Once outside, One Finger clapped me on the back lightly, only enough to buckle my knees, and said, "now dat were a good show. Almost wert da price of admission it were." May nodded her head in agreement, then chanted, "dip judge, dip bailiffs" a few times before barring her pointy teeth in a smile.

T'was high praise times two.

Lawyers aren't supposed to ask questions if they don't know the answer, don't want to hear the answer, or don't want to put the respondent in a position where they will have to lie. I knew this; I guess I was a little giddy after my victory, maybe even touched by the idea that the two cared enough to come see what happened to me. Either way, when I asked what they were doing here together there was a very brief, but very awkward pause before May explained that when she'd stopped by the inn to drop-off the proceeds from the sale of the clothes of those that attacked the Rider Reaper, One Finger told her she could find me here. Since he was going to the nearby training center, he figured he'd come down with her to find out if he still had me as a tenant. And that was how they 'just ended up' coming to court together.

It was a lie, and a pretty good one. Though it wasn't smooth, creative, or - even accounting for May's odd diction - particularly well delivered, it had enough truth in it to be plausible. Even if you knew they were lying, you couldn't prove it. And most importantly, it give away what they were lying about. One might just think they were trying to hide the fact that they cared about me.

I knew their showing up together wasn't about business, or an interest in my well-being. This was a date. I'm not saying it was romantic or fun, though it does seem to have been entertaining, but it was definitely a date. Looked at it through that lens I realized that they made quite the couple.

May was decked out in a black bolo jacket that provided only a modicum more cover than the low-cut blood-red silk blouse she wore underneath. The blouse was tucked into black patent leather pants that tapered to an end well above blood-red 4-inch stiletto boots. The outfit was topped off with a blood-red pill box hat with a black veil that covered her short, black, and now randomly spiky hairdo. And, even in its weird and seemingly excessive application, May's make-up was perfect.

His outfit, loose fitting, light colored, cargo pants that were well worn but not worn out, a loose button-down shirt that was probably linen, long coat, and boots, was more subtle and required close inspection to fully appreciate. His clothes, and even more remarkably, his boots, were notable first in that they fit his exceptionally large proportions, and second, if you stopped to consider it, in that they were clean. Really, really, clean. Almost like brand new clean; no small feat in a place where soot fills the air and collects on every surface. Impressive as all this was, the thing that let me know he really wasn't there to see me, the thing that told me this was a special occasion, the thing that was most likely to give their illicit romance away, was his hat. Atop his recently shaved and perfectly polished head sat a simple black wool bowler ... with a small blood-red feather in the band.

You 're officially and undeniably a couple when you start dressing to complement each other's outfits.

These two were the closest thing I had to friends here in Purgatory. Ever the wingman, I realized the best thing I could do was to embrace the lie. I shifted the conversation back to business and let stand the suggestion that our deal carried an implied obligation that May track me down to deliver my share personally. Careful not to thank her, I asked May for my share.

After counting it out in a public display of distrust, to which May feigned insult, I turned my attention to One Finger.

"By my count, I'm paid up at the inn till tomorrow. But since it looks like I'm gonna be here a while longer, I'm gonna need a place to stay. I'm guessing I'll need a place for a week, maybe more - maybe less, depending on how soon I get a court date and how that goes."

He nodded his head in that way that says go on, without committing to anything other than listening. So, I told him, "but I'm also looking for a partner."

His initial reaction, holding up a hand in the universal stop gesture, caught me off guard. Hand still in the air, he looked around to acknowledge the various unsavory people around us, then after a glace toward May said, "Forus?"

Lucky for us, in Purgatory, like just about every jurisdiction I've ever been in, you can find a bar within a restraining order's distance of the courts.

After we got situated at a table and each of us was staring down a dark glass of Forus, I set out my plan.

"I'm going to hang a shingle and offer my legal services. With all the new arrivals running around scared and clueless, there's what looks to be an untapped and very lucrative market here. And let's face it, if opposing counsel in there is representative of the profession, well, Purgatory needs a better class of lawyer."

He nodded, pulled briefly on his ear as though in thought, then, having decided, removed his hat and ran a meaty paw across his bald head, and then just said it.

"And yer na troubled by da fact dat dey got no coin?"

"I'm counting on it" I said, then smiled and clapped him stiffly him on the back in a reciprocal gesture that cost me most of the feeling in my hand. After a little rubbing to get the feeling back in my hand, which he and May politely ignored, I explained.

"They contract to have me represent them at their

retention arraignment. Rule 5 provides that full payment is due on the completion of services and Rule 6, say that any fees I charge for representation before the initial retention hearing cannot exceed what the client could earn in the time before their hearing. So, a person on day five with no other debts, can't be charged for more than a day's rate, where a person that hires me on day two can be charged for up to four days.

"If they stay beyond the retention arraignment, payment will be due in a day. The same applies where they have more time before their initial retention hearing and I do more work for them. Whether they owe me for a day or six days, when payment comes due, and not coincidentally when they can enter into contracts without restriction, as an incentive to keep me on as their attorney, I offer between one and six days of free services that can be applied retroactively."

So ya offer ta let them em out a payin ya?

Yes, provided they agree to pay my non-refundable retainer fee.

And ow er dey gonna pay yer retainer if dey cain't pay wot dey already owes ye?

Over time. Say less than six weeks, or maybe just under six months.

Yer gonna wait six weeks, maybe six munts, ta get paid a retainer fee dat equals wot dey originally owed ya?

Before I could answer May, ever the sharp one, chimed in, "Interest! No?"

"Not just interest" I said. "Interest at usurious rates."

Because Rule 5 required that debts be paid as incurred, Purgatory hadn't seen the need for, hadn't bothered to establish or, as a matter of principle didn't care about even basic prohibitions against predatory lending practices such as charging absurd interest rates.

The retainer wasn't a debt being paid, but rather payment for services that would likely be rendered. As structured, it was an option being purchased over-time.

In addition to having to pay a ridiculous interest rate on whatever part of the retainer that remains unpaid, they won't be allowed to demand representation until the retainer is fully paid.

After a bit more ear tugging One Finger asked, "Well, it certainly seems dat ya taut dis out. And good on ya fer dat. Ya don wanna go messin about wit da rules all willy-nilly – dat's sure ta get ya dipped fas-n-long. But wot I'm not seein ere is wot s'xactly ya need ta partner wit me fer?

"I ain't big on business speculation and if yer looking fer muscle, well troof be told, I'm tryina cut back on da urtin folks type a work. Sides, sounds ta me like most of wot ya need is someone ta find, recruit, and collect from potential clients, maybe even andle da books. Now May ere is bout da best der is at dat sort o ting. Wot say ye bout dis May?"

I detected a slight blush, in spite of her thick pancake make-up. Though obviously caught off guard by his flattery, May responded without hesitation.

"Plan ok. Better too, go after just arraigned. Can contract, some pay immediate some make retainer. Already know who going to court."

It wasn't genius, but it was a definite improvement on the plan. I made May an offer on the spot. "Five percent of my billable hours for all your recruits?" She hissed at me in response, which I took as a good sign. When she saw her hiss wasn't enough to make me bid against myself, we began to negotiate in earnest.

For a while I thought I did pretty well. She'd get ten percent of my billable hours for the business she brought in, and two percent of all my billable hours for doing the book-keeping and administrative work. It wasn't until she described this as "an agreement in principle" that I realized I'd been out negotiated.

My stomach fell when she said, "Need Gunfighter agree," and I realized I'd made the mistake of negotiating with someone that would defer approval of the deal to someone else. In a desperate attempt to recover I said, "Of course. But how about we stop by the public housing first. I haven't interviewed anyone there yet, but I think talking to some of them will give us a sense of how little time and effort will be required of you."

One Finger actually did have to get to the training center, so we agreed to go our separate ways. Their goodbye was short if not sweet. He bowed slightly, tipped his feathered hat and said, "lady" to which she scowled and only half nodded. He then dropped a heavy hand on my shoulder. Maybe he was a bit gentler, maybe I was numbed by the Forus and the prospect of having to deal with The Gunfighter, but much to my surprise, his hand hitting my shoulder didn't hurt. After nodding in agreement with what he was thinking he said, "All n all, a good day dis were."

Unfortunately, we'd picked a bar that was on the other side of the plaza from the public housing. As May and I walked past the raised structure with the dipping pool at the top, I asked, "if this is where all souls are taken for dipping, why didn't it ever seem to be used?" May explained that this pool was for special, public occasions. Like when celebrities were dipped or when souls were dipped to oblivion. Other, less elaborate, but no less-effective pools were used for routine dipping. Looking down, she dragged her well shod foot through the ever-accumulating soot and noted that those pools, which were used almost around the clock, generated most of the soot.

I stopped in my tracks, looked around and ran my own worn shoe through the layer of soot that had settled to the ground. I didn't want to believe what I'd heard but couldn't stop myself from needing to know. Looking to May I quietly asked, "This, this soot is emitted by souls when they are dipped?" She answered my question with a barely perceptible nod.

We crossed the raised concrete platform, following a lane in the soot created by the passage of those recently before us. From a distance, the squat grey public housing buildings looked like any the other government building on any other square anywhere else.

As we made our way across the plaza the "gophers" that had occupied the seating area earlier in the day were far fewer in number. Perhaps because there were two of us, but more likely because we were headed away from the public dipping pool, those that bothered to sit up and take notice, seemed distinctly disinterested.

All this changed when we veered off the raised platform and headed toward the public housing building. Where we'd previously drawn scant attention, our change of direction brought all eyes upon us. Those that had sat up got up, those that hadn't moved before followed, others seemed to come from points unknown.

Our clothes made clear that we weren't there looking for housing, and marked us as potential employers, victims, or benefactors.

By the time we got to the building steps we were surrounded by people looking for coin in one fashion or another. It was like a scene from one of those depression era movies where the truck pulls up to the day labor spot and is surrounded by individuals so desperate for money that they'd do just about anything.

All too quickly, the clamors of "got work?" "what you need?" "right here boss!" and more than one plaintive "me, me" gave way to pushing and shoving. After the first bit of jostling May hissed and began mumbling.

I took action before things could get too far out of hand and climbed to the top of the stairs at the building entrance. With hand raised high I shouted above the growing crowd, "We're not hiring anyone or buying anything! We're here to make you an offer." The crowd's change in attitude was palpable. Almost immediately they started to disperse. I quickly added "but what we're offering is more than worth the cost."

It was a weak, quickly thought up, and poorly delivered sales pitch. For a moment, when the crowd turned its attention back to us, I thought it had worked. It was only when I heard laughter behind us that I realized the crowds' interest had been caught by another.

Behind us, in the now open doorway between the stairs and the building hallway, stood a blocky, marginally dressed and, notably, shoeless man. He was of indeterminate ancestry not in that he didn't look like any race in particular, but because he looked like some of every race. Behind him, nearer the building hallway, stood a few even more marginally dressed men.

He looked us up and down then, in an accent that matched his global ancestral roots, cocked his head toward May and said, "Well, ain't no amount of paint and bondo gonna hide the lack of meat on them bones. But if you've an eye toward humiliatin' her, and you're ok with charging by the hour not the man, I'm willing to take up a collection here so's me and da boys can help you out."

As I tried to explain our interest, May began to mumble in earnest. Before I got out much more than that I was a lawyer, Any-Ancestry guy silenced us both when he took May's chin and lower jaw in hand. Holding her face like you would a kid that had just said a bad word, with a lick of the lips and more lasciviousness than I'd have thought May could engender, he said, "Stop all that fussin little lady. The trick is to know when and what to use that pretty painted mouth of yours fer. And with them pointy little teeth of yours…"

That's as far as I let him get. I grabbed the wrist of his outstretched arm with my closest hand, then stepped between him and May while I and used my other hand to force his elbow across his body in an upward arc while I pulled the wrist down. He twisted as his shoulder started to dislocate and was screaming even before I kicked his leg out from under him. By the time he hit the ground I'd touched May on the elbow and back to signal our exit and, ever the lady, she was gliding down the stairs next to me.

We headed back to the inn. May had said she wanted

to straighten herself up, but I suspect she was hoping One Finger was there to comfort her. Unfortunately, when we arrived he was nowhere to be found. May excused herself to one of the downstairs rooms and when she emerged her make-up was once again perfect.

No one says "thank you" in Purgatory. May's hands are small and, though usually gloved, they're thin and both fragile and cold looking. That they were strong, warm, and ungloved surprised me almost as much as her taking my hand in both of hers and holding it for a second before shaking it and promptly leaving. I guessed good etiquette demanded some acts be acknowledged.

Now, alone in the inn I pulled out my newest books to study. But try as I might, I couldn't take advantage of the quiet time. Between getting little rest the night before, my court appearance, the Forus, and my scuffle on the steps of the public housing, I was both pumped up and worn down. Napping was out of the question; I was anxious about when I'd be called back to court and at the same time, too tired to study. That I'd had a brush with violence most every time I went out, made exercise seem like a good option.

There was a small dirt patch in the patio. After warming up with some jumping jacks, kicks, and shadow boxing, I went through my blocks and strikes. I was walking through my stances when I heard the now familiar swish, swish of the broom as it moved across the courtyard pavement behind me.

I turned and asked One Finger if it was ok that I was practicing my fight techniques in the dirt patch.

With a half chuckle One Finger said, "Fight wot? N'ere I was wonderin wot all dat jumpin and stumbling

ye was doing was bout. Fer a bit I taut either da Forus ad
got to ya, or ya'd just plain lost yer mind and was doing
some sort a rain dance ting. T'was actually opin ye was just
tryin to spread da dirt around since ye were havin a bit a
luck wit dat." With a smile he added, "I adn't seen nutin
to make me tink you was practicin fightin.

"And wot tis it dat's got ya goin on like dis anyway?"

Then, almost as an after-thought he added,
"Mr. Lawyer-man."

I told him I was too tired to work yet too pumped
up to sleep from events at the courtroom and the public
housing and thought some exercise might push me in one
direction or the other.

There was a noticeable shift in his focus when he said,
"I know wot appened at da court. Wot appened at da
public ousing?"

He began sweeping again while I told him about my
conversation with May on the way to the public housing
and nodded in understanding if not empathy at my revelation about the source of the soot.

His smooth, rhythmic sweeping gradually eased me
into the part of my story about the crowd that had gathered around May and me, and my attempts to focus their
attention and pitch my services. He listened intently and
neither his broom stroke nor focus faltered when I got
to the part about May mumbling and Any-Ancestry Guy
grabbing her and making lewd comments.

But for the crack of the hard-wood broom handle
under his tightening grip, one would have thought the
story as uneventful and expected as my realization about
the soot. I quickly told him that, other than having her

make-up smeared, which she'd come here to fix, May was fine. I made it sound like I was boasting about my fighting skills rather than acknowledging his feeling for May when I told him how I twisted Any-Ancestry Guy's arm and how he'd started screaming even before he hit the ground.

I was surprised when he stopped sweeping to confirm that I'd grabbed Any-Ancestry Guy when he put his hands on May, and I was caught completely off guard when he asked if May had touched or examined my hands afterward. I told him about May's out-of-character two-handed handshake before she left, to his visible relief.

"Aye, dat'll do it." He explained. "Dat make-up on er ands, arms and face responds ta er spells. Any part of any soul dat gets it on em will ventually dissolve. Fact is, folks used ta call er "Powder Lady," a name she were na too fond a, till dey saw dat stuff work.

"Sure, most injuries will heal – I seen limbs dat er chopped off grow back in a few weeks. But wit dat stuff - dependin on ow much ya get on ya and wot er spell is - it kin take years maybe even an eternity to grow back wot gets dissolved. And trust me, it urts like da dickens. Ye mite'a woke tamara missing sometin if'n she adn't neutralized any ya got on ya wit dat anshake.

"Oh, an na ta burst yer bubble, but I spect May is wot ad yer man screaming.

After a brief moment of reflection he added, "I also spect dat since yer business requires dealin with dat sort, developing yer fightin skills is gonna ave ta be a part a yer business model."

A few days wiser now, I didn't even think to argue his point.

"Now ah aint seen dat dere's alot ta work wit ere but if yer goin to be a continuing tenant," to which I nodded my agreement, "and ya can't seem ta stay outta trouble," to which I could only shrug my shoulders, "it's in ma best interest ta elp ya develop some skills. Better dat dan me avin to go get ya all da time."

"Best interest" was the giveaway. I'd only been in Purgatory five days - by pretty much any definition, I was still a newbie. But even I knew this was, no pun intended, 'one hell of an offer.' His being one of the few fighters to be asked to train the Reapers was no small feat. I'd no doubt that being trained by him would usually cost more than the inn's accommodations. I figured it was his way of thanking me for stepping up in defense of May, something he could never actually acknowledge, and preparing me in case the needed to do so again arose in the future.

With nothing more in the way of fanfare, he said, "let's start by cleanin up da mess ya made wit all dat stumblin around ya call foot work," and tossed me the broom. I started sweeping; instead of hearing a swish, swish, with each stroke of the broom I could almost hear *wax on, wax off.*

After sweeping the patio, I swept the entry way to the inn, the sidewalk in front, the sitting room, and the downstairs room where May had refreshed her make-up. He followed me throughout, adjusting my posture, correcting my balance, and encouraging me to work from my core. At one point he stood behind me and pressed down on my shoulders, forcing me to work just to stand.

After a few hours the downstairs was clean, and I was exhausted but no longer anxious. When he finally asked for the broom back, I was no longer pumped up, just thoroughly worn down. After walking across the room, he opened the door to a small, very neatly arranged storage closet and placed the boom inside next to several other differently sized brooms.

The darkening had come, and I was looking forward to laying down on my cot, so I took this as a sign that we were done for the evening. With a vague nod in his direction, I turned and headed up the stairs toward my room, only to be waved back and offered a seat at one of the small downstairs tables. As I slowly lowered my now bone-weary soul into one of the seats, he went behind the bar and came back with a couple of glasses of Forus. Apparently learning to handle my Forus was going to be an essential part of my training.

He sat and, with no more in the way of preamble than a sip and spit, jumped right in.

"Da two tings ye can do ta best elp yer self is first ta practice, and second, ta understand ow tings ere work. We'll get ya plenty a practice but wot ya gotta understand is dat fightin ere is a bit different. Fer starters, folks don't ave bones in da usual sense so da joint locks n breaks ya fancy er an iffy proposition at best. Fact is, ya can twist a limb all da way round and, if der committed, a bloke'll keep on fightin. Pain, like speed n power, is mostly a matter a perception.

"Wit dat in mind, we're gonna focus yer training on survival skills. Dat means getting yer mind rite, learnin wot yer actually capable a doin, and learnin ta do it wit out esitation wen ya gots ta do it. We'll be takin all dat up soon enough."

I stood, nodded my agreement then turned and made for the stairs. I hadn't touched the Forus but I was confident that it wasn't going back into the keg.

The soul, like all things, needs purpose.

DE TENEBRA

CHAPTER 17

UT AD OMNES METUS

(The Fear Of It Should Affect All)

I WOKE THE next day later than expected. Though I've always tended to wake at first light, the always hazy full light of day already illuminated my room. I was still tired and would likely have slept longer but for the fact that someone was knocking on my door.

Still half asleep but awake enough to know it could only be One Finger, I yelled through the door. "If this is the part of the training where you wake me up and make me drink raw eggs and run around the streets in dirty sweats to inspirational music, I'll pass."

"Wot? No. Ya gots visitors." One Finger said from the other side of the suddenly flimsy seeming door.

In a voice that sounded far more awake than I was, I asked the question that had no good answer. "Is it someone from the court?"

"No. Member wot I said last nigh about lettin people

know wot yer capable a doing? Well, I tink yer bout ta get advance trainin rite-way. Best be down lickity split."

I was wide awake before my feet hit the floor.

When I got downstairs May and The Gunfighter were waiting, impatiently. I looked to One Finger to see if he had a clue about what this was about and found him fastidiously cleaning one of the glasses he kept behind the bar and making a poor showing of being disinterested in what was going on.

With nothing other than One Finger's wake up warning to go on, I played it low key and offered what I'd seen used as a respectful greeting. "Gunfighter."

By way of acknowledgement, The Gunfighter turned and walked out. After barring her teeth at me in what was either happiness to see me, or sympathy for what was to follow, May followed him out. Again, I looked to One Finger for direction. His nod toward the door told me to go - either to follow them, or so that whatever was going to happen next didn't happen on his property.

By the time I got outside they were several doors down and walking away at a good clip; I ran to catch up. Just as I pulled even with them, they turned and started down-hill and I realized we were headed back toward the courts.

A part of me was hoping I was being escorted back to court – I knew Reapers brought in those that didn't show up for their court dates. But as far as I knew I didn't have a new court date yet and, even if I hadn't made an appearance yesterday, I'd have all day today to get myself to court. Since I couldn't rule out some sort of judicial shenanigans, I mentally ran through my court options - a continuance, multiple meaningless objections, if pressed

I could even rough out my substantive arguments. Somewhere during the review of my arguments, I calmed down and asked myself, why would The Gunfighter bring May if he was just going to drag me to court. Since he wouldn't, I assumed we were going somewhere to negotiate the deal May and I had discussed the day before.

Not wanting to 'ass-u-me,' I jumped right in and asked. "Are we going to discuss the deal I talked to May about yesterday?"

His head seemed to dip a little lower than on his previous stride and I took that as a yes.

Since I was now talking with 'the boss,' I thought I'd better gain back some ground if I was going to get the deal May and I had agreed on. So, after acknowledging that I'd agreed to a ten and two percent deal with May, I started trying to weasel out of it.

By then we'd reached the middle of the stone civic center plaza. Rather than head to yesterday's bar where the negotiations began, we veered toward the public housing. At that point, had I even known it, that I'd been out negotiated again would have been the least of my concerns.

Turns out, after she'd freshened up and left the inn, May had gone to the training center. Her appearance there was both an obligation and a showstopper.

It wasn't that there were no female Reapers, there were. Rather, by default if not fiat only Reapers and their trainers were usually allowed in. All other entrants were viewed and dispensed with as challengers. Their training was private almost to the point of being secretive. Even the presence of Reapers' servants, like May, was frowned upon. If and when servants showed up, as May did, it usually signaled that something had happened that all Reapers should or would want to immediately know about.

Apparently, some time ago one of the Reapers had gone to the public housing on some type of business or other. The then head administrator of the public housing organized his people in opposition to the Reaper, in the mistaken belief that he was the Reaper's target. By virtue of sheer numbers, the Reaper was moved-on. Seeing this as the challenge to their position that it was, the Reapers banded together, and went to each of the public housing buildings. They moved on all the lieutenants, captains, and employees of the administrator, along with numerous unwitting residents. The only ones that were spared were the arrivals that managed to get out of the way, the head administrator of the public housing, and a promising junior administrator.

The head administrator was dipped to his shoulders in a bath that leaked into a second bath. The lieutenant was laid in the second bath and given a bowl to use to bail the liquid from his tank into a bucket, that was regularly poured back into the boss's tank. It took several days for the boss to stop screaming and twice as long for him to dissolve fully.

Though he bailed nonstop, the lieutenant couldn't avoid some contact with the acid. He rolled and shifted from side to side so that parts of his body would recover while others dissolved. But, according to rumor, he spent so much time dissolving in and recovering from the lye that he was permanently thinned, and his skin took on a gray hue.

When May showed up at the training arena and stood

demurely to the side, at least as demurely as one can in a low-cut blood-red silk blouse, clingy black patent leather pants, and four-inch stilettos, everything stopped - knives were sheathed, holds released, the sparring halted, even the talking ended.

May curtsied when The Gunfighter approached and when prompted, said there'd been a problem at the public housing, then paused to allow those further away to move within ear shot before speaking. And move they did.

At the mention of the public housing, to a man ... and woman ... the Reapers turned and approached. While The Gunfighter and other Reapers looked and listened with dead-eyed intensity, May told the same story about the public housing that I'd related to One Finger.

Neither The Gunfighter nor any other Reaper seemed moved by May's story; she told it from start to finish without interruption or question. When it was clear that May had no more to say, The Gunfighter glanced skyward, then spoke to May for all to hear.

"Darkening nears. Meet me at the inn at first light tomorrow." By word and tone, he'd made clear to everyone what they'd all anticipated – this was his affair to handle, theirs if he failed. Then he turned, drew his long knife, and along with the other Reapers, returned to training.

My knowing about this beforehand probably wouldn't have changed anything. I'd still be headed for the same public housing building we'd stopped at the day before – I could no more peel off and leave the two of them alone now than I could have refused to go with them in the first place.

Looking down the plaza to the raised fountain, I was

relieved to see a small crowd had gathered there. It meant there was no one on the benches or stairway that would surround us as the crowd did yesterday.

My hopes rose when we got to the public housing building. While the outer doors were open like the day before, the big double doors on the inside of the vestibule were closed. I hoped more than believed that maybe the building was closed, or perhaps no one was home. My hope was dashed when we got to the inner double doors.

He didn't bother to knock.

Flanked by May and me, The Gunfighter simultaneously shoved the doors open and drew his long knife. It took a second or two for my eyes to adjust to the darker Hallway we'd entered; by then two bodies were already starting to shimmer and dissolve. A shove from May's gloved hand kept me moving forward on The Gunfighter's flank. I was too shocked to keep count, but by the time I got my feet under me and was moving forward on my own power The Gunfighter had moved-on at least half a dozen souls.

Unlike me, the people in the hall caught on quickly. Trying to distance themselves, those closest to him shoved back against those that pushed forward to see the action.

All this changed when he drew and leveled his .44. The boom of the first shot left a clean hole all the way through the first guy's head, removed the back half of the second guy's head, and left a pulpy mush in place of some woman's face. The three bodies crumpled to the ground and began to dissolve right about the time the shock wore off and the screaming began.

Suddenly this was no longer a spectator sport - all

knew they were fair game. Everyone tried to run at once. The fast led the pack, the slow were pushed, and those clumsy enough to trip were trampled. The second boom of the .44 took out two more spectators and made clear that no quarter would be given. Those that fell crawled and scampered away as best they could. The fast and lucky had already made good their exit.

By the time we crossed the 20 feet to where a stairway joined the first and second floor, some shimmering goo was all that remained in a hall that had been full of souls.

The contrast between the eerie silence in the hall now and the chaos and carnage mere moments before was nothing compared to the calm of the lone man standing at the foot of the stairway. Being fully clothed, he was, relative to the masses in the hall, well-dressed. After a cautiously slow yet surprisingly graceful bow, his baritone voice boomed out,

"Greetings Gunfighter."

As soon as he said it, I realized that, unlike May who stood behind and to the side of The Gunfighter, I was hiding behind, and indeed peeking over, The Gunfighter's shoulder. I discreetly took a step to the side.

With a movement so fluid it belonged on a ballet dancer the man gestured up the stairs.

"I am here to assist. This way if you please."

The Gunfighter paused and without taking his eyes off our new guide replaced the spent cartridges in his gun in a single movement so fluid that the graceful assistant was noticeably impressed. The Gunfighter holstered the weapon, then gave a nod that said, "after you." The assistant, who hadn't moved a muscle during the reload, turned with a deliberate slowness and led us up the stairs.

The stairway was a worn, rough-hewn stone affair that doubled back once then opened into the middle of an empty hallway that ran above and parallel to the hallway that The Gunfighter had just "cleared." We turned and continued up more flight of stairs until we came to the top floor's parallel hallway.

The hallway to our left was clear. To our right, men and women each with shaved heads sat on the floor, with knees and heels under them, and their hands on their thighs. Sitting side-by-side, they lined both sides of the long hallway. The assistant turned right and headed down the path between them. As The Gunfighter passed each of the kneeling souls that lined the sides of the hall bowed. The two sides of the hall fell into a rhythm; left hand down when the assistant passed, right hand down in the space between the assistant and The Gunfighter, forehead to floor as The Gunfighter passed.

We passed several rooms with open doors. Most were filled with non-descript boxes; a few had a bed or two, others were filled with bunk beds, none were occupied. Eventually we came to the room at the end of the hallway.

It was a large room, easily occupying the space of four of the rooms we'd passed. Empty chairs lined the wall on both sides of the door we entered, while the two connecting walls were lined with desks. Recent looking scratch marks on the floors suggested the desks had been hastily moved. Beside each desk, individuals in varying states of dress knelt on one knee, with head bowed.

In the middle of the wall opposite us was a small, raised platform. A beautiful, threadbare rug hung on the wall at the back of the platform and a roughhewn chair was centered just in front of it. Rugs and pillows were spread across the platform, both creating an entry point for the now vacant chair, and seating for the chair occupant's guests and underlings.

On each side of the platform were contrasting sights. Toward the left stood a pencil-thin, gray-skinned man with a fuzz-bare balding head, and non-contrasting pale gray-green eyes. He stood motionless, head bowed slightly in deference and arms spread wide in welcome. His clothes, a loose fitting, earth toned pant/shirt combination, with comfortable looking sandals, confirmed his position of wealth. The assistant confirmed The Thin Man's authority when he walked over to him, bowed deeply, then dropped to a knee behind and to the right of him; his was not mere politesse.

On the other side of the platform, to The Thin Man's left, four individuals huddled together doing their best to imitate the formal bow of those in the hall. Behind each of them stood a larger individual whose bowed head, sinewy muscles, and full-length staffs made clear that they stood guard over those kneeling in front of them.

The Thin Man beckoned us forward toward the chair and pillows with a fluid, inordinately compelling, sweep of his arm. But for a restraining touch from May, I'd likely have bumped into The Gunfighter on my way toward the chair and pillows.

Rather than move, The Gunfighter's only response was to fix our hosts with his dead-eyed stare. Then, without preface or acknowledgment, he spoke into the silence that no one dared interrupt.

"It seems I and mine aren't welcome here."

The Thin Man seemed to bow a little lower and spread his hands a little wider. "No disrespect was intended Gunfighter. Those who were … less than cordial were new. They sought advantage, not knowing May was yours."

After a barely perceptible nod The Gunfighter asked, "and where are these 'less than cordial' individuals now?

The Thin Man clapped his hands and on command the five guys that had been standing guard grabbed those that were kneeling by the hair, neck, or whatever they could get a hold of, dragged them to The Gunfighter's feet, then bowed a quick retreat.

The Thin Man continued while the mass of bodies that was thrown at our feet disentangled itself and generally tried to assume a formal bowing position.

"Those who offended lay at your feet. I would not presume to interfere with your justice; they are as they were when they committed their despicable deed, untouched by my hand. He who dared put hands on yours bears her mark. Those who stood with him then, kneel with him now."

Clearly unsatisfied, The Gunfighter barely glanced at the souls cowering at his feet.

"These are newbies. They'd have known better if your people had done their job. I am here because your people didn't do their job, which means you didn't do your job. Your failure may cost me position and coin - and you offer these crumbs to make me whole? Where are yours that were in charge?"

The .44 boomed in emphasis of his point. He'd fired from the holster, neither drawing the gun nor looking at his target. It took me and everyone else a moment to figure out what had happened. It was only when the now formerly one-handed Any-Ancestry Guy started wailing that I realized The Gunfighter had shot off his other hand.

The Thin Man didn't miss a beat. But for the fact that he bowed lower still, I'd have thought that he hadn't even heard the gunshot. If anything, his voice was even more calm and deferential.

"After I had the head lieutenant that was on duty whipped, I sent her and all the others that were on duty to the public bath for dipping until your arrival. My building Captains have stood guard there around the clock, announcing their offense to all who come within ear shot. The Captains have orders to bring the lieutenants here at your signal."

Apparently the "public bath" was the raised area at the end of the plaza that I'd explored days before, and the "signal" they'd been waiting for was the boom of the .44 that they rightly figured would follow The Gunfighter's arrival.

I didn't see The Gunfighter nod his agreement, but the Thin Man apparently did. He bowed again slightly, then clapped his hands together twice.

Rather than being dragged before us like the five newbies, the four lieutenants, fresh from the baths and a march across the plaza, entered unescorted – a professional courtesy I suspect.

They shambled in at a what only their minds thought was a synchronized march. Naked and oddly thinned from being dipped for almost a full day, they did their best to form a straight line. Looking at them, it was obvious that the Thin Man had been more than a little generous in his claim that they were 'standing' in the hall.

A single individual stepped forward from the line. The dipping had been especially unkind to her. Raw, blurred and mottled scars on her back and shoulders marked her as the lieutenant in charge yesterday. I couldn't tell if it was part of their training, or if they'd been practicing while being dipped – perhaps for lack of anything better to do – but on the lieutenant's signal the others stepped forward, then, as one they placed a fist across their chests, bowed their heads, and knelt.

"And what happened to you not presuming to interfere with my justice?" I couldn't tell if The Gunfighter was joking, mocking, or just pondering the issue.

If there was a question about this in his mind, the Thin Man decided to err on the side of caution. With another bow he said, "These four hall lieutenants failed to adequately represent my interests in this regard and for that I have used those means available to me to punish them. They have thereby also insulted you. As your abilities in this regard are … unique, I entreat you to dispense any additional punishment you see fit."

Enroute to becoming a senior associate I once had to go to management training. While most of it focused on hiring, firing, sexual harassment, and other things you need to know to avoid costing your employer money, there was a useful a section on employee feedback and discipline. The takeaway from that section was that feedback should be immediate and impersonal, and any consequences should be clear and significant. Apparently, the Thin Man took this philosophy to heart.

The Gunfighter faced the lieutenants, drew his firearm slowly, then let his shooting hand drop so that the gun hung loosely at his side. He turned and walked toward the four bowed lieutenants without acknowledging or giving quarter to the four newbies that still knelt at his feet.

The newbies moved quickly, but in an uncoordinated and erratic fashion; like blind, deep-earth insects, they bumped and blocked each other in their attempts to get out of The Gunfighter's way while remaining bowed. Now without hands, Any-Ancestry Guy moved slowest and made the least progress in his attempt to get out of the way. Though he passed within inches of him, The Gunfighter ignored him, neither bothering to slow his stride as Any-Ancestry Guy wrist-nub hobble-crawled to the side to make a path for him, nor bothering to look at him when he shot Any-Ancestry Guy in the head.

Stride unbroken, The Gunfighter continued walking till he stood before the lieutenants, clearly unimpressed by their synchronization, wretchedness, or subservience. He faced the lieutenants but seemed to address everyone.

"You have failed to fulfil your obligation to familiarize those of yours with those of mine. It appears a personal introduction is necessary to ensure that mine are recognized and respected in the future." With that he waved May over.

Heads still down, as one the lieutenants rose in their synchronized and practiced manner. May left my side and, after grinding her foot in the goo that had been Any-Ancestry Guy, took her place next to The Gunfighter. After a pseudo bow to May, The Gunfighter addressed the four lieutenants.

"This is May. You will step forward … and take her hand in greeting."

Seemingly by way of example, The Gunfighter reached out for May's hand. When she presented her hand, he took it lightly in his and leaned forward, air kissed just above it, then tugged deftly as he released it. It was a subtle move, but a move that all were meant to see. With him holding the glove, her powdered and activated hand hung exposed in the air.

The practiced order the lieutenants had shown took on a panicked undertone. Two of the lieutenants took a step back. One of those two bumped into a third lieutenant who stood frozen, his gaze locked on the still shimmering goo that had been Any-Ancestry Guy. Another of the lieutenants let out a series of small whimpers.

The Thin Man stilled his people with an almost imperceptible shake of his head. Whether this was disapproval, sympathy, or warning was beyond me.

The sound of the .44's hammer being cocked back focused everyone back on The Gunfighter. He spoke in a voice that brooked no argument and gave no quarter.

"I'll give you till the count of three, then I'm gonna take offense if you don't shake her hand."

He counted one and shot the first of Any-Ancestry Guy's accomplices in the head to emphasize his point. He waited until that body fully dissolved then counted two and moved on another accomplice with another head shot.

That's when the handshaking started.

In short order the first two lieutenants that shook May's hand were staring at stumps where their hands had been. A third was holding his own wrist, squeezing it and his eyes tightly as though one or the other would stop the pain or process that was turning his hand into a puddle on the floor. The last lieutenant, the one that had been in charge, stood fast, tears streaming down her cheeks, arm still extended. Either unaware or unable to understand that the hand with which she'd taken May's hand had lost both grip and substance. Whether they knew it or not, and some clearly didn't, all the lieutenants were screaming.

The screaming stopped when The Gunfighter shot the last of Any-Ancestry Guy's accomplices in the head.

*Obstacles, temptation, and free will challenge
the already perfect soul to grow.*

DE TENEBRA

CHAPTER 18

CONTRA PROFERENTUM

(Against The One That Makes The Offer)

THE THIN MAN spoke into the quiet that stretched beyond the dissolution of the bodies and body parts.

"Eloquently done Gunfighter. As I said, your abilities in this area are … unique."

With his head still bowed in deference, he opened his arms in a manner that said his message was intended for all to hear.

"By The Gunfighter's decree the lieutenants now bear May's mark.

"The mark will serve as a reminder to all that the comings and goings of the Reapers are not to be hindered, and that theirs are our honored guests."

He almost made it sound like a gift had been given.

Almost mindlessly, using more muscle memory than thought, The Gunfighter flipped the lever on the .44 to release the cylinder. He shook the gun once and the spent cartridges dropped into his other hand. He bounced the cartridges a couple of times in his hand before pocketing the empties. When he pulled his hand out, he held fresh cartridges.

His reloading was nonchalant, mindless, and much faster than should have been possible. He clicked the newly loaded cylinder home, started to holster the weapon, then paused and quoted himself.

"Position ... and coin!"

Emotion flashed over the Thin Man's face for the first time in spite of all that had transpired.

He regrouped quickly and bowed a little lower before adding, "of course, and we look forward to the opportunity to make you whole."

For a brief moment I wondered if this pun was intentional - who am I to say what passes for humor in Purgatory.

"I have been told that yours came with the intention of offering legal services?"

After a barely perceptible nod from The Gunfighter the Thin Man made a sweeping gesture with his arm.

"If you would follow me please."

He started past us and his assistant fell inline immediately behind him. When they reached the doorway leading out of the room into the hall, he stood to one side and his assistant took up a position at the doorway opposite him. As mirror images they bowed and waved us into the hall. As The Gunfighter passed them, the Thin Man fell in just behind him - in front of me and May, his assistant fell in a step behind us.

Those that had lined the sides of the hall were still on their knees, heads still touching the floor. Either they hadn't watched the earlier spectacle, or they were well practiced at discretion.

We walked down the hall, past the stairs we'd come up, to the other end. There, three stones were placed together to form a hard, armless and backless bench under a square opening in the wall that formed an open window.

With a grace that reflected equal parts caution and respect, the Thin Man stepped around The Gunfighter to stand on the left side of the end of the bench facing us. His assistant, also no slouch in the grace department, deftly mirrored the Thin Man's movement and took up a position at the other end of the bench. Once they were both in position, the Thin Man pushed open the door to the room on the left and waved us forward.

The Gunfighter said, "Mr. Lawyer-man," then looked at me, toward the room, then back to me. A discreet nudge from May's now thankfully re-gloved hand confirmed the two things I feared: I was supposed to 'check out' the room, and I was stuck with the "Lawyer-man" name.

Begrudgingly, I moved forward to check out the room. I moved with what I hoped looked like a casually cautious gait and when I got to the doorway, I did what they do in every cop and spy movie ever made – I bobbed my head in and out for a quick look. Seeing nothing untoward, I stepped in and looked around.

A chair sat with its back to the interior wall on the other side of a heavy wooden desk. Rugs of the same type that lined the other room's platform were hung on the wall and laid in front of the desk, separating it from two guest chairs. A small bookshelf sat below a window which was opposite the door.

That I hadn't set foot in the room didn't stop me from offering my expert assessment. "Um, it's a room."

I was quickly corrected by the Thin Man.

"No, no Mr. Lawyer-man. It's an office. Indeed, it's your office should you deign to do us the honor of hosting your practice."

We can of course add accommodations for resting or any other ... activities you wish." Caught off guard, I was wary and attentive.

I turned away from the room, back toward the group just in time to hear The Gunfighter's single word response.

"And?"

The Thin Man was ready, "And if you'll permit, I personally would like to be the first of what I'm sure will be your many clients." Looking briefly from The Gunfighter to me he said, "May I offer you a retainer?"

On cue his servant produced a handful sized sack of coins and dropped it into The Gunfighter's instantly outstretched hand.

The Gunfighter bounced the sack in his hand a couple of times then held it at eye level between us. "20 and 10, you get the office, the clients, and May to do the book-keeping."

Though it almost looked like he was talking to the sack, it was as obvious to everyone that he was speaking to me, as it was that I had been thoroughly out negotiated.

I acquiesced with a nod and The Gunfighter turned to May. "Details."

Quick as a whip, May rattled off a bunch of terms and conditions that would have made her the belle of any contract lawyers' ball. Client access, security, various good-faith provisions, she even thew in provisions about routine cleaning and maintenance.

I really don't remember all the terms May set out. The realization that much of the shooting and torture I'd witnessed was likely equal parts reputation and negotiation left me mired in a sense of revulsion and guilt that should have been shared.

While I stood there wondering how many souls had been moved-on just to get the percentages I'd agreed to, The Thin Man, an obvious veteran of such 'full contact' negotiations was, none too discreetly taking my measure.

When May finished with the details, I turned to the Thin Man.

"You should be advised that the retainer is non-refundable, our agreement is non-exclusive, and when, whether, and how I or my assigns decide to take on any legal work you may require or desire is a matter wholly and solely within my discretion."

He accepted these harsh terms and acknowledged that I was 'in the game' with a nod of his head and a slight bow. Since I'd made clear both that he wasn't getting his money back and that I wasn't required to do much of anything, he was caught off guard by my next question.

"What is the nature of the legal work you desire?"

The thought of actually getting something for what he'd paid brought him up short. When he hesitated, I offered assurances.

"Any information you provide me will be privileged and kept confidential. It will not be shared without your express approval. The usual penalties apply to me, and by that I mean dipping, for violating this agreement, and of course, any soul that seeks to ... compel my disclosure will have to address such inquires to my silent partner here."

The Gunfighter cut me a sharp look, and May began an in-depth inspection of the hallway, looking for nothing other than not to be involved. I'd just cut The Gunfighter out of the information loop and the running of the business. The Gunfighter affirmed this addendum to our agreement with a glare and a nod, May bared her teeth, and the barest hint of a smile flitted across the Thin Man's lips.

Where I previously had his money, now I had his business. With a sentence I'd sweetened his deal and forced an implied obligation on him, while gaining major concessions from The Gunfighter in the form of protection and non-interference with my practice. Where the empathy he had perceived made me suspect, as one who appreciated the value of leverage and manipulation in negotiations, the Thin Man now respected me.

The Thin Man didn't hesitate. He accepted the additional terms, by dully stating, "contract review ... for starters." Then called his assistant close. After a terse but discreet exchange, his assistant walked to and opened the door directly across the hall from my new practice, and waved me in.

Even though this was Purgatory, and I was the one that said it, and even then, not out loud, I couldn't help but like the sound of "my new practice."

Since no one had laughed the first time and nothing bad had happened, I again moved at a casually cautious gait and did the cop/spy head bob thing. After a quick look and a long sigh that combined relief, resignation, and a bit of awe, I went into the room.

The room was the mirror image of my new office, but unlike my office there were neither chairs, a desk, nor rugs.

Though there were no filing cabinets, boxes, or other means to contain them, the room was filled with papers. The papers were stacked neatly, one piece of paper on top of another all around the room. Some stacks reached shoulder height, and each stack was topped with a heavy stone that held the top piece of paper, the one with a number on it, in place.

The stacks lined the walls and took up most of the open floor space. A maze-like aisle allowed access to the row after row of stacks, which were separated from each other by about three inches - a width I later learned was roughly equal to two hands with palms pressed together in prayer.

Once inside, I quickly perused several documents in the stacks. There were stacks of agreements going to room and floor space rental, labor, and construction. There were partnership agreements and thinly veiled loans. There also appeared to be a surprising number of stacks of what I call Purgatory-specific agreements; agreements to arrange beatings and kick-backs, to provide services such as blackmail and seduction, and those documenting pay-offs and bribes.

I didn't want to keep my new partner waiting too long because I didn't know what The Gunfighter would do if he got bored or suspicious, and I didn't want to find out. After my initial pass through the stacks, I called the assistant over, told him I would start with a random spot check of the contracts and, in what I hoped actually seemed random, directed that those sections be delivered to my office.

In truth my selections were made with an eye on the

special agreements. I was pretty sure how the labor, rental, and construction agreements would read so I only planned to review a few of them. The partnership and loan agreements were of personal interest since I'd just entered into a partnership agreement to run a business that relied upon not-too-thinly veiled loan agreements. But the Purgatory-specific agreements were a potential gold mine. If I was gonna get out of here I was gonna have to understand how Purgatory really worked.

As any honest lawyer - and most dishonest ones - will tell you, even within the legal profession, contract law is considered boring, tedious, detail-oriented work ... of necessity. At their core, contracts are about apportioning risk; as a general rule, the shorter the contract, the less risk that's apportioned. So, while any hack can draft a contract, a good contract attorney can craft a document that makes all the disclosures and demands required, while at the same time denying or shifting risk and responsibility.

Good contract drafting is an art. Akin to a Jackson Pollock painting, a good contract takes time to understand, and often morphs into something completely different from what it first appears to be as your angle and approach changes. And, as with a Pollock, once it's truly understood, a good contract conveys a wealth of information about the drafter, the client that commissioned the work, and how the world around it operates.

By the time I'd returned from the file room, The Gunfighter was gone. With the return of his assistant, the Thin Man gave a shallow bow and the two departed. When I questioned where The Gunfighter had gone, May made clear that she and he took their silent partner role seriously.

"Gunfighter gone," she said. Then, after handing me my share of our first client's retainer, she curtseyed and left.

I stood by myself in the hallway far too long, wondering what I should do next before remembering that I now had an office. I opened the door, stepped inside my new office, sat down at my new to me desk, put my feet up, and began contemplating my next move.

The universe wastes nothing.

DE TENEBRA

CHAPTER 19

A FORTIORI

(From A Stronger Argument)

THE MOMENT OF my reflection was short lived. A knock on the door announced the arrival of a few of the scribes I'd seen along the side of the hall and kneeling by the desks in the larger room. Bald, skinny, and barely clothed, it was hard to tell one from the other. There was a lot of bowing and hand waving before the papers I'd requested were brought in from the other room. After no small amount of pointing on my part, and repositioning by them, the papers were neatly stacked next to the wall opposite the window in my office.

When they started talking about how I could and should keep the documents neat and in order, I figured they were finished enough and unceremoniously ushered them out.

I started with the labor, rental, and construction agreements, both as a warm-up and to make sure there wasn't anything completely out of left field in them. Other than some Purgatory-specific, if not appropriate clauses, like provisions for dipping and beating, and the duration of the agreements – suffice it to say that there was no rule against perpetuities – the contracts were fairly typical.

The partnership agreements differed from most contracts in that there were numerous forfeiture provisions – this made sense in a place that embraced the schadenfreude defense and excused pleasure in the pursuit of harm to another.

As expected, among the documents were numerous attempts to circumvent Rule Number 5 which requires that debts be paid within the time required to incur them. For the most part these were uninspired, often poorly conceived, and only marginally effective attempts that any judge who was paying attention and not on the take would throw out. If I were planning to stay in Purgatory, revising and perfecting these agreements would provide a good and steady income.

By the time I finished perusing the partnership agreements I realized both that the bulk of the day had passed, and more importantly that I hadn't heard from or checked with the court about my next hearing date.

And that's when it hit me. I hadn't filed a notice of appearance, motion for party status, or other pleading that would typically be used to let the court know how to get in touch with me. I'd been thinking like a newbie again.

This being Purgatory, there were no phones, emails or, for all I knew, mail delivery. The judge had only agreed to "provide notice." At best, a notice would be posted - at or near the courtroom if I was lucky - in some obscure and unexpected place if I wasn't. It was a small thing with very large consequences.

I beat myself up for being stupid for the very few minutes it took me to gather my things to leave. I glanced at the no-longer-neatly-stacked, but still in order documents as I turned to leave and realized there was no lock on the door as I pulled it closed. Even though May had included provisions for security for the office in her terms, I wasn't comfortable leaving client documents unsecured and out in the open. After a moment of deliberation, I went back and grabbed one of the blank sheets from the top of a stack. As I stepped out and pulled the door closed, I inserted the paper in the door frame so that the top of it was barely visible. It was shit for security, but it would likely let me know if someone had entered my office while I was out.

I trekked across the plaza, passed the administration building, and entered the hall just outside the court where I'd appeared the day before. I looked in and around the courtroom and found nothing other than the signs noting the two daily sessions. After a walk down the hall, where I found similar schedules posted outside each courtroom. Swallowing my anger and frustration, I accepted that I would have to check every courtroom on every floor and, with a heavy sigh, headed up the stairs.

Five flights of stairs, five hallways, and 17 courtrooms later, I'd determined that there were no postings about my hearing outside any of the courtrooms, that the stair landings needed cleaning, that my shoes were an integral part of Purgatory's torture, and that it was time to head back to the inn.

I took my time and used the walk to release my frustration and review yesterday's lessons. I focused on walking; first synchronizing my breathing with my gait, then maintaining balance between steps to eliminate any bounce and unevenness from my stride - no small feat given the uneven cobblestone streets and my ill-fitting, clunky shoes. Eventually the walk became a meditation. As I thought about yesterday's training with One Finger, I could almost feel the broom in my hand. Where I'd been pushing the broom and trying to maintain balance, I felt that if I just held it as part of me and let it move with me, I'd maintain balance and sweep with little if any physical effort.

By the time I got back to the inn, the feeling was too strong to resist. I went to the broom closet, grabbed the first broom I could get my hands on and continued my meditation. That it was a push broom barely registered and didn't matter in the least. With a feather light grip and balanced stride, I steered the broom forward. Each exhale produced a smooth, effortless, and efficient stroke. It was like finding the sweet spot with a tennis racket, lucking up on the perfect golf stroke, or any Ken Griffey Junior home run swing; each was a perfect moment in itself.

My meditative mind followed the floor plan I'd unconsciously learned and in short order I'd swept the entryway and most of the courtyard. I'd rounded up the accumulated soot and was working on the beginnings of a small dirt-devil, when I felt more than heard something coming. I let my broom stroke carry me away from the object and brought the broom up with both hands in a defensive position, just as a pebble flew past where I'd been.

One Finger smiled as he walked over to pick up the projectile he'd launched.

"Na bad, na bad a'tall. Wy dint ya catch it?"

I smiled back. "It's not like you're living in a glass house."

He chuckled lightly then quickly moved into teaching mode.

"Yer balance is much improved" he said while tossing the stone up and down in his hand in thought. "But ya gots ta learn ta tink outside yer physical limits and get past da constraints of yer earthly perceptions."

When I looked at him skeptically, he nodded and explained.

"On earth ye learn ta push wit yer arms, den ya learn ta use yer core, back and tummy muscles. By da time most folks learn ta use all dare muscles, dare bodies er usually start'n ta fail. Da few dat get past dis point learn not ta rely just on muscle."

Both as a question and statement I said, "You're saying I should practice using my *Chi*."

"I don know wot all ya seen on yer field trip dis mornin, but from wot ah I do know, in da time ya been ere ya seen dat cuttin off a limb or two won't stop an attacker, and learnt da ard way dat twistin an arm won't stop it from workin. Seein folks do more, do it easier, n do it faster dan da mecanics of musculls laus mite get ya tinkin dat da rules of physics ya lived by surely don't apply ere, if dey applied anywere. Let's ave at wit an example."

With that he squared up in front of me, crossed his arms across his chest, and assumed something of a front stance. Once settled he said, "try'n move me back, I'll old ma stance but won't resist."

I'm not small, but this guy was super-sized. This was going to be a challenge. I hesitated for just a moment before mirroring his front stance, then I placed my hands on his hips, took a deep breath and pushed forward from my core as I slowly exhaled. True to his word, he didn't resist. Instead, he became a rigid object that allowed all my effort to be transferred through him to overcome the inertia of his mass on the floor.

My efforts weren't wholly in vain; he slid back a foot, maybe two. After another deep inhalation, I exhaled and pushed again and again, until we reached the wall near a large stack of 2'x 2'x 2' stones.

"Dat weren't bad" he said as he bent and picked up one of the large stones.

With barely a hint of exertion he carried it back to near where we'd started and set it atop the pile of soot I'd collected.

"But yer still focused on muscles dat ya don really gots." He picked up another stone and, carrying it as though it were a beach ball said, "ya cain't let yer self be limited by da expectations ya developed on da earthly plane."

When he returned, he picked up a third stone, casually handed it to me, and nodded toward the two he'd already stacked across the room.

The weight of the stone was near crushing; I staggered forward, unsure whether my legs or grip on the stone would give out first.

Slapping the stone dust from his hands and clothes, One Finger pointed back to the pile. "Set it wit da udder two n try pushin da pile back over ere. Tis like da broom" he said as he walked past me toward where we'd started, "da trick is ta let go of wot ya tink ya cain and cain't do."

The weight and bulk of the rock made for slow, unsteady progress that had me staggering toward the spot where the other two stones were stacked. By the time I got to the stack of stones my fingers had taken the lead in the race with my legs to see which would give out first, lifting the stone higher to stack it on top of the others wasn't going to happen. As I closed on the spot where I was going to drop the stone, which wasn't where I was supposed to put it, One Finger picked up the broom I'd been using and corralled a bit more soot into a landing zone next to the two stones he'd placed. I dropped/placed the stone mostly on the soot he'd gathered.

Using the broom, with little more effort than he'd afforded the soot, One Finger nudged the stone forward until it came to rest neatly against the other two stones.

By the time I was able to stand up straight One Finger had crossed from the courtyard to the entry-way with the broom. "I'll be putting dis away. Ya can take it up again after ya can move dem stones back n fore witout gettin in too much of a state." Then, after pausing to smile he added, "Took me almost being broke down by stonework ta learn dis lesson; I ope it don't take ya near dat long."

I spent the rest of the day and a good part of the night pushing, pleading with, and sometimes just sitting on the stones. In small increments, I'd moved the pile about four feet and was now standing in, and occasionally slipping because of, the soot that the stones had ridden on. When my eyes grew heavy and my body tried to coax me into lying on the stones, I called it a night and headed upstairs.

I woke early the next morning reenergized, refreshed, and luckily not the least bit sore. At some point during my stone labor I'd come up with a few ideas for small but useful additions to the contracts I'd looked at yesterday. I wanted to get to my office to get started but didn't want it said that I'd left this morning without trying again. So, I grabbed a couple of the borrowed books off the table in my room and headed down to the rock pile in the courtyard.

More as a formality than a renewed effort I dropped into a front stance, lowered my center of gravity, and gave the pile the type of effort I'd found had produced the only bit of movement I'd been able to achieve. After enough tries to show that I'd made an effort I realized two things. The first was that I'd expended only the amount of energy I'd expected and moved the stones the exact distance I'd anticipated. The second was that almost half of the times I pushed I'd slide backward in the soot. I've never studied physics, so I've nothing beyond a working familiarity with gravity and friction, and a rudimentary understanding of the workings of a lever and fulcrum. Still, I was pretty sure that what just happened shouldn't be possible – the times I slid backward the stones shouldn't have moved forward much if at all - isn't there some rule about an equal and opposite reaction for every action?

I stood still, perplexed and starring at the stones for who knows how long. In my mind I watched One Finger sweep the stones together with the broom again, and again. Where I'd earlier chalked it up to his great size and strength, I now realized that not only hadn't he shown any sign of effort, but also that what he'd done should have been impossible: The broom handle was sturdy but certainly nothing special, it should have snapped under the effort of pushing the weight of the stones forward.

Reflecting on the moment, I recalled that he'd said not to let myself be limited by my expectations and realized that last night I'd expected the stones to be heavy and only move a certain amount given the effort I could muster; after they'd done so a few times I expected to be exhausted, and I was. Then, when I felt certain that I couldn't do anymore, I couldn't. This morning I'd expected the stones to move the same distance given the same amount of effort on my part, and they had - in spite of the fact that the force of my effort was compromised by my sliding backward in the soot. Once I eliminated other possibilities, such as gravity changing, or me being made stronger by rest, I realized it was my expectations rather than my effort that produced the result.

I told myself that the stones would move, then tried pushing them again with minimal effort. Nothing happened. I told myself over and over again that they'd move then gave another shove, again to no avail. After a few more failed attempts I realized the problem wasn't that I wasn't trying, but that I was only trying. I wasn't wholly committed.

As in dreams where what you fear happening happens, or that original Star Trek episode where they'll die if they don't unequivocally believe that the shoot-out they're in, at the O.K. Corral, is an illusion. Any lingering doubts about what will happen, dictate what will happen.

Maybe I hadn't been here long enough - yikes! Or maybe I hadn't seen enough - double yikes! Because, in spite of all that I had seen and the logic of the situation, at some level I had lingering doubts. I hoped, but didn't believe, and since I didn't believe, I didn't expect.

∽

Can free will exist in the absence of truth?

DE TENEBRA

CHAPTER 20

VERITAS ODIT MORAS

(Truth Hates Delay)

I LEFT THE inn a short while later and, even though it was early, there was already a small crowd of people in the streets. I skirted the edge of the crowd and took the first street down toward the civic center. It didn't take long to get to my office in the public housing building.

The large front doors of the public housing building were still closed. I thought back to what seemed like long ago and remembered how easily The Gunfighter had flung them open yesterday. I gave them a shove before I could think about how it shouldn't be that easy. While they didn't burst open like they had when The Gunfighter shoved them, they parted more than enough for me to enter.

Stepping inside I saw that the full swing of the door had been blocked, by sleeping souls. The hallway floor was packed, and in some areas stacked, with mostly naked, mostly sleeping souls. They were everywhere, from the entrance to the stairway. This is where and how new arrivals usually lived; this is where I could and perhaps should have wound up.

I was standing at the entrance trying to eyeball out a path down the hall when a guard, who'd been standing to the side, saw me and stepped forward. She had a patchwork haircut - the kind you get when you use a knife such as mine to cut your hair. The longer hairs on her head were twisted around and held in place by slivers of wood that could serve as weapons if needed. A strip of cloth pulled tight across her chest highlighted a muscled physique and olive colored skin, while loose cargo pants provided for both modesty and ease of movement.

She snapped to attention, bowed deeply and said, "Please to follow me." She banged her long hard wood staff on the stone floor three times, then walked forward at a casual pace. Where I'd sought a path through the masses, she made one. Those that heeded the warning of her staff rolled or scrambled over each other to get out of her way. Those that didn't or couldn't move fast enough were kicked or knocked out of the way. I followed in her wake, feigning indifference.

We were met by another similarly attired, similarly built guard at the bottom of the stairs - he could for all intents and purposes have been her brother. No words were exchanged, after a brief nod each banged their stick on the floor. When she stood to the side, he beckoned me to follow. We made our way up the stairs then past more sleeping souls to the next stairway where, after another nod and stick bang, another guard took the lead. This ceremony was repeated at each landing until we reached the top floor. Here the guard, a squat, beer bellied guy that would look equally at home on a Harley, merely bowed and stayed that way until I turned and headed toward my office. There was no need to bang his stick as there was no one sleeping on the floor - the area was reserved for the scribe types, all of whom had already risen and assumed their tasks.

When I reached the door to my office, I breathed a small sigh of relief when I saw the tip of the paper still crammed in the door frame where I'd left it. I pushed the door open and just managed to catch the paper before it fell to the floor. That's when I saw him. He sat on the client side of my desk, feet up, hat pulled down low over his eyes, and apparently asleep. Even with his hat pulled down and from behind, I recognized him immediately - it was the guy I'd talked to at the intake office - The Fixer.

I took my time getting to my chair. I stopped at one of the stacks of paper to grab a contract of the type I'd been thinking about, while casually checking to make sure nothing had been rifled through. I made my way over to my desk while scanning the document, looking for the provision I intended to change. I was neither quiet nor particularly concerned that he was there. Taking my seat, I worked on the contract for a short while, even managing to jot down some of the modified terms that I'd come up with the night before. Eventually, with hat still pulled down low, he spoke up.

"Nice digs."

If there'd been any doubt, and there wasn't, this made clear that he wasn't here to make chit-chat. He wanted something. What I said and did next, and the tone I set would likely go a long way toward defining whatever relationship we might have.

Rather than stop reading, make eye contact, or acknowledge what he had said, I ordered, "Feet off the desk."

He knew the game and, as anticipated, saw my command for exactly what it was, me not at all politely suggesting that he had nothing to offer and preparing to give him the boot.

He could have taken his feet off the desk and tried to pitch me something, but that would have looked desperate and conceded too much. He could have challenged my authority and taken issue with my tone, but since he knew that I knew he didn't have any way to back up a challenge, that would have labeled him as a poser and earned him an introduction to the rough hands and hard sticks of the guards on his way out. So, he did the smart thing under the circumstances, he mostly ignored my directive, but only mostly.

Feet still on the desk, with a single finger he pushed his hat far enough up to allow eye contact and grinned as though we were old friends. "You were no more discreet about checking to see if I'd gone through your documents than you were with your paper-in-the-doorframe security."

I put the contract aside, face down, and nodded my acknowledgement. "After yesterday's events, I'm assuming that you and anyone else that could get past the guards are well aware of what the penalty would be for prying into our clients' confidential information."

My use of the term *our* wasn't lost on him. I was going

to sit back and try to relax into my really hard and only marginally more comfortable than his chair, but well before I could, he thumbed his hat all the way up and asked, "Our?"

He'd shown his hand and all but conceded the new dynamics of whatever relationship we were going to have, so I sat back and took the time to get, relatively speaking, comfortable in my chair. Then, instead of answering his question, I pointed out the obvious. "Your feet are still on my desk."

He jerked his feet off my desk and quickly sat forward, more likely out of enthusiasm and anticipation than in deference to my response, then all but blurted out, "So, it's true. You're working for one of the Reapers?"

His enthusiasm was genuine and calculated at the same time. What he was really asking about was the nature, rather than fact, of my business relationship.

I couldn't help but like him.

"I have a legal practice. A Reaper, The Gunfighter, is something of a silent partner in that practice." Then, in keeping with our 'give-some-to-get-some' history, I asked, "now, how and why is that any of your business?"

Though he tried to tamp it down, his interest was obvious. "Well," he said, "I'm here to make you an offer." I doubted he had much to offer but saw no harm in hearing him out, so I urged him to go on with a raised eyebrow and head nod.

"I'm thinking you need another partner…"

My skepticism was both immediate and obvious enough to let him know that no matter what he had in mind, he'd over-shot the mark. But he regrouped quickly.

"Or perhaps a partner-track associate. You've obviously got all the muscle you need. And," with a quick glance around the room, "since you were able to convince The Gunfighter to get you installed here, I suspect you've got more than enough brain power to get the job done. But what you don't have is someone that will make this business a going concern."

I was genuinely unimpressed and maybe even a bit disappointed. I used all of five words to burst his bubble and let him know he was about to be sent packing. "May comes with The Gunfighter." He smiled slightly, just enough to suggest that he'd intentionally ignored May's participation as a set up for his pitch. He relaxed back into the chair again and continued.

"Ah yes, the witch. Yeah, I hear she's something alright – smart, well organized, a fair negotiator, good accounting skills, and a bit of magic to boot. Word is she's even quite the lady, long as you're on her good side."

Unlike the now evaporated blob of goo formerly known as Any-Ancestry Guy, there was nothing salacious in The Fixer's remarks. On the contrary, somewhere in his impressive display of intel gathering and character assessment, I detected a hint of admiration.

"But there's two things that she isn't. First, she's not a salesperson." He held up a hand, correctly sensing that I was inclined to disagree, then went on before I could. "Oh, she can negotiate a number and dictate terms with the best of them, but she isn't really the customer-facing type now is she? Sure, she can walk over to the sheep at the intake and enough of the few that aren't scared off by her will jump on board with your program to keep your partner happy, but she's not gonna bring in the big fish. She's not, in your parlance, a rainmaker."

He had a point. But given my current obligations and ultimate objective of getting out of Purgatory, it wasn't a particularly compelling point. I was non-plussed.

After a glance at the stacks of paper around the office, I rhetorically asked, "This is day two for my practice. Does it look like I'm hurting for business or in need of someone to bring in the big fish?"

He'd obviously thought this out and was unfazed.

"To bring them in? No. Not if your business plan is to shoot up half of your current and potential customers, and then extort an agreement that has you doing the work of a junior associate."

I wanted to take offense but, my revulsion at yesterday's events lingered strong enough to give me pause. After playing to both my conscience and pride in my work, he gave me just enough time to realize my conflicting feelings, then threw me a line.

"What you need is someone that makes potential clients want to wade through the unwashed mass out there and hire you. Someone who also has their pulse on enough things to make sure your silent partner can stay silent while bringing in the big fish. Right now you're dependent on your silent partner and his agent for clients, protection, book-keeping, and most importantly, information; everything the business needs except someone to do the actual work.

"There are a lot of other lawyers here that would love to have this office. You need to make sure you don't end up being demoted from partner to employee. You need someone to make sure that yours is the face of this firm. You need someone that works for you."

He made a good point. Like I said, he was sharp.

I liked and trusted May, but she served The Gunfighter. That I could threaten to reveal her and One Finger's affair to assure her loyalty never crossed my mind. If I wasn't intent on getting out of Purgatory, I'd have started talking terms with him right then. As it was, I was on the fence. With the outcome hanging in the balance, he played his trump card.

"So, I've made my pitch. But I can see you're not wholly on board with my proposal. I get that. The kind of value I bring isn't something that always shows up on the books. So, how about I give you a sample of the value I offer. If it's the kind of thing you're interested in we talk terms right here, right now, if not, I'll be on my way."

We both knew I wouldn't and, in some sense couldn't, say no to his offer – curiosity aside, the rules of Purgatory pretty much required me to have a good reason to pass up the chance to get something for nothing. I said, "deal" and locked in this preliminary agreement.

He said it without preamble or fanfare.

"One thing your silent partner might not know or want you to know is that notice of the mandatory meet and confer has already been posted. You're due in court later today."

He'd caught me off guard and finished quickly, before I could regain my composure.

"As I suspect you know, if you don't show up for the meet and confer, your jurisdictional claim will be dismissed."

If I'd had my feet on the desk, I would have jerked them off. As it was, like him moments before, I quickly sat forward. Unlike him, when I opened my mouth to speak, I caught myself before I blurted something out.

He'd played me and played me well. He knew I'd want to head-out immediately to read the notice and start prepping for the hearing, but he'd already got me to agree to stay and negotiate terms if I saw value in what he offered. Obviously, I did. I'd been knocked off the fence and now found myself negotiating against the clock. I clenched my jaw a few times, both to keep from blurting something out and because I didn't like the position I was in.

Sensing both my mood and predicament, he eased in to close the deal. "By way of payment I'll require a percentage of all the business I bring in, a moderate salary, and incentives in the form of bonuses for the particularly useful bits of information I will occasionally provide."

It was a well-made offer; high, but not high enough to suggest that he was taking undue advantage of our timed negotiations – which might foster ill-will between us. Though his offer allowed both of us to claim that it reflected the value of his services, I was sure he'd built in some wiggle room, so I stopped clinching my jaw and countered.

"Your only regular payment will be in the form of you and only you, being able to reside here during non-business hours. You'll work as a consultant. That way, if you want, you can do side jobs - as long as they do not conflict with the interests of this firm. Indeed, you may only reference your relationship to the firm, for protection or otherwise, if and when you are conducting business on behalf of the firm. I strongly urge you to use both caution and discretion in this and all matters related to the firm as our termination policies are severe to say the least."

I didn't want any implied obligations between us and I'd long since learned the value of tipping well when you're a repeat customer, so I pulled out one of the coins I had from my share of yesterday's retainer and slid it across the desk to him. His eyes widened in anticipation when he saw it was a DieBus.

With my finger still on the coin I added, "This payment, which is consistent with the bonus incentive agreement we discussed, recognizes the value of the information you have just provided. Subsequent bonuses, if any, will be given at my sole discretion, to reflect my assessment of the value of the services provided.

"All the terms of our agreement will be placed in writing and said writing will be the sum and entirety of our agreement. Any and all subsequent modifications to the agreement will be presumed to have been negotiated at arms-length and will be in written form. There will be no implied agreements between us. In addition to your signed agreement to these terms, I'll need a signed confidentiality agreement. Agreed?"

It was a good deal, and he was too smart to try to improve upon it. When he said, "Agreed," I took my finger off the coin and rose to leave.

I wasn't worried about leaving him in my office with clients documents. The guards wouldn't let him leave with anything and he, like anyone who'd be interested in buying the information, knew that The Gunfighter wouldn't hesitate to move him and them on.

I had one foot out the door when he called out to me.

"Counselor? Do you want to know when and where to show up for the meet and confer, or at least where the notice is posted?"

A few seconds and some precious information later, with *Usu Apud Inferos Iudicii* in hand, I closed the door behind me and headed out to see the notice for myself. I could hear him laughing as I made my way down the hall.

I had no doubt that he had his feet back on my desk.

The man who is promised tomorrow is already dead.

DE TENABRA

CHAPTER 21

VOLENTI NON FIT INJURIA

(No Wrong Is Done To One Who Consents)

LIKE MOST CIVIL courts, Purgatory's courts require counsel to meet and confer before a matter can be heard. And while the meet and confer is mandatory, there's no guarantee or requirement that anything will be resolved. In civil courts the meet and confer ensures that the parties have and take the opportunity to discuss settlement, with the intention of preserving judicial time and resources. In Purgatory the meet and confer mostly serves as an additional obstacle; even if you know that it is required, you have to have some means of finding out when and where it will be held.

I could see how The Fixer might have learned that I'd had my case referred to a higher court, but I couldn't fathom how he learned when and where the settlement conference notice was posted – seems that bit of information wasn't for sale. One thing was for sure, I'd never have found the settlement conference notice if he hadn't told me where to look. Even then, finding it took some searching - it was buried under several unrelated documents that were tacked to a bulletin board, in the basement of a storage building that was so far out on the periphery of the civic center that it didn't even seem to be a part of the square. Thinking I'd find it by wondering about the courts was the kind of naïve, earth-side thinking that could leave me trapped here for an eternity. My DieBus was well spent.

I double and triple checked the notice to confirm what I'd been told - I was due in court on the second floor for the day's second session. Law books in hand, I made my way to the court and even managed to arrive with time to spare.

After going through another set of ass-backward doors, I entered the second-floor courtroom.

I was early, but I wasn't the first to arrive. The galley was sparsely populated with tentative looking people, and toward the front, sitting at counsels' table, was a relatively well dressed, briefcase carrying kind of guy. Head back, feet on the table, and mouth open, he seemed to be sleeping soundly despite the mild commotion going on around him. Further forward, on both the sides of the bench, sat two court clerks who looked for all the world like twins. He was a slight bird-like man with thinning hair that he combed straight up and around an obvious bald spot; she was of a similar build but as a woman carried it better. But for a general sagginess of body, and dour face, she might have been attractive. They moved about, exchanging documents and harping on each other in a manner that suggested neither purpose of deed nor thought.

Though the room was neither loud nor crowded,

when the judge came in through a side door his entry went unacknowledged, if not unnoticed. He stopped after a few steps to take in the room as though confused about where he was and how he'd come to be there. Torn, dirty, and threadbare though it was, but for the black robe, I'd have thought him just another poor lost soul.

Rather than head for the bench, he wandered forward toward the crowd then alerted, as though he'd heard something or received direction. He then staggered backward in no discernable direction until he came to a stop near where he'd entered. He stood momentarily motionless, swayed left, faded right, then turned and, while facing counsels' table, listed to the side toward the bench.

His steps up to the bench were precarious and he fell into, more than sat on, the chair behind the large wooden dais. Once situated he shuffled through the various documents that had been left for him and reorganized them into three piles, those on his left, those on his right, and those he threw on the floor. The court clerks went about their business, ignoring all that transpired, until the bailiff entered.

The bailiff burst through the wooden doors at the back with such force that they banged against the stone walls on both sides. The effect was like the bang of a gavel: Counsel for the state jerked awake and swung his feet off the desk, the court clerks ceased their bickering and busied themselves with the papers the judge had dropped, even the judge sat upright and focused.

If one was being kind, the bailiff could be described as a stout, barrel chested man. Since such kindness has no place in Purgatory he was more likely described as short, fat, and ugly. His hairline had receded fore and aft, no doubt the two would soon meet in the middle. This, combined with his generally sloped forehead and large protruding jaw gave the impression that he was stalking forward, even though he stood still. Whatever chest muscle he may once have had long ago gave ground to the fat that swelled around, and extended up from his belly, and threatened to consume his chin. His legs, though hidden by trousers that did nothing to hide his large posterior, likely mirrored his arms – short stubby things that were large at the top but lacking any definition.

He stalked around the front of the court room, eye-balling everyone while rubbing his hands together in a physical manifestation of threat and avarice. Between his small bent arms, large gut, big butt, and stalking-predatory gait, he brought to mind a small tyrannosaurus rex. After fixing the judge and court personnel with a domineering and, in the case of both clerks, lascivious glare, he har-rumphed and said to everyone within ear shot, "Well, let's get started. I don't want to be here all day."

After a wobbly nod from the judge and a brief rustling of papers, the male clerk stood and recited a well-practiced line, "All rise and come to order." At which point the bailiff took his seat.

"We'll start with the mandatory status conferences scheduled for today. When your name is called you will form a line at the front. All parties will then adjourn to the hall to discuss settlement, and the parties will return to the court once all parties have discussed their case with court counsel and reached either settlement or an impasse."

There weren't a lot of souls in the courtroom, but serial

meet and confers with just a few parties was more than enough to make this approach to settlement conferences a needlessly long process - exactly what I'd come to expect in Purgatory.

The clerks took turns calling out names. As proof that most souls didn't know their settlement conference had been scheduled, the bailiffs read more than a dozen names off the list before the first soul stood and marched to the front. More than a hundred names were called before mine, yet only four souls lined up ahead of me.

A lot more names and a very few responses later, counsel rose from his table and a small group of us followed him out into the hall.

There were two chairs in the hall, no table, no bench. When the lawyer took a seat, the first soul followed suit. The rest of us stood nearby or sat on the floor.

Most of the settlement discussions were a forgone conclusion. When the first soul started talking about her case court counsel cut her off and asked, "name and request?" She didn't blink, nod, or hesitate before answering with her name and requesting the "assistant deputy director, office of requisitions and returns" position. Court counsel checked his own list and nodded his agreement, then she got up and took a seat on the floor off to the side.

This process repeated itself with the next three individuals and, except for the guy that tried to upgrade his agreed upon position, went without a hitch. I found myself seated in front of court counsel much sooner than I'd expected.

He didn't look up from his list on hearing my name and he was still flipping through his papers when I broke the news that I was requesting to be returned to the earthly plane. After a beat he stopped flipping through the papers and blurted, "Wait, what?" After another moment, realization crept over his face and, with more than a little trepidation he said as much as asked, "You're not on my list, are you?"

I had a theory, and I went with it. "If you mean the list of people that you've been paid to offer certain choice assignments to, no!" It seems the others in line here knew to show up because they or their benefactors were connected enough to get notice of where the hearing was held and willing to pay to get particular and conveniently open positions.

Once he got over the initial shock, of having to actually discuss settlement, he shifted to negotiation mode. Apparently, this wasn't his first rodeo.

"So, let me make sure I've got this straight. You want to be sent back to the earthly plane just because you say you don't belong here? If that's the gist of your argument, the place you don't belong is in this hall meeting with me. I don't know how you managed to avoid having the idea of returning to the earthly plane dipped and beaten out of you, but that's a windmill you don't want to tilt at here."

He was down-selling me; trying to convince me that I didn't have a chance of winning and was about to lose big. If I showed any sign of doubt, after a bit more down-selling, he'd offer me a pittance, 'just to get rid of me' or, more likely, for a small fee.

I cut him off at the knees and, after explaining how I came to be here, noted that I'd already rebutted the presumption that I belonged here and established that the courts don't have jurisdiction over me.

If I'd cut low, he cut deep when he dismissed all that

I'd said. "That's the how and why you're here, and I'm not really a how and why kind of guy. I'm more of a percentages man and the way I see it the odds are so far against you it's almost laughable.

"Before you even get a chance to get into all that legal mumbo jumbo about jurisdiction, you'll have to convince the court that your matter won't be settled; or more specifically, that you're not going to settle. You'll need more than luck and a few choice Latin phrases to get over that bar. If I'm generous, and I mean really generous, I'd say your odds on that front are about one in a hundred. But hey, let's assume you're tougher than you look, Lady Luck smiles on you, your stars align, and whatever else needs to happen happens and you beat the odds. Let's also assume that this court, for some magical reason, doesn't just reverse the lower court's findings related to jurisdiction and the presumption that you belong here – *sua sponte*.

"Even if they allow you to argue the point, and that's a pretty big if, whether they are able and willing to find in your favor is a fifty-fifty proposition at best. So, odds are that you'll never even get the chance to ask the court to convene a Council of Special Masters to hear your matter. And while I'd like to factor in the odds of a Council of Special Masters sending a soul back to the earthly plane, which are slim to none, the fact is the idea of a court requesting that council be convened is so far removed from memory that it's more a matter of myth and folklore than practice. So, even before we consider the ultimate merits of your argument, the feasibility of the relief you're requesting, and about a hundred other variables, the odds of your prevailing are pretty much zero to none.

"So, what do you have in your favor? An interpretation of something you read in one of those books you're carrying around, and the fact that you were able to baffle or coerce someone into helping you get to this meet and confer. All that amounts to is moxie. And, much as I appreciate moxie, it's like they say, 'if all you've got is moxie, you gotta have the clothes to match.'"

He paused and took a moment to casually look me up and down, "and I think we can agree that no one is going to be asking you for the name of your tailor anytime soon.

"But like I said, I appreciate moxie. That and the fact that I've no desire to spend the rest of my day in the courtroom listening to you lose is why I'm willing to offer you a job. Am I offering you a good job? No, it's for a low-level position with little potential for advancement. But hey, if you're the kind of player that your moves thus far suggest, you should be able to overcome the limitations of the position in fairly short order. Is it better than what you'll get if you go back into the courtroom and say we're at an impasse? Definitely.

"And just so we're clear, this is a one-time offer made in confidence; I don't want every desperado out there thinking I'm hiring creative nuisances."

We'd come full circle and back to the part where he was down-selling, fluffing, and time-pressuring me. At least he wasn't asking me for a fee!

I thanked him and said, "We're required to meet and confer, not to agree. Having fulfilled that obligation, I suggest we declare an impasse and return to court."

He nodded in a way that said both "Suit yourself and vacate that seat," then waved the next person over. His remaining meet and confers went without controversy, and in mere minutes we were filing back into the courtroom.

Little had changed in our absence. The judge sat face down at the bench, emitting a slight but uneven snore. The female clerk had again been cornered by the bailiff. Where he was taking every opportunity to press his body close, she stood, backed against the wall, holding a stack of papers between them as a desperate, make-shift shield. The shortcomings of her shield were evidenced by her having twisted her head further to the side than should have been possible in an obvious attempt to distance herself from the bailiff. The male clerk sat shuffling papers and feigning disinterest, apparently happy that he wasn't the object of the bailiff's attention and intent on keeping things that way. With obvious relief, he cleared his throat and nudged the judge when he saw our group return.

The judge awoke and came to in the slow, hazy way that's typical of those that seek to distance themselves from reality with drink. His head swiveled left and right, he looked up and down then, when his brain registered the movement of our returning to our seats, he blinked repeatedly in an attempt to track and focus on our group. By the time we'd taken our seats things seemed to have gelled for him and, after slapping the bench with his hand, he said "please come to order." After a few more or less deflected paws at the female clerk, the bailiff grunted and sauntered across the room to a small uncomfortable looking chair. Once seated, he crossed his arms, extended his legs, leaned back, and closed his eyes.

With the bailiff seemingly situated, and without direction from the court, the male clerk rose and called the name of the first of those that had shown up for their settlement conference.

A frail and confused looking woman started, then stood and raised her hand. When she realized that neither the clerks nor judge, and certainly not the bailiff was looking out into the audience, she let out a timid, "Here."

Before she could say anything more, opposing counsel, who also didn't even bother to look up, let alone stand, spoke the magic word. "Settled."

The terse exchange that followed was the first evidence of efficient process I'd seen in Purgatory.

The female clerk said, "Cause of action" and opposing counsel summed up the complaint with "Contested." Then the male clerk shot back, "Settlement terms," and opposing counsel identified a job, its classification, and a pay rate. After that, the female clerk said "Consideration" and opposing counsel said something along the lines of "Waiver of cause plus costs."

The first exchange ended when, after the male clerk said, "agreed," opposing counsel said, "agreed" and turned to the woman who'd stood up. When she looked at him in confusion, he gave her the universal wrist rolling, 'spit it out so we can get on with this' sign.

As soon as she said, "agreed" the female clerk called the next name and the process started all over again.

Not surprisingly, my case was the last to be called. Where things had gone quickly before, they ground to an abrupt halt when, instead of the expected "Settled," opposing counsel said "Impasse."

By the time I got to and seated myself at counsel's table the clerks, unsure of how to proceed, had gone back and forth, looking for guidance from the judge or opposing counsel, a couple of times. After three or four rounds of this, opposing counsel threw up his hands and said, "I'm sorry your honor."

The bailiff who'd fallen into a light rhythmic snore, woke with a snort at this relative outburst.

He rose before he was fully awake and took a position center court. Then he turned a full 360 degrees, scowling at each person in the room, not fully aware of the thing that had irritated him to wakefulness.

When his sour gaze fell on opposing counsel the suit folded immediately and all but pointed a finger at me as he blurted out, "we're at an impasse, he won't settle!"

The foul man zeroed-in on me. He approached slowly, rubbing his bald head and scratching at beard stubble as though thinking through his options, even though his intent to do harm was as clear as the fact that he'd enjoy doing so.

I looked to the judge to see if he was going to intercede. Before he could stop himself, the shame of cowardice drove his hand to the inner folds of his robe. He produced a small bottle of Forus and quickly tilted it up. Then, like his clerks, the judge turned his eyes down and began meaninglessly shuffling papers.

I assessed the situation in a stark, almost disconnected way.

Fighting wasn't my best option. Even though I'd just started training under One Finger, I was pretty sure that with some luck and a few well-timed moves I could take the bailiff. But, even if I won, fighting him wouldn't get me any closer to my goal. So fighting was plan B, something

I'd stoop to only if and when it became clear that he was more interested in beating me down than merely slapping me around.

For lack of a better option, I figured I'd try to alter my reality like I'd done with the rock. I calmed myself and cleared my mind.

Apparently, this was not the reaction he wanted or expected. Like most untrained fighters he puffed up his chests and clinched his fist, a subconscious act designed to intimidate. When I didn't respond to this threat, he pulled a small leather-encased object from his pocket. He wrapped the retaining cord around his wrist, going slowly to savor the moment, then slapped the small blackjack against his palm several times, making both his intent and the weapon's effectiveness clear.

It was time to commit. I decided that in my reality, he wasn't going to hit me. I closed my eyes and, in my mind, pictured him putting his hand down and stepping back. I shaped the thought clearly in my mind, gradually adding detail and struggling to release both doubt that this would work and my fear of some imminent impact.

I sat like that for a while; hoping that it was working, fighting doubts that it would. It wasn't long, but it was too long. I should have been hit, someone should have said something, or I should have heard him walk away. It dawned on me that he might just be waiting for me to open my eyes, so I'd see it coming. Seeing no other option, I opened my eyes – one at a time.

He stood in front of me, exactly where he'd been before I closed my eyes, ugly sap still in hand. But now the scowl was gone. Instead, his mouth hung slightly open, agape and agog, and his eyes were too wide and unblinking. For a moment, just a moment, I thought maybe it had worked. Then I heard a familiar voice; raspy, dry and emotionless, so close that I felt as much as heard it when The Gunfighter said, "I'll be have'in a word with my partner here."

Somewhere during my 'meditation' The Gunfighter had come into the courtroom. Call it balanced walking on his part, deep concentration on my part, or whatever you want, he'd taken up a position close to and directly behind me without me even knowing he was there. I looked from The Gunfighter to the bailiff, opposing counsel, the clerks, and back to the bailiff. The bailiff, like the judge, counsel, and clerks seemed frozen; their relief at realizing that The Gunfighter wasn't there for them, replaced by the shock of hearing him claim me as his partner.

I was the only one that didn't jump when he told everyone, and the bailiff in particular, "Now."

The bailiff's body jerked and spasmed into action, his nerves responding in an act of self-preservation before he could consciously direct them. He staggered back two uneven steps before realizing both that his legs were retreating and that he still held his hand in the air … with a weapon in it. He spasmed to a stop, as he fought the urge to snatch his hand down in what might be seen as an aggressive move. Reason eventually won out over fear, and he slowly lowered the offending arm to his side, half bowed, and took a couple of more controlled steps back. He tried to pocket the sap then broke out in a sweat-panic when he realized that he couldn't pocket the sap with the cord still around his wrist, couldn't leave his hand in his pocket without looking rude and suspicious, and couldn't pull it back out without looking like he was again drawing the weapon. After a few attempts to get the cord off without pulling the sap out, he resigned himself to fate and slowly pulled his hand out without touching the sap, instead allowing it to dangle from his wrist.

There was a collective exhale when the bailiff finally stood fast. The twin clerks, fairly confident that they'd done nothing to offend, seemed disappointed that The Gunfighter hadn't come to dispose of the bailiff. The judge, who'd been far more worried about The Gunfighter's purpose, took the opportunity to calm his nerves with another swig of Forus.

After taking all this in, I turned to opposing counsel, who'd done his best to remain perfectly still in an apparent attempt to achieve invisibility, "It's not just moxie if you can back it up." I turned away from counsel's rapid-fire nods of agreement to address The Gunfighter.

Rather than risk getting into a staring match that I had no chance of winning, I jumped right in.

"How and why do you come to be here, Gunfighter?"

The bailiff stepped to the side; hoping or assuming that I was or soon would be The Gunfighter's target, and not wanting to be in the line of fire. Nearer to me, opposing counsel cringed at my direct, non-deferential tone, then closed his eyes and went still - apparently adopting the childlike belief that what you can't see, can't see you.

The Gunfighter, neither fazed nor challenged by my lack of deference, responded without hesitation.

"By way of introduction your new associate did me a 'favor' and told me you were arguing your case before a 'judge' that had no control over his courtroom, and a bailiff that had no control over himself."

We both knew there were no favors in Purgatory, only implied obligations and payments therefor. In case The Gunfighter's disdain at having been lured into an obligation wasn't evident in his raspy tone, he added, "You cost me coin."

In the silence that now shrouded the courtroom his low raspy voice carried well enough for all to hear the threat inherent in his words. I heard a gulp from the judge behind me, then the sound of the bailiff's feet as he discreetly tried to move even further away from me.

"He even offered to bet me a DieBus that the first thing people would hear about our firm was that you got beat down by this pudgy bastard of a bailiff in our first court appearance."

Telling The Gunfighter that I was making this appearance was a smart move on The Fixer's part, as was trying to get The Gunfighter to bet a DieBus on the outcome. If he lost he'd be no worse off than before we'd talked, if he won he'd have double what he started the day with. Either way, proved himself of value to The Gunfighter and complied with our agreement. That he'd withheld information from me about the judge and bailiff was largely immaterial. Had I known, I'd have shown up and done pretty much what I was doing.

Rather than acknowledge the dire nature of my situation - and make no mistake, pissing off a Reaper should always be considered a dire situation - I responded in a Purgatory appropriate fashion.

"You should have taken the bet! The first thing people

are likely to hear about our firm is that you moved on several potential clients to up your percentage of the partnership. And you should have listened more closely when he said, I'm here to argue *my* case."

As always, or at least whenever he wasn't killing or maiming, The Gunfighter stood deathly still, arms at his side, back board-straight, eyes scanning the room; assessing the threat posed by each individual and every corner. If you were lucky, this was his parley position.

After what seemed like too long, he dryly said, "What you do as a lawyer, even on your own case, reflects on our partnership!"

I wasn't having any of it. I had no intention of renegotiating the terms of our partnership agreement, and I certainly wasn't giving him any say in how I determined to litigate cases, especially my own case.

"Need I remind you that our arrangement specifies that you are the silent partner and I, the lawyer, am in charge of legal strategy. Especially when it's my case!"

"And what exactly was your litigation strategy? To sit there with your eyes closed and try to, to … what's the word your time uses … Jerrico? Jettison?"

"Jedi?"

"Yes, yes. … were you trying to 'Jedi' that oaf into not beating you? I don't know what nonsense you've heard, but this place isn't about what you expect of other people or other things, it's about learning to be in control of yourself!"

When he put it like that, what I was doing, sitting there with my eyes closed, sounded as silly as it probably looked. Since it wasn't something I wanted to own up to, I was planning to deflect and move on.

Then the .44 boomed out across the courtroom.

To drive home his point, or points, with a single shot, The Gunfighter had blown the sap out of the bailiff's hand and shattered the judge's jug of Forus. He held the still smoking gun in his left hand; our only proof that he'd reached across his body and shot left-handed. As usual his draw had been faster than anybody could see.

So much for deflecting.

"Point made and taken," I said. "However, I do have a plan. Sure, it's not as loud and intimidating as what you have to offer, but if you'll allow me to do what we both know I'm good at, I'll get the people I need to do something to do what I need them to do."

After a moment of tense silence, he leaned forward, fixed his dead eyes over my shoulder on the bailiff and, still loud enough for everyone to hear asked, "Do you really need the bailiff?"

It was my turn to speak to the court indirectly. I said, "*if you're good at something, never do it for free*," and turned away from The Gunfighter. After a glance at opposing counsel, I cast a withering stare at the bailiff, then faced the bench where the judge, like the court clerks, sat with equal amounts of fear and disappointment. Before taking my seat, I half glanced over my shoulder toward The Gunfighter and added, "however, a sliding scale can be arranged in some cases."

Once seated I briefly ruffled through my books then said to opposing counsel, "since this seems like more of a how and why than a percentages situation, I'll handle things from here out. If that's ok with you?" I addressed the judge without waiting for a reply.

"As opposing counsel noted, having met and conferred, the dispute remains unresolved, and we are at an impasse. I believe the law makes clear that, where there is such an impasse, for good cause, and on request, this court is required to convene a council of Special Masters. For the record, I hereby request that a Council of Special Masters be convened. If it pleases the court, I have reviewed the procedures and requirements for convening the Council of Special Masters and, if your honor would be so kind as to direct the bailiff to close his mouth and sit down, I'd be happy to assist your Honor with the process."

The judge was a drunk and very likely a coward, but he wasn't stupid. The 'sliding scale' on The Gunfighter's services that I'd mentioned came with an implied obligation. He looked to his two court reporters with a silent question. They'd either worked together long enough so that words weren't necessary, or previously discussed the matter. Either way, a subtle nod from the reporters confirmed that, given the chance, they'd be more than willing to contribute to a future purchase of The Gunfighter's discounted services.

Like that, the bailiff's world was turned on its head. He scanned the room, looking desperately for an out or an ally. Where opposing counsel looked away, suddenly preoccupied with his papers, the twin clerks took full advantage of the schadenfreude exception and laughed at him – openly reveling in his fear and desperation.

The judge, sobered by the gunfire, the opportunity to rid himself of the bailiff, or both, pulled himself up straight and locked eyes with the bailiff. When the bailiff looked down in submission, the judge spoke with a vindictiveness that his years of hard drinking hadn't diluted.

"You heard the man, shut-up and sit your fat ass down."

"We forge ourselves in the hearth of our will."
And what is will if not an expression
of our earnest expectations.

De Tenebra

CHAPTER 22

EX CONCESSIS

"From What Has Been Conceded Already"

Things went smoothly once the bailiff was out of the way. I pointed out the relevant code provisions and requirements in *Usu Apud Inferos Iudicii*. The suddenly sobered judge took of all this with a spark of understanding and nod of agreement.

Unfortunately, *Usu Apud Inferos Iudicii* doesn't say how soon the panel must be convened and only makes vague references to "higher being" when it comes to who will sit on the council as Special Masters. So, in spite of my urging the court to interpret *Usu Apud Inferos Iudicii* as requiring that a qualified group be convened as soon as is practicable, the best the judge could offer was assurances that he would investigate the matter and fully comply with whatever was required.

Given the penalties for noncompliance – extended dipping, and the possibility of another meeting with

The Gunfighter, I accepted these assurances. Opposing counsel's only contribution to this discussion came via assurances that someone in his office would no doubt be submitting a notice of substitution of counsel on his behalf.

Lest I make the same mistake twice, before the court was adjourned, I requested personal service of the notice of the convening of the Special Masters.

As expected, The Gunfighter was nowhere to be found when the judge slapped his desk to adjourn the hearing.

I headed back to my office, intent on finishing a list of proposed contract amendments for my sole client. It was too early for anyone to bed down for the evening, so the hall was almost empty. As I approached, the guard bowed in deference and made eye contact with the next guard, who bowed and urged me forward and upstairs. This continued until I reached the top floor where my office was located. When the last guard urged me forward, I stopped in my tracks. After a moment of assessment and consideration I turned back to the guard and, while pointing down the hall toward the cluster of people in front of my office asked, "who are they?"

As though he'd anticipated and prepared for the moment which, in hindsight I realize he probably had, rather than look down the hall where I was pointing, the guard offered another, slightly deeper bow and, without making it sound like he was stating the obvious, which again, hindsight tells me he kinda was, said, "They are those that seek your counsel."

I tried to take a head count as I approached but when they realized I was the 'Lawyer-Man' they sought, those that were lying on the ground or sitting stood, and everyone began jockeying for position. By my best estimate there were more than a dozen souls waiting at my door.

I approached and, before it could turn into a repeat of the chaos I'd witnessed outside the courtroom when I made my first appearance, I held up a hand and in a tone that brooked no discussion demanded, "Silence!

"You will arrange yourselves based on who has their preliminary hearing soonest. Among those that have a hearing on the same day, it will be first come, first served. If you're here for something other than your preliminary arraignment make a second line, again in order of arrival."

I stood in the frame of my office door while they shuffled and bickered themselves into something resembling two lines, then walked into my office and, before anyone could move to follow, returned with paper and pencil. After looking the line over briefly I asked two of those in line, "can you write?" When they nodded yes, I gave them the paper and pencils then directed, "write this down. Everyone else pay attention because I'm only going to say it once.

"First, my new arrivals practice is generally geared toward those of you that have been here fewer than six days, have yet to make an appearance, and want to contest being sent on. I am willing to represent you on the following terms …"

My offer to waive their fees was taken with varying degrees of skepticism, desperation, and opportunism. But, since my terms were non-negotiable and they were still interested, how they felt about the offer wasn't my concern.

"As an initial matter you'll need to think about how

you wish to contest being sent on, and what you'll do while you're here since you'll have to work, and you'll need to pay for my services.

"Second, if you're willing to move on, go. You don't need my assistance. You're just stalling and wasting everyone's time standing around here. If you want to negotiate certain terms as part of your departure the state's attorney will be more than willing to make a deal with you. Be advised however, such deals are suspect. It is unclear if you'll get what you bargain for and, if you do get what you bargain for, who's to say if that will be anything other than what you would have gotten anyway.

"Third, if you are beyond your first six days and haven't made an appearance, you should make every effort to do so immediately. I can help you with that if you have the coin, but let me be clear - I'm a lawyer, not a magician. With or without my assistance, your options are both limited and unappealing. You will be dipped - how long depends on how late you are. The only thing you have control over now is whether you walk in of your own accord, or are stripped of whatever you have, beaten, and dragged in by a collection gang or a Reaper."

I was giving it to them straight-up without a buffer, sales pitch, or lifeline; crushing both hopes and rumors. It wasn't what they wanted to hear, but it was a truth they couldn't turn away from. If giving it to them like that was a mistake it was probably the best mistake I made while I was there.

When I mentioned being dipped a ripple of fear passed through the crowd. The ripple grew to a wave when I mentioned the possibility of a Reaper coming for them.

And the wave became a Tsunami when I talked about moving on.

As one, the small crowd stepped back from the threat, then pressed forward in a desperate and physical reach for help. Some were pushed-down, others just fell to their knees on the floor. From somewhere in the crowd, a slow moaning-wail took form. Though it never rose to more than an undertone, the desperation it conveyed was palpable.

This, the sound of fear, was the soundtrack of Purgatory. A fear that first gripped, then passed through, before coming to rest at the back of everyone's mind. There it held constant sway - grating like an itch you can't scratch and playing like a song you can't get out of your mind – constantly threatening to overrule one's reason and dictate one's actions.

I'd seen and felt something like this before - outside the courtroom where souls fearing the unknown had made desperate deals with the state's attorney, and in the public housing hallway when The Gunfighter 'secured' my new office space.

I'd contemplated but underestimated fear on my walk back through the streets of Purgatory after my first court appearance. This wasn't the fear of not having enough that leads to greed, theft, and violence; or of not being good enough that leads to jealousy, insecurity, and envy; or even the fear of losing face that had prompted The Gunfighter to offer to move the bailiff on. No, this was a more basic fear. One that carried a certain sense of familiarity.

For anyone who grows up abused at home, black in America, closeted of necessity, or any place where oppression is a harsh feature of daily life, fear is a familiar friend. Familiar because you accept it as an ever-present feature in your life; a friend because, bad though it may be, it is reliable, predictable, and for better and more often worse, motivational. Those that would avoid or deny this fear evidence a belief that it cannot be overcome, and a loss of faith. They are the lost, the down-trodden, and often the perpetrators. Moving forward in the face of our fears is an act of faith – be it in a higher power, the self, the universe, or whatever sustains you. Those that survive, survivors if you will, well know that fear, not doubt, is the opposite of faith.

It is this faith that is tested in Purgatory. Souls that give in to fear and are too afraid of what would happen to them if they moved on, stay and become stuck here. Those who overcome their fear – be it out of desperation, love, hope, or whatever, leave Purgatory.

I couldn't help but wonder, what is it that I fear and how does that fear affect me? Unbidden, a line from *Dune* I'd memorized so long ago that I thought I'd forgotten it, roiled across my mind; *"Fear is the little-death that brings total obliteration."* And there it was, right in front of me - the answer I'd been unknowingly seeking, to a question I hadn't truly understood.

Fear stops us from fully committing. It is in the voice that says you should have a backup plan or safety net in case your dream fails; the thing that says don't prepare or work as hard as you possibly can because your best may not be good enough; and it is there in the lingering question of whether you've given up on a relationship, job, or desire too soon. It wasn't the fear that I might fail, but rather the fear that I might not be worthy of succeeding that was the difference between my wanting and expecting the stones to move.

I wrapped things up with the potential clients and decided on the spot that, starting tomorrow, I would only interview new clients at the beginning of each day, every other day. I posted my schedule then headed back to the inn to move some stones.

When I reached the inn, I settled myself on a stone that lay directly in front of the stones I'd tried to move. Rather than attempt to move the stones right away, I remained still and quietly let myself accept the new reality I was in. I heard One-Finger enter a long but indeterminate time later.

He entered quietly, more the result of habit than any attempt at stealth. I was all the more impressed with his balance when I saw that he carried a small table in one hand, and a couple of cups and jug of Forus in the other. He placed the table to the side, poured a couple of fingers worth, and took a seat across the stones from me. After waiting a respectful time, then a while longer, he spoke.

"Yer na tryna Jedi da stones er ya?"

Apparently, word of my antics with the bailiff had spread.

I smiled, genuinely bemused. Then, in answer, I referenced our earlier discussion of Sun Tsu.

"Just trying to learn not to fight uphill." Without getting up, I used my foot and far less effort than should have been required, to push one of the stones a few inches along the floor.

"Well dat dair's da ting now innit?

"In spite o wot ya see, wot ya ear, and wot ya knew er tought wile ya was on da earthly plane, wot ya cain do ere is about wot ya spect o yerself. We're not in da fizzical realm and dem laws don't apply here, if dey even did dair! Wot you cain do ere is bout you n wot ya truly spect o yerself. So, ya can be faster n stronger, n wit practice n discipline ya cain make yerself a bit eavier n arder ta move, er lighter n more nimble. But ere's da ting, far as I know dair ain't no 'mind trick' dats gonna make odders bow to yer will, n ya certainly cain't make tings levitate n fly true da air.

"Me, da Reapers, and dem dat joins us usually only work on tree tins - tecnique, strategy, and lettin go. Da first two er relatively easy - ya do countless repetitions to perfect yer skill, and try ta read erey tin dat dose dat ave passed true ere before ave written."

A light clicked on in my head and I all but blurted out, "so you're familiar with works other than the Art of War?"

He took a brief and wistful look back in time before he spoke.

"Sure Sun Tsu, Africanus, Subutai, dey all been true ere. N wile dey weren't all prolific writers, most ad notes, diagrams, or playbooks. But da fact is, most of us ere study strategy just ta find ways ta beat dem dat er a slave to it. Da ting most of us spend most our time practice'n, da ting dats ardest ta do, is lettin go a da fear n doubts.

"Doubt n fear take from and lessen us. Dey make ya esitate. Fin ya gets distracted by em ya may need an instant ta refocus, or ta give yerself permission ta act. Ya may even need time to reassure yerself dat ya cain do wot ya needs ta do. Fact is ya don't usually get to prepare yerself ta act.

Sumtimes ya just gotta react. Practice is how we unlearn our limits, rid ourselves of esitation, n learn ta keep focus on wot we gots ta do."

Without getting up, he kicked one of the big stones toward me - something I wasn't expecting. I thought about the harm it would do if it hit me, about stopping it with my foot, about getting out of the way. Before I'd decided what to do, the stone slowed and came to a stop a few inches away from me.

He moved his chair to the other side of the table, and over the night's Forus we discussed a schedule for me to begin my training in earnest.

⅍

*Time, as a relative commodity, generally bears an
inverse relationship to our wants or needs.*

DE TENEBRA

CHAPTER 23

AD ABSURDUM

(To The Point Of Preposterousness)

MY SIXTH DAY passed without notice or event. Over the few days that followed, in addition to client meetings, I reviewed hundreds of The Thin Man's documents, revised several of his contract templates, and consulted on some of his planned acquisitions. I needed to burn through the retainer as quickly as possible; I wanted out of Purgatory and didn't want it to be said that my not having exhausted the retainer amounted to my having implicitly agreed to stay.

Apparently, my work ethic hadn't gone unnoticed. On the afternoon of my tenth day word came, by way of yet another tall, inordinately graceful underling, that The Thin Man wished to meet with May and me to discuss additional work and payment. Since graft and corruption are generally considered a part of doing business in Purgatory, it was no surprise that The Thin Man insisted on a meeting with both of us - he didn't want to end up in the middle of an accounting dispute between me and my soul shooting partner.

May, with her uncanny sense of timing, appeared at the door just as the underling delivered his message. Today's outfit featured a light blue A-line maxiskirt, white lace up ankle boots. She wore a matching light blue frock jacket with white frill edging on the cuffs, collar, and button placket. A blue and white lace-fronted hat was complemented by a white and blue parasol, and small blue clutch purse. Her always-present gloves were white satin.

Out of both habit and good manners, I stood in greeting. Then, in mild mockery of The Thin Man's lackeys, waved May in with a swing of my arm that was far more dramatic than graceful.

May entered with a pointy-toothed smile and brief flutter of her eyes, then seated herself. After carefully smoothing her skirt, she curtly directed the lackey,

"Get master. Go." Then turned to me.

"Lawyer-Man busy! Retainer exhausted. Court appearances soon. Clients many."

She said it as a matter of fact, with so little question or concern about whether it was true or how she knew it, that it seemed like she was discussing a point of common knowledge. After a moment of reflection, I concluded that by now it was probably just that.

Before I could agree she slid a piece of paper across the desk to me. At the top in perfect, handwriting was the word "ledger." Beneath that were columns with work dates, hours, and amounts due. Not to be out-done, I slid my own, nowhere-as-neat-or-organized ledger across the desk to her. A moment of silence later, I looked up from the ledger she gave me to see May, who'd already completed her review of my ledger scrawl, patiently waiting for me to finish. Both our documents showed the retainer had been exhausted and a small amount was owing. A pointy toothed smile from her and a nod from me signaled our general agreement with each other's accounting.

Moments later the same or perhaps another baldheaded underling returned. After another typically graceful bow and wave of his arm he stepped aside and announced The Thin Man's 'personal envoy'.

The Envoy was lean muscled in the way that swimmers often are, with close-cropped hair, a neatly trimmed beard, and eyes so light they were more hazel than brown. Where all The Thin Man's other assistants wore scant clothing that, for good or bad, highlighted their bodies, he wore a loose-fitting short sleeve button-down shirt, cargo style pants that ended just above well-defined calves, and well-worn low top boots. All in all he looked like he'd either just come in from a trail hike or been prep'd for an outdoor magazine's cover shoot - he even had a pack slung across his shoulders.

He shooed the underling away with a wave of his delicate hand, then turned to May and offered up a bow that, while as graceful as I'd come to expect, was more gentlemanly than deferential. She was moved by the gesture and tried to hide it by waving him off dismissively. Something he'd apparently anticipated; he caught her glove ensconced hand in his and, in true southern gentleman style, bent and air kissed just above it before announcing, "It is a pleasure to make you acquaintance Ms. May."

After pausing just long enough to allow that he'd taken

in her attire he added, "Oh, and such a lovely outfit; blue really should have its own season."

It was complimentary without being flirty, the observation of a fashionista rather than a sycophant.

He'd read her fast and true, then instantly matched his manners to her neo-southern belle style and temperament. We were both caught off-guard. I was still about mid surprise when he stepped forward, smiled, and extended his hand to me. I rose, more out of habit than purpose, and took his hand.

A handshake can convey many things. He offered up the kind of handshake that people who are single or on the make know well. The grasp lingers a bit too long, and is often accompanied by a slight pulling, lingering eye contact, or a quick body review. It expressed interest and availability, while at the same time providing discretion and plausible deniability – after all, it was just a handshake.

While this kind of handshake may cause mild discomfort in those who are not interested, it opens the door to the next move for those who are and becomes the stuff of fantasy for those with constraints.

He released my hand with a smile, took a seat next to May, and jumped right in.

He saw the ledgers May and I had traded and, after asking permission, perused them sharply. After a moment he declared his agreement and, with a subtle nod toward May, noted that "the accounting detail was impressive" then rolled his hand around in an apparent reference to the entirety of Purgatory.

"It's such a rare pleasure to meet someone here who

understands that the intersection between math, fashion, and art rests in one's attention to detail."

After a gracious nod toward me he continued.

"Don't get me wrong, there is always room for the creative and the disciplined. You're contract modifications have been nothing short of inspired, particularly given the pace you've set for yourself. But our May here well, even if we ignore the ledger, her clothes, makeup, even her lovely speech patterns mark her as the gold standard of efficiency and detail."

He paused just long enough to subtly blink-look me up and down, then, almost apologetically added. "But really May, how it is that you let a man of his position and 'stature' walk around in clothes like that is really quite beyond me."

This seemed all too familiar. For a moment I couldn't place it, then it dawned on me, he'd 'combinated' on me. He was 'negging' - saying something mildly negative about me to up his desirability, and at the same time pulling a *Hitch* - positioning himself to get close to me by trying to make a good impression on May, the closest thing I had to a friend. He angled himself slightly more toward me, just enough for me to realize how focused he'd been on May.

"You should be wearing clothes that drop the 'D' and emphasize the other two parts of 'war-d-robe'. Clothes that let clients know they're getting the real deal and put the opposition on notice that you are not to be trifled with."

He sat back, more than a little self-satisfied, then got to the point.

"Luckily, with the retainer I've been authorized to offer

you for your continued work, you'll be more than able to buy clothes that speak well of you and your position."

When he clapped his hands twice two underlings, who apparently had been waiting just outside my door, entered. Their clothes and downcast eyes immediately identified them as clerk type functionaries: mid-level bookkeeping types who were trustworthy enough to be allowed to carry significant coin. Each carried a bowl filled with coins that easily doubled the amount of the first retainer.

Again, I rose automatically, this time without much in the way of conscious thought. As though drawn by, and intent on intercepting the coins, I walked over to stand between The Envoy and the money-carrying underlings. After a brief examination of the money and a withering stare toward the underlings, in one smooth and not at all gracious move, I turned, grabbed The Envoy by his shirt and pulled him up and out of his chair.

I can't say whether it was because he was shocked, all too familiar with rough treatment, or just had a flexible sense of foreplay but, rather than squirm or struggle he accepted my rough handling with an almost flirty smile. I shoved him back a step.

"Points to you and your boss for your research and planning, but we need to get two things straight here and now. First, I don't want or like to mix business with pleasure, especially where the deal being offered is contrary to my or my partner's interest. Don't get me wrong, I don't hold anything against those who are in the business of pleasure, but if that's your primary occupation and agenda, you have no place here."

He cut me off before I could get to my second point and spoke a bit too dismissively.

"Oh, come now. There's no need to act all butch-n-feisty. I'm open to negotiations. If any part of the retainer package isn't to your liking, I'm sure we can work something out." He moved forward slowly, arms up and hands open in a show of conciliation not to be confused with threat. Like a partner leading a waltz, he placed his left hand on the back of my bicep and directed me back toward my chair with his right.

I wasn't having any of it.

True to One Finger's training, I moved without doubt or fear; I didn't think about how to do it, let alone the potential consequences, only the outcome I desired.

I reached across my body and cover-grabbed the hand on my bicep with my left hand, then pivoted on my right foot slightly away from him as I brought my right arm around like a swimmer taking a stroke. Halfway through the "stroke" he lost his grip and by the three-quarter mark my right arm was resting on the back of his elbow. I bent the wrist I'd captured with my left hand hard and brought my weight down on the back of his elbow. On the earthly plain his elbow might have dislocated; here it became a fulcrum. Lifting the forearm, which now served as a lever, prompted him to slam his face into the desk in an attempt to get away from the pain of his hyperextending elbow.

Still holding on to his bent wrist for good measure, I turned to the now cowering underlings and said, "get him out of here. Then go tell your boss that neither I nor The Gunfighter will be bought into servitude. Hence forth he will be billed on an hourly basis." Before either envoy or underlings could recover from the shock of what was happening, I shoved May's account ledger into The Envoy's pocket, eased the pressure on his elbow enough for him to start to rise then, while still holding the forearm lever, pivoted sharply. When I suddenly released my grip, he went stumble-staggering toward the underlings.

"There is a payment showing due on the ledger. I suggest your boss make said payment in a timely fashion."

After a doomed effort to straighten my ever-ill-fitting shirt and jacket, I made my way back to my chair, then looked to May to make sure we were still on the same page. She smoothed her skirt in a calculated display of disinterest, then sighed in exasperation.

I thought the sigh was uncalled for until I realized she was looking past the departing envoy and underlings, toward the door. Following her gaze prompted equal parts of excitement and concern.

Just outside and to the left of the door, allowing just enough room for the underlings, The Envoy, and the money to exit, and looking all the sadder for the loss of the latter, stood The Fixer.

He turned and entered slowly, more a function of his repeated looks back toward the money than out of deference or caution. Once inside, after a brief nod toward May, he took a seat.

Rather than immediately ask what brought him to the office, I folded and put away the remaining copy of the ledger then, just to make sure they knew where they stood with respect to each other said, "May, permit me to introduce my associate." Both understood that my asking her permission to introduce him indicated his lower status;

he took it in stride. When I started to tell him that May worked for The Gunfighter, he cut me off with a nod.

"Really, there's no need to introduce May. Even before those in this place bore her mark, anyone that's paying attention knew of her."

It was smooth, gracious even. I suspect it had May reconsidering her exasperated sigh, … until he said, "But has she brought you the latest news?" With a smirk and shrug of her shoulders May all but said, "See, I told you so," and went back to looking exasperated.

Rather than push his luck, The Fixer, who was obviously quite content with himself, leaned forward conspiratorially, briefly eyed May as though making sure it was ok to talk in front or her, then turned to me and said, "I guess there's no need to hide behind formality here."

I spoke before the hiss I knew would come from May could manifest. "Don't push your luck. Do I have a court date, or what?" My cutting to the point clearly took the fun out of it for him.

"Well, since it's obvious that you're itching to know what I know, I won't be coy." He slumped back, dug in his pockets even though it was clear that he wasn't looking for anything, then mumbled out that he hadn't heard anything about a court date. He let that hang in the air long enough for my disappointment to show before looking at me half coyly, then exclaimed, "but, the General Counsel has asked for a meeting with you!"

His drama had the desired effect – after a brief pause during which I said some combination of why, who, and what that probably came out sounding something like "whywhowa" - chaos broke out.

The two of them spoke at the same time, but to different questions. He started talking about the General Counsel, while she spoke to what the General Counsel might want with me. I was trying to listen to both and couldn't follow either.

"Ok" was the only part of 'Ok, one at a time' that I got out. For some reason they both took that "ok" as my agreeing with what the other had said.

Before I could get another word in, they switched and started talking about how what the other had said was wrong. I said "No," both to get them to stop and because I hadn't understood, let alone agreed with anything. Only to have them both agree with me that the other was wrong, then go back to arguing their original claims.

Seeing no timely end to this chaos, I slapped my hand on my desk and said, "Enough!"

After a moment of blessed silence from the two, I pointed at The Fixer and said, "You. Tell me about the General Counsel."

The Fixer spoke with unmasked admiration.

"The General Counsel is a shot-caller, and not just some upper level shot caller. The General Counsel sits as close to the top of the bleachers as anyone can get and has a finger in everything. The courts, sure." After a brief look around, "the housing, all of it." But also manufacturing, labor relations, retail sales, you name it, on the books and off. You can't even get a drink of Forus around here without a percentage going to the General Counsel."

I waived him to a stop with the same hand I'd slammed on the desk, then turned to May. "Is this true? If so, why meet with me?"

May glanced toward The Fixer, sighed again heavily, then said, "General Counsel hold lawyer contracts. Mostly. Know people." Her response brought a snort from The Fixer. To which May responded by pulling out her handkerchief and shaking it back and forth in his direction as though doing so would ward off his cooties.

After returning the hankie to her purse May continued. "General Counsel know you request Special Masters, will appear or appoint state counsel."

"And what do you think the General Counsel wants with me? "

When May hesitated, The Fixer sat back. As the silenced stretched on he scooched yet a bit further away. Apparently neither wanted anything to do with this question.

May took a moment to reflect and gather herself then said, "Likely deciding if move you on or allow trial. Question if worth it."

Though I'd seen and aged a lot in my almost two weeks in Purgatory, I was still a little shocked. "He thinks I'm going to pay him just to have my day in court?"

It was May's turn to snort, and The Fixer's turn to speak up.

"Not if. The General Counsel will want to know how much you're going to pay to make it worthwhile to let you go forward."

For better or worse, when I opened my mouth to say something, nothing came out. Quietly, in the silence that now sat between us and without any of the niggling animosity he'd characteristically shown, The Fixer said to May, "Tell him."

May paused just long enough to pull out her hankie

again. She held it at the ready as she leaned forward then, in perfect English said, "the General Counsel is a demon."

The man who lives for tomorrow
never lives.

De Tenebra

CHAPTER 24

CONTRADICTIO IN ADJECTO
(Contradiction In Itself)

ALL THINGS CONSIDERED I'd say I took the news that the General Counsel was a demon well. I made several starts and stops at speaking – repeatedly opening and closing my mouth without saying anything; there was a lot of blinking – as though that would somehow help me see what they were talking about; and I took a lot of deep breaths – which did absolutely nothing to calm me. In the end, right about the time I'd sagged forward and dropped my head into my hands, it was The Fixer that spoke to the moment.

"Yeah, demons are a thing. No pun intended but that's certainly a Hell-of-a-lot to swallow.

"Now, while I'm generally not a half-full kind of guy, there's a few pluses to be found here. First and foremost, it's not like the General Counsel is gonna try to buy your soul and send you to well, … Purgatory. Also on the bright side, as I understand it there's no fangs, flaming hair, or bright red skin to deal with – sure some consider that kind of stuff mere aesthetics but still, those things tend to freak folks out, way out.

"You? Well, you just gotta look at this for what it is, either an investment opportunity or a sign that it's time to fold. Your hand is about to be called; you either gather up your chips and go all in or look for a way out of the game."

May, ever the model of oratory efficiency, nodded her agreement.

After a few more deep breaths, and a little hand wringing, I gathered myself and, looking to May, asked the question I'd been struggling to put into words.

"And what exactly does it mean to be a demon?"

"Boss rarely around, lots to do, Purgatory divided into many territories. Souls do administration, demons manage as executive staff. Come in different flavors. Senior ones know other Hells, no obey six rules, report to boss direct. Have big appetites - cigars, booze, sex, power. All resist injury, magic, and curses."

I didn't want to ask, but I needed to know.

"How senior of a demon is the General Counsel?"

They both shrugged, May seemed to think the General Counsel was significant among demons, but certainly not senior-most. The Fixer acted as though the conversation in general and this question in particular were beyond his pay grade.

After another pause, albeit briefer and without any hand wringing or deep breaths, I looked out the window at the soon-to-be darkening skies and made ready to leave.

By way of goodbye, I gave The Fixer a few Horis and

asked May to bring my share of the payment due, by the inn the next morning. Though she claimed my request was an imposition, I sensed excitement under the surface of her complaint. When I suggested this was part of her other duties under the partnership agreement, she acquiesced – even though we knew it wasn't and that she knew the terms of our agreement better than anyone.

Once the two of them were out of my office, after a bit of organizing, I too left. I snaked my way through the now much more crowded first floor of the building, then headed back toward the inn along Purgatory's hard stone streets.

With no one to talk to and only the light of the now dusky skies to distract me, my thoughts turned inward. For me there was no choice, I wasn't going to give up, I was going all in. This meant I was going to have to give up the only thing I had of value, my interest in the partnership. If I lost my case also losing the partnership would be bad but nothing I couldn't overcome. The real problem was that my share of the partnership wasn't worth much without me. For my offer to be worthwhile I'd have to agree to work for the business as well. I could end up being the General Counsel's employee; working in servitude until I decided to move on.

I needed a hedge; I needed to buy an option to purchase The Gunfighter's share of the partnership so that if I lost, I'd still be in charge of my destiny. But since the General Counsel would also want all my cash assets, I'd need to front load the hedge so that the post-loss purchase price would be nominal. And I'd have to do this without raising any suspicions about what I'd done with my money.

I'd have to make it look like I'd squandered the money I'd earned from the move on with The Gunfighter, the implied obligation of the Rider-Reaper, the retainer, and the payment due. Even to me, it sounded more like an act of desperation than a plan.

I spent the rest of the walk back to the inn trying to think of other options, or ways to improve my plan. All to no avail.

When I found myself in front of the door to the inn, I paused and took a few breaths.

Wholly committing to act within the space of three breaths was a Sun Tsu tenet that One Finger had embraced. Clearing one's mind and being present in the moment, was the first thing we did each time we trained, and training started as soon as I returned each day.

Today was no exception. I cleared my mind of any doubt or concern, committed to the plan, then opened the door to the inn and went up to my room to put away the few books and documents I'd brought back with me from the office. When I returned to the lobby One Finger was waiting.

The drills we did started basic, sticky hands, off-balancing, even an occasional waltz. On the surface the objectives were familiar, cleaner technique, improved balance, learning to feel one's partner's energy, and so forth. But the focus here was different; I was being pushed to maintain my commitment while letting go of distractions as we practiced technique after technique. Gradually both the drills and our practice became more advanced.

Through such drills I'd come to realized that, like the drills themselves, my skills were relatively basic. Under the guise of working on basic techniques, One Finger was helping me declutter my mind, my commitment to the act, and my expectations. Even when I had in mind what I wanted to do I'd often get distracted by whatever obstacles my mind anticipated or imagined.

Each day we seemed to practice just a little longer. I was getting accustomed to the darkening, but only gradually. My energy still waned as the darkening rose, but it was much better than my first day here, when I'd fallen out under the dusky sky. When my fatigue became obvious One Finger would call an end to the physical part of our training. Today we finished well after the skies had gone to dark.

Rather than stretch or warm-down, we customarily concluded our training with some Forus and conversation. In one of our earlier conversations One Finger explained, that the difference between fighting and winning is often one's focus. I'd heard this concept voiced before. The baseball player that sees the rotation of the seams on the ball coming at him at almost a hundred miles an hour, the basketball player for whom the rim looks huge.

One Finger spoke of these times as the moment. In what was both an act of introspection and confession, he acknowledged, "Taint da roar of da crowd or da fall of yer ponent, tis dat pure and perfect moment dat, once fount will be sought again. Tis a powerful drug; one dat even da dead-eyed, emotionally dulled Reapers can nah resist."

In addition to the interplay of focus and doubt in life and fighting, our talks ranged from military to street fighting strategy, religion and violence as tools of oppression, and philosophy and discourse as full contact sports.

But our favorite topic, or at least the one we most often returned to, was whether there was any real difference between fighting here and on the earthly plane.

While we both agreed that the difference was less than one might think, I maintained that our physiology on the earthly plane limited how much speed and power we could expect to generate. Rather than disagree, One Finger off-balanced me with the force of my own argument, asking if maybe our expectation of the physical body was limiting how much speed and power we generated.

Like any good master, his *kuzushi* extended to verbal as well as physical exchanges.

Of necessity, I guided tonight's conversation to matters of finance and fashion. I started by asking about the cost of my stay – what his best room, which mine certainly wasn't, would run me, how much lessons like his would normally cost, even what my Forus tab would be – were it not part of the training.

Once it was clear that I wasn't trying to renegotiate our terms or worse, looking to make the case that I was getting a favor, he answered questioningly, but unguardedly. When I told him of my predicament, plan, and possible needed to shelter some assets, he spoke more candidly.

Since his nicest room had been and would be vacant, no one would know different if I claimed to have moved in there after starting my practice. Nor would they know that I hadn't been paying the higher daily rate instead of the weekly rate, drinking the more expensive brand of Forus each night, and paying dearly for his instruction.

One Finger noted that if I was going to claim that I was burning through my money, I needed to start looking the part and, after noting that 'cheap is relative,' told me one of the best places to buy 'imported' goods like clothes at a reasonable price was the central market down the street. I asked how much I should expect to pay for lawyerly looking clothes, clothes that "pulled the 'D' out of wardrobe," and he chortled at the bad pun.

"Well, fin ya gets dair early n pays wots asked, ya can ease-ly get in ta some DieBus. But fin ya gets dair later when deys woe'n bout cartin stuff back, den ya pays wot ya should."

I told him waiting till later in the day, after May dropped off my share of the retainer, would work. But at the mention of May's name, One Finger changed his tune.

"Coarse, fin ya wait too long yer like ta miss out on da good stuff. N ya really don wanna come up lackin ere. Specially on da shoes."

And, after a pause that seemed long only in relationship to the millisecond that it'd taken him to reverse his position,

"Fin ya want, I cain send a body round ta da clothiers ta ave em send wot ya buy ere - wit payment on delivery. Fin it gets ere fore ya return to da inn I'll front da cost and ya cain pay it back later."

Now it's not that I can't take a hint - in my mind I'm still the best wing-man Purgatory's ever had - it's just that I'm not above giving a good ribbing when the opportunity presents itself. After all, by definition, *kuzushi* is a two-way street.

Knowing full well that he wanted me gone when May arrived, I asked, "what's your interest here?"

The question caught him off guard. But before the

moment could become awkward, I added "if you have to front me the cost of the suit, what interest rate will you charge?"

After a brief and deep chuckle, he nodded toward the jug on the table. "Well, dis ere jug a Forus is gettin a lil low."

I bowed in gratitude, and by way of good night, tossed back the little Forus that remained in my cup, swished it around my mouth and spat it out.

Stress the root, strengthen the vine.

DE TENEBRA

CHAPTER 25

QUOD MEDICINA ALISS NON MISER LEX ET ANIMA

(The Miserable Have No Other Medicine)

ONE FINGER SAID that at this time of day it'd be easy to find the market.

"Jest turn rite and foller da crowd."

But, as I made to head out the door, he urged caution since, "dey buys n sells much more n clothes dair." With that warning in mind, I went back to my room, secreted my only somewhat trusty knife in my waist band, and left the inn.

I turned right and after a few blocks it was clear that I was headed in the right direction. At each intersection people merged and joined a flow that I'd unwittingly become a part of. These people were dressed in clothing of every sort. But unlike the crowd at the intake, other than me and a few others, they weren't just making do with whatever rags they'd scrounged. There were kimonos, some elaborately decorated headdresses, and more than a few studded velvet loin cloths of varying colors and girths. There were even hints and dabs of make-up but of course, nothing that compared to May.

In marked contrast to their gaudy, almost festive dress, the crowd moved with a low, grumbling murmur. As the crowd shuffled along gaining mass, my discomfort grew.

I don't like crowds. Under even the best of circumstances there are too many people, too close. The pushing, bumping, blocking, and general closeness make crowded places a playground for thieves, perverts, and worse … the inconsiderate. Being in Purgatory raised my distaste for crowds to near paranoid levels.

But for the fact that my shabby attire earned me a small but noticeable amount of additional personal space, I'd have likely broken with the crowd. Absent resistance, I moved along with it for several blocks, with minimal bumps and numerous looks of disdain, until we came to a large intersection.

Across the street was an arch that marked the entrance to the open-air market. The crowd passed through the arch and fanned out toward the stalls like water coursing around rocks.

At first glance the market seemed like almost any other open-air market. Stalls and squares defined by tables, mats, and the occasional canopy were loosely arranged toward the center. On the sides, tents and more formal structures housed the more established businesses and gave the whole thing a sense of permanence. Over the crowd, I could see the occasional raised platform where barkers shouted and cajoled would-be patrons.

There were no birds squawking, music playing, or cars passing, but the loud haggling, merchant banter, and calls to customers gave the place a lively, active air. Sensing a potential customer in the form of a well-dressed passerby, I heard a nearby merchant cry-out,

"You sir, yes that's it, come, come. Tell me, have you ever seen such a beautiful mat as this one? Made from the center wood of trees brought straight from the far shores. It's far superior to those shit-rags they sell at the stalls down the way; I wouldn't let my mother-in-law wipe herself with one of those. Take a good look - here, feel the craftsmanship."

Poorly dressed as I was, I moved about the market freely, accosted only by looks of distrust and suspicion. Until one merchant, a lanky, heavily bearded man took an interest in and reached toward me.

"Yes, yes. This way please. We offer a 70/30 split, much better than you'll find elsewhere."

I put my hand on my knife when he put his hand on my shoulder. I set myself and drew the blade, butt forward, parallel to my forearm, and point back, with the business edge on the outside, when he tried to pull me along.

Either my immobility, the blade, or my apparent willingness to use the knife caught his attention. He took his hand off me and raised both hands in a placating gesture.

"Apologies, apologies, good sir. Fool that I am, I thought you interested in earning coin at our post."

Intrigued by his explanation, I asked without thinking. "You have a post?"

"Yes. Yes and no good sir."

I sheathed my knife, and like any good salesman he

took this as a sign to continue his pitch. With a grand gesture that both drew people in and ushered them along, he announced, "We don't just have a post, we have the best post and most complete equipment you will find in any market!"

He was good; he'd seamlessly transitioned from critical-eyed buyer to sycophant-salesman. He warmed his mark, me and all within earshot, with a practiced pause of appreciation and intentional widening of his eyes to mimic the sparkle of enthusiasm, before continuing.

"And let me just say, we offer men and women, both willing and conscripts. All fresh and reasonably priced.

"Oh, and the wheel! Did I mention that we have a breaking wheel as well?" He paused again, as though appreciating a fine wine. "Ah yes, the wheel is special indeed."

I only belatedly realized that he'd fallen in beside and was subtly guiding me along.

"For a mere pittance you can torment the rich, celebrities new and old, perhaps even someone you know. All fresh and contracted for by time - do as you like, they can beg, cry, and plead, but they can't back out. The only limits on their pain are yours. Connoisseur that you clearly are, let me assure you, we have the best equipment - ropes, chains, whips, stones, spikes and other instruments - to choose from. Why, we even have a cat-o'-nine-tails that you can whip them with!"

"Whip them?" I all but blurted out.

"Ah yes, I see you are a man of purpose, the hands-on type. Of course, you may also beat them. With your fists, our clubs, or perhaps you have an instrument of your own particular fancy! You may, at your own risk mind you, even use that well-crafted blade you so kindly displayed for me. All for the most reasonable of prices. We are not cheap, but you will find the experience is worth every pittance you'll spend."

The rest of his fluffing was lost on me. The street we were on converged with a couple of others at a group of double-stacked stone squares that formed a stage. Front and center on the stage was a knee-high post; solidly anchored and with various hooks, loops and other attachment points. On the side of the stage were two things. The first to catch my eye was a well-worn breaking wheel that screamed of years of hard and hardy use. But it was the second thing that held my attention. Loosely corralled, like horses in a makeshift pen, were several nearly naked, ragged individuals.

I've often wondered why horses don't simply push through and out of their corral, here it was obvious that these unfortunate souls were trapped by more than the rope surrounding them. My being mistaken for one of these poor souls confirmed that I needed new clothes.

In well-practiced synchronicity, two other groups approached the stage from different directions, mirroring our approach. Each group was lured forward with the song-sale-pitch of an individual like the salesman who brought the group I was in forward.

When all three groups had converged at the stage, his colleagues took-up positions on opposite sides. Working in concert they baited and coaxed and cajoled the crowd into a fervor. The bearded man that had led me over then took center stage and, while pacing back and forth between the corralled and the crowd, barked out insults to one and encouragement to the other; skillfully working up the crowd even further.

When the crowd seemed to peak and was beginning to grow impatient, 'The Barker' took up a position in front of a table in the center of the platform behind the post and stood silently with his hands raised high overhead. On cue, his comrades grew silent and he slammed his hands down, focusing the crowd's attention.

With great and intentional fanfare, he tossed one of the rags that covered the table aside to reveal a coarse stained, and knotted rope. A loop at one end served as a handle, while the other end was frayed and uneven. He picked it up, pulling at it and ostensibly testing its strength. The first time he slammed the rope down on the table the crowd jumped as if snatched awake from some stupor. As he continued to beat the table the crowd yelled its approval. It was only when he stopped, rope in mid-air that I noticed his colleagues yelling and cursing from their new positions just outside the corral.

With rough hands and tones, they shoved and sorted through their cowering inventory of souls. Eventually they settled on a dirty, threadbare, wisp of a man whose attempts to placate them by prostrating himself, only resulted in his being dragged to the center of the stage and chained to the post.

Only after his two colleagues stepped aside did The Barker move. He rushed forward, adding momentum so as to deliver a nasty blow with the rope, only to stop short, arm still in the air.

The whoops and hollers that were slowly building into

a cheer from the crowd morphed into a collective sigh. He slowly brought his arm down, gradually turning on the rope and looking at it as if anew, then bringing it in close to touch and inspect. Decision made, he stormed back to the far side of the table and tossed another of the rags aside to reveal a length of rusted old chain.

He picked up the chain, pulled it tight, swung it around several times then brought it down with a sharp crack on the table. There was a brief startled gasp, before the crowd again erupted in a cheer.

As I said, I don't like crowds.

Rather than look around to see what new threat approached, eyes closed tight, The Wisp grabbed onto the post with both hands, holding it close like a lover that whispered sweet things in his ear. But there were no sweet entreats. What The Wisp heard was the irregular stomp and crack made by The Barker as he did a jumping-skipping dance toward the post. With each landing he brought the chain down in a crack against the hard-stone stage. The Wisp involuntarily joined the dance, starting and jerking in rhythm to the crack of the chain as The Barker approached from behind. With his final leap The Barker landed astride the trembling Wisp's legs.

If he'd had anything in his bladder, The Wisp would surely have let it go. Failing that, The Wisp took to moaning out some incoherent plea. The only response he got was the tender touch of rusted steel upon his skin as The Barker gently cascaded the chain across his head and back again. Whether momentarily soothed or just caught off guard, this seeming kindness caused The Wisp to make the mistake of looking back toward his tormentor.

The Barker smiled and, now holding the chain with both hands, took the opportunity to drape the chain around The Wisp's neck, then drove his knee into The Wisp's back while pulling the chain taut. The Wisp was in Purgatory's version of a yoga sun-salutation before he even realized what had happened.

Like a train wreck that you can't look away from, all this seemed to be happening slowly enough that I couldn't miss any detail, but so fast that I could do nothing but watch. The crowd, already an irritant, pushed in on me like a stench that I couldn't get away from.

Already egged on by The Barker's insults and taunts, The Wisp's new predicament was all the encouragement the crowd needed. The growing cacophony of calls for him to be beaten, choked, and even sent down, was joined by random pebbles, sticks, and other small objects, thrown with varying levels of vigor in the general direction of The Wisp. While The Barker's colleagues discreetly collected these small and seemingly worthless projectiles, The Barker moved to seal the deal. Shifting the chain to one hand, he waved the crowd closer with the hand other as he made his pitch.

"Yes! This one's primed, ready, and worthy of your worst punishment."

He carelessly slapped The Wisp about the head as he spoke, then pointed to one in the crowd.

"You there, fancy a go? No?" Then, pointing to an old woman, and subtly shifting his accent. "How about you marm? Surely he's been a naughty boy!"

Calling to one of his colleagues, "fetch me marm ere da paddle. Come on now marm, fer you da first one is on da house."

I heard her cackle with glee well before I saw her step up on the stage.

She was a short plug of a woman that moved slowly and seemed unsteady. The crowd, worked to a fervor, wanted blood not the dawdling of an aged and infirm woman. You could feel disappointment race through them; it mixed with muted laughter that would surely morph into taunts.

We were all shocked into silenced when, in one fluid motion she snatched the big flat wooden spoon and took a practice swing. The swooshing sound it made as she swung it through the air left no doubt that she was a journeyman hitter. With her second practice swing the crowd broke into cheers and started egging her on, and by her third swing the crowd was again calling for pain and blood.

She sidled up to The Wisp with a confident ease. Sensing, as had the crowd, that she was well familiar with paddling and punishment, The Wisp's eyes darted around in what would in other circumstances have been a comical fashion. As she drew close, he half consciously pulled away, until the chain drew taught on the post.

She closed to well within arms-reach of The Wisp then held the paddle so close in front of his face so that it blocked his view of her and almost everything else. This unexpected sensory deprivation quickly took its toll. When he furtively tried to peek around the paddle, she viciously rapped him across the bridge of the nose. His howl of pain was cut short by another vicious rap, and when he tried to pull further away, he was herded back to his original position with cuffs to the sides of his head. She kept at it till he was on his knees with his back toward the crowd, still and quietly whimpering, as he starred at the paddle inches from his face.

The crowd ate it up. What had been random insults and calls for violence blossomed into blood chants. When she slowly lowered the paddle, she held both The Wisp's and the crowd's full attention.

"Now that'd be a good boy. You just sit still and let old marm ere get a good look at you."

She reached down and gently caressed his chin; a almost sensual act that made him start and shudder. After squeezing her hands together to force his mouth open, she tugged on a couple of teeth to satisfy herself that they wouldn't, or perhaps would come out easily enough, then took a slow walk around him. When she was halfway around him, standing directly behind him, between him and the crowd, he turned his head just slightly to follow her progress. As though expecting it, she viciously cuffed him on the ear and admonished him.

"Now don't you go payin them shit bags out there no never-mind."

After a dismissive glance toward the crowd, she continued. "And oh, what a collection of broke-ass, shit-for brains turds they is."

I couldn't fault her assessment of the crowd.

After a full circle inspection, she extended a single dirty and bent finger and used one of her chipped and blackened fingernails to brush an errant hair from The Wisp's eye before addressing him in an almost motherly fashion.

"Well, ya aint much fer the eye, not much at all. But ya deserves better than some old lady with a piece-a-shit cookin spoon that this lyin ass is tryin to pawn off on these shit-brained folk as a paddle."

She turned back to the crowd and, playing to their bloodlust, asked rhetorically, "Am I to make do with this?"

Turning back to him, with the same hand that had brushed away the errant hair from his face, she grabbed a hand full of hair and pulled his head back, forcing him to stare up at her, wide-eyed and open mouthed. When his eyes locked on the spoon's worn sharp handle, which was pointed at his throat like a dagger, she said again,

"Am I to make do with this!" Her statement was loud, declarative, and no longer rhetorical.

The crowd, now on the verge of becoming a mob, responded with boos and hisses, then launched a volley of small stone projectiles at The Barker and his colleagues; they let these stones lay.

Holding the spoon overhead, starring at The Barker, she looked for all the world like someone's homicidal grandma, threatening far more than a spoon spanking.

"Am I to make do with this!" Now it was a threat - aimed squarely at The Barker and backed by the power she now held over the crowd.

Whether motivated by fear of the crowd, loss of potential business, or both, The Barker moved quickly to appease. With only the slightest hint of resentment he offered her the chance to pick both the instrument and individual she thought should inflict punishment.

She accepted his proposal with a broken and black-toothed smile, looked down on The Wisp, then, after throwing her head back and barking out a cackle, whispered loud enough for all to hear.

"We're a team we are. I'll pick the weapon and when I point to yer huckleberry you just give yer ole marm here the signal."

After a half pat - half slap on The Wisp's cheek, she said almost conspiratorially, "Trust ole marm here, I'll get ye what ye need" then she went to inspect The Barker's instruments.

Another loud, head-back bark of a cackle told us she'd found what she was after. She returned to stand in front of the kneeling Wisp, threw one leg over the semi-slack chain, and looked down on the pitiful figure in front of her. Holding a pointy pick like a tool high for the crowd to see, she told him,

"We're a team we are. I've picked the instrument and now you get to help pick yer tormentor. I'll wave this shiv around at the crowd and whoever it's pointin at when you give me the signal, well they'll be your huckleberry."

Then she leaned in and again took his face in her hands, "But there ain't gonna be no cheatin here."

After a cutting glance at The Barker, "You don't get to pick some weak looking old lady. No sir, you'll be doin yer pickin in the dark."

And with that she lifted her skirt – not high, but high enough to see long, grayed-out pubic hairs, framed by the same crusty layer of soot that covered everything else in Purgatory.

Like The Wisp, I and the rest of the crowd instinctively gasped and pulled back in sympathetic retreat. With her pinky fingers pointed up daintily, like she was taking noon tea, she held her skirt up and sauntered forward toward The Wisp's kneeling form. The crowd snapped out of its revulsion induced stupor and erupted in a fevered roar as The Wisp retreated backward on his knees.

For a brief moment his retreat kept pace with her approach. Clearly this wasn't the deal he'd bargained for. He continued his scooting away well after the chain grew taunt, wearing and grating his knees on the stone stage, but making no progress. In a last futile act of defiance, he extended his arms and threw his head back in a futile attempt to delay her approaching womanhood.

As she pressed forward and closed with her uplifted skirt, she cooed out to him, "Now don't you pay them fools out there no never-mind. You just give ole marm the right signal and we'll have you right as rain in no time."

She draped her skirt over his head and, pulling on both his ears, secured his face to her crotch. Rather than halt her approach on contact, she pushed forward further still. As he fell backward, his knees trapped under him, she rode him to the ground. When they came to rest, she sat balanced on her knees, toes, and his face.

The crowd went wild.

I dry swallowed instinctively - had I eaten it would have surely come back up - then uttered a tight-lipped curse of crowds.

With her thighs clamped tight to his head and her dress ridding high, his sparse hair mushroomed out from between her legs and mingled with her dirt crusted crotch. He squirmed and writhed trying to get away. But with his legs trapped under him and his arms held taunt by the chain, all this did was draw a few coos and cackles from the old woman and send the crowd into a fit of laughter and applause. Perhaps in shock but more likely in defeat, after a few more spasm-like jerks, The Wisp went still. Clearly disappointed, she spread her legs slightly so he could hear and told him,

"Lie slack if'in you want, but if ye don't signal me yer preference, I'll have to find another use for this little goody."

With that she stabbed him in the head with the pointy end of the tool. It wasn't a deep penetrating stab, probably not even bone deep. But it became obvious that it was painful as she repeatedly stabbed him. After the first few stabs, I could hear his crotch-muffled cries as he struggled to get out from under her dress. A few more poke-stabs and his squirming attempts to dodge the blade seemed to produce the desired effect. She tossed her head back and with a lust-driven cackle alternated between grinding back and forth and bobbing up and down on his face; all the while waving the knife around like a drunk in a bar fight and vaguely pointing it at the crowd. In between pointing toward random people, she'd occasionally stab him in his head then cackle, either with the joy of the deed or otherwise.

Soon, and to a general round of hoots and hollers, she pulled up violently on his hair while crushing down on his face. She came with a few guttural grunts and hisses, then sagged forward into a lewd, one-armed parody of "child's pose." Spent and half breathless, talking more to herself than The Wisp or the still yearning crowd, she gasp'd out,

"Ah that be a fair signal, fair enough indeed. I guess you made yer choice clear enough with that one."

She looked down her arm to the pointy pick like a tool she still clutched in hand and let her gaze run along

it, then out in the direction it was pointing until she was
staring into the crowd, straight at me.

Disbelievers have their own faith.

De Tenebra

CHAPTER 26

MALUM IN SE

(Wrong In Itself)

A WAVE OF disappointment swept over the crowd; it soon turned into a steady stream of boos and boo-hoos from those not chosen. The Barker quickly stepped in to wrest control from the still prostrate hag.

With a grey-toothed smile and an excess of hand waving he urged the crowd to make way for me to come forward. While those in front of me stepped aside, those behind pulsed forward. The push of the crowd quickly escalated into a series of rough shoves that thrust me toward the stage in a herky-jerky series of stumbles.

The crowd was almost out of control; they wanted blood. Mine if I didn't get a move on, at my hand if I did. This brought to mind what The Gunfighter had said to me in court after my meet and confer, that 'this place is about learning to be in control of yourself.'

Half-way to the stage I accepted that one way or

another I was going to be part of this show. By the time I'd been punch-pushed to within arm's distance of the stage I had both a realization and a plan.

I'd seen too many cons to believe that my being called to the stage was a coincidence. Given the other relatively more affluent people in the crowd, I knew this wasn't about coin. The only things I had of value was a growing practice and a good cause of action. The question was which of those two was this about. To get an answer to that question I'd have to work this con to my advantage.

Spotting a con is easy once you realize you're the mark, beating the con is an altogether different matter. You have to con the con man into believing that you don't know you're the mark, that you're buying into the con, and that you're responding in a genuine but unexpected way.

After being shoved to the front I drew my knife and swept it in a slow, lazy arc around me that gave those in the crowd who were still pushing and shoving just enough time to step back. This, along with the rags I wore, earned me enough breathing room to get into character. Like a lot of litigators, I've always thought I'd be good on stage; I was about to find out if I was right.

With a healthy mix of rage, confusion and indignation, I turned on the crowd and, stealing a Dorothy Parker line, demanded of them, "What new Hell is this!" Where the question was rhetorical, my disdain for the crowd was genuine.

The stage was low. I stormed it in two quick steps, all the while muttering to myself, shaking my head, and in general, making a spectacle of my anger and confusion. I was trying to look disturbed, just shy of unhinged; disappointed yet resolved; and most importantly, like a man ready to jump into the abyss - desperate enough to do what they dared not.

After pacing back and forth a few times I ceased my muttering and scanned the crowd, hoping that I appeared to be looking for one that could answer my seemingly existential question. Frustrated and annoyed at not finding an answer, I made a couple more trips back and forth across the stage, then alerted on the old hag who was surreptitiously trying to crawl away. I didn't hesitate, in far less than three breaths - Sun Tsu would likely have been proud - I stormed over to her semi fetal form and unceremoniously push-kicked her off the stage.

My ranting, raving, and kicking the hag off the stage established my bonafides as an unknowing mark and sold the con men on the idea that I was buying into their con. Now all I had to do was convince them that they'd lost control of the con, in order to figure out exactly what they wanted with me.

Sparse laughter murmured up from the crowd. They were confused by my ramblings but encouraged by this preview of dark entertainment. I wasn't having any of it. Rage renewed, I turned and insulted them in my best Yoda idiolect.

"Fools are we?"

With the crowd rebuffed into silence, to no one and everyone, I again asked, "What new Hell is this, where loving an old whore with your face passes as torture?"

I picked up the hag's ice pick, then after some more mumbling and pacing, hefted it a few times, then threw it aside disdainfully. With a heavy sigh I drew my knife and pointed it at The Barker with one hand while reaching out toward the now silent crowd with the other and begged of them, "… and where we are sold a beating with a spoon as the sweet promise of redemption."

I strode back to The Wisp, knelt and stared at him intently. After sniffing and baring my teeth at him, I suddenly alerted. I looked over one shoulder, then the other, then furiously started slapping at my ears with both hands, as though I were being attacked by a horde of flies. When I'd gotten rid of the non-existent flies, I looked upon The Wisp anew. I helped him to a seated position, stroked his hair, seemingly an act of genuine kindness, then firmly took hold of a handful of that hair.

The crowd went silent, both confused and enthralled by my actions.

Holding The Wisp by a snatch of his oily hair, I did my best imitation of Horatio as he looked upon poor Yorick. Summoning all the day's sadness I said, "Come friend, let us cast off the last of our mortal coil. We shall flee this false new Hell for a truer path."

Still holding him by the hair, I drew my knife and pressed its edge tight against the back of The Wisp's neck, then put my knee on his chest, I was poised to decapitate him.

The crowd - still, silent, and enthralled - hung on my every word. I knew I'd conned the con men into believing they'd lost control when The Barker tentatively placed a hand on my shoulder.

"Come friend, judge us not too harshly. All have borne witness to thine penchant for self-sacrifice." Then, ever the showman, to the crowd he exclaimed, "And we are made better for it.

"But as I look upon this piece of a soul before you, I find him lacking commitment and unworthy of your sacrifice. I urge you, mete out a more tempered justice."

And there was the answer I needed.

If I'd lost control and tortured The Wisp, whether because of peer pressure, frustration or whatever, I'd lose my case. I wouldn't be entitled to the equitable remedy I sought because I'd be acting unethically, like I belonged here. Call it Purgatory's version of the *Unclean Hands* legal doctrine.

The Barker wanted and had likely been paid to get me to beat The Wisp. He hadn't counted on my knife or my seemingly unstable disposition and was now afraid that I'd move The Wisp and myself on. Whoever was behind this didn't want me out of the picture, they just didn't want me to have my case heard by the Special Masters.

Satisfied that I had my answer, I only needed to 'cool' the would-be conmen. I tentatively withdrew my knife from The Wisp's neck, trying to look somewhat mollified and as though I just needed further convincing. But when I looked The Wisp in the eyes, expecting to see relief, I saw I'd made a mistake.

I'd approached him thinking it was a "Three Musketeers." A con where two or three players are actively working the crowd. A fourth player, who looks and acts like a mark, is there to allay suspicion – like the guy at the crooked dice game, who's there to win just so the marks will think they can win too. But this wasn't a Three Musketeers, it was a "Focus," and The Wisp was the Scared Mouse – a person who, because they aren't in on the con, reacts in a genuine but predictable way that gives the con credibility.

The Wisp really was some poor soul off the streets.

Looking in his eyes I saw that the fear and distrust he'd shown the hag were gone. In its place was heart rending sadness and disappointment. He too had bought my con. He'd seen relief and redemption, seemingly at hand moments ago, now painfully slipping away. The hag's pain and humiliation was nothing compared to what I'd done.

Still holding him by what little hair he had. I leaned down and in, then spoke conspiratorially. "It is him I find lacking commitment and unworthy of your sacrifice."

When I loosened my hold on The Wisp things seemed to slow down. The Wisp blinked slowly in dawning comprehension of what I'd said, someone in the audience yelled "Kill the old coot," and one of the attendants on stage snickered in disgust.

I had time to see and hear everything. I was, as One Finger would put it, in the moment. I might have lost the moment but for the squeak like creak the wooden planks made as The Barker shifted his weight. The sound brought back memories of my arrival here, reminded me that I didn't belong here, and told me that The Barker had leaned in too far and was likely off balance.

He reached out, likely intending to help me to stand, but encountered only air. I'd pivoted while still kneeling and turned my shoulders away from him. The Barker seemed to fall forward in slow motion. By the time surprise at falling began to register on his face, well before he could react to arrest his fall, I was pushing up with my legs, letting this drive my arm up toward the target his face had become. I heard The Wisp gasped the instant before the blow connected.

There was no satisfying crunch or eruption of blood that comes with a broken jaw or nose, but the force of the blow lifted him clear of his feet. He rose and seemed to hover for the briefest instant, then gravity prevailed, and he came crashing to the ground in a heap. I heard The Wisp chuckle and, just as time resumed its normal course, the crowd erupted in cheers.

If I'd been holding a mic, I'd have dropped it. As it was, I shoved the blade back in my pants and leapt off the stage. I didn't need the knife anymore; a hard look and purposeful step in the direction I was going parted the crowd and I stormed forward. Driven by claps on the back, I stormed through the crowd on my way back to the inn.

Like I said, I don't like crowds.

Hope springs eternal, so it's used to being crushed.

DE TENEBRA

CHAPTER 27

BENEFICIUM PACISCI INGRESSUS
(The Benefit Of The Bargain Entered Into)

I'D RIDDEN THE meandering wave of people into the market. Now, as I stormed out, the late comers and bargain hunters that were just now making their way into the market couldn't get out of my way fast enough.

I headed back toward the inn bristling with what I wanted to believe was anger but knew was actually fear. There were only two explanations for what had happened at the market. It could have just been my bad luck. But bad luck really didn't explain why The Barker was worried that I'd actually move The Wisp and myself on. More likely, I'd been a target, in which case my presence at the market was anticipated.

I needed answers and assurances.

When I reached the Dark Light Inn, I threw open the doors and stormed inside. Intent on making a ruckus, I dragged one of the heavy tables and a few chairs across the stone floors into the courtyard where the blocks I once struggled to move sat neatly stacked in a corner. I then went behind One Finger's intake desk and grabbed the waning jug of Forus, three cups, and a spit bowl.

Before I could make my way back to the table, One Finger appeared, more than a little disheveled and sporting blotches of white powder in many and, might I say, odd places. This was the same powder that May used as a weapon and for self-defense - I'd seen it dissolve limbs on contact. No doubt it was neutralized for his benefit.

I slammed the Forus and cups down in the center of the table and, ignoring both One Finger and discretion, shouted for May. One Finger quickly assessed the situation and determined that patience was the better course. He stood casually, while discreetly trying to arrange his clothes and brush off some of the more obvious and telling powdery residue.

I was about to shout for May again, something that One Finger seemed to be trying to Jedi me into not doing, when she entered the courtyard. Other than an errant hair or two, a slight unevenness to her lipstick, and her skirt being on backward, you'd have thought she'd just come from a business meeting. One Finger and I were still standing when May arrived at the table. He saved me from letting my angst get the better of my manners by pulling out a chair for May.

Once we were all seated, I picked up the jug of Forus, poured a couple of fingers in each cup, then put the jug down without touching my cup or saying a word. After waiting three breaths, during which no one so much as blinked, I related the events of the morning.

I talked without pause or interruption, relating the story from beginning to end in great detail. One Finger spoke first when I was done. Always the teacher, he wanted to talk about the "moment" I'd had.

May, more than a little put out by being interrupted and yelled after, wasn't having it,

"Not point."

Her words were terse even by her frugal standards. Perhaps sensing the mood slipping, One Finger tried to regroup.

"True. De portent ting is dat ya were able ta maintain yer composure n foller wot were goin on."

Before he could get any further, May cut to the chase.

"Him expected. How?"

Realization dawned on One Finger and he gave voice to the facts no one wanted to say. "True, I were da one dat suggested ya go dar." And even before I could nod my agreement, "and t'was ma idea fer ya ta go early too.

"Well, dats grounds fer concern alrite. But ere's sumptin ta consider. First, me let'n on where ya wuz goin would mount ta a breach a da terms of yer lodgin agreement."

May interjected. "Need keep finances, comings, goings, visitors confidential."

"Aye," said One Finger, "n dats n agreement dat I made wit Da Gunfighter; na one I'm cline ta break. Sides, fin word got out dat I was sellin info bout ma guest, I'd be closed up in no time.

"I spect somebody got ta the lout I sent ta da market bfer ya, n paid em ta know yer business. Dat be'n da case, I gots a beatin ta dole out, and ya gots more problems dan a new outfit's likely ta cure. Da Barker probably ain't da only one out dair lookin to trap n trick ya."

We sat in silence for a while, each keeping their own counsel. After a time, I slid the Forus I'd poured toward them and picked up my glass.

"I suspect you're right. But this may be more of an opportunity than a problem – imagine what their spy will report when, instead of giving him a beating, you tell him his services won't be needed because my funds are running low."

After a smile from May and a nod from One Finger, we tossed back the Forus.

I quickly swished and spit mine out, then waited. Just as One Finger leaned over to spit and May reached for her hanky, I added, "but I still need better clothes, preferably clothes that won't be worn backward."

One Finger, who I suspect was aware of, but hoping no one else noticed or would say anything about the wardrobe malfunction, involuntarily gasped - before he'd spit out the Forus. He gagged on, then involuntarily swallowed the Forus causing him to break into a coughing fit. May who hadn't realized her mistake, looked down at what One Finger was eyeing, her outfit, then lurched forward and spat out the Forus. Some of it made it into the spit bowl on the floor but the bulk of it landed on the table – where it would soon be rubbed to a fine luster.

I excused myself while I could still hold back my laughter and headed back up to my room to grab a few things I'd need at the office.

I returned to find One Finger rubbing the 'spilled' Forus into the tabletop, feigning concentration. May, still seated, but now with her skirt properly oriented, sat all too nonchalantly touching-up her makeup.

After a nod toward One Finger I said to May, "I've got to get to the office to meet with some potential clients."

Still smarting from my earlier tease, by way of a response May stopped reapplying her makeup just long enough to incline her head toward the desk then said, "retainer share."

When I asked if I should count it, she snapped her compact shut causing a small plume of powder to rise, then blew it in my direction.

Hint taken.

I took a big step back, told her I was sure everything was accurate, and headed for the door. I paused at the door threshold and, once I was sure I had her attention, asked May to, "ask The Gunfighter to stop by my office at his earliest opportunity," then left.

When I got to the office there was a small grouping of potential clients waiting.

Apparently, word had spread about either my case, my services, or the success I'd had thus far. Either way, several souls were waiting for an initial consultation. As had become my practice, I gave those awaiting my arrival the same three-part speech I gave before.

My potential clients generally fell into one of three groups; those looking for free advice or assistance, those who sought a way to beat or circumvent the system, and those who might actually have something I could help them with. "The speech" as I'd come to call it, generally got rid of the first two types which, on a typical day, left me with just a few folks to interview. While there were slightly fewer new arrivals than I'd expected, there were a lot who sought help with other legal issues; housing and construction disputes, purchase and sales agreements gone awry, and the occasional employment dispute - if you count indentured servitude as a form of employment.

As far as new clients go, today was typical. Of the eight or so people that were there when I arrived, only three stayed through the end of the speech. The first two clients had criminal issues, something I hadn't taken into account in my original business plan.

Around here the punishment of dipping was handed out like candy on Halloween. But for most souls the real punishment, the kind that actually dissuades them from misbehaving, was asset and property seizure. And, since Purgatory considered itself at least generally civilized, a whole body of law existed to govern such seizures.

The first of the two clients was a long-term resident of Purgatory that had run afoul of Purgatory's Rule Number 6. He'd been running a fairly basic scam where he sold his goods at inflated prices to company buyers to whom he was paying a small kick back. To hear him tell it, an inadvertent bookkeeping error had led to his paying a few buyers a few days late. Rather than interest on the oversight, the buyers were trying to blackmail him into paying them more of his profits in kickbacks. When he'd refused, they'd turned him in.

What he really wanted was to hire The Gunfighter to move the leader of the group on and scare the others out of talking. Because he either lacked the connections or the nerve to approach one of the Reapers, he was hoping I'd broker the deal.

Arranging hits for hire wasn't one of my practice areas. After hearing the amount at issue, I tactfully suggested that it would probably be cheaper for him to pay off everyone except the ringleader, so that it would be just one person's word against another's. This would make the complaint easy to defend against and dissuade others from organizing against him. He left more than happy with this "free" advice, but clear that he was obliged to hire me if he followed my advice.

The second client needed help with an upcoming arraignment – she'd been in a relationship that appeared to violate Purgatory's Rule Number 2, which forbids things like altruism, mercy and kindness, and Rule Number 3, which forbids pleasure for the sake of pleasure.

After I politely refused her offer to exchange her "personal" services for mine she expressed an interest in signing a retainer agreement. We went over the ins and outs of the agreement, then I suggested she take some time to think on it.

I never found out what the third potential client's issue was. He was a squirrely looking man whose habit of looking about furtively only added to the impression. After he introduced himself and looked around the office at everything and nothing, he grasped the sides of the chair as though to prevent it from getting away, and took a seat. Whether paranoid or prescient, fate proved him right.

The Gunfighter entered just as the would-be client was lowering himself into the seat. The Gunfighter grabbed the chair, turned it toward the door, and ejected the squirrely looking man with neither concern nor ceremony.

I doubt the man ever even saw The Gunfighter. That

something had suddenly intervened and ejected him from his seat was more than enough for him; he hit the ground running and never even looked back.

The Gunfighter seated himself effortlessly. He only half turned the chair away from the door back to face me. After smoothing his poncho down, he crossed his arms under it, and said "Go on," as though I'd been talking to him the whole time. Maybe I'd been in Purgatory too long. But the only thing that stood out about all this, the thing that gave me pause was the realization that I'd never before seen The Gunfighter sit.

I jumped right in.

"I want to buy your share of the partnership. And, while I'm only willing to pay one DieBus for your actual share, I'm willing to pay considerably more for the option to buy your share at that price."

I expected either a long pause or a perfunctory rejection. Some part of me even wondered if I'd hear the boom of the .44 if he blew my head off. What I got instead was a considered and neutral rejection.

"Whatever money you've made has been from the partnership. If you paid me everything you've earned, I'd be selling to you for 40% of what was, when I'm entitled to 60% going forward if you don't get your chance in court or lose. Conversely, if I accept your offer, win or lose I'll get nothing going forward."

The good news is that he hadn't said "no," so we were negotiating. The bad news is that he was right.

I countered before things could become either awkward or deadly. "Well, the first thing to keep in mind is that while the cost of the partnership is nominal, the price of the whole package is, I think, reasonable. Especially since technically, I'm just buying an option. That said, I'd be amenable to putting some additional conditions in the agreement that could make it more worth your while."

After a pause that I interpreted as him urging me on, I continued. "For example, perhaps you'd be willing to sell me an option on a percentage and an agreement not to sell."

I was opening high, arguably expecting, but in reality, just hoping he'd counter with something I could live with, which would be pretty much anything that would keep The General Counsel from gaining a controlling share of the partnership.

He stopped looking out the door and fully focused those dead eyes of his squarely on me.

"No. I won't sell you my share of the partnership."

That was it, negotiations were over. I didn't realize there was still a deal to be made until, after a long pause, he spoke again.

"You can have my share or an option. But only if you try to get me out of here too."

The one-armed man rows his boat in a circle.

DE TENEBRA

CHAPTER 28

AMORIBUS MISERIAE TURBA

(Misery Loves Company)

THAT BLANK SPOT? Yeah, that's everything that passed through my mind after his counteroffer.

Where he'd anticipated and prepared for this shift in the conversation, I'd done neither. Completely caught off guard by his counter, I stalled to think.

"And by 'out of here' you mean what exactly?"

"I mean, like you, I take up residence on the earthly plane; like you I regain the struggles of the mortal coil; and like you I get assurances that the forces of Purgatory will not interfere with that mortal existence."

This was a nightmare that I hadn't seen coming. I needed his share of the business if I was going to have a shot at getting out. But getting it would require me to do the impossible. Worse, even if I succeeded, I'd be doing the unthinkable and unleashing this horror of a soul on the world, and likely sentencing myself to a return to this horrid place.

Under the circumstances, I did the only thing I could, I looked him square in the eye and conceded everything he thought gave him the advantage.

"So, aside from the fact that I can't pay you what the business is worth, and I need your share of the business if I'm going to have any chance at even getting a shot at getting out of here, why on earth would I help you get back to the earthly plane?"

He held my gaze without flinch or tell. Only the time that passed before he spoke let on that he'd been caught off guard by my candor. It seems I'd unwittingly called his bluff.

After a while, he blinked a couple of times, apparently affirming his decision, then slouched back into the uncomfortable chair. When he finally spoke, he didn't stutter, stammer or look away.

"There's a reason Reapers never move each other on, why we practice our craft religiously, why we stay here so long. There are versions of Hell that make the things I've done and the worst deeds I've even contemplated seem almost pedestrian. It's been said that some people – like Hitler and priest-pedophiles - deserve a special place in Hell. While I've not seen the Hell I'm headed to first-hand, I've no doubt that it is indeed special.

"If I thought I could, I'd probably stay here for all eternity. But I can't - none of us can. Whether it's because of the boss, politics, some subconscious desire, or just bad luck – eventually even reapers move on. So, I'm going to that special Hell of mine, … unless I can change who and what I am enough to change my fate."

It was my turn to be shocked. The candor and content he conveyed caught me off guard, but it didn't render me stupid. I'd already seen so much that I'd never be able to unsee. I didn't want to know what he'd seen, but I had to know if he was desperate enough to try and change or just scared and looking for a way out.

The problem was that like him, I was desperate and out of options. I couldn't wait to see if he was genuine, and I didn't have anything more to dangle in front of him as an incentive. He'd already raised my raise, so I went all in and called.

I managed to combine venom, ridicule, and challenge in one or two not particularly well thought out sentences; exactly what you don't do if you hope to walk away from a conversation with a Reaper. He'd either move me on and go about his business without a partner, or cop to his real plan out of desperation.

"And what's your plan? How long do you think you can hide out on the earthly plane and avoid your comeuppance? Or is it that you've got an itch for another lifetime of maiming and killing."

When I was done ranting, I locked eyes with him. I saw everything and nothing. A dryness of the lips that, try as he did, couldn't be licked away, a slight slouch of the shoulders that marred his usually perfect posture, an unevenness in his usually steady breathing. And then I saw it; the path of the fearful thing that he was, flowed from the fear that he held.

He looked away briefly, exposed but not shamed, then

returned my stare with something I'd not thought possible of him, need.

"No. Here, by nature, deed, and the fact that this firearm continues to function, I am a Reaper. I've never felt compassion, love, empathy, or a host of other feelings that you take for granted. They are as foreign to me as their absence is an asset in this desolate place. I would return to the earthly plane in the hope of changing my destiny; if I cannot come to feel such things, I hope to at least learn to understand and value them."

He seemed earnest and his words heartfelt. Had I not seen and heard of his prior deeds I might have been touched. The fact that he was the one who had brought me to this place didn't help him.

"So, what? Your plan is to wander the earth, maybe do a carrot avocado cleanse, take a retreat, and spend some time in a monastery not talking in the hope that you'll catch some newfound feelings along the way?"

I'd tapped into an anger that I hadn't realized I was holding. The heat of it birthed an epiphany that pulled me up short.

It wasn't that I'd suddenly come to like or believe him, but I had to ask, "Aren't you worried about making an enemy of The General Counsel if you help me? As I understand things, The General Counsel has got a lot of pull here and elsewhere."

For the first time since I'd met him, and probably the first time in a long time, he smiled. It was an ugly, half measure of a thing – his lip curled more than raised, and rather than a slight closing of the eyes as his cheeks raised, he squinted as though his sharp eyes had faltered and he was struggling to see something. It looked almost painful. Mercifully, for both of us, his "smile" was fleeting. He blinked a couple of times, marking its passing, then turned those dead eyes on me.

"No. There's no love lost between me or any Reaper and demons, particularly The General Counsel. After all, it's demons that run the Hells we Reapers are headed to."

His answer suggested our deal brought long and severe consequences if I failed and he stayed.

I dialed back my anger and reconsidered his request. "And how exactly would this you returning to the earthly plane thing work anyway?"

If he was taken aback by my sudden shift and interest it didn't show. He answered with the simplicity of one explaining the mundane to a child.

"The body to which you seek return is now unoccupied by a soul. There are many others like it, bodies that the soul vacates because of injury, neglect, abuse, or plain old disuse. You can find one at almost any hospital, drug den, or nursing home. With state authorization, all that's required is for me to find a vacant body or a soul that has vacated or is willing to forfeit the rights to its body."

I was thinking while he was talking, and by the time he finished I had paper and pencil in hand and was writing at a fevered pace. To his credit, when he finished answering my question, he didn't ask what I was doing, or even lean forward to steal a look. He just stopped. He stopped talking, he stopped moving, he even stopped looking back and forth between me and the door.

Two pencils and some thirteen pages later I presented him with a rough draft of two agreements.

The first agreement was an amendment to our partnership agreement. It required that I provide my best efforts, to secure his return to the earthly plane if and when I appeared before the Special Masters, in exchange for his agreement not to sell, trade, or otherwise dispose of his partnership interest. It also provided for the transfer of his interest in the partnership to me should he leave Purgatory for any appreciable time. Lastly, it provided me full and immediate control over any and all office staff.

The second and far more substantial agreement contained provisions governing his release. I included every safeguard I could think of. There were provisions related to slavery, indentured servitude, homicides and other felonies, prohibitions against war crimes, breaches of the Geneva Convention, and references to both the International Covenant of Civil and Political Rights and the Universal Declaration of Human Rights. In addition to being contingent on my release, his release was subject to compliance with, and immediately self-terminating upon contravention of, any or all provisions that I, in my sole and unfettered discretion might subsequently deem necessary or appropriate to add.

Perhaps most important, his time on the earthly plane was limited. His possession and presence terminated at the end of the normal life in being of the body he was possessing or on my death on the earthly plane, whichever came first.

After I finished, I read it, reread it twice, then slid it toward him for review. He answered quickly and without even bothering to pick it up. I figured he wasn't going to bother reading it because he either realized my terms were non-negotiable or he was so desperate that he'd agree to whatever I proposed. It wasn't till he suggested I change, "death" to "death or incapacity" that I realized he'd been reading the document upside down as I was writing.

"Give the final draft to May, I'll sign it and she'll make three copies - one for me, one for you, and one for a third party of your choice."

I incorporated his suggestion then gave him the bad news. He was the missing piece of my case - a witness, and not just any witness. A witness with firsthand knowledge, who's credibility came from his position. I told more than asked him. "I'm probably going to need to call you as a witness. Is that a problem?"

"If you're going to call me as a witness it will have to look spontaneous. If you tell The General Counsel that you're going to call me beforehand, I can all but guarantee that I'll be somewhere outside the court's jurisdiction when you need me, at least until I can't be of any use to you.

"Also, if you get me on the stand, I will be obliged to answer whatever questions you ask. But there are some questions that you shouldn't ask since I, like any other, Reaper would be obliged to move you on then and there rather than let the answer be spoken in open court."

It reminded me of a time when, during trial, a junior lawyer for the opposition asked my expert-witness a question without knowing the answer. It took a couple of seconds for the junior lawyer to realize his mistake, at ten seconds he was trying to withdraw his question, and within thirty seconds my expert had scuttled the opposition's entire case.

The Gunfighter was warning me. Purgatory had its

own version of the lawyer's rule, that you never ask questions that you don't know or want to know the answer to. And, like all things in Purgatory, the consequences for violating the rule were dire.

"Rather than me finding out the hard way what these questions are, how about you tell me what questions, or at least topics I should avoid?"

He stared at me in silence for an unnerving moment of reflection before answering.

"You don't want to ask me any questions about who I work for, what all I do, how I'm able to do what I do, or that would lead me to implicate anyone else in any way. Stick to the facts pertaining to our interaction, avoid questions about my employer's rules or motives, and stay away from existential issues, like what happens to those who leave voluntarily."

"So, nothing related to your normal practices or patterns, prior wrong doings, or agency policy."

I was going to have to fight with one hand tied behind my back. It wasn't fair, but it was par for Purgatory.

In keeping with the dark sense of humor I'd developed in Purgatory I laughed and said half out loud, "At least if I got moved on in the middle of direct examination the court would likely rule in my favor."

"No, they'd find your appeal moot and dismiss your case on the spot."

He said it without hesitation or irony - as if he'd seen the issue resolved first-hand, more than once.

So much for humor in Purgatory.

As he rose to leave, he threw back the poncho he

wore that had covered his lap and the .44 which he'd been pointing at me the whole time.

For a moment I couldn't decide which was more striking, that he'd contemplated using the gun, that he'd pulled it out and not used it, or that he'd bothered to pull the gun out in advance of deciding to use it – we both knew that even with all the practicing I'd been doing, he was still so fast that even if he told me he was going to draw his gun and took his time doing so, there was nothing I could do to stop him.

It seems he mistook my contemplations for umbrage. Perhaps by way of apology, perhaps as a first step toward change, he holstered the .44 and explained.

"This, or something like it, is how partnerships usually get dissolved around here."

᪣

Fear best be a familiar friend.

DE TENEBRA

CHAPTER 29

IN TERROREM CLAUSE

(A Clause Used To Frighten)

IT WAS A long and draining day. I struggled with even the mundane task of preparing the final draft of our agreement for signatures. Just after I'd given the draft a final proof-read, May showed up at my door.

I didn't risk reminding her of the morning's wardrobe malfunction by commenting on her change of outfit. Her once backward skirt had been replaced with a long, emerald-green coat, worn with the collar up. Shiny black boots peered out from under the hem of her coat and subtly transitioned to tight black pants. An untucked black satin shirt was cinched around her tiny waist by a thick belt that matched the emerald green of her coat. With her hair spiked up on top and worn close on the sides, she looked like one of Cruella DeVille's siblings who'd gone shopping in the Emerald City of Oz.

As had become my habit, I stood in greeting before

inviting her in with a wave and a "please." She walked in gracefully and, after inspecting the chair, seated herself and assumed a lady-like position – legs crossed with her wrist resting atop her knees.

"Here get contract."

Perhaps she was still smarting from this morning, perhaps she realized that the contract she was picking up meant that she was not likely going to be part of the business we'd started, or perhaps I was just a bit paranoid. It was hard to tell given her usual verbal elides, but I got the distinct impression that she was being more curt than usual.

I was too worn to worry about it and, knowing that training awaited my return to the inn, more than a little motivated to move things along. I slid two contracts across the desk to her.

She looked from one document to the other, then back to me quizzically so I explained.

"These are both final versions that have been signed by me. The contracts are identical but for one provision." After a nod toward the one on her left, "that version includes a provision that allows you, in your sole discretion, to elect to continue as this firm's bookkeeper for as long as you, again in your sole discretion, see fit. It also provides that, should you elect to continue as the firm's bookkeeper, whatever salary you and the majority owner of the firm agree upon shall be paid to you personally and not subject to any prior, and now subservient, agreements with the signatories to the contract, or any successor(s) in interest."

Her reaction caught me wholly off-guard. I thought

she'd be happy with this proposition; figured there'd be a pointy toothed smile and a thank-you, maybe some hand clapping, at most a little bouncing around in her seat. Instead, she pulled out one of her hankies, a white one with emerald-green embroidery around the edges, then alternated between dabbing furiously at her eyes and flashing me her pointy toothed smile. She was genuinely touched.

After a few attempts at talking caught in her throat, she waved the emerald green trimmed hanky furiously in surrender of both gratitude and composure, then scooped up the documents and rushed out.

She moved so fast, she was barely still within earshot when I yelled after her, "you'll need to destroy one and have The Gunfighter put his mark on the other."

I sat back in my chair more than a little self-satisfied. I'd gotten the better of May not once, but twice, on the same day!

With spirits buoyed by the exchange, I breezed through my remaining tasks, grabbed a few books and documents, closed up shop, and headed back to the inn. Even before the market incident, I was in the habit of taking a different route home each time I left the office. These walks which had only been intended to help me get a better lay of the land also allowed me to clear and focus my mind. Tonight I took a meandering, circuitous route through back streets and alleys, into neighborhoods that I'd not seen before.

Perhaps not unexpectedly, my thoughts were drawn to my upcoming meeting with The General Counsel and how it could affect my getting out of Purgatory. In the relative coolness of the darkening I saw and embraced my anxiety for the fear that it was.

I was afraid of The General Counsel, afraid of what he could do, afraid of what he'd say, afraid of what would happen if things went wrong. Rather than fixate on these fears I tried to look at them dispassionately. Was I really afraid that I wouldn't get out? That maybe I belonged here? That I didn't deserve what I was after? Whatever I feared was just that - fear - not reason, not justice, and certainly not destiny. I had to see it for what it was, so it wouldn't guide, control, or compromise me.

I arrived at the inn just as One Finger put the broom away. He clapped his hands together a few times then slapped imaginary soot off his already all too clean pants as he approached. By way of greeting, he inclined his head toward my room.

"We're gonna work on sumptin a lil differn ta nigh. Best ya urry up wit yer tings so's we can get started."

Now curious and a little more invigorated after my walk, I didn't dally. I took the stairs two at a time and pushed the door open without breaking my nice and balanced stride.

I didn't notice the items laid out on my bed until after I'd put my books and papers on the desk.

The thing that first caught my eye was the suit. It was medium blue with crossing lighter blue and faint gold lines that created a subtle plaid pattern. It was accompanied by a light blue shirt, blue and yellow silk tie and matching pocket square, brown belt, and brown leather shoes. The pièce de résistance, the thing that completed the ensemble and afforded it an air of authority was a relatively nondescript brown briefcase. It wasn't the nicest suit I'd ever seen; in fact it probably wouldn't have stood out for the better or worse in my, "there's never casual Friday at the FRAT," suit rotation. But here, in Purgatory, it was high fashion.

I was fighting a losing battle with the temptation to try the suit on, and when I heard a burly voice yell from downstairs, "Well, puter on sos we can ave a look-see!" I succumbed.

I'd been working, training, and even sleeping in the only clothes I had for so long that it wasn't until I peeled them off that I remembered how uncomfortable they were. About the only good things I could say about the clothes was that the slippery shoes had forced me to improve my balance, and the button up fly that had led to my fall-rolling into the pants, hadn't proved to be an issue since I'd never had to take the pants off, to go to the bathroom or otherwise.

I stripped naked and walked around the room a few times - 'airing things out' if you will. Right about the time my feet let go of the shape of the ill-fitting shoes, I heard a mockingly impatient "Well!" bellow from below.

For the briefest moment I was tempted to walk downstairs *al fresco*. But a glance at my new outfit banished the thought. I started with the shirt and by the time I'd buttoned the cuffs I'd fallen into my old routine: Socks first - yes honest to goodness socks, then pants - belt taut but not tight, and lastly the tie – knotted with a classic double Windsor, of course. The pocket square, gold with blue dots needed little attention – it was already in pocket and folded in a four-point Cagney; not lawyer conservative, but suit-appropriate enough to work.

I saved the shoes for last. Not because they were the

best shoes I'd ever had; they were just well-worn mid brown, no brogue, lace-up oxfords, that had been cleaned and polished. But, by virtue of the fact that they actually fit, they were a monumental improvement over what I'd been wearing. Before putting them on I undid the casual left-to-right, right-to-left lace-up job, and laced them up properly. Once the laces formed parallel bars going up the shoe, I finished with an under-looping knot.

I felt like I did when, fresh out of law school, I first started work at one of the big firms. Having put myself through school, money was tight. I spent my first two weeks on the job making do with conservative looking thrift-shop suits that I'd had re-tailored for job interviews. A big part of my first paycheck was spent on the trappings of the profession, more fashionable suits, monogramed shirts, silk ties, newer versions of the classic oxford, a nice watch, even an expensive pen. This wasn't a splurge, or mere investment in my career. It's about giving people, and not just white people, every opportunity to question their assumption that you're not all that you are. A Blackman in a law firm is assumed to be support staff – the guy that works in reproduction, or maybe an investigator; in medicine, without the white coat and stethoscope you're an orderly or nurse, rather than the doctor. Give that man a broom or package that looks like it needs delivering and he can go almost anywhere; but he'll need a suit or other uniform that says money, power, or both to be seen as more than the help.

While I couldn't pass for more than a new or "B-grade" lawyer on the earthly plane, I was looking like money by Purgatory's standards.

It wasn't until I'd headed out the door and gone halfway down the stairs to the inn's main room that I realized my outfit was wholly at odds with the type of physical training we usually did. Before I had the chance to over-think the matter One Finger called out.

"Well, tis bout time. Ya'd tink I was waitin on May erself. Truth be told, I was beginin ta tink she put some sorta slow spell on dem drapes fore she left em for ya?"

"Ah, so I have May to thank for this sartorial splendor?"

"Aye, dat ya do. Didn't leave ya no bill eider. Fact is, she made quite a fuss about it-tall. Claimed you wuz tryin ta pull a fast one and saddle er wit some implied obligation."

I doubt she did a good job selling that line to him, as he was only making a token effort to sell it to me. I let it go, mostly. "Yeah, I reckon she showed me alright."

I tried to move back to the topic at hand. "Well, now that I've taken a turn on the runway, I'll go back and change into something more appropriate for our training." He waved me off with a meaty paw.

"Non-sense. Ere we do full service, all-purpose training. Ta nite yer gone learn two tings. First well cover da difference tween da crappy Forus we usually drink, and one a da more expensive but only a bit less crappy brands a Forus. Second, we'll see ow ya andle yer liquor wile talkin - by drinkin and talkin."

In short order we'd settled into a nice rhythm of drinking and talking, mostly drinking. We didn't talk about my case, our businesses, or the various characters we knew. We did the kind of drinking poor people, oppressed people, my people, often do to set aside their concerns, blunt fears, and accept the bad possibilities. Somewhere along the line you may swap stories, tell a few jokes, maybe share a dry laugh or two, but really, mostly, you just drink. You drink in the hope that it will take your mind off the bad times that may come; you drink because thinking about the bad times and terrible things is a double-edged sword. Too much thought leads to paralysis; too little thought leaves you unprepared. You drink because misery loves company much more than sobriety.

Like an old friend of mine once said, 'you won't find the answer to your troubles in a bottle, but with some luck and effort you may forget the question.'

Though it went well into the darkening - through the less crappy stuff and well into the crappy stuff - it ended far too soon.

I woke with the light, more rested and refreshed than I had a right to be. It was only when I glanced across the room at my new suit, which I'd refused to sleep in and had draped nicely over the chair, that I thought about what the day before me held.

My plan was to peruse the books I'd brought home, possibly hit up the Bureaucrat for a few more books, or even better, information about the Special Masters, before making my way over to The General Counsel's office.

Thus far none of the books I'd read said anything about the procedures or rules of court that govern appearances before a group of Special Masters. I didn't have a clue who the Special Masters were, who was going to go first, or whether I'd be allowed to introduce new evidence. I didn't even know if today's meeting with The General Counsel was a required meet-and-confer type thing, something along the lines of a professional courtesy, or just your basic extortion meeting.

It was a lawyer's nightmare … pretty much what you'd expect in Purgatory.

I got dressed in my nice new-to-me suit and made my way down to the inn's lobby, fairly sure that my plan was DOA.

There, sitting in one of the inn's less uncomfortable chairs, talking to One Finger with all the familiarity of a drunk speaking to whoever's nearest them at last call, was The Fixer. He rushed toward me and started talking at me even before he would have been within earshot if he weren't almost yelling.

"Come on, come on. What's taken you so long, you're on the verge of being late when you're supposed to show up early!"

Then, as though he'd just looked at me for the first time, "Nice suit. But we've really gotta get a move on. You don't want to start by getting on The General Counsel's other bad side."

"I thought The General Counsel wanted to meet with me today, not this morning?"

"Yeah, today. And when you're dealin with The General Counsel 'today' means you get there just before the office opens and wait to seen."

One Finger, who up until now had been less than discreetly listening in under the guise of cleaning an already spotless table, dropped all pretext and joined in the conversation.

"So, da General Counsel makes everybody fight uphill from the start eh. Well, good on em."

Not fighting uphill, along with creating chaos in combat were two of One Finger's favorite topics, and to hear him tell it, "Two sides a da same coin." I cut him off before he went too far down that familiar road.

"I'll be taking a different tact."

"Eye, no use fightin more upill dan ya needs ta. Er ya gon make em wait fer ya? Or maybe even come ta ya?"

I feigned offense and took-on a mock formalness.

"Heavens no good sir. That would be … rude. I shall have my valet announce my forthcoming presence and be most grievously insulted if the office is not prepared to receive me upon my arrival."

As usual The Fixer was quick on the uptake.

"Oh, so now I'm your "valet" am I. Fine, as long as it pays. But since we all know The General Counsel won't give two shakes about you being insulted, I'm guessing this charade is for the underlings."

"Exactly. You'll have to make it clear to them that I'm someone important that's enroute for a meeting with The General Counsel but be careful not to make enough of an impression to prompt them to actually check with The General Counsel about it.

""When I get there, I'll raise a fuss and threaten to storm out. Any smart underling will try to cover their asses by keeping me happy until The General Counsel will see me."

One Finger nodded approvingly. "Aye. If'in it werks da General Counsel will tink ya at least got anuff pull n influence ta ave da staff git ya ta da top a da list."

The Fixer chimed in, "and if it doesn't work, we'll end

up sitting there most of the day, till they bother to get to you."

"Which we would likely end up doing anyway, and for which you will receive fair compensation." I added.

The prospect of a day's pay, mostly for doing nothing swung his mood in my favor. He changed his tune without missing a beat.

"Fair enough. Good plan. I'm in." Then, after a graceless and mocking bow that was notable only for the number of hand circles made, he said, "I shall take my leave of you, ma Lordship."

∽

Fear is the avalanche wrought by the
snowflake of oppression.

DE TENEBRA

CHAPTER 30

NUDUM PACTUM

(Naked Promise)

ONE FINGER WENT back about his cleaning as soon as The Fixer left, and I went over everything I had. Unfortunately, I found absolutely nothing that would help me prepare for my meeting with The General Counsel or the Special Masters. It was a necessary waste of time, but a waste of time, nonetheless. Since I needed to make up for my lost time, I decided to forgo the stop at my office and just go by The Bureaucrat's office to swap out the books I had.

The Bureaucrat wasn't there so I left the two books I'd borrowed last time on his desk and took two others. They didn't look particularly promising, but I'd already gone through his more helpful sounding tittles. At this point I was just hoping to luck up on some useful law. I stuck the books in my brief case, latched it closed, and headed for The General Counsel's office, resigned to the fact that I was going to have to and try to *finesse* The General Counsel into giving me the information I needed.

Though The Fixer hadn't bothered to say where The General Counsel's office was, I had a pretty good idea. I headed to the fifth floor of the main building, toward the largest door.

I went with The Gunfighter's public housing strategy, minus all the shooting and maiming. I didn't break stride or stop to focus. I pushed the double doors open and entered a bit more forcefully and faster than either possible or appropriate. I ignored the half dozen or so people who had startled and turned to look at me from the seats and benches lining the outer office's walls. Bypassing the few folks in line, I casually walked up to the desk.

Before the receptionist, a purse-lipped, bouffant-wearing woman, could bother to stop doing whatever she was doing and look up to ask what I wanted, I rapped sharply on her desk. Then perhaps a bit too authoritatively said, "Please tell The General Counsel that I am here for our meeting."

Apparently, this wasn't her first rodeo. She didn't even deign to look up when she asked, "And whom, exactly are you?"

The Fixer was at my side immediately. He snatched off a worn and tattered hat that I'm sure he hadn't been wearing before, and with head hung low, shoulders hunched, and eyes cast down, responded with a single word. "Sir."

Between his fidgeting, twisting his newly found head gear, and furtive glances back and forth between me and the ground, he looked for all the world like a puppy that had peed on the floor and was expecting punishment. Basically, like a good minion.

Where I'd shown her the rudeness of the privileged, his act conveyed the threat of power. I locked eyes with her, never even bothering to look toward The Fixer as I addressed him.

"Did you not announce my arrival?"

He rushed to answer, as though I might not give him a chance to do so before inflicting some dire punishment.

"Aye sir, that I did. Was nearly the first in line and spoke to the very same Missus here."

After shooting a scared and vaguely threatening glance at the receptionist, he cast his eyes down and went back to fidgeting with his prop hat.

I drew my lips tight, into the type of smile generally associated with sales managers, psychopaths, and the *Grinch*. "Surely madam, you have informed The General Counsel of my pending arrival?"

She knew that, even if I was as powerful as I pretended to be, I couldn't touch her directly. But she'd been around long enough to know that if I was someone important, there'd be consequences for her failure to announce me. As I'd hoped, she was smart enough to avoid taking needless chances.

Rather than answer my question, she pursed her lips into a simile of a smile and rose quickly from her seat.

"It's been such a busy morning. Let me make sure the General Counsel is ready to receive you. If you'll just have a seat, I'll be right back."

I stopped her with the raise of an eyebrow and cursory glance around the room. "Have a seat? Out here? Me? Oh, I think not.

"Please inform The General Counsel that I was here and will be happy to host our meeting at my offices at some other time. Oh, and be sure to provide my assurances that, if properly announced, The General Counsel will not be kept waiting."

On cue, The Fixer reached down and picked up my briefcase, as though our departure was imminent. Since I didn't know where else to take this charade it's a good thing it didn't go any further.

"No, no good sir," said the receptionist. "I didn't mean to suggest that you wait here. The executive conference suite has been prepared for you. This way if you please."

With The Fixer right behind me, I followed her through a side door into a room that was at least as large as the reception area. A window, with actual glass in a stone surround, made up the better part of one wall, while the other three walls were paneled with a well-oiled burl wood. Plush rugs were situated to create different functional areas in the large space. We walked past a highly polished wooden conference table that could easily accommodate ten persons, over to a group of couches that made up a seating area, between a fireplace and bar.

I seated myself without asking or waiting for an invite. The couch, the first comfortable thing I'd experienced in Purgatory, was upholstered in real, honest to goodness leather. It was so comfortable that I struggled to look put upon when the receptionist excused herself to "go see what's holding The General Counsel up."

As soon as she left The Fixer started looking about, inspecting the room. He ran his hand across the table then checked his fingers for soot, sat down on the couch and bounced a couple of times only to be distracted by an errant thread, then got up and, after wiping away a smudge, stared out the window for way too long. Eventually, he summed it all up with a high-pitched whistle, snicker, and shake of his head.

The receptionist returned in short order, but by then The Fixer was standing dutifully behind me, hat in hand, back in the role of bootlicking minion.

She was still playing it safe; more polite than she would have been if she'd previously announced my arrival to The General Counsel, and less curt than she would have been if she'd come clean to The General Counsel and found that there was no need to announce me.

"The General Counsel will be here shortly." And, before I could feign offense at further delay, she appeased. "May I offer you a drink in the meantime? She won't be long at all."

The "she" part caught me off-guard. I had no idea what a female demon would be like, and my mind raced to figure out what, if any, role this would or could play in our negotiations. By the time I figured out that it really didn't matter since I knew nothing about demons, male or female, the receptionist had poured two fingers worth of a dark liquid in a crystal glass, placed it on the nearest coffee table, and excused herself.

After what I'd been through just to get here, I certainly wasn't above a late morning Forus. Besides, I'd trained for this very eventuality with One-Finger. I reached for the glass but before I picked it up I realized there wasn't a spittoon to be found in the room. The Fixer, seeing that I was confused but not understanding why, stepped forward to my side.

"What, you think it might be drugged?" He picked up the glass, brought it to his nose, and took a sniff. But for the way he jerked his head back, I'd have thought his sniffing the drink the olfactory equivalent of raising the hood when your car doesn't start – an act that's strictly for show.

Before I could ask if it was indeed drugged, he said, "It's scotch!" then took a well measured and long savored sip. His eyes rolled back, and a brief tremor passed over his body – almost as though he had indeed been drugged – but when he opened his eyes he smacked his lips and smiled. "Islay style, nice and smoky, aged at least sixteen years." Then he stiffened, handed the glass back, and added a "sir" before quickly stepping behind me and back into character.

I turned to see that it was the entry of The General Counsel that had caused The Fixer to snap back into character.

Rather than the horn headed, boisterous, and buxom demon caricature that I'd conjured, she was lean, almost androgenous. Coarse, jet-black hair was pulled back tight, in conjunction with heavily lined eyes and fire engine red lipstick, it gave the impression that she was of vaguely Eurasian ancestry.

She wore black thigh high leather boots. Muscular thighs provided a transition from the boots to a black leather micro skirt that barely covered the crease of her tight, well-defined butt. The black mono chromatic theme was broken by a red silk lace camisole, so sheer and low cut that it highlighted her otherwise easily overlooked breasts. But for its being ensconced in the black full-length coat that sat square on her broad shoulders, the camisole would have left little to the imagination. All and all, the look suggested a rich and full sexuality that needed minimal decanting to reach full bloom. Women would be drawn to her like flies and men who took notice would be well rewarded.

"If it's a day under twenty years old someone's going to lose a hand, … for starters."

Caught off-guard by her all too soon entrance, I parried. "One can never be too careful, bad liquor may be the worst drug there is around here."

"No, it's not. But I do appreciate your taking the precaution of bringing a taster. In fact, I'm not sure which to give you more credit for, having someone who is actually willing to serve as your taster, or finagling your way into the first open spot on my schedule. I'd give you extra credit for weaseling your way into the executive conference suite here, but this is where I usually do this kind of business anyway."

She'd leveled the playing field, but in doing so opened the door. With nothing to lose, I jumped in head rather than feet first.

"And exactly what kind of business are we doing here anyway? Are you going to demand some sort of payment just for the privilege of having me kick your ass in court?"

She made a bee line for the bar, poured herself a scotch, and after a couple of swirls and a "must we bandy-about" sigh, got down to business.

"If I had any reason to think you could make me look bad, let alone win, I'd have had you moved on long ago. And yes, if you insist on duking it out in the courtroom across the hall, it will cost you the little bit of cash you have, your share of your firm, and pretty much everything else you own."

Then she paused to look me up and down with an appraising eye, "Except the suit you're wearing. That you can keep; call it professional courtesy, an appreciation of good taste or just pragmatism on my part.

"Since we both know that all you have couldn't even buy the bottle of scotch that your man over there is still savoring, you'll also have to agree to work for me if you lose. Then, after you lose, I will buy out The Gunfighter's larger ownership percentage and both you and your little firm will be mine to do with as I please.

"So, rather than go down that long, arduous, and oh-so-predictable route, what say we cut to the chase and talk about why you're really here."

In response to my "And why is that?" silence, she spread her hands in reference to the room and all its trappings and chortled, "You're here so I can offer you a job," then upended the drink she'd poured herself and wiped her mouth with the back of her hand.

Her lipstick didn't even smear.

"You're going to work for me. Whether you have your day in court first, only goes to the compensation you will receive."

When she again looked to me for a response, I swirled the scotch around in the glass a few times then put it down without drinking or saying anything.

"Ah, you doubt me. You're thinking, you're a good lawyer and with a little more of the same luck and chutzpah that got you here you might prevail.

"Fair enough. If you weren't a good lawyer, I wouldn't be offering you a job. As for luck, well trust me, that's overrated. And The Gunfighter? Well, he isn't going to risk crossing me for the sake of his partnership interest. Especially since if you lose, my owning your part of the partnership and you, would drive up the value of his end of the partnership.

"But really, you haven't even heard my offer yet."

She poured herself another drink then settled into the lounge chair opposite me in the sitting area. Setting her drink down, she dove into the details of her offer. And a good offer it was. I thought so, she thought so, and when she threw in, as a sweetener, allowing me and mine "personal access" to her and just about anyone else on her staff, The Fixer's face suggested he thought so too.

In truth, I was almost as surprised by the generosity of her offer as I was at the tingle of interest I felt in response to her offer of personal access. In the end those very things, and of course, the fact that I was in Purgatory where I didn't belong, worked against her.

I picked up my glass and swirled around the scotch - just enough to aerate it.

"Now that is a good and, dare I say, generous offer. In fact, it's a bit too good, and maybe a bit too generous.' Since we both know my case, I suspect you're counting on my slipping up on some rule or technicality, or that I'll get hung up on some other aspect that I don't know about."

"Oh, heaven forbid - literally. There are no unknown rules, no hidden processes, not even secret handshakes where the Special Masters are concerned. At least none that I or any of my people are aware of.

"The only rule seems to be that neither side gets to know anything more about the process than the other. Apparently, they make sure the field is level by making it up as they go along. At this point, there's only one thing I know about the hearing before the Special Masters that you don't, and I'm obliged, though certainly not happy, to share that with you.

"So again, no. I'm not worried about you winning.

"I'm making you this offer because of all the things that I am, the thing that's most often overlooked about me," and she paused to run her hand down her waist and along the outside of her thigh, "is that I'm a damn good manager.

"I'll be honest with you, pride and ego are pretty much my stock and trade, and I do so love the taste of a spirited soul that is willing to bet it all on himself. Normally I'd be looking forward to your crushing defeat. But you strike me as more of a top than a bottom - I don't believe that you'll perform as well for me beaten as you will if you go out on top. Sadly, crushing you isn't in my best interest.

"You see, unlike most idiots, egotists, and lawyers that represent themselves - no exception intended - good managers don't gamble. Under the circumstances, though it is contrary to my ... instincts, it's in both our best interest, that I buy you out."

She smiled when I failed to respond to her very backhanded, and still only marginal compliment.

"Apparently, I need to make it clear just how very much it's in your interest to be part of the team. So here, take this."

She reached into the inner pocket of her jacket and

pulled out a black card with an address handwritten on it in white. It took only an instant to read, but several seconds for what she was suggesting to sink in. And in that time she had changed. Her skirt seemed to ride higher; there was definitely more leg showing. I could feel intense heat coming off her body and see the flush of it in her face. When she first licked, then gnawed at her lower lip, it was like she was both thirsty and starving ... for me.

Stunned, I turned in my seat and looked back at The Fixer to see what he was making of what I was seeing. She lurched forward and was in my face before I could turn all the way back to face her. Now standing, she'd bent at the waist with her back straight, allowing the top of her camisole to fall open more than enough to give me and The Fixer an unobstructed view of her more muscular than busty chest. Long, hard, and dark nipples stood free inside her blouse, promising play and pleasure. She looked The Fixer up and down –briefly lingering on the growing tent in his pants that confirmed that he was indeed seeing what I was seeing – and with her voice licked a whisper into my ear.

"You and your *taste tester* should come by tonight ... to sleep on it. Oh, did I just objectify myself?" She bit her lip in mock guilt, hard enough to cause real pain, that revealed itself in a shudder of pleasure.

When she pulled away, the delicious smell of her lingered behind.

I sat still, clear about her message, confused by my response, and unsure of what to do or say.

Then, as quickly as it came, it passed; what she had become, whatever it was, was gone. Her exasperation was obvious and unfiltered. She stood up straight, adjusted her skirt, then smiled professionally and turned to leave.

Just before she reached the door I stood quickly, almost spilling the drink that I forgot I was still holding. "Wait, what's the one thing?"

She seemed almost pleasantly disappointed - perhaps because I hadn't figured out that she'd already told me and had to ask, perhaps because in spite of everything that had just transpired, I'd remembered to ask.

She looked over her shoulder and spoke without pause or break in her stride. "You are going to work for us voluntarily or you will work for us because you are mine. I'm hoping you'll accept my invitation and come by tonight. If you don't, I expect to have your assets before first light, and your ass after you lose at tomorrow morning's hearing, across the hall." She smiled at her own wit, winked, then closed the door behind her.

Somewhere in the long pause that followed her departure The Fixer came around and took her seat. Rather than apologize, offer wit or insight, he let the moment sit. After a while he raised the half full glass she'd left and said, "L'Chayim."

There are always pluses and minuses. Here the pluses are greatly outnumbered and hard to find. But this being Purgatory, what else would you expect?

DE TENEBRA

CHAPTER 31

IN OMNIA PARATUS

(For All Things Prepared)

BEFORE WE PARTED ways, I asked The Fixer to come by the office a while before the darkening. I needed to pay him and had another task that needed doing.

When I got back to my office, I went through the new books I'd borrowed from The Bureaucrat. I found exactly what The General Counsel said was out there - nothing. Confident as I could be that I knew everything I was going to know, I pulled out a clean sheet of paper and started preparing a document that would transfer all my assets, including my share of the partnership, to The General Counsel and have me work at the firm at the partnership's discretion. It didn't take long to prepare.

When I was done drafting, I left the transfer papers on top of my desk, in about the same place The Fixer had rested his feet, along with a few Horris and instructions for him to deliver it to The General Counsel's office asap.

I gathered my things and left before I could start thinking of my office as a cage.

When I got back to the inn it was silent and deserted. After dropping off my things in my room and changing into my only other outfit, I made my way back downstairs. Though it was about the time we usually started training, One Finger was nowhere in sight.

I started in on some forms without him. These were patterned movements that he and I had developed together. Each could be practiced as a solitary exercise, either slowly, at a normal pace, or together with a partner working in opposite to provide isometric benefits. After only a few times through, I felt more than heard One Finger join in behind me. I pivoted on a forward step to bring us face to face, and we engaged in the pattern as isometric opposites.

I'd learned early on that maximum focus was required just to make One Finger feel my presence because, as he put it, "unlike da rock, I ave ah will ah ma own." But honestly, it wasn't till I did the form with him that I truly realized how much more of an obstacle he was – the stones were easy in comparison.

My focus was good, but after a brief time, I was inordinately fatigued. In short order, One Finger called an end to the physical part of the night's lesson, and we retired to our usual table where cups and a jug of Forus awaited.

He cracked open the jug as soon as we'd seated ourselves. "Tought ya mi na ah been up fer it ta-nigh. Ya did ok in yer meetin wit da Genral Cousel did ya?"

Tradition if not good manners forbade a response before the pour. He started pouring and, as demanded by the same tradition and etiquette, stopped only when I began to speak.

Rather than describe generalities he likely already knew - that my hearing with the Special Masters was tomorrow, or that the terms The General Counsel had required were harsh - I spoke to what troubled and stood out to me. It wasn't that I still had no idea of what was going to happen tomorrow, or even that I might lose. What bothered me was that I'd felt off, and outside of myself around The General Counsel.

Sure, I admired her fashion sense and style, but I was genuinely surprised by the desire she stirred in me. Her allure was an almost tangible thing. I couldn't fault The Fixer for his obvious response to her attentions because I too was affected.

I'd been rendered near speechless today and couldn't help but be worried about how I'd perform tomorrow. I peered into the acidic brown liquid, looking beyond the contents of the cup for answers. When none came, I swirled, swigged, swished, and spit a couple of times, then tried to explain.

He matched me swig for swig and spit for spit, listening without interruption. When I finished, he tossed back the Forus that remained in his glass, held it a beat too long before spitting, then leaned closer, like he wanted to make sure we weren't overheard.

"Even on da earthly plane, ya don git ta be General Counsel by playin fair n talkin strait. Yer dealin wit a demon ere, ya know, da scavengers of Hell and tormentors of da damned. Dey's mean, lyin, n sneaky, on der good days.

"Don't be fooled by wot ya eard n saw. She weren't dair ta argue superior litigation position er use err femnin wilds. Ya were spectin da furst, n ah've no doubt she'd done nuff research ta tink da latter woodn't werk. Na, I spect she were werkin sum serious who-do on ya. Ya know, May ain't da ony one with dem gifts round ere.

"Wit er deep pockets da General Counsel can ire da best. And wit dat kinda mojo on ya, tis a wonder ya didn't sign over ereyting and sign up wit er rite den-n-dare."

He rubbed his large rough hand with, then against the grainy stubble on his head a few times in thought then suggested, "why ount ya bring down dat fancy suit ya gots."

When I came back down with the suit, he draped it over one of the chairs and began rifling through it like the veteran of searches and pat-downs that he was.

He spoke as he searched.

"Magic abounds ere. Folks like May stays warded up. Fact tis, fin ya get nere er an on er friendly side, er wards will bleed over n on ta ya. Taint like yer gonna grow anoder ead, er start see'in n ta some udder dimension, but yer like to be a bit faster, feel a bit more on top ah tins and, fin ya could see it, yer aura'd be lit up like a firecracker.

"But dair be a price ta be paid. Folks dat'er used ta it, like May, sleep like da dead, literally. But newbies, well der like ta just drop in da street."

By this time, he'd gone over the suit a couple of times and found nothing. He stepped back, took a look at the suit anew, then snorted.

"Member da first nigh wen ya came ere, so worn out dat ya fell out on da floor o're dare?"

He pulled out the pocket square and opened it to reveal a stone, no bigger than a kidney bean, resting in the center fold.

"Well, dis be da kinda ting dat could drop ya."

It was a talisman. Tiny script in some unknown language and cryptic symbols covered its entire surface. He brought it close for inspection, while making sure not to touch it.

"I, ya musta dun May a right solid. Sumptin like dis, tailored ta ya as tis, be sure ta run ya more'n dis whole get up a yers. N worn o're yer eart like dat, it be sure ta generate some serious pertection."

"So this, this is why I was near speechless at the meeting today, and why I'm so tired now?"

"Dat yer tired iza sign dat da ward wuz werkin, n werkin ard indeed. I spect fin ya ad'nt kept yer yap closed, da wrong ting woulda come out. N since by not sayin nuttin ya seem ta ave come across as cagey, well ya can tank dis fer dat.

"My advice, specially since ya already ad yer complimentary carry ta bed n tuck in, is dat ya take yer self ta bed fore ya end up spendin da darkenin bent over dis table. Get yerself some rest so's you and dis ere stone er rested n ready fer tamara.

I didn't question his conclusions or argue his suggestion.

When I awoke the next morning, I barely remembered getting up from the table or climbing the stairs, and I had no idea how I actually got into bed. What I did remember was that my hearing before the Special Masters was today.

I gathered the books and papers I'd brought home and put them in the briefcase; more to give it heft and me a sense of purpose than for anything else. But it was only when I started to remove what I now call my "street clothes" that I realized my new suit was nowhere to be found. In a flash of panic, I realized I'd left it downstairs last night.

I all but ran downstairs, and there it was. The pocket square was neatly folded and back in place and, though I couldn't swear to it, the whole suit looked to have been brushed clean. With One Finger nowhere around to not be thanked, I grabbed the garment and headed back upstairs.

Moments later I was dressed and out the door headed to court. It didn't dawn on me till I was well down the street that there was far more foot traffic than I usually encountered on my early morning departures. I'd over-slept! This was the morning rather than early morning crowd, luckily it wasn't the late morning crowd.

I'd hoped to be the first to arrive at court. Now I would barely get there by the start of usual business hours. Since there was no official start time, "technically" speaking I wouldn't be late. But this being Purgatory, I was as sure that if I wasn't there on time, The General Counsel would move to dismiss my case, as I was sure that the Special Masters would grant her motion.

I picked up my pace.

The General Counsel said the hearing would be in the room directly across the hall from her office, another room where you entered through two sets of those treacherous double inward swinging doors. By the time I arrived though several people were gathered in the main lobby, the hall upstairs was mostly empty. I popped my head in The General Counsel's office reception area to see if the workday had started. I was only there long enough to see a few people waiting before the purse-lipped receptionist fixed me with a stink-eyed stare.

I was cutting it close.

I shoved through the first set of inward swinging doors across the hall and in my haste almost ran into a lean old guy who was standing there between the two sets of doors. His slight hunch and casual attire suggested a life of honest labor and made one wonder what he was doing in Purgatory. The apology I was about to make for almost running him over stuck in my throat when I saw that he was not just blind, but blind and without eyeballs. If his eye lids remained there, they'd sunk inward to become part of the black craters that marked where his eyes once had been. I took an almost involuntary step back, and only then saw that that he was carrying a cane like walking stick.

It seemed he'd worked his way into the vestibule between the treacherous doors and, after pushing on the inner door that only opened inwards, had become confused and, at least momentarily, trapped. Once I regained my composure, both by way of apology and to expedite my own entry, I spoke to him.

"I'm sorry, I almost ran into you. But I'm glad to see that I'm not the only one who finds these doors difficult." Then I stepped past him to the court side door, pulled it toward us, and held it open for him. "Here, it's probably easiest for both of us if you go first."

I said it both in deference to Purgatory's first rule and to make clear that there was no implied obligation here. He offered up a wry smile and spoke as he passed into the courtroom.

"Difficult is an understatement. If I had my way, whoever designed these things would be dipped long and deep.

"I'm Lucky. You came along just in time."

I took the hand he'd offered and realized this was the first time I'd shook hands in Purgatory.

Midway through the hand shake his brow furrowed and his nosed pinched, if he'd had eyelids, I suspect he'd have been squinting. After a moment he cocked his head in curiosity, then nodded in understanding.

"That's a nice suit, and the pocket square is a beauty. I'm bettin you're The Lawyer Man," and as he swept his other arm around in reference to the crowd inside, "that we've all come to see try to work your way out of this place?"

The crowd inside told me I was later, or things were starting sooner, than I'd thought. I needed to get to my seat at the plaintiff's table, but I couldn't help but be drawn in by his folksy friendliness.

"Indeed. I'm afraid I am. And you are?"

He smiled and slapped me on the shoulder in a friendly fashion with his free hand as he let go of my hand. "I'm Lucky."

I got the sense that he got a lot of people with that joke; the wry smile was still on his face when he turned and headed down the aisle to find his seat.

With a little humor and a handshake, he'd given me a lot of perspective. I'd gone from seeing an old guy with craters in his face where his eyes should have been, to exchanging pleasantries with someone who seemed to take the stride of this dark world at his own pace. I gazed after him with a renewed sense of purpose then took a moment to really consider the room.

If I was impressed with the executive suite in The General Counsel's office, and I was, I was stunned by this courtroom. It was beautiful. The same stones that served as flooring in most every other building in Purgatory did so here. But now they were polished to a mirror finish, etched, and inlaid with what I later learned was the same wood that was used to make coins.

Where other courtrooms in Purgatory used stones and mismatched chairs for seating, here there was row after row of identical Mission-style benches. Each was rubbed and polished to a deep luster. On the whole it reminded me of the Red Room in the Ninth Circuit Court in San Francisco. Built in 1905 by skilled artisans that were brought in from Italy, the building was designed to represent the affluence and increasing importance of the United States. After surviving both the 1906 and 1989 earthquakes, it was remodeled in 1993 by family members of the original artisans who were again brought over from Italy.

I would have been fixated by the festoons and fixtures, the detailed carvings in the ceiling, and the strange and horrifying sconces that depicted souls on fire and abominations doing abominable things, but the truth is, I stopped looking about the room when I looked past the waist-high balustrade to the dais for the Special Masters.

It wasn't the dais itself, a solid, dark almost burnt sienna, slab of wood that, though polished, absorbed rather than reflected light, that caught my attention. It was Lucky. He was seated on the far right of the dais, wry smile still intact, and seeming for all the world to be looking right at me.

I made my way past a short wooden retaining rail that separated the audience from counsels' tables. All the while I was simultaneously praying that I didn't look as taken aback as I was, thinking that maybe he had taken the wrong seat, and hoping that he wasn't in the wrong seat.

The General Counsel was seated at the table next to me, smug as the cat that ate the canary. Though backed two rows deep by several well dressed minions, she stood out. She wore a dark navy skirt-suit. The fitted, structured blazer complemented her strong frame, and the side slit skirt provided an immodest view of her muscular legs. Golden cuffed platform shoes were accented by gold Tiffany Knot cuff links on a white silk shirt. A thin gold chain was knotted tight at the neck; it ran down between her cleavage to serve as both a mock tie and ode to bondage. Where the suit reeked of power, her hair, was swirled casually into a top bun. Two strips of hair that she left free to fall down evenly on each side of her face suggested whimsey.

She blew me a kiss when she saw me looking in her direction.

Just as I was about to take my seat, I heard someone directly behind me in the audience say,

"Aye, ya must be doin sumptin right. Yer gettin da stink-eye from dem suited lackeys and da kissy-face from da General Counsel."

Though his laugh was cut short by what I suspect was a sharp elbow to the ribs, I immediately recognized the speaker. Distracted as I was when I had entered, I overlooked my favorite hecklers, May and One Finger, were seated on the bench right behind me. At the other end of the bench, with a couple of people between him and them, as though he wasn't really with May and One Finger, sat The Fixer.

He looked like he'd had a long and draining night that had stretched into the morning. His shirt was hastily and only partially tucked in, and while the cuff of one shirt sleeve extended beyond his coat sleeve and over several knuckles, the other was nowhere in sight. His hat, which was pulled down low to hide rest-deprived eyes, was on backward.

Seeing an opportunity, I turned and discreetly asked May, "who is that guy?"

May, grasping the need for discretion, mouthed more than whispered, "Luck."

"I know he calls himself Lucky, but who or what is he, and what's he doing up there?

"Name Luck. Lucky nickname! Chief Special Master."

"Aye, n Blind Luck at dat! Well, least dey din't send is bruder, 'Bad Luck.'"

I was off the bench, but still the 'slow on the uptake' rookie. There'd been far more behind the old man's wry smile than a simple joke. I looked back to the dais and saw him chuckle as though he knew that I finally got the real joke. I couldn't help but smile.

My smile vanished when the door behind him at the opposite end of the dais opened.

In my time in Purgatory I'd befriended a witch, almost been seduced by a demon, partnered up with a Reaper, and seen more souls than I could count dissolve into nothingness. None of that prepared me for the next two people that entered the room.

The first was a woman. I initially thought she was wearing a faded yellow burqa. As her approach brought her into fuller view, I saw that what I'd taken to be a burqa was actually long, thick, dull yellow-blonde hair. This covered her face and front, as well as her head and back. It went down well past her waist, and with her slight, utterly non-curvaceous frame, when she stood still it would be hard to know if she were coming or going.

She moved slowly, making good but clearly unnecessary use of a long smooth walking stick on her way to the opposite end of the dais from Lucky.

In an effort to be more discreet, rather than turn to ask, I leaned back in my chair toward May and tilted an ear in her direction.

"Lachesis, Fate sisters. Say little."

"Don be fooled needer; taint no walkin stick dair wit er. Lease er sister Atropos taint in charge. Ya don wan yer fate in da ands of a mad woman wit scissors."

An "umph" signaled that there'd been another correcting elbow from May.

Once seated, Lachesis laid the stick across the dais, crossed her hands, then sat utterly and completely still. That's when, out of the corner of my eye, I caught a glimpse of something low to the ground as it peeked around the door and, in a blink, retreated.

The minions that had gathered close around The General Counsel, no doubt to go over the emerging cast of characters just as we were doing, had all stopped. They too were staring at the door.

Me, I didn't know what to expect – a gnome or dwarf, perhaps even a small dragon of some sort? Having met Fate and Luck, by my mind it was pretty much anything goes at this point.

With all eyes turned to the front of the room, Lucky leaned forward and appeared to offer a few kind words of encouragement. And I must say, kind and persuasive he seemed to be, especially for a guy with sunken black holes in his face where his eyes should be. Eventually, with continued coaxing, a mop of dark wooly hair appeared at the lower edge of the doorway. The hair was followed by a dark patch of skin and then a single, olive-green eye that opened almost comically wide on seeing the crowd. The latter presaged a retreat back behind the door frame.

Before Lucky could go back to his coaxing, someone somewhere in the crowd barked out a laugh. This was followed by a guffaw then a growing chorus of chuckles.

The click of the hammer on The Gunfighter's .44 being pulled back, silenced the crowd.

I and just about everyone in front of him swiveled around to see The Gunfighter, holding the finger of his right hand on the trigger of the .44, tracking it around the general vicinity of where the laughter came from. He held the index finger of his other hand to his lips, silently shushing the crowd. He simultaneously lowered the .44 and brought his shushing finger up to push his hat back off his head, until the lanyard caught and held it across his back in a casual display of respect for the court. His spurs bounced off the hard, polished stone, clicking and chiming in an uncharacteristically loud announcement of his arrival as he calmly walked down the aisle toward the front.

While all eyes were fixed on The Gunfighter, I stole a look back at the door behind the dais. The first olive-green eye had been joined by a second, then a nose, and a mouth. Finally, the full body of a small boy, looking no more than six years old made its way through the door to get a better look. Curiosity had proved more alluring than Lucky; the boy stared out at The Gunfighter, in rapt wonder.

When I turned back toward The Gunfighter, I saw that he had made his way to the front and was standing next to the bench by The Fixer. With gun still in hand, a momentary glare from his dead eyes was all it took to prompt the two people between May and The Fixer to vacate their seats. The Gunfighter mindlessly spun the .44 around and back into its holster then, with the same hand that had moved on so many souls, beckoned the child forward.

When The Gunfighter took his seat, the child smiled then half-ran, half-skipped over to his seat; making sure to touch everything within reach along the way.

I turned to May and let the dumbstruck look on my face voice my question.

As though it were so obvious as to be unworthy of explanation, May identified the child with a single word.

"Hope."

❧

Why is hope so nerve wracking?

DE TENEBRA

CHAPTER 32

FUMUS BONI IURIS

(Smoke of a Good Right)

THIS WAS THE first child I'd seen - or even heard of - in Purgatory, and from the audiences' reaction I wasn't alone. My experience with May on my first day here had taught me that things are not necessarily as they appear. Still, I struggled to grasp that Hope appeared as, and from every indication actually was, a child. I needed to come to grips with the fact that the child seated at the dais, the third Special Master, was the embodiment of hope. I thought I was having an internal dialogue, but I guess I let slip, "So hope really does spring eternal."

Ever sharp of ear if not timing, One Finger quickly chimed in, "Aye, n tis wit da mind of a child dat e'll be judgin ya. In dis case ya gots ta fight were Ope is."

Before I could ask or May could explain what One Finger meant, Lucky banged his walking stick sharply to get everyone's attention, then he banged it once again, apparently just because he could. Gone was the wry smile, replaced by a perfect, if not practiced look of judicial neutrality.

"Well young fella, you got us all here so you could speak your piece. You should probably get to it about now."

When he was done, all eyes looked to me ... except his.

Following the 'go with what got you there' philosophy, I'd planned to use pretty much the same opening that worked well in my first appearance. Just as before, I stood, approached the balustrade and, after a short pause, smiled.

Unlike before, this didn't get me the higher ground. Lucky leaned back looking for all the world like he was preparing to take a nap. The General Counsel ignored what sounded like snarky commentary from her minions, smirked and mouthed, "tonight." Lachesis continued to sit still as death. Only the child, Hope, seemed interested. He smiled back and waved then, after glancing self-consciously from side to side at the other Special Masters, lowered the errant hand and hid it behind the bench.

It was an inauspicious start but, for lack of a better plan, I continued.

"May it please the court. As an attorney admitted to the bar on the earthly plane, I am representing myself - *pro hac vice*. Several days ago, I made a *special appearance* to contest this court's personal jurisdiction over me and request immediate release and relocation to my former life on the earthly plane."

I expected the court to interrupt me at any time, but was taken aback when The General Counsel cut in.

"Objection. Counsel's claim that this court lacks jurisdiction is untimely and counter to his presence here under the *res ipsa loquitur* presumption."

I didn't wait for permission to respond.

"As I explained in the lower court, it is true that *res ipsa loquitor* or 'the soul knows best' doctrine gives rise to a non-rebuttable presumption that the soul that comes here willingly, belongs here. However, whether a soul has come here willingly is a question of fact that must be determined in order for the non-rebuttable *res ipsa loquitur* presumption to apply."

Thick with boredom and disdain, it sounded more like a man talking in his sleep than a ruling from the bench when Lucky mumbled, "Overruled."

I called it a win and ran with it.

"Because I was brought here under color of state authority, it cannot be said that I in any way chose to be here. Therefore, the *res ipsa loquitur* presumption has no application and the courts here have no jurisdiction over my person."

I glanced toward The General Counsel's table - she was opening and closing her thumb against the four fingers of her hand, and silently mouthing out "blah, blah, blah." Apparently, she was not alone in her assessment of my opening. Hope sighed and put his head down on the desk. I was on the verge of losing the only interested entity I had on the bench.

When The General Counsel rose to give her opening statement, she walked toward my table and ran a finger along its edge in an odd parody of Hope's entrance then, after winking at me, began. In doing so, she discreetly positioned herself so that she stood directly between me and Hope. It was a nicely executed spin on the classic litigation move where you block your opponent's view.

"Your Honors. Counsel uses legalese and artifice in an attempt to blur the distinction between being brought here against one's will and tacitly agreeing to come. He's trying to avoid telling the truth and to suggest that he was "kidnapped" when in fact there's no evidence of any such thing. The fact is, he, like many others, was provided an escort with whom he came here willingly. That Counsel now proffers arguments that distort this truth and abuse your largesse further evidences the appropriateness of his presence here."

She sashayed back to her seat having achieved exactly what she needed. She had cast me as a shyster-lawyer, and put the burden of proof on me.

We were all caught off guard when Hope raised his hand. Though he pouted like a disappointed child, there was nothing childlike in the way he stared through me.

"I thought we were gonna hear a story!"

I'd made a mistake, a big one, and I was on the verge of losing because of it. The three people before me were judges and jury. As any veteran trial lawyer knows, it's not so much the facts and even less so the blackletter law that wins over jurors - it's the story you tell.

Good lawyers weave the facts, the law and their theory of the case into a simple, plausible story; better lawyers make the story compelling; and great ones make it of personal interest to the jurors. I'd done none of that.

I had a story to tell and though it was a good one, I feared that it might not be enough. The General Counsel was a demon and from what I'd just seen she was as adept fighting in the trenches of the courtroom as she likely was in the trenches of Hell. I needed to let go of my fear and, as One Finger had put it, show my mastery of the unusual while advancing the unexpected. My pivot was quick and smooth.

"And a story you shall get young sir. But not just any story. This is a story about a cowboy."

I can't say whether it was the promise of a story, the mention of a cowboy, or some combination of the two, but whatever it was, Hope's eyes lit up anew. Bouncing in his chair with excitement, he pointed an excited finger at The Gunfighter. "Is that him, is that the cowboy?"

I teased to draw him in, neither answering the question, nor looking back at The Gunfighter.

"A cowboy that gets lost in a desolate land where he wanders aimlessly about year after year after year, for eons. Eventually, he gets so desperate to find his way, that the cowboy forces someone to help him."

Hope's disappointment in the cowboy was as obvious as it was tentative. He now saw The Gunfighter, who'd just come to his aid and stopped the crowd from laughing at him, as a flawed hero at best.

I needed and wanted to lighten what could easily become a dark narrative and make it more child friendly. With nothing to lose, I reached for something the likes of which Purgatory probably hadn't heard. I began riffing off *Dr. Seuss*, *Fractured Fairy Tales*, and any other childhood story that came to mind - I advanced the unexpected.

"*The man he brought back seemed ordinary - as ordinary as ordinary can be. As ordinary as you, and as ordinary as me.*

He wasn't too smart, he wasn't too tall, but for a special gift he wouldn't have stood out at all.

"*Like you, he asked himself what his special gift might be.*

Well, with the help of a princess and a Giant, in the land of the lost, he soon came to see."

Hope could barely contain himself. He all but stood on the chair and with both arms, one for each, pointed at One Finger and May. "He's the Giant, isn't he? And the pretty painted lady, is she the princess? Hi Princess."

I suspect it was the best poorly phrased compliment May had ever received. But apparently Hope had gotten ahead of himself. When May waved back at him, he realized everyone could see him, suddenly took shy, and all but dove for cover. Finding none at the front dais, he settled back into his seat and shyly waved back.

"Now, some words will be like birds, about they'll flitter and fly. And some claims will be strained or just an outright lie.

But if you pay close attention, then through it all you'll see. The heroes of this story are really you and me."

I stepped back, a physical move that gave Hope a small reprieve and suggested I might go on this journey without him. Then, I fixed him with my kindest, most beguiling stare.

"Are you ready?"

He couldn't shake his head in agreement fast enough. He was in.

"Good. Because the lady over there," I pointed toward The General Counsel, "she's gonna say the cowboy didn't make the man come back with him."

I leaned in conspiratorially. "I say he did, but for a very good reason.

"What do you say, should we ask the cowboy?"

His eyes widened and he jolted back, then quickly lurched forward and began nodding short, fast, and non-stop.

Avoiding the temptation to approach the bench and ruffle his hair, I turned to Lucky.

"With the court's permission, I call as my first witness, the Reaper known as The Gunfighter."

Chaos broke out at The General Counsel's table. After Lucky banged his walking stick The General Counsel quelled it, silencing her minions with an ugly sneer. She rose from the table, cinched down her jacket, then lit in. "Your Honors, I object! There's been no advance notice of this or any other witness being called."

Again, following the "better to seek forgiveness than ask permission" rule, I didn't wait for Lucky to allow me to respond.

"Your Honors, I can't speak for The General Counsel, but I only learned yesterday that this proceeding was scheduled, so there hasn't been time for notice or sharing witness lists. Moreover, I hadn't the need to call this witness until The General Counsel disputed my recitation of the facts. Also, *on information and belief*, there are no rules that bar the unnoticed presentation of witnesses in a proceeding such as this. Apparently, allowing witnesses is entirely at the court's discretion."

The bang of Lucky's staff on the hard floor preempted any further response from me or The General Counsel.

"Overruled."

On cue, The Gunfighter stood up and began to make his way toward a large wood-hewn chair that was positioned just off the end of the dais, directly across from The General Counsel's table.

While most folks were watching The Gunfighter, Hope sat as low at the table as his pushed-all-the-way-back chair would allow. Only the tips of his fingers were actually visible; his elbows hung low, likely touching his knees, and his chin rested atop his finger tips. But for his eyes – wide, unblinking and tracking the stride of The Gunfighter in rapt fascination - you'd have thought a disembodied, wooly haired head had been placed on the table.

I took my time approaching The Gunfighter, more because I was unsure of whether there was any swearing in or other antecedent to his testifying than any need to let him get situated. Before my lack of familiarity with court procedures became obvious, I stepped between The Gunfighter and where The General Counsel sat, intentionally blocking her view of my witness, and began.

"We came here to Purgatory together did we not?"

"Yes."

His oratory efficiency would have made May proud.

"Please tell the court, in your own words, exactly how it was that I came here from the earthly plane that night.

His response was as direct as his shooting.

"Don't know who else's words I would use, so ok. I detached you, the soul, from your comatose body. You were confused and bewildered, as souls tend to be right after being detached from a still live body like that.

"In order to get you here I had to get us to the transition point between that world and this. These days transition points mostly appear as elevators, but in my time I've seen stairs, trails, rivers, even cliffs. Anyway, since there was a rickety chair with wheels nearby, I sat you in it and off we went. Then, when we got to the elevator, I chucked you in."

"And by "chucked," you mean?'

"I grabbed you by the shoulders, hauled you up out of the chair with wheels and onto your feet, then threw you in the elevator."

Then to no one in particular, but likely for my or Hope's benefit, he added. "You took the throw well; even managed to stay on your feet. For a minute you looked tempted to try and run or fight, but being the thinking type, you opted to try and talk your way out. I suspect you may still be questioning that decision."

Having seen him do what I'd seen him do, I wasn't questioning that earlier decision at all.

"Anyway, as is often the case we arrived right about the time you accepted that what was happening, was happening."

Rather than risk snatching defeat from the jaws of victory, I ended my direct examination right there with a "thank you."

I'd gotten what I needed from The Gunfighter and apparently done so without asking anything that would get me moved on.

After again silencing her minions, The General Counsel stood and addressed the court.

"Your honors, this testimony was, to say the least, unexpected. May I have a few moments to confer with opposing counsel in my office?"

Lucky didn't bother to consult the other Special Masters, he banged his stick once and said to anyone that was paying attention, "We stand adjourned till the afternoon session," then stood and, using it once again as a cane, started tapping his stick against the back wall as he headed toward the rear door.

Having once left some relatively unimportant documents at counsel's table during a court recess only to find opposing counsel perusing them when I returned, out of habit, I quickly gathered my documents into my briefcase and started up the aisle. When I passed The Fixer, he staggered to his feet, silently offering to accompany me. He was in bad shape; unkempt of clothing and unsteady afoot. I said "You can sit this one out" when I got within ear shot. He sighed in relief, and I heard the thunk of him collapsing back into his seat as I passed.

Other than the pursed lipped bouffant-wearing receptionist, the reception area of The General Counsel's office was now empty. Rather than dwell on yesterday's deception, she stood and, after a "this way please," led me back to the executive suite. For a moment I thought she was being professional, then I entered the conference room.

Seated around the large wooden conference table were The General Counsel's minions from court. The General Counsel herself was seated at the head of the table. A small and rickety, hardwood chair that appeared to have been stolen from some kiddy table was the only seat left at the table for me.

In parody of her actions in the courtroom, I walked over to the chair, ran a finger through the layer of soot that had managed to survive the chair's being brought to this room then, without saying a word, seeking permission, or even looking back to acknowledge them, walked to the bar, put my briefcase down, grabbed a glass, poured myself a couple of fingers of scotch, and took a seat there.

"Now that's how it's done! You see why I want this guy? I told you he wouldn't disappoint. Now pay up and get out." As several Horis and even a few DieBus clinked and clattered onto the table The General Counsel turned and said to me, "grab another glass and the bottle. I'll meet you halfway, in the seating area."

She sat across from me on one of the comfortable couches in the lounging area and crossed her legs in that Sharon Stone, *Basic Instinct* way that both leaves little to the imagination yet sparks great interest.

"Shame on you," I said. Then after a pregnant pause, "Taking advantage of your people with a bet like that. The old dirty chair was so far over the top, you should have at least given them odds."

She smiled before responding - both in appreciation of my double entendre and for love of the game.

"And you, coming in here all by your lonesome. Where's your 'valet'? When he left this morning, he was light afoot and riding high."

"Well, apparently he's come crashing down." Then, after I took a sip of scotch, "And speaking of crashing down, is there something you want to say?"

"Yes, as a matter of fact, there is.

"I have to say, I am impressed. Pandering to a child and convincing a psychopath to speak on your behalf; to be honest, if I'd thought you had that kind of moral range, I'd have offered you much more yesterday. But no matter, now's my chance to make amends.

"How does Assistant General Counsel sound. You'll make almost double what I previously offered, making you the highest paid soul on my staff, you'll have your own group of minions to do with as you please, and of course, you can still have any or all of the other … benefits I offered."

I stood up, saddened only at the thought of leaving the scotch behind.

"Thank you. If that's all, I'll be going"

"No, that's not all. That's my offer, and the second one I've made might I add. So now it's your turn. Give me an ask. If you know what you're doing, and you wouldn't be here if you didn't, I won't agree to it. But maybe I can come close enough to make us both happy."

"Ok, a counter you want, a counter you shall have.

"I want out. I want out of Purgatory, away from these games, and away from you in particular. I want to get back to the earthly plane. And I don't want to waste my time 'negotiating' with someone that doesn't have the authority to give me those things."

She took my little outburst well, much better than I expected. After she tossed back the scotch she smiled, whether at my play or just savoring the scotch, I couldn't tell.

"True enough, I can't, and might I add, wouldn't, give you all that. But just so you know, while you've been here drinking my scotch and making unreasonable demands, my staff has been in the hall talking to The Gunfighter. Telling him that he has a choice, work with me when we get back in the courtroom and have an only moderately unpleasant hereafter - perhaps something as simple as licking up the shit of those that have been disemboweled, or continuing to stand against me and having a stick shoved up his ass so he can be passed around like a popsicle, to every lower demon that wants to work their way up the chain by impressing me with the depravity they can stoop to and pain they can inflict on him.

"Besides, even if, and I don't see it as at all likely, but if he is stupid enough to stand with you against me, I will so thoroughly vilify and discredit him that when you lose, and lose you will, you will wear the stink of it around this office for eons.

"So, I suggest you lower your firm little ass back into that chair, and very, very politely ask for something more realistic."

Both scared and intimidated, I was tempted to reconsider.

Luckily, the .44 boomed in the hallway before trepidation got the better of me. There were so many shots, in such rapid succession that it sounded like a single long explosion.

A new strategy hit me, dare I say, like one of the slugs from the .44. I was talking my way out of her office before the gun's echo faded away.

"If I'm not mistaken that was the sound of stupidity, and you're now short a few minions. So, if you'll excuse me, I have to check something at my office before returning to court."

I made sure to pick up my briefcase on the way out.

By the time I got to the hallway there was nothing left to see. Neither The Gunfighter, May, or even the clothes that whoever had been moved on was wearing remained.

Half-way down the hall I ran into One Finger.

"Dit ya see enny a dat? T'was da art a da moment. An, dim be-in da General Counsel's staff, I spect he wuz showin a bit o'restraint. Stood dere n let dim well-dressed fellas talk ard at em e did. N din, only moved on da two dat put ans on em. Din't even draw fer dat, used is bare ans. But wen da udders rushed em, well, he emptied dat weel-gun so fast, dim dat weren't down din't know de udders ad dropped, dat he'd reholstered da gun, or dat he'd drawn is knife.

An o wot a sight is knife tecnique were; is foot werk lone were nuff ta bring tears ta a dancer's eyes."

I'd clearly underestimated One Finger's love of what passed for 'a good dust up' in Purgatory. But, while part of me was appalled by the story he told, my lawyer brain was hearing a self-defense claim and figuring out how to integrate that into my evolving strategy.

No doubt One Finger would have continued to wax poetic about the gruesome act had I not cut him off.

"I need to get some things from my office so I may need you to stall for me. If nothing else, tell the court that I'm on my way back."

He pulled himself up, even beyond his already substantial height.

"Me, speakin n court n playin da barrister? Well fancy dat." Then, more seriously and in deference to our surrounds, "Well, dough I won't charge ya barrister coin, … ."

I cut him off as I went past him. "Two Horis if you have to speak, one if you don't."

I took the stairs two at a time, and all but ran across the courtyard to my office.

The halls of the public housing were mercifully empty, so there was no need to hop-scotch over bodies or wait for the guards to get to my office. Once there, I retrieved and reviewed my copies of the contracts I'd entered into with The Gunfighter and The Fixer. After emptying my briefcase, I shoved the contracts and the copy of *De Tenebra* I'd borrowed into the briefcase and hustled back to court.

I'd made good time. So, when I entered the courtroom, I wasn't surprised to see both that the Special Masters had yet to return, and the courtroom was nowhere near as full as it was before. It was only when I slowed to get back into the moment that I realized the audience was not only smaller, but also markedly different.

Gone were the looky-loos and bystanders – likely scattered by the gunfire or lost to the threat of future violence. In their place, strategically seated around the room, but clearly positioned around The General Counsel's minions, who themselves had doubled in number and now sat four rows deep, was a motely band of no-nonsense looking men and women. They varied as much in physical appearance - being of various heights, sizes, and skin colors - as they did in dress and choice of weapon.

I made my way to counsel's table up front and was relieved to see that my Four Musketeers still occupied the bench behind me. I was about to ask them what was going on when the door that was made to open out toward the hall was forced inward. Seeing the smooth, bone-white skin and emaciated head, I shuddered with the realization that it was the Rider Reaper even before I could make out the two slit openings of his nose, dark sunken eyes, and hollowed cheeks.

I scanned the rest of the room in mouth open shock. My gaze was returned by the dead eyes of more than a dozen reapers. Some were fairly obvious, if not by reputation, by nom de guerre, like Scythe, and Samurai. But there were others too; one man dressed in a leopard skin, another in the all black of a ninja. One guy looked like a simple farmer, who just happened to be carrying a blood-stained axe. There were even a few women; one, almost predictably, appeared to be a 'painted lady,' another, an older woman wearing a loose-fitting floral dress, looked like anybody's favorite aunt. And yeah, there was a guy in a clown suit in their midst.

Toward the back were several other people who clearly weren't Reapers, but certainly wouldn't fall into the category of general public either. A small older gentleman holding a stout stick was accompanied by a lean young man, I figured they were "Stickman" and "Speedy". I assumed the others were also instructors at the school.

The Special Masters had yet to arrive, so I asked my Four Musketeers the obvious question, "what happened?" When no one answered I started working my way through the lineup.

It was like dealing with miscreant children.

I started with The Gunfighter who stood, more petulantly than in defiance. Rather than speak he walked over to the witness chair and took a seat, removing himself from the conversation entirely. When I looked to May she began searching through her handbag, looking for nothing other than a way to avoid eye contact. One Finger looked around the room, either for a distraction or trying to look like he hadn't heard the question. When that didn't work, he said, "Wot? I told ya wot appined in da all din't ah?" Then, as though that explained everything, he bent and began fussing with his shoelaces.

The Fixer went on the offense when I got to him.

"Oh, so I get the short straw! Fine. But let's all be clear, I was right here and didn't have anything to do with whatever may or may not have happened. I'd likely still be catching up on my beauty sleep if it weren't for all the noise."

Then, to the whole and completely silent room, "I ain't no snitch but, since I have a contractual obligation to provide you information, here's what I know.

"By the time I made it through those damned doors to see what the ruckus in the hall was about, other than almost a dozen recently vacated suits on the floor there was nothing to see. Someone" at which point One Finger subtly inclined his head toward May, "then got the idea, perhaps from someone else," at which point The Fixer glanced at One Finger, "that it might be a good idea to tell the other Reapers that one of their own had been set upon at the behest of, or perhaps even by a demon. Either way, here we all are!"

With that, he slapped his palms across themselves quickly twice, threw them up briefly, then folded his arms over his chest, thrice signaling that he was done talking.

I wasn't.

Looking out over the audience I counted over two-dozen potential combatants. This had the look of a long simmering powder keg of a feud. The kind that would make the Hatfield and McCoy spat look like a playground tussle.

I turned back to The Fixer, "and how is it that this apparent détente was so swiftly arrived at?"

The General Counsel, who like everyone else, had overheard the whole exchange, decided to chime in at that moment … not in a good way.

"Arguably, your little band of badly dressed idiots may not be the complete idiots that mine are. When I assured them that I am more than capable of disciplining my staff, if and when I see fit, and reminded them that our boss genuinely frowns upon … interdepartmental squabbles, they stood down."

After a dismissive flip of the wrist she added,

"So, with peace now reigning over the land, his Reaper pals and their groupies decided to stay to watch me kick ass in court - his and yours."

Her snarky commentary was neither entertaining nor politic; it didn't go over well with either of the two groups. Where the minions grumbled and some appeared to clutch at secreted weapons, the Reapers responded strategically. Where they had positioned themselves to repel reinforcements that might enter, they now shifted seats to assume flanking positions and create kill zones.

From the Reapers' perspective, the only thing worse than an organized group trying to move on one of their own, was that the group being led by one of their hereafter tormentors.

Looking at it from that perspective, I realized that The Gunfighter's relocation to the witness chair was at least as much about taking up a better shooting position as distancing himself from my questions.

The path to light is clearest in the dark.

DE TENEBRA

CHAPTER 33

NE EXEAT REPBLICA

(Let Him Not Exit The Republic)

THINGS WERE GOING downhill in a fast and dangerous fashion, and I had no idea how to slow, let alone stop the slide. Given the tension in the room, I think it understandable that I almost dove for cover when Lucky, who's entrance I hadn't noticed, banged his stick on the floor.

Where Lucky got everyone's attention, it was Hope that broke the now almost palpable tension. He came skipping out from the back room after Lucky banged his stick on the floor. When he saw the new composition of the room, he stopped in his tracks and stared, his mouth open in silent joy. The circus hadn't just come to town, it had come to the courtroom just for him.

After a few giddy claps, he tried to get ahold of himself by clasping his hands together. Then he all but bolted back to his chair so the show could begin, only to stand next to it fidgeting - so excited that he forgot to or couldn't sit down.

Lucky banged his stick a second time when Fate entered. Hope snapped out of his spell and took his seat, and the whole room seemed to sit back and exhale.

With The Gunfighter already in the witness chair, Lucky simply turned to The General Counsel. "You have cross." It was a statement, not a question.

She stood easily and answered without a hint of the snarkiness that had brought us to the verge of chaos moments ago. "Yes, thank you."

She approached The Gunfighter like a young man who had lost his virginity the time before – still eager, but now intent on savoring the experience.

"You are a Reaper. Yes?"

"Yes."

"And as a Reaper, how many souls have you moved on?"

"By myself, probably a few hundred."

"And does that include the dozen or so members of my staff that you moved on during the recess?"

"Yup."

"That's an impressive number. But oh, you do have that sidearm. That makes you special, even among Reapers doesn't it?

"It's different."

"Well, all Reapers are 'different' aren't they. Like you, they can move souls on without repercussion, and like you, they don't have to tell the truth all the time. Do they?"

He didn't shift in his seat, look up and to the left, or show any type of tell. Instead, with a mixture of indignation and animosity he simply said, "I don't lie."

"So you say. But let's get back to all the bad things you've done.

"Back when you were mortal, on the earthly plane, did you ever kill a man?"

"Yes."

"A woman?"

"Yes."

"Children?"

"Yes."

"How many? You can guesstimate if you've lost track."

"More than fifty, less than a hundred."

"Fair enough. What about rapes? Ever force yourself on a young cowgirl or cowpoke?"

Then, before he could answer, "And how many people have you robbed and stolen from. Beaten or abused? Threatened or lied to?

"Or are you telling us that you just now stopped lying?"

And again, before he could answer any of that, "perhaps we should stick to what we know to be true and can prove. Are you in business with opposing counsel?"

"Yes."

"And is the business you two have making what you consider decent money?"

"Yes."

"And you do realize don't you that, among other things, opposing counsel seeks to have this court order his departure and return him to the earthly plane do you not?"

"Yes."

"So tell me, why are you providing testimony that might help your partner weasel out of what has been a profitable business for you?"

She took a moment to both relish and emphasize the threat and malice inherent in the question before asking,

"You do know you can be dipped for doing favors like that, don't you."

"T'aint no favor. I came here, he called me as a witness and, having taken the stand, I'm obliged to answer all questions, truthfully."

If she was taken aback by this answer, and she should have been, it didn't show.

"Really, are you saying your partnership agreement requires you to defend counsel, even in this court?"

"The partnership contract, no."

She heard his qualifier, and all too quickly asked, "Is there another contract between you two?"

"Yes. Counsel has agreed to make his best efforts to help me relocate to the earthly plane."

It may have been the perfect answer. He told the truth without telling her everything, and what he said was so shocking that everyone focused on it, rather than what he didn't say.

Even better, now that he'd chummed the waters, she stopped circling about and went in for what she thought was the kill.

"And there you have it your Honors. Counsel is so desperate to avoid being here or moving on to his rightful place that he would do anything. He's used legalese to avoid telling you his truth and induced this wretched soul to lie and say that counsel did not come here willingly. And a lie it clearly is."

She started counting things off on her fingers in a way that reminded me of my first talk with One Finger and I knew she was going all-in.

"His own witness, poorly coached and lacking credibility as he is, has made clear that" and she raised a first finger, "Counsel was on his feet when he entered the transition point." She raised a second finger, "he made no actual attempt to escape, and" raising a third finger, "he willingly stepped out and into Purgatory proper."

She was making me look like some failed mastermind that needed to be in Purgatory just long enough to be sent on to somewhere worse.

I wanted to object then and there but, as they say, timing is everything. Stopping her now, before she got everything out would make me look guilty of what she'd said, and fearful of what she was going to say.

"And, even if he's not suborning perjury, and there's no reason to believe he isn't, consider this - counsel has knowingly agreed to unleash a soul, no - a thing that has no conscience, no remorse, and no regard for humanity, unto the earthly plane. A soul that, by its own admission, has killed, stolen, beaten, likely broken every commandment there is, and probably done stuff that wasn't, but should have been included on that list of no-no's and bad acts.

"Counsel has done all of this in order to avoid his comeuppance, no matter what the costs to others. And he has the audacity to claim that he doesn't belong here!"

Finally, it was time for me to speak up.

"Objection. I may have missed something in all that, but I don't believe I heard a question of the witness. Have we skipped any further examination of the witness and moved directly to closing arguments?"

"Sustained." Luck said it dryly, apparently not a fan of lengthy cross or brief cynicism.

She dismissed me, my objection, and The Gunfighter with a wave of her hand,

"Withdrawn. I have no further questions." Then, with an unnecessary, but admittedly well worked sway of her backside, she made her way back to her seat.

I half rose from my seat and asked, "Redirect your honor?" I stood fully when he nodded his permission.

"Gunfighter, you previously stated that we entered into a contract whereby I would make best efforts to get you residency on the earthly plane did you not?"

"Yes."

After digging briefly through my briefcase, I pulled out my copy of the agreement. "Your Honors, I have here a copy of the contract he's referring to and would like to ask him questions about some of the express conditions therein. May I approach the witness and give him a copy of the agreement?"

The General Counsel spoke up before I could start forward.

"Objection. Counsel has not provided copies of the purported contract to me, or your Honors. For all we know that piece of paper could contain more directions on how the witness should answer questions!"

The Gunfighter chimed in before I could respond to the objection.

"Don't need a copy. I know every condition of every contract I've ever signed."

After asking for permission to approach, I stepped forward and handed Lucky my copy of the contract and gave The General Counsel the third copy.

"Well then, Gunfighter. Would you please be so kind

as to list the various provisions of the contract that relate to your return to the earthly plane." He listed every one of the conditions I had written into the contract to ensure he didn't run amok if he returned to the earthly plane, all in order. He then identified the harsh and immediate consequences he'd suffer for violating any provision of the agreement, and specifically acknowledged that the contract both required my affirmative permission for him to remain and gave me unfettered discretion to terminate his time on the earthly plane.

On the whole, he made it clear that he wouldn't be running amok on the earthly plane either without consequence or for long. When he finished, I retrieved my copy from The General Counsel and asked Lucky to mark the copy I'd given him as an Exhibit, and to place it in the record.

So, at that point my witness had made it thoroughly clear that I hadn't come to Purgatory willingly and refuted The General Counsel's intimation that I wasn't concerned about public safety. The odds were in my favor, but they weren't good enough.

I didn't just need The Gunfighter to convince the Special Masters that my agreeing to help him wasn't out of self-interest, I needed him to show them why I agreed to help him.

"Thank you, Gunfighter. That was an impressive display of both intellect and recollection. I just have a few more questions. Now this may be a bit hard for you, so I want you to take all the time you need to answer.

"Let's go back to when we discussed you returning to the earthly plane. Do you recall what I said when you first asked for my help?"

"Indeed, I do. Yours was more of a question than a statement. You asked why, despite the fact that you need me to testify, would you help me get back to the earthly plane? Then you asked what I planned to do if I got back."

I was working on the fly, not just asking questions that I didn't know the answers to, but asking questions that might get me shot, decapitated by sword or hatchet, or moved on by whatever means any one of the Reapers in the room chose.

"And why is it that you said you want to return to the earthly plane? What did you say that convinced me to help you?"

A pained look passed over The Gunfighter's face, then he cast his eyes down, and started speaking quietly. Every soul and other thing in the courtroom leaned in slightly, desperately clinging to his word and deathly afraid they might miss what he said next.

"I want …"

I cut him off. "Want?"

He looked up at me sharply, then after a soft conceding nod, "Well, I more than want, I need …"

With my soul on the line, I was going all in. I wouldn't, couldn't brook half measures on this point. "Need?"

Where he'd looked at me sharply before, he now seemed slightly lost and more than a little desperate. When I nodded encouragement, he took a deep breath, then stared intently at the ground between his boots. All eyes were focused on him. Even Fate leaned closer to listen.

When he finally voiced it, it came out with a whoosh. Everyone who was leaning in was knocked back by the force of what they heard.

"I hope to change. To rehabilitate my soul, alter my destiny and change my fate."

In spite of all the speed and skill in the room, Hope was the first to react. He sprung up and with arms raised high yelled out either, "Yippee!" or "That's me!" I couldn't tell which because at the same time, there was a vast, collective gasp from Reapers, and the minions fell into chaos.

Lucky banged his stick several times, calling for order, but it took some harsh words and a few stiff blows from The General Counsel to get her people settled down and thinking about re-cross examination.

I wasn't done.

As soon as the crowd quieted, I moved in to finish.

"Thank you, Gunfighter I have just one more question.

"Why do you think I agreed to help you?"

The General Counsel saw where this was going and reacted quickly. She jumped out of her seat, all but knocking her chair over, "Objection! The witness cannot speak to opposing counsel's motives."

I started to respond to the objection but didn't even get a word out before Lucky raised his hand and stopped me.

"Overruled, the witness can provide us his impressions, prescient and otherwise. We will weigh it appropriately. The witness may proceed."

I can't say it was The Gunfighter's preferred ruling. When I first asked the question, he turned his head askew for a moment, clearly trying to make sense of this thing that he was hearing. And when Lucky directed him to answer his real struggle began.

He started tentatively, speaking in a broken and disjointed way; it was almost as though he was trying to speak in a new and foreign tongue. Gradually, he warmed to his own story, and started reliving the moment out loud.

"My offer to testify didn't seem to hold much sway. You weren't interested in negotiating anything and seemed on the verge of telling me to get out. I realized, if I was going to have any hope of making a change, I had to start then and there.

"So, I told the truth, all of it. And you seemed to get it; not just hear it, but to really understand it. It was like this heavy thing in me had somehow not only been shared, but somehow lessened in the process.

It was his story and while I didn't want to interrupt, I needed to focus him on one part of his story in particular.

"And what was this thing in you?"

"Objection" said The General Counsel, "he's leading the witness!"

Lucky saw this for what it was, an attempt to break my rhythm and throw my witness off. He wasn't having any of it.

"He's supposed to lead - it's his witness! Overruled."

The General Counsel put her hands on her hips in preparation for what I suspect was going to be another snarky comeback but was interrupted by Lucky before she could start.

"Say something sassy and I'll have his friends in the back of the courtroom stake you to that chair and sew your mouth shut."

Apparently, contempt has consequences, both serious and immediate, in Purgatory.

After she smoothed her skirt down and took her seat, Lucky turned to me. "To your witness sir."

Fingers clasped in front of me, I leaned forward then, quietly so as to pull everyone that was listening back into the story, I asked, "And what was this thing we shared?"

"It was more than an idea, but less than a thing; perhaps a chance, but not yet a belief. It was that maybe, just maybe, I could be uncoupled from what and who I have been. I'm not saying I was suddenly freed from my sins and burdens, if anything it was the opposite. Putting my cards on the table, getting my thoughts and desires out in there in the open made those things real, and all the more frightening."

Though his answer was obscure, its significance was clear. A Reaper, dead-eyed and unfeeling for hundreds of years, had both expressed hope and spoke of feeling.

I thanked The Gunfighter and told the court, "I've no more redirect for this witness your Honors."

I took the opportunity to assess my position as I walked back to my chair. Fate was still Fate - inscrutable under her mass of hair. Blind Luck was still blind but, he seemed to nod in my general direction, as though he knew I was taking stock. Hope, who had gone all in earlier, was spent. He looked like a kid who had spent too much time in the bouncy house; arms slack at his sides, he sat back limply, his head resting against the chair, staring up at nothing, with a contented smile on his face.

But when I looked to opposing counsel's table, I didn't like what I saw. There was chaos, but it was controlled and seemingly of purpose; she was on the ropes but not yet beaten.

After a time, Lucky spoke up. "Counsel, do you have any re-cross examination?" Though things at The General Counsel's table became more animated, she didn't respond. By the time he asked again, they were quietly yelling at each other, fingers were being jabbed, there was even a shove or two.

He banged his cane on the ground twice more. "It's now or never, counsel."

At that point, one of her overzealous minions made the mistake of trying to force some papers, presumably more cross questions, on The General Counsel.

She pulled him in by his wrist and an ear, bit a sizable chunk out of his cheek, then shoved him away. She straightened her jacket as she chewed and savored the piece of soul she'd bitten off before turning to the court.

Lucky was nonplussed. "Does The General Counsel have anything more for this witness?"

She wiped her mouth, with the back of her hand. "No, your Honors. Thank you."

I'd pushed The Gunfighter as far as I could, and gotten all that I'd hoped for, yet The General Counsel still seemed to believe she was in the fight. With everything to lose, I played the only card I had left.

"Your Honors, at this point I would like to call a second witness. With your permission, for reasons that will become readily apparent, I would like to treat the next witness as hostile."

With that I opened my briefcase, pulled out the contract I'd entered into with The Fixer and read the signature line again.

"Your Honors, I call Roberto BeElsa to the witness chair."

If he was surprised at being called to the stand, it didn't show.

The Fixer casually took the prop hat he'd acquired for yesterday's theatrics off his lap, picked off some invisible lint and gave the brim a new fold making it look almost new when he put it on his head. When he stood, he pulled on the sleeves of his jacket, straightened the lapels, and flapped the jacket open and closed a few times, as though putting on a new garment, and it too now looked new.

On witnessing this transformation One Finger who was sitting between The Fixer and May, slid both away from him and in front of May. If nothing else, his mass muffled May's hiss. Apparently, I wasn't the only one that had been fooled.

When he walked to the rail separating counsels' tables from the audience he paused and held on to the rail, as though for balance, while he cleaned his worn, dusty shoes by rubbing them on the calves of his pants. The shoes as well as the pants came out of it for the better; the shoes took on an almost new luster, and the pants fell, creased and crisp.

The audience sat in stunned silence. When he passed The Gunfighter on his way to exchanged places in the witness chair, he touched his finger to his hat in acknowledgement. As The Gunfighter nodded his acknowledgement, opposing counsel slouched down into her seat. Whether she was embarrassed because her boss was being outed, because she hadn't known it was her boss, or because he was being called to testify was anybody's guess.

As soon as he'd situated himself on the stand, The General Counsel stood and addressed the court.

"Your Honors, at this point I'd like to ask that the court adjourn for the day to allow me to meet with opposing counsel and attempt to resolve this matter."

When Lucky looked to me for a response I stood and pressed my position.

"Your Honors, I've met with The General Counsel twice already and we've gotten no closer to resolving this matter. We're all here now, ready to go. In addition to seeing no point in further fruitless settlement discussions or unnecessary delays, I am concerned that the witness I just called may not be available at a later date."

He who had been known as The Fixer spoke without prompting.

"Your honors, I plan on attending the settlement conference in the hope that it will be more fruitful. As for reconvening tomorrow," with a smile and glance toward Hope, "I suggest we take that off the table; we don't want to wait that long to hear the end of this story."

The purpose of the soul is to pursue growth.

De Tenebra

CHAPTER 34

QUID EST VERITAS

(What Is Truth)

WHEN I ARRIVED, he who was known as the Fixer was relaxing on one of the couches in the executive suite, all too much at home. The General Counsel sat curled up like a cat on the couch tucked up against him.

He motioned for me to take a seat on one of the facing couches, then spoke in a voice and manner that harkened back to the first time we met.

"Tit-for-tat?"

He jumped right in when I nodded my agreement.

"As a professional courtesy, tell me, when and how you knew that I wasn't just another lost soul?"

"That's two questions," I told him, before I went ahead and answered.

"It wasn't a single thing. I got suspicious when you found and provided me the notice - it was too well and intentionally hidden. It was unlikely that a newbie, even a well-connected one, would have the contacts to find it. Another hint was you going to the training area to tell The Gunfighter about my first court appearance. Even if I didn't know that regular folks aren't usually allowed there, it would have been an inordinately gutsy move. Then yesterday, the way you looked about this suite – it was like you were inspecting rather than appreciating it. And when she invited me over – her looking at and inviting you, a lackey, to join us was a lesser tell. The clincher was today, when The Gunfighter stood next to you, gun out to prompt someone to move, the thought of doing so never crossed your mind.

"Those things combined made me think that something was amiss. So, I reread our contract. Mostly I was looking for loopholes, making sure you'd actually signed was just a detail.

"Then I saw your name. In all the contracts I reviewed for The Thin Man I never saw what sounded like a real name. Sure, there were a lot of nicknames, some logos, and more than a few had just made their "mark". Yours was the first and only real sounding name I've come across since I got here. It made me think about what The Gunfighter said when he brought me here, that 'souls are more aptly referenced on the basis of their character.' From there it was either luck or fate. My father's name was Robert; I never really understood how you get Bob from Robert, but after years of hearing it, whenever I read Robert, I hear Bob. That and my having filled out way too many of those 'last name first, first name last' forms, led me to Belsa Bob; after that Beelzebub was obvious.

"My turn. What do you want with me?"

He half-laughed. "I've been called many things: Son of Perdition, Little Whore, The Deceiver, The Trickster, He of The Forked tongue – that's her favorite, not mine - and quite a few others. But the truth is, I don't lie, and I take no joy in deceiving. There's no challenge in the former and the latter is bad management. Instead, I gather information, put it out there for all to see - hence the role of The Fixer - and let the chips fall where they may.

"Do I find most souls predictable, certainly." Then, with a nod toward a stack of coins on the table, "Am I above putting a bet on the expected outcome, not at all.

"In your case, it's pretty much like she's been telling you. This has been a job interview.

"Here's the thing, Purgatory evolves to reflect the human condition. Arena and intellectual challenges were being replaced by rap battles and chess games, now those are being replaced by litigation – if Purgatory could support technology, we'd probably be having video game contests. And, while litigation requires lawyers, me winning requires that she have good lawyers.

"It's like I said when we first met, I'm part of a very large and complex organization. Though it isn't any of the organizations you had in mind, like any organization we're always in need of talent. Finding ruthless people is easy, finding talented ones, … not so much. When I see a talent gap developing, I move to fill it; I recruit when I can and groom when I must. But honestly, you weren't on my radar for either.

"I'd been grooming Christina for a long time. I knew her parents, I am an alumni booster for several of the fraternities where she partied during college and, as one of FRAT's major clients, I was instrumental in her being hired.

"When I closed my account with FRAT they had no reason to keep her on so they started making moves to get rid of her. With no savings and no family or friends to fall back on she'd have then made her way to us in short order. But you stepped in and sidetracked my plans. Not only didn't you fire her, you put it in her mind that she could succeed, and on her merits no less. That's when you caught my attention.

"Whiskey?"

My head nodded, in understanding. I hadn't considered that I was a late addition to his grand plan. He took my head nod as agreement and cut The General Counsel a look.

She begrudgingly detached herself from his arm and sashayed over to the bar. She returned with three glasses and the same bottle we'd sampled yesterday. After three fat pours, she sized-up the still half-full bottle then went back and got a full one.

"In case we get lucky and make a deal – or vice versa – or either one." She then reattached herself to, more than seated herself to him, and took to doodling on his arm and neck - digging her fingernails in deep enough to leave marks.

Drinks untouched, and apparently unphased by having his body treated as a canvas, he continued.

"I'm prepared to offer you your own district. I'll set you up with everything you need, office, staff, big budget, fat salary, you name it."

Without either looking at me or bothering to stop doodling on his arm, The General Counsel chimed in.

"And we can 'visit' each other whenever we like."

We weren't really doing tit-for-tat anymore and I was dying to know. So I just asked him, "Are all demons, you know, … like her?"

She leaned forward in a sensual, snake-like fashion until she was just close enough for me to feel the heat coming off her, did that lip licking-biting thing again, then inhaled deeply, more taking in my essence than smelling me.

"Oh, you sweet naive soul, there's no one and no thing like me!"

Still leaned back on the couch, but now behind and to the side since she'd leaned forward, he rolled his eyes and nodded yes.

I shook my head, snickered, and began to stand. "Well, as tempting as your offer may be … ."

Without bothering to sit back or look away from me, The General Counsel said to him.

"See. Told you so, pay up."

He stalled my departure with the classic double palm out, 'wait a minute' gesture. Then reached into his pocket, pulled out a hefty stack of DieBus, and handed it to her.

After she put the DieBus on the table, she sat back next to him and roughly renewed her artistic efforts - now high enough up on his inner thigh to suggest that their wager involved more than coin.

"Ouch" I said. "Did you at least get odds?"

"No. But I plan on getting it back shortly."

Intrigued, I sat back down. "Well?"

He smiled all too confidently.

"No salary, benefits, or protection from me. I set you

up with an office, staff, and incidentals. You work as a contractor, billing by the hour to serve my interests and the clients I send you. Your free time is your own."

He paused, to whet my appetite before throwing in the clincher.

"And you split your time between here and the earthly plane – for every day you spend here, you get an hour on the earthly plane.

In my experience, there comes a point in negotiations where, based on what the other party says, you know you're in striking distance of a deal. This was that moment.

Where I'd been sitting forward, ready to leave at any moment, I sat back. Even before I countered, he saw it for what that it was, an acknowledgement of the potential for a deal.

My counteroffer was simple but pricey.

"Your best efforts to make me whole. If I decide to go out on my own, you pay the first year's rent for an office. I'll find my own staff. Either way, I live on the earthly plane, and I represent who I want, if I want - including or excluding you and your friends."

It was my turn to pause.

He should have waited, both to make sure I was done and to 'cool the mark' - by taking enough time to give me the sense that I'd negotiated well, and that he was thinking about the deal, perhaps even struggling to figure out how he could live with it. He didn't.

Instead, he nodded his head and smiled. When he scooted forward to voice his agreement, I cut him off.

"And The Gunfighter comes with me."

Throwing The Gunfighter into the pot seriously upped

the ante. Now we were negotiating over something that really mattered to them.

He leaned back and made a 'whooshing' sound as The General Counsel pushed further forward. I could feel the heat coming off her again and this time there was nothing sexy about it.

"You've gotta be kidding me!" she exclaimed. "Why would we let that thing go anywhere, let alone back to the earthly plane?" Besides, I have some serious, ass flavored karma for him to chew on for a very, very long time."

I'd struck a nerve, but I doubted it was the one she was protesting about.

Up until he explained his plans for Christina, I'd wondered, but knew better than to ask, who decided to bring me here - whether The Gunfighter was acting on orders or on his own.

Now, I had my answer. The Gunfighter probably didn't know I'd interfered with their plans and had no reason to care if he had known. Besides, as evidenced by our argument in front of the bailiff, The Gunfighter hadn't had enough faith in my lawyerly abilities to want to bring me here on his own. He on the other hand had been working the long game with Christina – grooming her to become one of The General Counsel's minions or maybe for one of the jobs they'd offered me.

Knowing that The Gunfighter was just following orders solidified my resolve. I was going to get out of there and I was going to get The Gunfighter out too.

Rather than end the negotiations by rejecting my offer, he countered with a question.

"Why would I agree to let The Gunfighter go? You do

know that he's a psychopath, don't you? True psychopaths, which is pretty much a minimum requirement to become a Reaper, are very rare. At best they have an intellectual understanding that something is wrong, more often they're compelled to commit such deeds in the hope of feeling something. And, they have neither empathy nor a sense of remorse; that's what allows them to move others on. It also makes them difficult souls to deal with. An individual's Hell is created by that individual's remorse, guilt and self-loathing. Since Reapers don't feel any of that, they can't create an appropriate scenario for growth through penance."

The General Counsel explained, "Purgatory is the best place for Reapers. We put them in positions where they're allowed to wreak whatever havoc they wish in the hope that they'll eventually tire of it. When they are moved on, and one way or another they all are, my people make them suffer long and hard so that they at least come to associate pain and suffering with their deeds."

I answered their question with one of my own. "Yes, but that hasn't worked, has it?

"The Gunfighter's trying to get out is just a symptom. The real problem is with your business model. Sure, the rules and the whole fear thing have worked well for a long, long time. If anything, it's worked too well. Souls are so afraid of what comes next that they've lost sight of the end game.

"This place was supposed to be a way station; a few lashes, maybe a hair-suit, or some navel gazing, and off they go to their next, next. But now, souls are so afraid of what's next, that you're over-populated – look at the public housing, the lines in the administration building, and of course, the courts. A whole preindustrial economy has sprung up and is thriving out there. And, with 7,500 people dying each day in the U.S. alone, your new arrivals far exceed your departures - so it's only getting worse.

"The Reapers used to transport folks, then with their unique ability to move souls on they also served as a stop-gap measure. Now they're just something else to be feared. You need to change all this. You need to get a different message out there, and freeing The Gunfighter gives you an opportunity to do just that."

The General Counsel looked to him. When he nodded, she dropped the sex-crazed demon act and sat back, now more interested in solving the problem than posturing and playing angles.

"And what is this new message?"

I'd hit the nail on the head. Now that I'd piqued their interest I had to play a hunch. I looked from him to The General Counsel.

"It's the same message your boss here tried to send when he wrote this."

I pulled *De Tenebra* out of my briefcase and slid it across the table. It came to a stop somewhere between one of the untouched glasses of whiskey and the coins she'd stacked on the table. Then I combined two quotes. "The purpose of the soul is to pursue growth," and "Purgatory must evolve to fulfill its purpose and foster spiritual growth."

It was his turn to speak up.

"And how do you propose we get that message out at this junction?"

I relaxed into the couch and took my time answering. We'd agreed in principle and were now just hashing out the details.

"Technically, and for all anyone knows, we've been working together from the time I arrived. Now that I've called you as a witness, you're gonna go back on the stand and let everyone think that The Gunfighter brought me here on his own, that you've always known what he was up to, and that while you may not approve of his methods – kidnapping me – you support his objective.

"You're going to agree that he and I should be returned to the earthly plane based on the need for the soul to seek growth. You can claim that you're running an experiment, starting some sort of pilot program for dull and stunted souls, or whatever, but you're going to insist that I be returned, and that The Gunfighter go with me."

Voice full of resignation, The General Counsel spoke up. "The Special Masters will see you as the conniving, scheming bastard that you are, those in the audience will be wondering what you know about their various schemes, and I, of course, will end up losing."

After an exasperated sigh, she turned around, so her knees rested on the couch seat and bent over the back of the couch to where she'd put her briefcase. Her position wasn't lost on him.

After slapping her nearest butt cheek to, as he said, "tenderize it," he leaned in and brutally bit the now 'tenderized' spot. After some cursing, a moan, a grunt, and a few not-at-all-discreet tremors, she exhaled deeply then turned back around and produced two stacks of DieBus and placed them on the table.

Apparently always one to say, "I told you so," he offered her a taunting, yet still salacious smile.

"See, I told you he'd figure all this out and save everybody's ass in the process."

He picked up and raised one of the thus far untouched glasses of whisky and said,

"Deal."

After we'd all thrown back our shots, The General Counsel, red cheeked from the slap, the bite, the whiskey, or just because, sat with her lips pushed out in a faux pout. But for the fact that she was a lawyer and a demon, I'd have been tempted to think her disappointment genuine.

"Yeah, everybody's ass gets saved except mine. You and The Gunfighter get out, He gets his grand vision pushed forward, and I get a loss on the big stage." Then, with feigned horror, "Whatever will my boss say about this."

He ran his finger around the inside of his glass, coating it with some of the residual whiskey that had pooled in the bottom, then turned to her and responded with great interest but little concern. "I guess you'll just have to sully yourself and do whatever it takes to make it up to him." Then he deftly slid his whiskey-coated finger under her skirt. She responded with a deep, bestial moan and, in one deft move, hiked up her skirt, lifted a leg, and went full cowgirl on him.

With our negotiations apparently done, I opened my briefcase deposited *De Tenebra*, then prepared to take my leave.

Barely upright and wholly distracted, he halted my departure with a grunt.

"Normally I'd insist that you join us, … to seal the

deal," a suggestion that elicited a groan and more frenetic movement from her, "but we really don't have time to do a threesome justice if we're going to wrap things up in court today."

I started to leave, then, seeing an opportunity, picked up both bottles of scotch and held them up.

"In lieu of a raincheck?"

I put the bottles in my briefcase when he waived me out, and quickly closed the door behind me to muffle their grunts and groans.

What purpose serves deception but to subvert free will?

DE TENEBRA

CHAPTER 35

RESPONDEAT SUPERIOR
(Let The Master Speak)

When I got back to the courtroom little had changed. The detente between the *Hatfields* and the *McCoys* still hung by a thread, One Finger sat protectively close to May, and The Special Masters had yet to return.

I made my way down the aisle to counsels' table in front, took my seat, closed my eyes and, intent on taking full advantage of this momentary break in the action, slouched way back in the chair. Though it felt like I'd just closed my eyes, I may have been snoring when I was roused by a stiff poke from One Finger.

If I'd had a hat on, I would have had it pulled down and I'd have answered without lifting it. As it was, I only half sat-up and only half turned around to see him sitting there with shoulders shrugged, arms half lifted and eyes wide in a "Well, what happened?" expression.

I sat up, turned to face him fully and with less than a

word erased whatever question he had in mind. It wasn't what I said, or how I started to say it, it was the scent he caught when I started to speak.

"Whiskey!"

He said it with the kind of awe and reverence generally reserved for great feats, lost treasures, and exquisite lingerie.

Without bothering to explain, I started in again, and got as far as telling him that we'd reached an agreement before he cut me off.

"Scotch, aged about, umph."

I doubt May's sharp elbow focused him, but it certainly shut him up. With priorities clearly established, May leaned forward.

"Agreement?"

Before I could continue, he who was the Fixer walked in. The General Counsel demurely followed a respectful distance behind.

But for a new wrinkle here and there and the slit of her skirt being relocated to her other thigh, one would have thought nothing of their arrival. Or at least nothing more than one would usually think when the Prince of Hell enters with a demon in tow.

Had there been any civilian spectators left in the courtroom there'd likely have been a bit of a hubbub. As it was, a slight murmur went through the trainers, and the minions sat-up a tad bit straighter. The Reapers, including The Gunfighter, were unperturbed.

The Council of Special Masters arrived immediately after. Once the three were seated, Lucky got things underway with nothing more by way of fanfare than an empty socketed glare at The General Counsel and derisive, "Well?"

I and The General Counsel stood. After a look to and nod from her boss, the General Counsel addressed the court.

"May it please the court. After well considered, arms-length negotiations, the parties have agreed to a resolution of this dispute that is both fair and in the interest of all. The terms of the settlement, ..."

I was about to interject, since The General Counsel dryly discussing a settlement wasn't what we'd discussed, when Fate found her voice.

"We will hear this from him!"

And a terrible voice it was. In the space of those six words, three different voices spoke up. Where the voice that best fit her body was light and somewhat tentative, another was high pitched and urgent, while the dominant one seemed raspy and strict. With each voice apparently competing with the others to be heard, both tone and cadence were uneven, and some words were said two or three times - near, but not always at the exact same time.

The Fixer nodded graciously in response and took the witness chair, as both I and The General Counsel took our seats. This was their plan – a little something they'd worked out between grunts and groans no doubt.

He started slowly, with just enough reflection, defer-ence, and regret to cast himself as the gracious loser. Then, before anyone could latch on to the idea of his losing, he pivoted and allowed what had seemed like a loss to morph into a sacrifice he had hoped to someday make, for a cause he had long championed.

There were references to "inspired" writings ranging from *The Missing Piece* to the *I'Ching*. He drew liberally from *De Tenebra* and his other writings and spoke in languages that probably hadn't been heard in eons and others that were never meant for mortal ears.

It made my earlier efforts to sway the court with my opening statement look like high school show and tell.

He sat in the witness chair discussing the events that had brought us here for I can't say how long. With Lucky nearest to him on the bench, it seemed natural when he turned to Lucky and acknowledged the good fortune I'd had in Purgatory and how my starting a practice to help new arrivals and standing up for The Wisp were not the deeds of a soul that belonged in Purgatory. By the time he got around to talking about The Gunfighter, praising his desire to rehabilitate himself, basking in, and relating to The Gunfighter's and all entities' hope for redemption, he was standing so close to Hope, that theirs almost appeared to be a private conversation, albeit one-sided, between two kindred souls.

Well before he got within arms distance of Fate, he'd acknowledged my humanitarian efforts, commended The General Counsel for her public service, and spoke about the need to find one's higher path, to an audience that went well beyond the occupants of the room.

Though this had been my idea, by the time he turned to address Fate, even I had brought into his speech. I couldn't help but wonder if this was really my idea, or just me following the path he'd led me along.

Fate brought my contemplations and his presentation to an abrupt end.

She banged her stick on the bench and, using only three garbled words, was mercifully terse.

"Enough. Be seated."

He bowed in a graceful façade of politesse and deference, then took his seat.

When The General Counsel nodded at me and started to rise, I joined her and stood to request the verdict that would decide the fate of my soul.

"We stand submitted, and ask that the Special Masters accept our settlement," she said. I noted my agreement then, for lack of any other ideas, waited in silence.

Lucky spoke without hesitation. "The settlement agreement you propose provides for extraordinary relief. While well within the purview of this Council's authority, such relief can only be granted on a unanimous vote by the Council. I will vote first."

Lucky dug in his pocket, produced a coin, looked at me as best a man with no eyes can, then said, "call'er 'fore she drops" as he flipped the coin in the air."

Caught completely off-guard, I blurted out "tails," which drew a snicker from The General Counsel.

When Lucky caught the coin midair, I wondered how he'd be able to read the coin, then realized he probably shouldn't even have been able to catch it. He chuckled as though he'd been watching me as I figured all this out, then pronounced his verdict.

"Tails it is. I vote to accept the settlement."

When Hope's turn came, he stood slowly, placed both hands on the bench, and locked eyes with The Gunfighter in a most unchildlike manner. As the moment stretched out, I hazarded a glance back at The Gunfighter. His gaze though unflinching as always, seemed a tad softer, perhaps even less dead-eyed. If this was the mother of all staring contests, as all knew it to be, it ended in a most unexpected fashion. The Gunfighter broke first, a slight upward curl at the edges of his mouth evidencing his 'devastating' loss. But Hope broke hardest, laughing out loud and collapsing back into his chair. His fist shot up as he went down, and he signaled his agreement to the settlement by raising a single thumb.

All eyes then turned to Fate. For the longest time she seemed to just sit there, as still and silent as she'd been throughout most of the hearing. Even from the proximity of Counsel's table, I almost missed the slight movement of her fingers as she ran them along her staff. It was almost as though she were reading and writing brail. After some time and what sounded like muttering, she placed the staff on the bench, nodded her head a few times as though resolving some internal debate, then and pulled back the dull blonde hair that covered her face.

That she was a young girl, just old enough to be called a woman explained her flat, boyish figure, and when she spoke everyone understood why she hid behind her hair. The first thing she said, "No," came out in a dry, raspy voice that reeked of anger and resentment. In the same breath, she said, "Yes" in a high, urgent voice that seemed almost desperate.

Disturbing though they were, the shifting voices paled in comparison to the rapid-fire facial expressions that changed with the voices. One instant she was scowling, with brow furrowed, nostrils flared, and an evil squint of the eyes; the next she was wide-eyed and furtive, looking to be on the verge of panic. When she spoke an instant later, she was calm, her face relaxed, and her voice light and almost soothing in its youthfulness.

"By majority I agree that counsel should be returned, that he should be made whole, and that no signatory to the agreement, party to this proceeding, witness herein, or agent of any of the aforementioned shall act against him here or on the earthly plane.

"However, not all that has been done can be undone. Having been brought here, counsel has seen and learned things that are beyond most on the mortal plane. Since counsel cannot unlearn what has been learned, you are admonished - be judicious in discourse related to these events. But do not let this judiciousness lead you to be cloistered or secreted away. Having seen another plane of existence, you cannot ignore those that dwell in the in-between. Be advised, the fate of your soul will now be held to a higher standard; determined not just by how you interact with other mortal souls, but also by how you interact, good or bad, with all beings.

"We are not in agreement about The Gunfighter. Either acting alone" and with a slight inclination of her head toward the witness stand, "or at the behest of another, The Gunfighter has interfered with the natural order of life and death," then looking back toward me, "exposed this being to things not meant for mortal souls to yet know, and generally shown himself to be worthy of his place in Purgatory and the hereafter. While the hypocrisy of his claiming to have done so in the hope of changing is not lost on us, neither is the significance of what is at stake here.

"Though one can no more deny hope than fate, we are neither blind to the facts nor willing to just leave things to hope. We will therefore require ongoing proof of progress. Just as The Gunfighter shall be released, so too shall he return. On each earthly solstice, The Gunfighter shall meet with a Special Master and make an offer of proof – showing what progresses he has made toward regaining his humanity. A failure to appear and show satisfactory progress will be grounds for The Gunfighter's immediate return.

"Moreover, while we appreciate counsel's efforts to ensure that The Gunfighter does no harm, we cannot leave the potential for such harm to the chance of a drafting oversight. We will release The Gunfighter but, effective on arrival, the terms of The Gunfighter's Reaper contract will be transferred to counsel for the duration of counsel's natural life.

"Consistent with said contract: Counsel shall have full ownership of The Gunfighter; any act of disobedience on the part of The Gunfighter will be punished as counsel sees fit; should mortal harm befall counsel prematurely The Gunfighter will return to Purgatory and his contract will revert to its prior holder. And if The Gunfighter, by act or omission, causes said mortal or other harm, he shall be dipped until dissolution and moved on from Purgatory to his next existence.

"These are our terms. They are non-negotiable."

With that, Fate leaned forward and with a slight shake, caused her hair to fall forward and again cover her face; she then sat back, still and silent once more. Apparently, she or they had said all they had to say.

Hope responded with a world-weary yawn and nod of

agreement. Lucky took it all in, thought for a second, then said "agreed," and banged his stick on the ground.

"We're adjourned. Now get out, and there better not be any shenanigans on your way.

Hope and Fate rose at about the same time. He took a half-skip over to her as she turned, took her hand in his and they walked out together. From the back it looked for all the world like an older sister walking with her little brother.

I'd won. I don't know what I expected, maybe some *Perry Mason* like moment, someone to cheer, maybe I'd even get carried out of the courtroom on everyone's shoulders. What I got was a bark of a laugh and a heavy-handed cuff on the back from One Finger.

Before I could turn to face One Finger, even before the shock of the moment could fully manifest, The General Counsel sauntered over.

Standing silently in front of me, she placed one hand on her hip, and casually undertook a detailed examination of the finely polished fingernails on her other hand. Eventually, after it was clear that I had to wait for her, but before the surprise of her approach wore off, she leaned forward, shamelessly providing a down-blouse view all the way to her well defined abs, then summoned me close with a come-hither finger.

"Before you go gloating about your victory, let me tell you what else you missed. I still own your share of the partnership. With The Gunfighter soon to be off on a brief holiday," she glanced over my shoulder at May, "the witch, as an employee, will be mine to do with as I please."

I shook my head and, after my own world-weary sigh, explained.

"It wasn't your fault; I took advantage. Not knowing who my witnesses would be, and not having time to do depositions, you were forced to choose. You either had to ask questions that you didn't know the answer to, something no seasoned attorney would do, or craft the best story you could from what you knew.

"And frankly, yours was a good story. Arguing that The Gunfighter only agreed to testify because I agreed to get him out made sense, even though it wasn't particularly ... inspired. It allowed you to use what you already knew about The Gunfighter and his 'misdeeds' to paint him as a villain and call into question both his credibility and my motives.

"But going with that story meant you couldn't ask him what he'd agreed to pay me for my services. A question like that would have undermined your story.

"Now I get it, you being a demon and all, it probably never crossed your mind, that since he had his own reason to appear, lest I violate Rule 2, I had to charge him something for my services."

"Did he agree to give you his share of the partnership in exchange for your services!?"

"Of course not. Had he done so I would have had to turn over that newly acquired asset along with my other assets. What he agreed to was three amendments to the partnership agreement. The first prohibits him from selling, trading, or otherwise disposing of his interest, subject to the second provision. The second provides for the transfer of his interest to me should he leave Purgatory for any appreciable period of time. And the third provision made May an 'at will' employee - she serves at the pleasure and mutual agreement of herself and the partnership."

"You let May become an at will employee?

"While I certainly appreciate both the thoroughness and spiteful nature of your getting her out from under my thumb, it does sound as though you did little May there no small favor."

"Not at all. I imposed an obligation on May." After a quick glance back in May's direction while I subtly patted the pocket where the talisman sat, "An obligation that has certainly been repaid.

"Besides, would you really want me to work for you if I couldn't stop you from getting control over me, my office, and my staff?"

"So, win or lose I'd be left with a minority interest in a firm with no lawyers, and a single employee that could quit if and when she wanted?"

She smiled, as I started to nod my agreement, then moved fast, Gunfighter fast. It didn't even register that she'd reached forward and grabbed me till I felt myself being pulled out of my seat. She pulled me close – we were both cheek to cheek and body to body. Heat roiled off her - intense, almost to the point of painful, yet intoxicating - as she cooed more than whispered into my ear.

"You don't know dick about me or what you're missing."

When her tongue touched my ear it was cool, almost refreshing compared to the heat coming off her body. It only took me a moment to realize that she'd extended her tongue and was gently caressing my ear, an instant more for my crotch to tell me that the bulge I felt pressing forward wasn't my own, and longer still to realize I was involuntarily doing her lip biting thing.

I inhaled, breath broken and urgent, just as she exhaled and was pulled away with a grunt. I didn't know I'd closed my eyes until I opened them and saw that Lucky had grabbed her by the scruff of the neck and pulled her away. She stood next to him, eyes wide and alight, skin flushed, and nipples painfully erect, smiling in a lusty, almost feral way.

When she took a lust-crazed half-step toward me Lucky shoved her back easily, with a force that was wholly incongruent with his diminutive stature and easy going, folksy style.

"Move on now missy, you've had your day in court."

She recovered quickly. In the time it took to pull her blouse together in an act of faux modesty, her eyes calmed, and her skin returned to normal, even her nipples retreated.

By the time my breath returned to near normal she'd gathered her minions and was preparing to leave. When she saw me looking after her, she held pinky finger to mouth and thumb to ear and mouthed, "Call me." Then laughed, draped herself on her boss's arm, and together they headed out of the courtroom.

I turned to Lucky, looking to find a way to convey gratitude for his actions of the day.

"Much obliged."

The significance of my phrasing wasn't lost on him.

"T'was my pleasure. I don't cotton to demons; all that plotting and scheming that they're so fond of generally

430 | DARWIN E. FARRAR

leaves little to chance. Truth is, I rather enjoyed seeing that sassy little girl get her comeuppance."

He paused, one hand in pocket, the other holding his cane; he seemed to be reflecting on the events of the day.

"Best of luck."

He said it as he flipped a coin toward me that I instinctively caught in the air. He was well on his way by the time I realized it wasn't a coin of the realm.

It really hadn't been that long since I'd seen one, but it was so at odds with my surroundings that it took me a moment and a few blinks to realize that it was a penny. May chimed-in right about that time.

"Lucky penny."

When I turned to face May I heard first one, then another, then several clink-clinks-clinks; the sound of coins hitting the hard-stone courtroom floor. I looked to One Finger, not wholly understanding, and saw him smiling unabashedly.

After another cuff on the shoulder - this one almost knocked me back into my chair - One Finger explained.

"Sure, da Reapers came ta back Da Gunfighter. But, once dey were ere, t'was suggested dat it mite be werf dare wild ta see ow you andled Da Genral Counsel. After I told em bout yer moves dus far, includin yer meetin yesterday, dey saw dis fer wot it were, da real game oh Purgatory. A game ware infermation, guile, n confidence battle again fear n doubt, wit souls ang'n in da balance.

"Dey's payin ya fer da lesson dey got taday. Ya bested Da Genral Counsel, sumptin dat ain't easy ta do, by turnin er strengths – suspicion and distrust –ta yer vantage. Ya got er ta say wot ya din't wanna say, dat he was a bad one, din used it ta set up yer redemption claim.

"Fact tis, after ya cross examined da Gunfighter n went off drinkin whiskey wit yer pals," he paused to puff up his already enormous chest and put his hands where his waist would be if he had one, "Ah was asked ta offer ya yer pick tweenst eider an instructor position er a services retainer if tings didn't work out in yer favor ere in court.

"Troof is, if'n ya could force dem Reapers ta tell, and ya really cain't, like Lucky, alf of dem would admit ta payin jes fer da pleasure of seein da lick'in ya put on Da Genral Counsel."

"And the other half?"

He rubbed his rough hand across his stubbled face and looked down, contemplating his phrasing.

"I suspect, ard pressed doe dey'd be ta mit it, dey'd pay fer da ope dat dair's sumptin fore dem in yer redemption story."

By the time he'd explained all this, The Gunfighter, the other Reapers, and the instructors had left. May excused herself when One-Finger and I took to our knees to pick up the coins. Apparently, the task of crawling around to find each and every coin ran contrary to May's lady-like sensibilities. Before she left, I asked her to stop by the office first thing tomorrow morning.

I paid One-Finger the customary 10% finder's fee - it would have been more if he'd been physically involved – then we walked out of the building and split up. He headed back to the inn and I to my office.

∽

What salve soothes disappointment?

DE TENEBRA

CHAPTER 36

TEMET NOSCE

(Know Thyself)

I WALKED ACROSS the plaza toward the public housing, trying not to disturb the ever-present soot on the ground and to get a handle on the moment ... and failing at both. Soon enough I found myself at the heavy doors of the public housing entrance.

This late in the day, when space was at a premium, the large heavy doors at the entrance were closed. I pushed them open without thought or having to break stride. The guard at the door was a thickly muscled woman who wore the breaks and scars of a hard life proudly and was thereby made beautiful. She stepped forward when the door swung open, back when she took in my suit and briefcase and saw that I wasn't there for casual accommodations, then quickly knelt with head bowed when she realized it was me.

A sparse crowd had already gathered in the hall with

many trying to stake out favorite and relatively prime spaces on the floor. The crowd began to part before the guard fully rose. By the time she banged her staff and took the lead walking me down the hall they'd pressed against the walls, creating a path at least three times wider than necessary.

"Lawyerman." A quick identification by a few became a realization by some, then a murmur that passed through the crowd – an eerie reminder of the day I arrived with The Gunfighter. I switched my briefcase to my left-hand, freeing up my right-hand to reach my knife, neither acknowledging nor ignoring the crowd, then followed the guard.

The guard at the foot of the stairs had already assumed a kneeling-head-bowed position when we arrived. Rather than the guards banging their staffs and passing me off, the first guard continued up the stairs, leading the way and the second guard fell in a respectful distance behind me after I passed. At the next landing, the guard, who was likewise kneeling with head bowed when we arrived, stayed kneeling until after we passed. Instead of joining my mini entourage, this guard rose and took off at a run down that floor's hall.

I was more than a bit unnerved by this change in protocol.

When we got to my office door, the scarred muscular woman that had become the lead guard brought us to a stop with an upheld hand. Then, staff at the ready, she opened my office door and went inside. She spent only the time it took to walk in, scan the box of a room and look behind the desk for intruders before coming back. Once back outside the room she bowed gracefully, waved me in, then took up a position on the far side of the door - the rear guard mirrored her position on the opposite side of the door.

I entered my office and closed the door – all the more unnerved by the guards' new protocol. After conducting my own paranoia-induced scan of the room, I took a seat at my desk.

Figuring it was better to get in and out quickly than sit around trying to figure out what was going on, I set about organizing the office for my departure. There wasn't much to do, and I'd almost done that when there was a knock on the door.

In response to my, "come in" The Thin Man entered with The Envoy following a respectful distance behind. They bowed deeply in unison, as I stood in greeting. The change in our power dynamic that The Thin Man's deep bow implied at was confirmed by his tone.

"Apologies for this unscheduled intrusion. I only seek a moment of your time."

"Nonsense." I replied, " I am but a guest in your house. You are always welcome. Please, take a seat."

The Envoy stood just within the threshold, silent and all but invisible. As The Thin Man hadn't bothered to reference him etiquette forbade, and history urged, that I neither address nor acknowledge him.

"You are too gracious. It is my house at the pleasure of the Reapers, and it is I who benefits from your presence. Which brings me to the purpose of my intrusion.

"It is my understanding that you and your partner will be taking your leave of us. Forgive my impertinence, but it is my hope that you will be kind enough to have your firm maintain a presence here in the building."

But for his phrasing I'd have assumed he was tactfully asking if and when he could have the space back. Given that phrasing, I simply queried, "Kind enough"?

Seems he'd tested and I'd unwittingly called. He did the smart thing and put his cards on the table.

"Ah, yes, please forgive my inaccuracy. I wish to know the terms you will require if we are to keep your firm here with us."

That's when it clicked. I was the first person in mostly known history to negotiate a return to the earthly plane – that I'd also managed to have a Reaper sent back under my authority meant that my stock hadn't just gone up in Purgatory, it had gone way up. Having the firm, even empty and partially owned by The General Counsel, located in his building would be a boon for him. Rates to rent space on this floor alone would double, triple, or more.

"As I have transferred my minority interest in the partnership to The General Counsel, I cannot speak for the firm. However, I am willing to speak to The Gunfighter and recommend the partnership remain here provided two conditions are met.

"First, I intend to make an offer to buy my partnership interest back from The General Counsel. That interest in the firm is of little value to The General Counsel, and little is all that I am willing to offer." I opened my briefcase, pulled about a quarter of the coins I'd gotten from the Reapers, and placed them on the desk.

"However, as it is very much in your interest to have

me rather than The General Counsel as an owner of the firm, you are free to supplement my offer."

Then, after an appraising look at the Envoy, I added, "As you see fit."

When he nodded his agreement, I grabbed a piece of paper and scribbled out *'consider the bearer my proxy… for the night.'* I folded the paper twice, signed the outside, then stabbed the ends of the fold through with the pencil to make it difficult to open without detection, then passed it to The Thin Man.

"The signature on the outside of this letter will get your man into The General Counsel's residence. Do not open the letter, and do not give it to one of The General Counsel's minions.

When The Thin Man held the letter up, the Envoy stepped forward immediately, took it and stepped back to his silent waiting position.

"And your second condition?"

"You shall not raise the cost of accommodations on the first floor."

He paused, unable to see an angle and either unwilling or unable to accept the demand as altruistic, then looked at me quizzically - wanting to ask but not daring to question.

"The newest of the new are an important part of the firm's practice; having them here makes the firm more accessible and provides us free advertising."

He nodded in seeming understanding of my request and clear acceptance of my terms, then sent the Envoy on his way with a dismissive wave of his hand.

He rose to leave easily but with a deliberate slowness,

then bowed deeply. I rose from my seat, our mutual respect acknowledged.

He made to leave but stopped just inside the doorway and turned.

"I have been here a long time, certainly longer than most. I have seen things change, but I doubt any have seen the kind of change your time here will soon bring. Should you return and find that I am no longer here, know that missing what next havoc you wreak will be only my loss."

It seems my words, or more accurately, my theory and the words of The Fixer, were already having an impact; reverberating and causing souls at all levels of Purgatory to reconsider their tenure here.

Still standing, I bowed in understanding, hoping that what I lacked in grace, I made-up for with sincerity. When I looked to the door after bowing, The Thin Man was gone.

With the darkening approaching and my office now in order, I picked up the pencil and scribbled out a note to May. The note informed her of my agreement with The Thin Man and committed the remainder of the funds I gotten from the Reapers to her salary and the firm's expenses.

When I walked out the office the guards again took up positions in front of and behind me. We made our way downstairs, through an ever-thickening collection of 'residents' on the third and second floors, without incident. When we got to the bottom level I saw that bodies had already filled the floor, making passage a tricky proposition. I stopped the guard in front of me before he could bang his staff on the ground to signal his intent to clear a path.

"Stay here," I told the two guards as I stepped forward into the sleepy mass. Briefcase in hand, mind focused on balance and opportunity, I made my way through the tangle of bodies on the floor. Those that were awake made space where they could, I stepped around those that already slept. Their courtesy and mine, minor anywhere outside of Purgatory, were made all the more significant by our unspoken agreement and the lack of an implied obligation.

I made it to the large inward swinging doors without a stumble or grumble. I pulled the door open easily, just enough for me to pass through it, then walked out into the warm air of the darkening.

*Victory in the unwinnable scenario is wrest
in the revelation of the true self.*

DE TENEBRA

CHAPTER 37

QUID DECEPTIONE MULCET

(What Soothes Disappointment)

I GOT BACK to the inn, put my briefcase behind One Finger's desk, and went upstairs to change. I hung my suit over the chair in my room, slapped off the loose soot that coated it, and quickly changed into my only other outfit. When I got back downstairs One Finger was warming up under the guise of sweeping.

By way of celebration, we trained well into the darkening. As was our custom, when we were done, we moved to one of the small tables for drinks and conversation.

I opened with one of his favorite topics, the transferability of our training here, to life on the earthly plane. He was mid-sentence, saying something about how perceived rather than actual limitations are the common denominator when he rose to retrieve the cups and Forus he kept behind his desk. Being closer to the desk, I cut him off with a wordless, "permit me" gesture that seemed both natural and intended to allow him to continue talking.

I returned just as he was warming to the subject - saying something about musculature and physiology being merely a psychological constraint - and put the cups and the half-full bottle of whiskey from The General Counsel's office on the table in front of him.

He stopped mid-sentence. Whatever he was going to say was lost to the ether; evaporated like the alcohol before us and replaced by a reverent silence. That silence was broken only by the sound of my pouring a finger's worth in each cup.

After the pour I took a seat across from him and sat silently. Trapped by custom - which dictates that he who pours takes the first drink - he sat there, looking back and forth between me and the whiskey.

After some none-too-subtle sniffing, a lot of head rubbing, lots of lip licking, and even a discreet bit of salivating, he broke.

"Well! Er we gon drink it, er just sit ere n watch it vaporate?"

"Sure." I said, picking up my glass. Just thought I'd give you the chance to try the whole Jedi thing on me before we started. He laughed low and hard then picked up his glass.

Where he sipped and savored, I threw mine back quickly and waited. A few sips, some lip smacking, and not a small number of grunts and sighs later, he put his cup down empty.

"I blame May" I said.

He looked at me quizzically, clearly not connecting the dots.

"You drink your whiskey slow, like an old lady. Next thing ya know you'll be pointing your pinky finger in the air. At this rate I might well be back here before you finish the other bottle I brought you."

He scowled without menace, reached for the bottle and poured us each another finger's worth. I reached for my glass when he nodded after the pour, intending to offer a toast; not knowing I was merely being given a head start. His empty cup bounced off the table before I'd even swallowed.

Four more fingers in, with the bottle dented but not beaten, I sought a dignified surrender. As both a truce and retraction of any slight to his drinking, I poured anther round and offered a toast. "*May your enemies be few, and their fight uphill.*"

Then we sat and drank the way good whiskey should be consumed; pouring the smokey smooth liquid-delicacy in our mouths, letting it swirl around there in a joyful mockery of 'drinking' Forus, then leisurely letting it ease its way down.

"So, yer gonna give me a noder bottle a dis fine hooch ere are ya?"

I scoffed out a laugh and in my best May imitation, slurred out "'no frees, no frees.'"

"Ay, so I taut. N wot, udder dan my not tellin May dat ya called er an old lady, would ya want from a lout like me?"

"When I first arrived, I needed a job and information. I've turned down several job offers today, but now find myself more in need of information than ever."

When he nodded, I poured another finger for each of us then, held up first one finger: "What happens next?"

Then another finger: "When?"

And a third finger: "Am I destined to come back?"

He picked up his cup and stared into it as though reading tea leaves, then swirled the whiskey around like he hadn't seen what he was looking for and stared into it again. Eventually he put the cup down without taking a sip.

"Since nutin like dis as appened as far back as any soul can member, we's all just speculatin on a pothesis at dis point. Troof is, I aint got a clue bout yer first two questions - fer all's I know da Reapers could come by tammara, dress ya up all purdy in pink, and old a parade as dey march ya off to a land called Anah Lee.

"But dair's two tings I do know dat mite be useful. First, ya gotta keep in mind dat da worse torment ah Purgatory is dat nobody is sure bout its purpose. Da optimists say it's a temporary stop ta llow ya to ta figer out yer best destiny, da fearful say it's da first gate ta Hell. T'aint jest dat ya did sometin nobody else had done by convening Da Special Masters and whopping Da General Counsel, as dat da speech, long wit yer bein returnt, sports da optimists view dat makes yer victory important. Da Gunfighter go'in back is proof positive dat we ain't all damned, dat wot lies fore us may na be sumptin ta fear, and dat dair is a bit a ope fer us all poor souls ere.

"Da second ting I know is dat ya needn't worry bout comin back ere."

That said, he emptied his glass then sat there reflectively, nodding his head in internal agreement with himself. Apparently, done talking.

When it was clear that he wasn't going to go on I impatiently asked, "And why is that?"

He smiled slightly, savoring both his drink and his revenge for my Jedi comment.

"Because dat oder bottle a whiskey will cover yer room n board fer a mighty long time, should ya side ta grace da place wit yer presence again."

If discretion is the better part of valor, humor must be the salve of disappointment. I poured us another round, then another, and another. We finished the bottle in silence, without a hint of trepidation or melancholy.

I woke sometime later, chair-sore and stiff.

One Finger sat across from me, resting deeply and snoring lightly as I silently rose and made my way upstairs.

*In our dreams, a charge of great emotion becomes
a most tangible thing that, like all save our
deepest regrets and most profound fears, with the
light of day fades to a vague remembrance.*

DE TENEBRA

CHAPTER 38

DONATIO MORTIS CAUSA
(A Gift Caused By Death)

I WOKE TO the familiar surrounds of the Line Hotel, feeling only mildly out of sorts. A feeling I attributed, along with my all-too-vivid dreams about Purgatory, Reapers, and Demons, to the combination of wine, beer, and mescal I'd drunk with Christina the night before.

When the bedside phone rang, I slapped at it several time before getting ahold of it. I thought about sitting up but the pain in my head - which felt like a stroke, and the pressure on my chest - which felt like a heart attack, argued against it.

After uttering what was supposed to be a warm hello into the phone that came out as a high-pitched rasp, a very polite young lady started talking at me.

"I'm so sorry to bother you, but a gentleman is here at the front desk for you. He says he's a little early for a meeting with you this morning."

Then to someone else, "Excuse me, what was that? Oh, yes." Then, after some flirty giggling, "Why thank you." When she turned her attention back to me the flirtiness was still in her voice.

"He says his name is Roberto BeElsa and that he's on his way up."

I suspect she hung up, I don't know what I did with the phone. What I do know is that I bolted upright into a seated position, then froze.

I didn't question if I'd heard what I heard, because I couldn't believe I was seeing what I was seeing in the blackout-curtain-darkened room. I fumbled for the switches that lift either of the two sets of curtains. Luckily, I hit the one that lifts just the black-out curtains.

Even before the shade was all the way up, under the half-light of the morning sun, I saw them. Two not particularly large but nicely shaped breast rested atop a mocha skinned chest that was, but shouldn't have been, mine.

I stumbled out of bed on unfamiliar legs, took a clumsy fall, then got up and staggered toward the bathroom, turning on every light in the room and touching every part of my body along the way. Once in the bathroom, the mirror explained the additions and significant deletions I'd felt when it showed a very naked and very shocked looking Christina Vic staring back at me.

I'd probably have panicked and run screaming from the room had I been able to wrap my mind around what I was seeing. Instead, I just stood in the bathroom staring at the reflection in the mirror as my mind tried to make sense of what I was seeing. Like a kid, I turned slowly to see if the reflection in the mirror kept up, then I tried it quickly all-the-while knowing it would. I got so close that my breath fogged the mirror - then ignored the mirror entirely because of what it kept showing me. When I worked up the nerve and turned full circle slowly to get a good look, I felt like a voyeur. For the longest time I just stood there frozen in mouth-open shock.

When I heard a knock on the door to the suite, rage replaced shock and confusion. I stormed to the door, threw it open and there he stood, impeccably dressed and smiling smugly.

I lit into him without regard for who he was, what he could do or, to my undoing, what he was holding in his hand.

Several flashes later, when he was buckled over in laughter and having a hard time holding his phone camera steady, I finally regrouped enough to slam the door closed.

I returned several minutes later draped in one of the hotel's fine brushed cotton bathrobes. I opened the door to find him dabbing at his eyes with a hankie and fighting off the giggles.

"Pictures!? Really?" With a hand wave I referenced Christina's body, "As if this isn't enough!"

"He shrugged, looked me up and down, said, "nice robe" then picked up a travel bag and the briefcase May had given me and entered.

"For what it's worth, The General Counsel actually got down on her hands and knees and begged me to let her come and 'help' you with this … transition. But, since we can't have you running around looking like you own stock in *Grindr* well, here I am instead." Then, he patted the pocket where he put his phone-camera, "honestly, the only way I could get her to stop pouting was to promise to bring back something to share.

"Besides, providing you information is one of the services I agreed to perform when I signed the contract with you at your office."

"Oh, so you're here to help.

"Ok, for starters," this time I pointed with both hands toward my body, "explain this.

"Is it some backhanded besmirch of my sexual preference, a truly lame attempt at humor, or just a petty act of revenge because I stole one of your pet Reapers?"

He brought his hands up in mock defense.

"Whoa there little lady, slow your roll.

"Permit me to take those in order of most to least stupid: First, the whole sexual preference chip you have on your shoulder, well that's just low-brow thinking - even for an earther. Sex is sex, love is love, and souls are souls. That souls manifest as male or female in Purgatory is a function of the recency of their arrival not some sort of predetermined gender order. And, as I suspect you've figured out by now, since demons are neither recent arrivals nor souls, they're not bound by your quaint sounding, but truly minor league, notions of gender.

"You know, you really should have taken The General Counsel up on one of *its* offers. Assuming you survived the experience, if nothing else, you'd have a lot better perspective on all this.

"Second, I'm pretty sure you're pointing the blame finger in the wrong direction. Did you really think The Fates favored you?

"Not to take anything away from your courtroom

victory, but honestly, The Fates aren't just cruel, depending on which one is in charge at the time, they can be mean, nasty, or petty, and sometimes all three. And honestly, with the three of them trapped in and forced to share that one body as they are, who wouldn't be."

He shuddered as if a chill had run through him.

"The Fates knew the outcome they wanted all along. Sure, asking that The Gunfighter be sent back may have thrown them for a loop, something I suspect they'll try to remedy at their first opportunity, but you were always just an unwanted party guest that they couldn't wait to send home.

"And me, I've no cause to seek revenge. If we're keeping score, I'd say you might have managed to break even, while I've certainly come out ahead. Sure, you got The Gunfighter, but only for a moment. Worst-case scenario – you two soon fail. That means that I get my soul killing machine back, and The General Counsel gets a new chew toy. Best case - when you're done, he's given up his soul-killing ways in favor of hugs and puppies. That proves me not just right but prophetic, maybe even revelatory. Heck, just on the basis of our little courtroom theater the Reapers are more thoughtful in their reaping, and the rate of uncontested departures has near doubled among the long-term residents.

"As for my sense of humor," he smiled and patted the phone-camera in his pocket, "while I'm not above candid camera shots, I generally favor irony.

"And speaking of which, did I mention that there's a promising new attorney in Purgatory? While she doesn't have your creative flair or political savvy, she's got potential and certainly isn't above the occasional devious act. Or have you not bothered to stop and ask yourself where the soul that used to occupy that body is now?"

"What? No. I wanted my life, not hers. How is any of this you keeping the deal we made?"

"Our deal was that I support your and The Gunfighter's return, I've done that. It was you that asked the court to order that you be made whole. This is us, but honestly mostly them, accommodating your request.

You see, the thing you didn't take into account when you demanded to be made whole is time. You didn't know that The Gunfighter didn't show up immediately to snatch you out of your body - several months had passed before he paid you a visit. And you couldn't know that time passes differently in Purgatory. The difference isn't linear. If I had to, I'd say the difference is more elliptically shaped - time it right and few will even know you're gone, get it wrong and you'll burn through a week's vacation time in a matter of minutes. So, between your time laying around in a coma and the time difference, by the end of your eighth day in Purgatory, about a year passed."

"I've been gone a year!?"

"More or less. But honestly, more.

"Of course, in that time you've lost your job, your flat, your car, pretty much everything. With nothing to refute it, even those at the firm that respected you and know that she's really "not your type" have had to accept Christina's claims that it was your own inept attempt to drug and take advantage of her that led to you being in a coma. More importantly, while your former body sat vacant and comatose, your muscles atrophied to the point where you can't walk or talk - right now just opening your eyes would be a challenge. Oh, and you wear a diaper 24/7.

"If we put you back in that brittle and broken thing, rather than the fun bags and multi-click mouse that greeted you this morning, you'd have woken to a sea of blackness and pain. By the time you got your eyelid muscles to function well enough to open, you'd probably be insane. Even if your mind survived, it would likely be weeks before you could talk, months before you could piss standing up, and you'd probably never be able to walk any better than an old whore that just finished a double-header donkey love show.

"So, while you may be smarting from the loss of your pull-toy, asking to be made whole was probably the right move. Fact is, you should be thanking me —because of the diet and fitness regime I urged Christina to embark on, you're in a younger body that is a lot more firm than flabby."

"And what happened to Christina?"

"If you mean what happened that resulted in her vacating the real estate that you now occupy? Well, let's just say that mixing episodic high intensity cardio with diet pills and alcohol can have unexpected and, in her case, dire consequences.

"If you mean where is she now? Well, without the benefit of an escort, she's likely standing in the new arrivals line and will soon head over to the public housing.

"And by the way, The General Counsel accepted your offer — even she had to admit that you sending her a boy-toy conscript was a nice touch. So, congratulations on reacquiring a firm that you're not there to manage. But, since you now have both your interest in the firm and an option on The Gunfighter's interest, might I suggest you have your administrator hire Christina."

"Why and how would I do that?"

"Why? Well, if having a law firm that actually has a competent attorney working there isn't enough, do it out of spite - to keep her from working for The General Counsel. Oh, and there is that old saying about *keeping your enemy closer.*

"As for how, I suggest you send your gunslinging errand boy. He knows the way and could probably use a break from trying to get that broken-down old shell of yours working again."

"You put The Gunfighter in my body!? I suppose you're going to say that was The Fates' idea too."

He held up a correcting finger. "Your *former* body. And no, that was my idea.

"The betting line on whether he'd make enough progress to pass his first probationary review to remain on the earthly plane was about 1:1 when he left the courtroom. Since I pretty much had to bet on his success after my speech at the hearing, I wanted better odds. Between the difficulty of resurrecting that old broken body, and the likelihood that you'll send him back at the first hint of trouble, since he's wearing your face and using your name, the odds dropped to 1:4 against him as soon as word got out that he was wearing your old husk."

I was speechless, angered beyond words. I did the only thing I could do under the circumstances - I refused to let any of it show. There was no 'stink-eyed' stare, jaw clinching, finger drumming, or muttering, I didn't even let my nostrils flare. Knowing not getting a rise out of me would bother him more than anything else I could do, I got right down to business.

"So, how am I supposed to live my or Christina's life when I barely know her and have no idea what she and the rest of this world have been up to over the last year?"

He shrugged his shoulder and sighed, his disappointment at not getting a rise out of me obvious, but only somewhat soothing.

"I wanna say you're thinking like an earther again but really, the problem is that you don't know what you know."

"But I know that I don't know."

"No, you just think you know that you don't know because you don't know how you know, and that's a whole different thing to know, or not know."

I stared at him in equal parts confusion and frustration.

"It's like when a name is on the tip of your tongue, or when you were just about to say something but then can't remember what it was, except you know it was on the tip of your tongue."

Arms crossed over a chest that felt wrong and unfamiliar, I silently challenged him to start making sense.

"The point is, when something slips your mind, you don't recall it by trying to remember what it was – that just focuses you on the fact that you can't remember and takes you further away from what you're trying to recall. You get it back by giving your mind the space to fill in the blank."

He'd said enough to make me think it had something to do with One Finger's lessons about expectations, letting go of doubt and self-imposed limits. I just wasn't sure what.

I sat there, thoroughly confused, brow furrowed in both concentration and an attempt at comprehension.

"I suggest you fill up the lovely soaking tub in the bathroom and relax over a long hot bath. Her soul is gone but her memories are still there.

"With some practice and the proper focus, you can know anything that Christina knows. That knowledge will give you access to Christina's bank accounts and other holdings and allow you to assume the position she now holds at FRAT - a junior partner position here at the firm's Los Angeles branch that, had things gone differently, would likely be yours. All that, along with the contents of your briefcase and the bag I brought should fulfill our agreement and the Special Master's directive that you be made whole."

He tipped his hat and turned to leave as though all was right in the world.

"Now if you'll excuse me, I have a brunch date with a deliciously naive aspiring actress/hotel receptionists."

He was just outside the door when I spoke up.

"One more thing before you go."

He turned and looked back expectantly, but not at all surprised.

"Why me?"

He paused. Not long, but long enough for me to wonder if he was going taunt me, go back to bargaining for information, or just walk away. Instead, he smiled.

"Here's where I'd usually go into a story about you being special. I'd talk about you having innate abilities and a unique skill set that will take you on great adventures enroute to some special destiny. I'd appeal to your pride and, more subtlety, to that sad little part of you that, despite all that you've done and learned, still fears that you aren't good enough. In short, I'd recruit you.

"But I'm not. Maybe because The General Counsel was right - 'some horses shouldn't be broken,' maybe because I don't want to risk violating the spirit of the Court's order, or maybe it's because you're not asking the right question. Regardless, here you go:

"Like you said, I had a problem with souls – you showed an ability to solve soul-related problems when you interfered with my plans for Christina. That got you on the board. Are you the only piece in play? No, you're just one of an untold number of conscripts brought in to address a problem. So, the question isn't why you but rather, why did you succeed."

I smiled back at him, unsure about the new face I was using, but hoping my smile looked as forced and disingenuous as it was.

"Per our agreement, there will be no implied obligations between us. Compensation is due for the information you just provided. To that end, you may collect on the implied obligation The General Counsel assumed when she accepted the boy toy I sent over. With our accounts now settled, as is my right under our agreement, said agreement is now terminated."

His bow was graceful, but shallow enough so that the door missed him when I slammed it shut.

What we do in life marks our souls.

DE TENEBRA

CHAPTER 39

HABEAS CORPUS

(You May Have The Body)

TEN MINUTES LATER the suitcases were sitting on the bed still unopened, the bathroom mirrors were steamed over, the hotel's fine brushed cotton bathrobe was lying in a heap on the floor, and I was stepping into an almost too hot bath.

Thirty minutes later I was used to the water, and I knew everything that I needed to get started and all too much about Christina. By then I'd almost forgotten about the luggage The Fixer had left.

I dressed quickly, going with the easy-on sports bra that looked and worked enough like an athletic style tee-shirt to not require instructions, some loose grey sweatpants, sneakers, and a Lakers tee-shirt that was in the gym bag she brought with her.

Once dressed, I approach the two bags The Fixer had brought.

First, I opened the briefcase May gave me. The original contract with The Fixer was on top. It now had "void" stamped across each page in big red letters. But any surprise or concern that I'd have had with The Fixer's having anticipated his termination was ousted when I saw the suit May gave me underneath the contract.

A quick and somewhat frantic pat-down of the suit confirmed that it had arrived complete with talisman and lucky penny in pockets. The suit was wrapped neatly around The Gunfighter's holstered and fully loaded .44, and the whole lot rested atop a copy of De Trenebra. Mercifully, the outfit I got when I first arrived in Purgatory was nowhere to be found.

All my other worldly possessions were in the briefcase, so I was worried about what was in the bag. I once again resorted to tried and true television safety precautions - I turned the bag away from me and jumped back when I opened it from behind. When nothing jumped, seeped, or rose from it, I cautiously circled the bed for a better view.

Even after I'd worked my way all the way around and had a clear view of the contents, I still couldn't believe what I was seeing. It was money; cash mostly, but also several bearer bonds, some stock certificates, gold, and even a few jewels. Whoever'd packed the suitcase must have been big on portfolio diversification. The contents were obviously worth a lot, but since I didn't have the latest stock market report or know the going rate of gold, I had no idea exactly how much.

I closed the travel bag and called down to the front desk to ask them to bring Christina's car - now my car - around as I was ready to checkout. I grabbed the travel bag, briefcase, her purse and gym backpack, then headed down to the lobby. By the time I'd signed out, my car was waiting for me.

As I approached, the valet opened the door to the car, a two-year old BMW M model that Christina had bought as a status symbol rather than the performance toy that it is. When I put the bags down to fish through the purse - which had poor visibility, limited access, and no discernable organization - for a tip, the valet upped the ante by popping the trunk and loading the gym bag, travel bag, and briefcase. Maybe I was jaded from my time in Purgatory, maybe I was just feeling flush, but the fact that he grunted with the effort of lifting the travel bag seemed like a nice touch, so I dug a little deeper into the purse and added a bit more to his tip.

Driving the car like it was made to be driven, I made it to the hospital where I'd been in a coma - the same hospital that The Gunfighter had taken my soul from almost a year, yet only eight days ago - in half the time it should have taken.

A few quick inquiries later, I walked into a hospital room and the mother of all out of body experiences. My own withered and bed-broken body confronted me. Though still and silent, it cried out to me. In that moment I understood why people sometimes try to crawl into the casket with their deceased loved ones, that the permanence of some types of loss is inconceivable - try as we may to accept it - and that grief is as tangible as the bitter taste it leaves in your mouth.

I wanted to both hug and hit the body that I couldn't help being repulsed by and drawn to at the same time.

Instead, I stood close, close enough to let the smell of piss, body rot, and bed sores drive home what my eyes still tried to deny; he'd been telling the truth. There was nothing left for or of me in that shell of a body. That body was the new Blain, that body only resembled who I used to be, that body is what I had been moved on from. After all that I'd done, seen, and gone through to get back here, what I now was, was all that was left of that me.

As I stood there grieving over my loss and contemplating the need for closure, the head on the body that was no longer mine lolled to the side. The eyelids fluttered as they struggled with the heavy effort of lifting, then opened just enough so that I stared into The Gunfighter's eyes.

Pain, surprise, understanding was right there. Like me, he'd gotten what he'd bargained for, but not what he wanted.

In that instant I felt a defining sense of clarity that was most notable for the lack of compassion it carried. I looked down on The Gunfighter dispassionately. When I spoke there was no mercy, kindness, or concern in my words or person.

"Either get that body of mine working and get out of bed or give up and go back now."

If he had any doubt who I was or where he was, it didn't show. Instead, the machines that surrounded him started beeping, sirens seemed to go-off everywhere, and doctors and nurses came running.

A finger twitch here and a grimace in response to some pokes and prods confirmed that things had changed and suggested that there might be something there to work with.

He fought long and hard with that body over the next few months. Loath though I am to admit it, I'd never have gotten the thing working. Desperate and disciplined though he was, even with me haranguing, harassing, and threatening him, it was weeks before he was able sit up in bed. Over the next month he went from being helped to his feet and shuffling along with two aides carrying him between them, to short trips with a walker. Much to his credit, and my concern, he started practicing his draw even before he could make it to the bathroom by himself.

Switching from a walker to a cane accelerated his progress dramatically.

As New Blain, The Gunfighter could access my memories - Blain's memories - the same way I could recall Christina's. During one of his jaunts into my prior life, he realized both that carrying the .44 wouldn't always be practical and that, with the appropriate medical documents, he could go anywhere with a cane. In short order he, and sometimes we, we're practicing cane techniques and forms.

While the medical staff thought New Blain's recovery was some sort of miracle, I saw it for what it was, desperation. In short order, as The Gunfighter he was going to have to show the Special Masters that he'd done more than learn to pee standing up to make a good impression. To that end, the first thing this New Blain was going to do was help me restore Blain's reputation.

*Those blessed with imagination are cursed
to die with regrets, and vice-versa.*

DE TENEBRA

CHAPTER 40

QUO FATA FERUNT

(Where The Fates Bear Us To)

OK, STOP ME if you've heard this one before - two lawyers whose bodies are possessed by other souls, walk into a law firm …

Yeah, it sounds like a joke, but a few months after waking up from a year-long coma, emaciated looking and gimpy though he was, New Blain walked into FRAT for a meeting with Messer's Fulsome, Rucker, and Taft. Even without the .44, who better than The Gunfighter in a New Blain body to go in and put the fear of protracted litigation on claims of wrongful termination based on racial discrimination, sex discrimination, and homophobia - a public relations nightmare - into the FRAT partnership.

If this was a joke, nobody was laughing.

Between New Blain's righteous indignation at having his good reputation sullied, and Christina's remorseless admission – that she left the shots she ordered sitting on the bar unattended while she took the other drinks to their table so anyone could have put something in one of the drinks - FRAT was more than willing to buy their way out of their predicament and our employment. Backpay, vacation pay-out, severance pay, and a - bigger than everything else combined - bonus "for the good work Blain did on his last case" required only mutual non-disclosures and a waiver of any and all potential claims. Christina received a six-figure severance check when she resigned and cashed out her share of the partnership.

Between the settlement with FRAT and the travel bag full of money, we were financially set. Not shoe room, shoe broker, personal cobbler comfortable - New Blain paid for those things, along with his titanium cane with the quick-release hide-away carbon fiber blade, and other personal items with money he'd made transporting things from and selling correspondences to earthside – but with a little sound investing we could live comfortably without ever working again.

But, between The Fate's cryptic warning, The Gunfighter's need to evolve, and the whole "idle hands" thing, doing nothing wasn't really an option.

Given The Gunfighter's impressive ability to recall contract details and his having Blain's legal training, experience, and still active bar status, opening a law practice together was a no brainer. But despite his knowledge of all things Blain related, there was no way New Blain was going to convince anyone close to him that he wasn't either possessed, cognitively impaired, or both. We couldn't stay in San Francisco and Christina had a place in Los Angeles but no friends, so we opened an office in Los Angeles.

Vic-Edward Investigations and Law, or *VEILaw* for short, specializes in issues related to business, estate planning and, occasionally, the interests of more unique clients. We are small and discreet, and intent on staying that way.

We'd leased a small - two office, conference room, reception area - space, located just far enough away from downtown to be chic. It was well appointed, but what we didn't have and sorely needed, was someone special to handle the day-to-day tasks of running the office. And, while New Blain's eccentricities and poor bedside manner might easily be overlooked as the entitlements of a named partner, we were looking for someone that was sharp enough to see, but willing to overlook, any of our more unique clients' oddities.

In the few minutes before yet another in what was shaping up to be a Purgatory like, endless series of uneventful interviews with inappropriate candidates, I was talking with New Blain about the trip he'd take back to Purgatory at the coming solstice.

With The Fates' admonishment – that I'd already seen things not meant for mortals to know – hanging over our souls, neither of us wanted to go too far into the details about how he went back and forth.

We were both relieved to hear the doorbell ring just after he'd told me that it involved a deep state of nothingness more akin to death than deep meditation. I rose from my desk and, making no attempt to conceal my relief at moving on from our prior topic, quickly pulled on my Hailey Bieber suit jacket.

I walked past New Blain toward the reception area without saying a word or otherwise acknowledging him.

He fell in behind me, cane in hand, and we made our way into and across the reception area. His slight limp - a remnant of his year-long coma – was little more than a justification to carry a short-sword concealing cane.

When I reached the door I stepped to the side, reached for the door handle, then paused to check with New Blain. Standing front and center, one hand resting more than leaning on his cane, he smoothed his lapel with the other hand before, true to the Boy Scout's 'ever prepared' motto, placing it on his hip - within easy reach of his gun.

Contrary to how I hoped it appeared, I wasn't opening the door to be the assertive woman or in deference to New Blain's senior, at least on paper, partner status; this was our security routine. I pulled the reinforced door open, all the while staying well behind it, then again looked to New Blain. I'd never expect him to relax since he never tensed, but when he forced a fully fake half smile and moved his hand a slight distance from the gun at his waist, I took that as a sign that things were ok and stepped forward.

As I rounded the door, I saw that things were much better than ok. It wasn't the curly dark hair, or the lean, muscular physique that even my personal trainer would kill for, at least not just that. Ok, bonus points for that.

The thing of it is, the guy standing there about to come in, the guy that had come to apply for a job, the guy that wanted to work with me at least five days a week for eight plus hours a day, … he smelled really, really good! I caught a whiff of him as I pulled the door open. And when he walked into the office and stepped slightly to the side, to form a perfect triangle between the three of us, his scent hit me full on.

It reminded me of a moment. Like the moment just before you bite into a cookie that just came out of the oven, the feeling that you get after you've climbed all the way up the ladder for the high dive, walked to the end and are leaping into space, or that first time you rode a bicycle by yourself, wobble-careening down the street on the verge of crashing, but peddling faster anyway. Your senses are overloaded, and somewhere in the back of your mind there's a ticker tape listing all of the things that can go wrong. You're on the brink of panic but you ignore it because somehow, perhaps instinctively, you just know that this is gonna be good - really, really, good. It's a perfect moment, and in that moment, it doesn't matter if you end up burning your mouth, belly flopping, or crashing into the bushes along the sidewalk. Giddiness and joy forestall what was and may later be, so you chomp down, jump higher, or pedal faster because you want it to last and because you know it can't.

It had been a long time since I'd ridden a bike, but I knew right then that this was a bicycle moment, and I definitely wanted a ride.

"Hi, I'm Mark. I'm here about the administrative assistant position."

Rather than make the mistake of shaking New Blain's hand first, a move that would have required him to turn his back toward me and hinted of misogyny, he turned and flashed me a smile that acknowledged my presence, my position as a named partner in the firm, and my femininity, without a hint of trepidation or creepiness. I was ready to hire him before we even shook hands.

When we did shake hands, my breath caught in my

throat. In that brief moment, before the fact that I wasn't breathing could become either obvious or embarrassing, he asked, "are you Edwards or Vic, of Edwards and Vic?"

It was a slight and unavoidable affront. He couldn't know that it was supposed to be Vic and Edwards. I'd had the office door stenciled four times by three different companies, was on my fifth set of business cards, and had threatened the landlord, our internet provider, and just about everyone we'd entered into contract to no avail. Everything we ordered came back with the name of our partnership reversed. And it seemed the more I tried, the worse things got.

For our partnership the name wasn't about ego. As part of our founding principles, and in deference to The Fates warning, we needed to take on certain "underrepresented" clients. Vic and Edwards Investigations and Law, or the acronym VEILaw, spoke to these clients. In the end, I'd been reduced to damage control and left to hope that no one read too much into the EVILaw acronym that we were stuck with.

Calling the firm Edwards and Vic didn't take away from the points he got for being unassuming and sensitive, but it was irritating enough to get my lungs and voice working again.

"Despite what is printed on the door, our cards, stationary, and just about everything we own, it's Vic and Edwards."

His smile said he understood my angst; his response "and you must be Vic," said he welcomed my correction, and his soft yet firm, hot but not too hot hand in mine brough back memories of lip biting.

And then, just as he let go and turned to shake hands with New Blain, it all changed. It wasn't just that he let go prematurely, it was more like something clicked to signal the start of a Rashomon moment – that moment when the same events the characters are witnessing are seen as something completely different by each character.

His brow furrowed and he looked back and forth between New Blain and me, head slightly angled to the side, obviously confused. For a moment he almost looked like a puppy. After a couple more looks back and forth between us, more to himself than to either of us he said, "This is wrong." When he did turn to us there was greater conviction and growing agitation.

"You two are wrong. What's going on here? Who are you and what are you trying to pull?"

I'm not sure what he was seeing, but whatever it was, he didn't like it.

For me, when his brow furrowed, he transformed. Suddenly he was flawed and less polished, even the fit of his suit seemed to falter. Now he was pissed and just slightly above average looking. And like that, all thoughts of cookies, high dives, and sadly, bicycle rides vanished.

I can't say what exactly New Blain saw. But it was like somebody flicked a light switch. One moment he was wearing his best phony smile, reaching out to shake hands, and preparing to fake his way through the painful civilities of an interview. Then, just about the time he got close enough to get a whiff of that delicious smell, his left hand produced the .44 and aimed it at the middle of Marks' newly furrowed brow.

Disappointed though I was about there being no

bicycle ride, New Blain's reaction struck me as a bit extreme, even for him.

"Ba-lain," I said it long and slow. I wasn't worried that I'd startle New Blain, that was an impossibility. I just wanted him to know that he needed to listen to me and not shoot Mark - at least not before someone explained what was going on.

Oddly enough, Mark seemed to take it all in stride. If not the speed of the draw, the fact that there was a gun pointed at his head should have completely unnerved him. Instead, almost as though it were a matter of bad etiquette, he told, rather than asked New Blain, "stop pointing that thing at me."

His words were met by an unflinching, predatory glower. New Blain had reverted to Reaper mode, and it was a fright to behold. It wasn't a large or difficult change for New Blain, it was more like taking your work clothes off at the end of the day than putting them on in the morning.

I'd been through enough with New Blain to heed this warning. But honestly, the guy seemed more weary of, than threatening to us. My gut told me there was something about him that was worth looking into, and this wasn't just the good smell talking. I figured there might be a real opportunity here … if everybody lived through the next few moments.

"Blain!" I wanted to get his attention.

"Baa-lain?" Mark said mockingly, "Is that what you're going by here? And just what are you doing here sneaking around in that dark and lovely new meat-suit? Trying to fleece those of us that work for a living? If so, you are definitely wasting your time on me."

He turned from New Blain to me, squinted, looked me up and down, then asked, "And what's your angle? Are you some quasi-femme fatale that's gonna play nice to offset his true and genuinely very, very bad cop persona? Do you even know who and what he is? Dare I even ask what you're preferred pronoun is?

Then, turning back to New Blain, "Oh, and again, get that thing out of my face!"

When that didn't work, he stomped his foot in frustration and, hands on hips, leaned forward to give New Blain the 'stink eye'.

He held New Blain's gaze longer than most folks, then snickered in equal parts concession and exasperation, straightened and, much to my surprise, greeted New Blain anew with "Gunfighter."

"Ba-lain?" The fact that I'd said it again, longer and slower, in no way masked my growing impatience. I wanted to know what was going on, I wanted New Blain to lower the gun so we could figure this out, and I wanted him to know that he needed to answer me, now.

For better or worse, before any of that could happen Mark, turned to the side, lunged for a nearby trash can, and vomited up the better part of a semi-digested lunch - salad and a side of fries, I think. Still bent over, he produced a handkerchief from his pocket, dabbed at his mouth, and in a snarky tone said, "I told you not to point that gun at me."

Briefly, and for the first time ever, I saw true emotion flash over New Blain's face. Disgust and horror passed through him with an intensity that, if he weren't so caught up in the moment, would likely have surprised him as much as it did me.

As one who's prone to trigger vomiting – vomiting at the smell of vomit - I understood New Blain's disgust. But it was only when I saw that some of the vomit had jumped the trash can and landed on his lower pant leg that I understood the depth of New Blain's fury.

Though New Blain's gun remained fixed on Mark there was something new. It was slight, significant more in novelty than in fact. New Blain's gun-hand had a slight tremor. Though barely noticeable it was like a quake compared to his usual steady hand. This wasn't fear, doubt, or nerves - I suspect those will always be foreign to New Blain. No, behind New Blain's dead-eyed expression a war was waging between his desire to shoot, and my direction that he not. Perhaps, in an attempt to marshal himself, but more likely in the hope that I would acquiesce and let him shoot, through gritted teeth New Blain snarled,

"Incubus."

It was one word, said as a greeting to Mark, an answer to me, and a warning to both of us.

END.

ABOUT THE AUTHOR

Darwin Farrar received his Bachelor of Science, Master of Public Policy, and Juris Doctorate degrees from U.C. Berkeley. He holds black belts in Taekwondo and Yong-modo (Korean Jiujitsu).

After more than 30 years of practicing law, including a decade on the bench as the Assistant and Acting Chief Judge, Darwin now serves as Chief Counsel for a very large and effective public interest advocacy organization.

Though he has written several newsletters, reports, and academic pieces, and is a lifelong reader of science fiction and fantasy this, the first in a trilogy, is Darwin's first writing in the genre.